Dear Reader:

D.V. Bernard is a phenomenal writer and having read all three of his books without ever putting them down, I am convinced that one day he will be one of the most celebrated authors of all-time. His books *The Last Dream Before Dawn* and *God in the Image of Woman* should be required reading at colleges and universities worldwide. In this effort, *How to Kill Your Boyfriend (in Ten Easy Steps)* he steps away from his normally serious subject matter and entertains readers with a humorous, intriguing tale of two women who get caught up in a journey of both self-discovery and mystery.

I have no intention of giving this book away. That would be nothing short of criminal, but suffice it to say that it is unlike any other book I have ever read. I love authors who write outside the box and take risks that others tend to shy away from. I am one of those who believes in creating something new or putting a different spin on an old storyline. D.V. Bernard pokes fun at society's tendency to want to do things in "numbered steps." Over the past decade especially, self-help books and programs that get people excited about being able to quit smoking in three steps, being able to cook a gourmet meal in five steps, being able to lose weight step-by-step, etc. have become a huge consumer market. That is what makes this book a page-turner. You will not be able to stop wondering what the two main characters are going to do next.

One day D.V. Bernard will write a literary work that will earn him the Pulitzer Prize in Literature. I believe that with every ounce of my heart because he has the talent, the foresight, and the gift of putting pen to paper that mark a great writer. In a million years, I could never write like him and I am not ashamed to say it. His skills are far and beyond what most authors could ever imagine. Please check out his other books as well; you will not be disappointed.

I want to thank those of you who have been gracious enough to support the dozens of authors I publish under Strebor Books International, a division of ATRIA/Simon and Schuster. While writing serves as a catalyst for me to release my personal creativity, publishing allows me the opportunity to share the talent of so many others. If you are interested in being an independent sales representative for Strebor Books International, please send a blank email to info@streborbooks.com.

Peace and Blessings,

Zane

Publisher
Strebor Books International
www.streborbooks.com

OTHER BOOKS BY D.V. BERNARD
The Last Dream Before Dawn
God in the Image of Woman

ZANE PRESENTS

HOW TO KILL YOUR
Boyfriend
(IN TEN EASY STEPS)

D.V. BERNARD

STREBOR BOOKS

NEW YORK LONDON TORONTO SYDNEY

Strebor Books
P.O. Box 6505
Largo, MD 20792
http://www.streborbooks.com

How To Kill Your Boyfriend (in Ten Easy Steps) © 2006 by D.V. Bernard.

ISBN-13 978-1-59309-066-1
ISBN-10   1-59309-066-8
LCCN 2006923547

Cover design: www.mariondesigns.com

Distributed by Simon & Schuster, Inc.
1230 Avenue of the Americas
New York, NY 10020
1-800-223-2336

First Strebor Books trade paperback edition June 2006

10 9 8 7 6 5 4 3 2 1

Manufactured and Printed in the United States of America

For information regarding special discounts for bulk purchases,
please contact Simon & Schuster Special Sales at 1-800-456-6798
or business@simonandschuster.com

DEDICATION

To crazy, homicidal women everywhere

When Stacy thought about it afterwards, she told herself that she had not intended to kill her boyfriend. It certainly had not been something she had planned. However, even she would have admitted that she had been somewhat annoyed with him lately. It had not been anything definite—just the usual ups and downs of a relationship. Once, he had bought the wrong brand of tampons, and she had raged against him mercilessly. If he had really loved her, she had argued, he would have gotten her the right brand. It had all been a sign from God, and she had wept bitterly while he clutched her shoulders and begged for forgiveness. After a few days of brooding and melodrama, she had been able to admit to herself that the entire argument had been stupid, and they had made love. Making love had always been her way of saying she was sorry. In fact, the week before she killed him, they had made love a great deal. It had gotten to the point where she had found herself being aroused as soon as she started yelling at him. And so, maybe the murder, unintentional as it was, had only been an escalation of their sex—a case of arousal gone too far.

Dr. Vera Alexander got out of the cab and stood looking at the storefront bookshop. It was in Midtown Manhattan—one of those trendy neighborhoods where everything cost too much and the droves of shoppers took a strange kind of pride from the fact that they were squandering their money. Vera surveyed her reflection in the bookstore's windowpane. She was a slightly plump 31-year-old who always had a tendency to look overdressed. The socially acceptable stereotype at the moment was that gay men had impeccable fashion sense, so she trusted all her clothing, hair and makeup decisions to a flamboyantly gay Haitian called François. The style that year was to have one's hair "long and untamed," so, on François' recommendation, she had adopted a hairdo that was so wild it seemed vicious. All the mousse and red highlights made her hair seem like some kind of diseased porcupine. Yet, it was the style, and she was pleased with her appearance as she stared at her reflection.

When she walked into the bookstore there was a smile on her face, because there were at least two dozen people there, waiting for her to sign copies of her book, *How to Have Great Sex with a So-So Man*. On the cover there was a picture of a beaming woman standing next to a slouching doofus. The bookstore patrons froze and stared at her when she entered; some pointed to her and whispered to their neighbors, as if in awe of her. A couple of them snapped pictures of her, or began to record on their camcorders. Whatever the case, the mass of them moved toward her and put out their hands to be shaken. Soon there was a line to shake hands with her. Of course, all of them were women. Vera shook their hands gladly, smiling at each one and thanking her for coming. The store manager was a bookish-looking woman in her late-twenties: gaunt and severe-looking, with a sarcastic look pasted on her face from years of suppressing her disappointment with life:

"Let Dr. Vera get set-up first!" she chastised the patrons like a kindergarten teacher telling two five-year-olds to stop pulling one another's hair. Some of them groaned in disappointment, but Dr. Vera nodded to them, as if to reassure them that she would shake their hands later. They made room for her to pass, and she walked over to the desk where she was to sign books. A line had already formed; two women tussled with one another in their desire to occupy the same spot on the line. The store manager gave them her stern kindergarten teacher look and they calmed down.

Vera smiled at it all. She got out her fountain pen and sat down at the desk. Soon, she was asking the women their names and writing the same message in their books. She had developed a bad habit of writing and looking up at the person she was signing the book to. As a consequence, the message she wrote was usually illegible. Many people later discovered that she had misspelled their names, or she had written it merely as a line with a squiggly thing in the middle.

She had a good tempo going. In fifteen seconds, she could sign a book, dispense advice on the mysteries of male sexuality and still have time to pose for a picture. Even the sarcastic-looking store manager seemed impressed. The woman did not exactly smile, but she exuded a kind of pleased smugness as she stood to the side, surveying the long line.

"Exactly," Vera said in answer to one woman's declaration of gratitude, "if you can teach a dog to shit outside, why can't teach your man to please you in bed!"

Everyone in the store laughed; some of them applauded. Vera had used that line about 80 times since she started her book tour a month ago. She had had a dream once, where it had been the only thing she could say...but people loved it when she said it.

She nodded to the woman who had made the declaration of gratitude (as to dismiss her) and the next woman on line stepped up to the table. People were still laughing at Vera's joke. However, the woman who stepped up to the table had a drawn, wretched expression on her face—like in those pictures of war refugees who had watched their children starve to death and their men butchered. The woman seemed about Vera's age, but could have possibly been about ten years older. With her thinness, the woman seemed frail and detached—except for the intensity with which she stared at Vera. It was off-putting, and Vera instinctively looked away. She noticed the woman's blouse: the nape of the neck was slightly frayed and discolored. Vera noticed a peculiar birthmark on the woman's neck. It was heart-shaped with a jagged line through it—a broken heart. The store manager looked at the woman disapprovingly, wondering if she could afford the $21 price of the book.

The woman handed Vera the book to sign, and Vera came back to her senses. She tried to reassure herself by smiling. "To whom am I signing this?" she said.

The woman's voice was low and ominous: "Don't pretend that you don't know me."

Vera's smile disappeared; all the background conversation in the book-store seemed to cease. "I'm sorry," Vera said, flustered, "...I don't—"

"Don't you *dare* pretend—*you* of all people!"

"I'm not—"

"I took the weight for you," the woman went on, suddenly animated. "I carried it while you were doing all this," she said, looking around the bookstore, as if all of it were Vera's and the woman's sacrifice had allowed her to attain it. "But when is it going to be my turn to be free?" the woman lamented. "...The things we did," she said, beginning to sob, "they're *killing* me—the weight of it all...! I can't take it anymore—it's too much for me."

Vera had sat stunned for most of that; the store patrons had stood staring. Vera remembered that she was a psychologist and stood up, to calm the woman. "Please—"

"I've lost everything," the woman cut her off, talking more to herself now than anything.

"Ma'am, please—"

"*Ma'am*?" she screamed, outraged by the formality and coldness of the term. "After *all* we went through—all those things we did...?"

The store manager came over, but Vera warded her off by shaking her head. Vera walked around to the front of the desk and tried to take the woman's hand.

"No!" the woman screamed, as if brushing off a lover's hand. And then, more calmly, "If you don't remember me, it's too late for that. It's too late." Her eyes were full of sorrow and desperation now: "You were all I had left."

"Maybe you should sit down," Vera attempted to reason with her once more. She again tried to take the woman's hand, but the woman pushed her hand away. And then, with a disillusioned expression on her face:

"You *really* don't know me...?" She stared at Vera's face, as if searching for some clue of recognition; but seeing none, she bowed her head thoughtfully and started talking to herself again: "I guess it's best that you forgot. I took the weight for you, but it's too much."

"Let's talk about it," Vera said, trying to think up every therapist trick she knew. "Maybe you can help me to remember."

The woman started to walk away, as if she had not heard.

"Please," Vera called after her, "—at least tell me your name!"

The woman stopped and stared at her as if considering something. At last she sighed, saying, "I'm the one who helped you to forget." At that, she walked out of the store. When she got to the curb, she looked back at Vera via the display window; then, she turned and took a step into the street. The speeding truck hit her instantly. She was sent flying like a cartoon character. There was something unbelievable about it—like a cheap special effect in a bad movie. The truck tried to stop, but the woman's careening body fell right in its path. There was the sound of tires screeching, and then a thud...and then silence.

For Dr. Vera, four years passed in a blur of success and controversy. As was usually the case, the controversy had fueled her success. The entire episode with the woman at the bookstore had been captured on some of her fans' camcorders. The story got international attention. People called it "The Forget-Me-Not" incident, because of the woman's rant on being forgotten. A couple of networks did exposés on Dr. Vera, trying to figure out the connection between her and the woman: if there really was some deep dark secret that they had shared...but there had been nothing. The woman had spent her entire life in a small town in North Carolina; she had had a history of mental illness and had been living with a family friend until she snuck away to come to New York the day before she died. With all the media attention, the camcorder scenes of Dr. Vera attempting to calm the deranged woman had made her seem compassionate and accessible; and within weeks of the incident, Dr. Vera had been approached to do her own radio call-in show.

Four years later, the Dr. Vera radio call-in show was not exactly a hit, but it was broadcast nationwide, and there was talk of a television version. Since the incident, her agent had been telling her how she was on the verge of greatness. Her last book, *10 Steps to Find Out if Your Man is a Cheating Bastard* had been a number one bestseller…but that was two years ago, and she could not help thinking that her career was languishing.

As for her personal life, despite the fact that she was a relationship counselor, she was single and childless. It had been over a year since she had had sex, and the more she thought about it, the more certain she was that the young stud her agent had set her up with the last time had faked his orgasm just so he could get away from her! In bed, she seemed almost mouse-like—nothing like the voracious sexual beast she wrote about in her books. In college, two of her lovers had fallen asleep while making love to her. Granted, they had both been drunk at the time, but it had all set off a lifelong sense of sexual inadequacy—which was probably why she connected so well with her legion of fans. She knew how they wanted to feel about their sexuality, because she wanted the same feeling—the same fantasy. Her greatest fear was that people would discover she was lousy in bed. To a certain degree, she remained single because she was afraid one of her ex-boyfriends would write one of those tell-all books on her, cataloguing the horrific boredom of her sex. Every lover was a potential blackmailer.

And if all that were not bad enough, she was growing tired of being Dr. Vera. Her last name was actually Alexander, not Vera, but it had become an accepted practice for media doctors to go by their first names—like Dr. Phil and Dr. Ruth—as to give a false sense of intimacy to their fans. Being Dr. Vera required vast amounts of energy—as was usually the case when one lived a lie. Every day, she told lies about lovers who were a figment of her imagination; she dispensed sexual advice on things that she, herself, was terrified to try. And with each passing day, it became clearer to her that she *hated* doing her call-in show. Five nights a week, it was the same tedious nonsense: women calling up to find out why their husbands or boyfriends did not love them anymore; people trying to manipulate their lovers into doing something (stupid), or who were merely calling to hear a psychological professional justify their scummy behavior.

She knew that something would have to change soon or she would crack. Every once in a while she would have a nightmare where she failed totally at this life and again had to return to being a high school guidance counselor. The nightmare would motivate her to work harder for a few weeks, until she again felt herself on the verge of cracking.

"Okay," Dr. Vera said after she had finished answering the last caller's question, "—we have time for one more call." She looked at the computer screen before her to see which caller was to be next, and then she pressed a button: "Matt from Minneapolis, how may I help you today?"

"Thanks for taking my call, Dr. Vera. I'm a longtime listener and first time caller." The man's chipper, excited voice annoyed her for some reason, but she retreated into her usual radio routine:

"Thank you, Matt. How may I help you today?"

"Well, Dr. Vera," Matt began, "I've come to the conclusion that I'm a lesbian."

"Aren't you a man?" she asked, frowning at the computer screen.

"Yes."

Dr. Vera frowned deeper, and looked through the soundproof glass, at the engineer/producer. When she made eye contact with the huge, woolly-mammoth-looking man, he shrugged and bit into a gigantic submarine sandwich. Vera sighed and stared at the computer screen again, as if the answer to everything lay within it. She had trained herself to always give kind, considerate responses—even to the stupidest questions—but all she could think to say was, "Look, Matt, to be a lesbian, you sort of have to be a woman."

"That's a pretty sexist view!"

"How is that sexist?"

"It's sexist to believe that a man can't be a lesbian, just as it would be sexist to believe that a woman can't be an astronaut, or have her own radio call-in show."

Dr. Vera shook her head: "To be a lesbian, you have to be a woman," she maintained.

"Not at all: a lesbian is simply someone who wants to have sex with a lesbian."

"So, if I had sex with you, I'd be a lesbian?"

"Of course!"

Dr. Vera groaned, despite her usual attempt to maintain a professional/unflappable radio persona. Maybe it was the fact that it was Friday night and she wanted to go home. She wanted to get away from people and their sexual problems—at least for the weekend—

"Anyway," she said to move things along, "you think you're a lesbian trapped in a man's body?"

"Not at all—I'm secure in my lesbian-ness," he said, making up his own terms.

A side of Dr. Vera wanted to say something sarcastic like, "Good for you, girlfriend!" Instead, she sighed and said, "So what is your problem then?"

"Oh," Matt said, as if he'd forgotten, "...you see, the problem is that my boyfriend doesn't want to be a lesbian."

Dr. Vera hung up the phone and sighed. The theme music began to play in the background, and she glared at the producer as if to say, *Aren't you supposed to be screening these calls!* However, he was too busy devouring his sandwich to notice her. "Cherished friends," she began her usual sign-off message without enthusiasm, "this brings us to the conclusion of another wonderful show. This is Dr. Vera, reminding you that every day can be a great day if you choose to see it that way. Until next time, my friends...!"

As soon as she was off the air she groaned again, grabbed her huge handbag and walked out of the studio. The summer night was hot and humid. The studio was in midtown Manhattan; when Vera got outside, there were thousands of teenagers milling about on the sidewalk. A rock star named Pastranzo had done an interview at the station about four hours ago, when Vera was coming in to work. Awestruck teenage girls had screamed and passed out at the prospect of meeting their hero; ambulances and huge phalanxes of police officers had had to be called in to quell the hysteria. The worst of it seemed to be over, but even though Pastranzo had left the studio hours ago (through a side entrance) the teenagers refused to believe it. They stood their ground, baking in the summer heat with the crazed obstinacy of goats. Vera, who had had to fight her way through the crowd when coming into work, was now forced to do the same thing upon leaving.

All of a sudden, a squealing 14-year-old ran up to her with arms open wide, perhaps thinking that Vera was Pastranzo. As Vera did not have the patience to explain the difference between herself and a stringy-haired Italian man, she put some sense into the girl's head the most efficient way she knew: with a firm backhand.

When she got to the curb, she hailed a cab and headed to Brooklyn. The cab smelled of vomit, curry and toe jam, so she opened the window and groaned again as she sat there brooding.

The two police officers exited the deli, each carrying a Styrofoam coffee cup in one hand and a paper bag of donuts in the other. Just as they reached their patrol car, the first officer bent his head to take a sip of his coffee and noticed the person standing across the street, in the shadows. The neighborhood always seemed as though it were in the middle of nowhere, even though the Brooklyn and Manhattan Bridges towered overhead. On the bridges, and the major thoroughfares that connected to these bridges, traffic zoomed 24 hours a day—except of course when there was a traffic jam. Either way, on the streets below the bridges, there was always a kind of loneliness. Most of the buildings were industrial ware-houses or warehouses that had been converted to luxury condominiums. After dark, the neighborhood was usually deserted. This was why the police officer found the person in the shadows so conspicuous. The first officer got his partner's attention, and then he gestured across the street. His partner stared quizzically in that direction before nodding. They left their coffee and donuts on top of the patrol car and began to walk across the street. Their hands automatically went to their guns. They did not grab them yet, but their fingers were within reach of their weapons. They made no attempt to rush; as they walked, they surveyed the person in the shadows. They took note of where his arms were—if his hands held a weapon. At last, when they were about to step onto the curb, the first officer called to the figure in the shadows:

"Is everything all right?"

Stacy stepped from the shadows, and they saw her. They surveyed her shapely figure—the way her cotton blouse was moist from the humidity and her sweat; they looked at the way her jeans hugged every succulent contour of her legs. She was like an angel standing there before them. Her hair was long and curly from the humidity; she tossed it over her left shoulder and the officers followed the motion as if it were something miraculous. She smiled, and they instinctively smiled. They forgot about their guns and whatever protocol they had learned in the police academy. There was something infectious about her smile, so that the more they looked at it, the more they smiled and felt overcome by an unnamable feeling that made them feel alive and intoxicated.

"Were you guys concerned about me?" Stacy flirted then, breaking the silence. She smiled wider, and the officers, to their amazement, found themselves giggling along, like two teenage morons. They were speechless in that "I wish I could say something cool, but I'm too overcome with awe" sort of way.

Stacy nodded at that moment, as if acknowledging that they were putty in her hands, and then she gestured toward the all-night deli: "Were you guys making a donut run?"

"Yeah, you know how it is," the second officer said, still shy; but looking at her now, and seeing again how beautiful she was, he suddenly remembered the strangeness of her standing in the shadows. "Is everything all right?"

"Sure, I was waiting for a friend."

"Your friend makes you wait here in the dark?" he said, trying to joke. He felt proud of himself; his partner seemed impressed, so they laughed too loudly at his joke.

It was then that a cab drove up and stopped in front of the deli. They all turned to look as Dr. Vera got out.

"There's my friend," Stacy said, smiling again. However, she made no attempt to get Dr. Vera's attention, and the woman walked into the deli.

Only after the cab had driven off did Stacy and the officers realize they had all stood staring at the scene. The officers looked at Stacy again, and giggled in the same nervous way as she smiled back at them. "Thanks for looking out for me, officers," she said then.

"That's our job," the first officer said with a strange sense of self-importance.

"Can I ask you something?" she said then, lowering her voice, "I mean, between friends?"

"Sure. *Anything*," the officers said in unison, enlivened by the prospect of being her friend.

"Did you ever shoot someone?" she said, gesturing to the first officer's gun.

The officers looked at one another uneasily.

"That's a strange question," the second officer said.

"It's a perfectly natural question," Stacy responded with a shrug. "You guys carry guns for a reason."

"We carry guns to keep the peace—not to shoot people."

She laughed heartily, while they stood there with gloomy expressions on their faces. "You don't need to justify it with me, officers," she continued. "The first time you pull a gun on someone, everything changes. Even if, in your mind, you're telling yourself that you're keeping the peace, once you get that close to death—*to killing someone*—something changes within you. There is a sense of power there that's difficult to turn back from...." She was looking at them with an odd gleam in her eyes; they shrunk away from it—felt cowed before it. They looked at one another uneasily again, but just then Dr. Vera emerged from the deli—

"I guess we'll have to discuss it another time," Stacy said, cutting off their conversation. "It's been a pleasure, gentlemen," she said, beginning to walk across the street. And then, winking at them mischievously over her shoulder, "Don't hurt nobody." Their faces were wretched as they watched her leave, but then their eyes navigated to her retreating buttocks, and they stood staring at the firm perfection of it. They were mesmerized now, forgetting the discomfort they had felt when she asked her strange questions. They forgot about the morbid gleam in her eyes, and the fact that she had been standing alone in the shadows. For those few moments, they became merely men staring at a nice ass.

Dr. Vera had developed a (bad) habit of stopping by the deli after her shows, in order to pick up some junk food. That was especially true on Fridays. Tonight, she was so tired that she would have had the cab wait, in order to drive her the last two blocks, to her luxury condominium, but she had endured enough of the vomit/curry/toe jam stench as she could stand. Even though the blocks of this neighborhood were dark and deserted, there were usually a few policemen lurking around the deli, replenishing their junk food and coffee stocks. That was why this was a relatively safe neighborhood. As she began the trek home, she placed the ice cream and cookies she had bought in her huge handbag. She used the bag to carry her gym clothes, but it had been weeks since she had seen the inside of a gym. Now, as she plopped her ice cream and cookies on top of her gym clothes, she felt no guilt. She was going to eat junk food all week-end. She was going to order pizza and Chinese food, and vegetate in front of the TV, and nobody was going to take that away from her.

Still high from her junk food manifesto, she turned to the right and continued down the block. She noticed Stacy crossing the street, but thought nothing of it. Yes, she would take a long bath and watch the most melodramatic love story she could find on cable TV. It would all be perfect, and she would be at peace…at least, until she went back to work on Monday. These were her thoughts when she heard footsteps behind her. She turned to see Stacy's smiling face:

"I'm a big fan of your show, Dr. Vera," Stacy said as soon as Vera turned around.

"Thank you," Vera responded before turning back around. She started walking quickly, hoping to get away, but Stacy matched her pace, her youth and grinning face seeming somehow inescapable. Unable to stand it anymore, Vera swung around and faced Stacy, who was walking by her side as though she had been invited home: "What do you want?" she said gruffly; but then, seeing Stacy's grinning, awestruck face, she sighed and reverted to her radio persona: "How may I help you today?"

Stacy squealed with delight, because that was the phrase Dr. Vera used to greet all the guests/patients on her radio show. Stacy was still beaming, like some kind of star-struck imbecile.

"How may I help you?" Vera said again, to bring Stacy from her trance. This time, Stacy nodded excitedly, saying:

"I'm the one who is here to help you, Vera. May I call you Vera?" she said, smiling again.

"Sure—fine," she said with a certain amount of annoyance. She started walking again—calmly this time, but nonetheless with the hope of getting away from the woman. "How do you intend to help me?" she said with the same twinge of annoyance in her voice.

"There's something in my car I want you to see."

"Something's in your car?" she said, fighting to understand. "What are you talking about?"

"Well, that's my quandary. If I tell you what it is, you may not want to come; at the same time, you may not want to come unless you know what it is. ...Will you come with me, no questions asked?"

"No," Vera said frankly.

"I understand," Stacy said, bowing her head thoughtfully. At last, she looked up and sighed, saying: "That leaves me no choice."

Stacy's tone and body language disturbed Vera, so that she was a little breathless as she said, "What do you mean?"

Stacy hiked up her blouse then, and pulled out a .22. Vera froze, but Stacy gripped her upper arm with her free hand and pulled her along, saying, "I need you to come with me, Vera."

Vera stumbled along, dazed.

Stacy continued: "As I tried telling you before, I need you, Vera. However, you need me as well—you just don't know it yet."

Stacy made Vera take a right turn, away from her condominium. After walking half a block, Vera began to regain her composure; her mind worked frantically.

"What's this all about?" she said, her voice hoarse.

"I need you to come and see what's in my car," Stacy said plainly.

Vera tried to think up everything she knew on escaping an abductor; for a moment, she thought about hitting the woman with her huge handbag. She shook her head. "Look," Vera tried to reason with her, "there is no need for a gun—the main thing is that we talk."

"I'm not one of your patients, Vera," Stacy said with a calm chuckle, "—but I'll talk if you want…as long as you come to my car."

Stacy's grip was firm and commanding; their pace was not exactly brisk, but in her dazed state, Vera found herself stumbling along. Her limbs felt like rubber. Her stomach felt queasy, so that she worried about throwing up over the designer outfit François had picked for her.

Stacy tugged at her arm again—she had been about to walk into a street lamp. Vera forced her mind to be still: she had to reason her way out of this!

"Hey," she began, trying to forge some kind of connection with her abductor, "you didn't tell me what your name is."

"My name is Stacy."

"Okay, Stacy," she began with new hope. "What's so important about your car?" As she asked the question, she suddenly remembered that people who got into a car with an abductor were more likely to be killed… or did that just apply to men abducting women. "What do you want from me?" she said at last.

"I guess that's a fair question," Stacy said with a shrug of her shoulders. "I suppose it can't hurt now, as we know where we stand." As she said this last part, she waved the gun ostentatiously in the air, like one would a diamond ring. There was a nonchalant expression on her face now as she began, "The fact of the matter is, Vera, that I killed my boyfriend tonight."

Vera stopped and stared at Stacy—to see if this was some kind of sick joke—but there was something in Stacy's eyes that told Vera she was looking at a murderer. She quivered; Stacy smiled, then tugged at her arm again, so they could continue walking. Vera felt dazed and wretched again.

"Before you get excited," Stacy continued after a while, "it's not what you think."

Vera had to take a deep breath before she could talk. "…It doesn't matter what I think," she started. "The important question is, what do you think it is?"

Stacy squealed with delight again. "Good, good—you have to keep the lunatic talking about herself. And you know what? I will keep talking—we have about fifteen minutes to wait anyway."

"Fifteen minutes until what?"

"Come on," she said, pulling Vera's arm again. "That's the big surprise… I've thought about it for a while now, Vera: if I tell you what has happened, you won't believe me anyway. The only way is for you to see for yourself."

"Okay," Vera forced herself to speak. "So, why did you kill your boyfriend?"

"I killed him so you would be able to see."

"See what?"

"The true nature of life and death."

Vera took another deep breath. "Why is it important to you that I see that?"

Stacy snickered. "You're thinking I'm some kind of celebrity stalker: that I've lost sight of reality and think a voice I hear over the radio is the center of my life. That's hardly the case, Vera. I actually think you're a spoiled, condescending bitch."

"So you're here to take revenge on me?"

Stacy laughed again. "Nah. Like I said, I'm here because I need you, Vera—and because you need me: mutual need."

"Why do I need you?" she said, still struggling to understand.

"You will know that for yourself, once you see what's in my car. Needs don't require justifications and explanations: that's the great thing about them. If you're hungry, you don't have to come up with a million reasons why you're hungry. You just have to say 'I'm hungry' and you go and get something to eat. In the same way, I could give you a million reasons why you should come with me, or what I need from you, but once you see the nature of our mutual need, you'll realize all those reasons are a waste of time. My car is right at the end of the block," she concluded.

"Where are you going to drive me?" Vera said uneasily.

"I'm not going to drive you anywhere, Vera. We're going to sit in my car for"—she looked at her watch—"another thirteen minutes, and then, if you wish, you can go home."

Vera frowned. "We're just going to sit in your car?"

"That's right. We're going to sit there, and you're going to see something that will change the way you think of yourself as a human being."

There was something ridiculous about the proposition, and Vera, despite everything, could not suppress her smile. Stacy smiled as well.

"Laugh if you wish, Vera. Twelve minutes from now, you'll thank me."

Vera stared at her for a while—as if some clue in her face would reveal everything to be an elaborate joke: one of those celebrity hidden camera shows, perhaps, where a celebrity was made to endure an embarrassing or frightening situation before the host came out and revealed that it was all a joke...but the streets were bare and dark. They had walked several blocks so far: unless there were cameras on every block, then Vera really was being abducted by a madwoman. A new sense of panic began to rise within her. She looked at Stacy anxiously: "...Did you really say you killed your boyfriend tonight?" She asked the question as if she suspected that she had misheard Stacy—as if this entire situation could be explained by some misunderstanding, but:

"Yeah, I killed him," she said simply. "I killed him so you could see that you need me."

Vera suddenly felt sick. She looked at Stacy pleadingly: "You keep saying that I need you, but it doesn't mean anything. I don't know you—I don't *need* you. And you don't need me. We're *strangers* to one another."

"You're the center of everything, Vera," Stacy countered. "I need you to be the objective observer in all this—the *skeptic*."

"So, this is all some kind of experiment?"

"'Experiment' makes it seem so sterile. This is about life and death, Vera, and those things are always messy."

Vera stared at her for a while, then she stared at the ground and shook her head. "You're really going to let me go after all this?"

"You'll be able to leave if you wish, but once you see our mutual need..."

Stacy did not complete the sentence, and Vera nodded. Her mind felt overwrought—on the verge of collapse. She looked over at Stacy again, still struggling to digest the few facts that would keep her in contact with reality.

"You said you killed your boyfriend *tonight?*"

"Yeah—about forty-five minutes ago."

"*What?*"

Stacy laughed. "You think I'm lying to you, don't you? Admit it: part of you thinks this is some kind of attention-getting stunt?" she said, smiling with an odd expression in her eyes.

The expression made Vera turn away; she felt queasy again. Yet, maybe it was to try to fool Stacy into believing she was not afraid that Vera said, "You don't seem like a murderer."

Stacy laughed heartily, so that the sound echoed down the long, empty, warehouse-lined blocks. "What's a murderer supposed to look like?" she said between laughs. "...You'd be surprised by what a murderer looks like, Vera. You'd be surprised to know how easy it is to kill someone."

By now, Vera could practically taste the vomit in her mouth; she had the urge to spit and lie down, but she forced herself to speak—to try to forge some kind of connection with her abductor. "Did you shoot him with that gun?" she said, gesturing to the thing in Stacy's free hand.

"No, I stabbed him with an ice pick." And then, with her usual frankness: "When you stab someone with an ice pick—right in the heart—there isn't that much blood. There's less mess."

"Oh," Vera said when she could think of nothing else to say.

"What are you thinking now?" Stacy said with a laugh.

"I don't know...You kidnap me and tell me that you've killed your boyfriend, and then you talk as though nothing's wrong—as though killing your boyfriend is no big deal."

"It's not—I've done it three times so far."

"What?" Vera said with an uneasy laugh, hoping beyond hope that this was all part of the sick joke.

"You still don't think I look like the type?" Stacy said, smiling morbidly.

The expression on Stacy's face made Vera shudder. She took a deep breath to calm herself. And then, in a low, non-threatening voice: "I told you before that it doesn't matter what I think. The only thing that matters—"

"Yeah, yeah," Stacy said in annoyance, "—the only thing that matters is what I believe."

They walked along in a brooding silence for a moment. The silence ate away at Vera more savagely than the horrible things Stacy had said. Vera felt somehow that she had to make peace:

"Maybe if you told me your motive in killing your boyfriend I'd be able to understand."

Stacy sighed. "Terms like 'motive' are irrelevant, Vera. I didn't kill my boyfriend for any of the usual reasons. He wasn't abusive; it wasn't a crime of passion or something like that. I didn't do it because I was bored and thought I could get away with it. I don't hear homicidal voices in my head. In fact, I didn't take any steps to get away with it: if my 'experiment,' as you called it, fails, my case will be the easiest murder trial in history—and you'll have something to talk about on your show on Monday. It will be like the Forget-Me-Not incident all over again. It will revive your career. So, you see, you win no matter what, Vera."

Vera was looking at her with a frown on her face, as if trying to tackle an equation that refused to add up. Stacy laughed at her expression. "Don't overanalyze, Vera. For once, just sit back and observe. You don't have to come to any conclusions right now; you don't have to treat me—I'm not one of your patients. And of course, there is no point in thinking you can escape me," she said, displaying the gun once again. "This is a great moment in your life," she went on joyously, "—remember I said that afterwards. I'm going to show you something beyond anything you ever thought was possible. Nothing I can say to you can express what I will show you in a few minutes. And, speaking of which, here we are," she said, gesturing to the utility van parked on the curb.

Vera looked at the vehicle warily. A van seemed to hold more unwholesome possibilities than a car—especially where an abductor was involved. It was a rental van—the rental company's logo was emblazoned in huge purple and orange letters on the side. It fit in with the other commercial vehicles parked on the block, but it seemed dark and ominous: there were no side or rear windows on the vehicle, so that no one would be able to see what was going on inside. While Vera was thinking these thoughts, Stacy let go of her arm and went to the side sliding door. In a deft motion, she pulled it open (it was unlocked); as soon as the door was open, the nude torso of a body flopped out. It was Stacy's boyfriend. There was a street-lamp nearby, and Vera saw the horrified expression that was frozen on his face. His eyes were staring into space; his mouth was gaping; and as the body was totally naked, Vera could see the handle of the ice pick sticking out of his chest—

"Oops," Stacy said, pushing the corpse back into the van, "I guess the body shifted while I was driving around."

Vera's handbag slipped from her shoulder; she took a step back and went to scream, but nothing came out—

"Don't scream," Stacy warned her, "—we don't want to attract any attention to ourselves."

Vera took some more shambling steps back; the scream that would not come was still reflected on her face—

"It's too late to walk away now, Vera," Stacy chastised her, as if disappointed. And then, as Vera continued to retreat, "Get back over here!" she said in an angry whisper. In three steps, she had Vera by the arm again.

"Leave me alone," Vera pleaded, "—I don't want any part of this!"

Stacy pulled her back over to the vehicle. "You don't know what you want, Vera…but everything will be clear in eight minutes. For now, let's wait inside—"

"You can't be serious!" Vera said when she realized that Stacy meant for her to go in the back with the body. Vera tried to make a break for it, but Stacy grabbed her and shoved her into the dark, gaping entrance of the van. Stacy was strong and vicious for a beautiful, waif-looking girl. Vera banged her knee as she was sent flying. She landed on top of the body; she felt the hard handle of the ice pick against the warm, clammy elasticity of the body. She squealed and scurried into a dark empty corner, in the rear.

At last, Stacy threw the huge handbag into the van, before getting into the vehicle and pulling the door shut. For a few seconds, they were in total darkness, but then Stacy turned on the ceiling light. Vera was sobbing by now, partly from the pain of her banged knee and partly from the terror that came with the reality she was trapped in the back of a van with a corpse and a gun-wielding murderer.

Stacy tried talking to her in a soothing voice: "There's no need to cry. I told you that you're in no danger." Nevertheless, Vera continued to sob. She sat with her knees touching her bowed forehead—like a child trying to hide in the back of a closet. With the outside heat, it was like an oven in the back of the van. Sweat was already streaming down Vera's face; and with the heat, the sickly sweet odor of blood seemed more sickening somehow.

"Come over here," Stacy said. She was still crouched by the body. Vera ignored her, or did not hear her. "Come *here!*" Stacy commanded, so that Vera jumped and looked up. Vera's face was lined with tears; her eyes were red. "Come here," Stacy said in a more neutral voice. She gestured with her hand for Vera to come—the way a mother gestured for a baby to take its first steps—but Vera saw that the gun was still in her hand.

"Please come," Stacy said at last, and Vera wiped away as many tears as she could, got on her hands and knees, and crawled over to Stacy and the body. As she crawled, she stared at Stacy's beautiful, encouraging face. She found that if she stared at the face, she could block out everything else: all the immediate realities and horrors. When she was close to Stacy, the young woman smiled, as if proud of her.

"Okay," Stacy said in a new voice, as if all that had passed before were forgiven and forgotten, "—I need you to do one last thing."

Vera tried to open her mouth to ask what Stacy wanted, but her jaw was tight and unresponsive. Stacy went on:

"I need you to check his vital signs, so you know that he's really dead."

Vera glanced at the naked body, then back at Stacy's beautiful face. She shook her head, pleading…

"Check his vitals," Stacy said, calmly but firmly, so that Vera began to sob once more. Vera looked down at the body and again noticed that it was nude. She looked away. "Go on," Stacy coaxed her again. At last, like a child ordered to do something onerous, Vera stifled a sob, reached her hand down and felt the boyfriend's neck. She did so without looking directly at the nude body. The skin was still warm and clammy, but there was no pulse.

Stacy laughed at her. "I didn't know you'd be such a prude, Vera. You have a problem looking at a naked man? Aren't you supposed to be a sex and relationship therapist?"

"I like my naked men breathing," Vera mumbled sarcastically.

Stacy laughed louder. "That's a good one!" She seemed pleased with the way everything had turned out. While she continued to laugh, Vera glanced down at the body again:

"Why is he naked?"

"I told you I planned everything, didn't I?" Vera nodded her head tentatively; Stacy went on—"…I didn't want to get any blood on his clothes. I hate making a mess."

Vera frowned in bewilderment. "You can kill someone, but you don't want to make a mess?"

"You have no idea what a headache it is to clean up blood. When you cut a major artery, the blood gushes all over the walls…clothes…*everything*? You can spend hours cleaning up afterwards—and I don't have time for that."

"That's understandable," Vera said when she could think of nothing else to say.

"Anyway," Stacy went on matter-of-factly, "since I've started using an ice pick, I don't have to worry about that too much anymore, but I still hate getting holes in shirts. I hate ruining perfectly good shirts. That's why I made him take all his clothes off."

That, too, seemed reasonable; and despite everything, Vera found herself nodding.

Stacy was still pleased with everything, and she smiled grandly all of a sudden. "Let me tell you how I killed him!" she started, seeming proud. "I told him that I had this fantasy to have wild sex in the back of a rental van!" She started laughing to herself as she remembered it all. "He's such a moron: You can get him to do anything once you tell him there's sex involved. You could get him to jump off a bridge if you told him there was an orgy going on at the bottom of it." At this, she threw her head back and laughed heartily. Vera could only stare. It left her stomach feeling unsettled, so she looked away. However, all there was to see was the nude corpse. She noticed, for the first time, that the boyfriend's clothes were heaped to the side, along with his shoes. Her eyes went to the flaccid penis, then glanced away—

"You can look at his cock if you want," Stacy said with a laugh, "—even though it's not that much to look at." Here, she pursed her lips and sat assessing his penis the way an art dealer assessed a painting. "But let me assure you," she went on thoughtfully, "that what he lacks in size, he more than makes up for in originality and imagination—"

All at once, Vera had to put her hand over her mouth to hold back the surge of vomit. She felt it in her throat, but mercifully, it went back down. She groaned and swayed—

"Don't you *dare* throw up in here!" Stacy warned her. "It's bad enough cleaning up blood. Just suck it up for six more minutes."

Vera felt dizzy. She glanced at the body again, before once more looking away uneasily.

"Don't be such a prude, Vera." Stacy laughed again. "Hey, you ever do it in public? My boyfriend liked to do it in public all the time—that's why it was so easy to get him into the van. ...This one time, we got caught by these two old ladies—"

"Would you *please* shut up!" Vera screamed, unable to stand anymore of Stacy's ghoulish bragging.

"That was uncalled for," Stacy said as if stung. "Besides, I'm talking like you asked me to. You have to keep the lunatic talking, remember," she teased her.

"You don't need to talk anymore," Vera whispered, fighting her dizziness. She glanced at the body again:"—Oh God!" she broke down, as if only just now grasping the situation. "He's dead—he's *really* dead! ...And you killed him."

"Yeah, he's dead all right," Stacy said with a shrug and a mischievous wink.

Vera tried to reason with her again: "What good is keeping me here going to do? Why don't you let me leave now?"

"After all the trouble I went through: renting the van, killing my boyfriend...? You're the key to everything, Vera—you can't leave yet. You're the one who will make all this real."

Vera began to sob again—she could not help herself.

"Don't stress yourself." Stacy tried to soothe her. "We only have five minutes left."

"Would you stop that goddamn countdown!" Vera screamed. "I feel like I'm watching the New Year's Eve countdown on TV! Just let me go. Turn yourself in..."

Stacy shushed her. "Don't come undone on me, Vera. I told you before that you had to be the skeptic in all this—the objective observer. We can't have you cracking up."

"You expect me to sit here calmly with your dead, naked boyfriend lying there, and you holding a gun on me!"

"Sure, why not? If I can stay here, then so can you."

"You're not well!"

Stacy opened her mouth to say something, but Vera interrupted her. "Please, don't talk to me anymore—do whatever you're going to do, but don't talk."

Stacy smiled at her. "Talk makes things go faster. Besides, don't you think it would be kind of morbid to just sit here silently in the dark, staring at a dead body?"

"I think it's morbid to kill your boyfriend and then abduct someone to brag about it."

Stacy laughed again. "I guess this is a little odd."

"A little odd!" Vera bristled at the phrasing. "He's *dead*. Doesn't that mean anything to you? ...Look, you're not well. I can help you if you wish—"

Stacy was laughing so hard that she looked as though she would collapse. "I told you before that I'm not one of your patients, Vera."

"You subconsciously know that you need help—that's why you kidnapped a psychologist."

Stacy scoffed: "You blasted psychologists and your subconscious motives!"

Yet, there was still a satisfied smile on her face. She was pleased with the way everything had turned out. She glanced at her watch now: "It's almost time," she announced. When she looked up, there was an excited expression on her face: "…We can start now."

"Start what?"

"Start cleaning him up." And as she said it, she reached into the corner, to her right, and picked up a plastic bag. She took a dark towel out of it, then she returned to the body and pulled the ice pick out of the corpse's chest. There was a trickle of blood, but she pressed the towel into it. Vera watched all this with new fascination, wondering what strange ritual Stacy was going to perform on the body. Now, Stacy was rubbing the towel over the body tenderly. There was something almost erotic about it and Vera's face creased when the thought registered in her mind.

"Did you love him?" Vera ventured.

"More than that, Vera. I need him."

"Just like you need me?"

"Exactly," she said, looking up at Vera with the same odd gleam in her eyes.

Vera forced herself not to look away: "Do you always kill the things you need?"

Stacy thought about it for a while, and then she chuckled.

Vera continued: "You said you've killed two other people. Did you need them too?"

Stacy laughed louder. "I told you not to overanalyze, Vera. Just wait three more minutes."

"Three more minutes until what!"

"Patience," she said with a smile. She finished toweling off the body and placed the towel back in the plastic bag.

"Why'd you do that?"

"I told you that everything has to be ready."

Vera groaned in frustration: "Ready for *what*?"

"Patience, my friend."

Vera glanced at the body again. "The other times you killed—were they men as well?"

"Yes," she said coyly, "—all men." And then, with another laugh: "You're thinking I have some kind of hang-up against men—some kind of insane grievance."

"Do you?"

Stacy laughed carelessly, almost falling over again. "You mean that I hated my father and I'm trying to get back at my first boyfriend for breaking my heart—that kind of thing?"

"You tell me."

"Nah," she said with a nonchalant chuckle, "men are just easier to kill than women."

"Why?"

"I don't know many women intimately enough to kill them."

"You only kill people you've been intimate with?"

"Of course: killing is a very intimate act, Vera—like sex. You can't go around doing it to everyone. …I mean, you can, but then it loses its significance."

"And what is the significance of all this," she said, gesturing about the van, "—proving your theories?"

"Proving them to *you*: I've already proven them to myself. …The truth isn't useful until it's known to others."

Vera stared at her for a while. "How long have you been killing?"

"Since last weekend."

Vera went to say something, but Stacy shushed her then. She was looking down at her watch again. "It's time, Vera," she said at last, her eyes gleaming with excitement. "Get ready!"

"Get ready for what?" she said in bewilderment.

Stacy smiled grandly then, and pointed down at the body: "…And, *now!*" she whispered.

As she said it, the corpse convulsed and took a long, rasping inhalation—as if the boyfriend had only been holding his breath all that time! Vera gasped and scurried back into the corner. She realized that she could not breathe. She lay frozen as the boyfriend began to move. For a few moments, inarticulate sounds escaped from his mouth—groans—as if he were having a bad nightmare. Then, all at once, the boyfriend sat upright and opened his eyes. Vera went to scream, but the sound again would not come, so she lay there, trying to breathe. Stacy held the boyfriend then, and shushed him.

"This is only a dream," she whispered as she caressed the nape of his neck. "Go back to sleep, sweetheart. We had wonderful sex, and this is merely a dream. Close your eyes and sleep." At that, the boyfriend lay back down and was soon snoring. Stacy smiled at him and caressed his hair. Vera still had not moved. When she could breathe again, she found herself hyperventilating. Stacy looked back at her and winked mischievously.

Stacy opened the back door, and they got out of the vehicle. Vera was trembling.

"Take long, deep breaths, Vera," Stacy advised her, to stop her hyperventilating. Stacy opened the passenger side door of the van then, and gestured with her head for Vera to get in. After Vera had complied, Stacy walked around and got into the driver's seat. Vera was sitting there, staring ahead. Only when Stacy slammed the driver's side door did Vera seem to come to her senses. She jumped in her seat and looked around as if just waking up.

"What just happened!" she said breathlessly.

Stacy smiled. "You saw for yourself and you still have to ask questions?"

"He was dead…" Vera whispered, staring ahead blankly.

"And now he's alive again."

"Are you saying he can't die?"

"I've killed him three times so far," Stacy said nonchalantly.

"The two other people you said you killed…you mean it was only him all the time?"

"Yes. He keeps coming back to life."

"How is that possible?"

Stacy smiled at her—as if she had said something stupid. "You ask the wrong questions, Vera."

"What do you mean?"

"When you witness something that is clearly impossible, asking 'why' and 'how' is a waste of time. The important thing is that we know the impossible is possible—that everything we thought to be real is irrelevant."

"You're saying you don't care how he comes back to life? You don't care if he's immortal—if there's something about his physiology that can make us all live forever?"

"Living forever is a fool's desire, Vera," Stacy chastised her, as if disappointed by the limits of her imagination. When Vera looked at her helplessly, she said, "You'll see what I mean."

Vera nodded her head, even though she still understood nothing. She sat silently for a while, staring out of the windshield blankly. At last, something occurred to her: "How'd you find out he couldn't die? There had to be a first time?"

"I don't like thinking about it," Stacy said flatly. She retreated into herself.

"Please," Vera pressed her. "What happened?"

"Okay." She sighed as she thought about it. "We went hiking last weekend—in Vermont. We were out in the middle of nowhere, hiking on this beautiful mountain ridge. We could see out over the entire valley. We could see for miles. It was the middle of the afternoon, and the scene was like a postcard. We were walking on this narrow ledge. It was just a few feet wide at most; to the left, there was a ravine—a drop of at least one thousand feet. My boyfriend was walking in front. I can't remember what he was talking about exactly—but he kept looking over his shoulder, at me, as he walked. He wasn't paying attention to where he was walking, and he had made a misstep. He tried to catch his balance; he waved his arms in the air and arched his back, trying to keep from falling over the edge, but it was no use. It happened so quickly...I was frozen in place. Soon, he was toppling over the edge, into the ravine. He disappeared into the shadows of trees. He brushed past some of them on the way down, and then there was this sickening thud. It seemed to echo through the entire valley."

"My God," Vera whispered. "What did you do?"

"For a while, I couldn't do anything. I stood there, frozen. It was as if my mind refused to accept it. I was in shock. If he had fallen, I knew that he was dead, and I could not bring myself to accept it. Maybe I stood there for thirty seconds or a minute, waiting for my mind to accept what had happened. ...And we were in the middle of nowhere. My boyfriend was the hiking buff, not me. I had no idea how to navigate the woods and read maps. If he was dead, then I'd be lost in the woods by myself. I'm not saying I was only thinking of me, but all these thoughts made my mind lock up—

"I remember that I screamed all of a sudden. It just came out of me—as if my mind had added up everything and the scream was the result. Anyway, the scream seemed to break the spell somewhat, because I began to run—or at least, to move as quickly as I could down the narrow path. The path meandered down to the ravine. It was a *long* hike—about an hour. I couldn't think anymore—I just jogged. Every once in a while, I would remember that my boyfriend had fallen over the edge and that I was alone. By the time I got down to the floor of the ravine my mind was like something that had been chewed up. I was expecting him to be dead. I didn't have any hopes. I was just rushing to...I don't even know why. I was rushing because it was something to do. Also, he had the cell phone. I was thinking that maybe I could call for help—even though that was stupid, as we were out in the woods, and there was no service. I was crying. The tears were streaming down my face before I became conscious of them. I was already mourning him. ...But when I got to the foot of the ravine, I saw him walking toward me, dusting off his clothes. I froze. He walked the rest of the way to me. There was this confused expression on his face. 'What happened?' he said. I grabbed him and hugged him, screaming, 'I thought you were dead!' I began to cry again, but now in relief. 'What happened?' he said again. I detached from him and stared up at him. 'You're really not hurt?' I asked. He said he was fine, but then asked how he'd gotten down there. I told him that he had fallen; and then, I pointed up to the hiking trail: 'You fell from *there*.' We both stared up at it. He seemed more shocked than me. I reasoned: 'You must have been knocked out by the fall. You sure you didn't break anything?' He said, 'No, I'm fine...but if I fell from there...'

"He did not finish the statement, but it was in my mind too. If he had fallen from there, then he should be dead. We continued walking, but I kept thinking, 'He should be dead.' Or, if not dead, he should have some broken bones or something. I was grateful that he seemed well, but I knew, deep down in my heart, that it was impossible, and something was wrong.

"We made it to the campsite. It was nighttime now. We were lying on one of those air mattresses. We had finished eating, and were lying there staring up at the stars. The fire we had used to cook earlier was dwindling down—but the moon was out, highlighting everything. It was peaceful, and I began to put thoughts of death out of my mind. Anyway, one thing led to another and we started making love. ...The sensation of the wind blowing on bare skin makes you feel alive and free. When you make love outside, you feel like you're making love to the entire world. It's almost like you're drawing off all the world's energy and using it for your pleasure. You feel limitless. I felt myself drifting off into the pleasure—*losing myself*— when my boyfriend suddenly stopped and looked at me with a terrified frown: 'You hear something?' he whispered. I held my breath and listened, but I didn't hear anything. 'Like what?' I whispered back. 'Footsteps?' he said, but there was a slight smile on his face now, so I knew he was kidding. 'I thought you liked an audience,' I teased him, and caressed his back, so he could continue making love to me. We liked to talk while we made love— to tell one another all kinds of crazy things. That's when I whispered, 'Wouldn't it be a turn-on if people could see us lying here: you on top of me while I take every delicious thrust?' He liked it when I said stupid shit like that. He groaned in agreement and pleasure. I went on: 'What if two Boy Scouts had wandered away from their camp and were watching us right now—seeing how a man does it to a woman; hearing how a man makes a woman moan?' And I groaned there and sucked at his neck. I was turning myself on—turning us both on, imagining two 12-year-olds gaping at us beyond the bushes...perhaps jerking their 12-year-old dicks frantically, fantasizing that they were my boyfriend—that they could make a woman scream like my boyfriend was making me scream. And I clawed at my boyfriend's back then: that was always the signal to go faster. Sometimes

I slapped his ass—like a jockey telling a horse to go faster…and I felt the tension building in my body—in *both* of our bodies. For those few perfect moments my boyfriend and I were one beast: muscles contracting and flexing, fingers clawing…and then I was screaming and shuddering; and then, after he had had his pleasure, all was still, except for our panting and the sound of wind blowing through the leaves.

"For a while we dozed in that position, with him lying on top of me. Maybe five or ten minutes passed that way. Eventually, he said that he had to use the bathroom. I wanted him to lie there with me. …Maybe I sensed something was going to happen to him if he wandered into the woods by himself; maybe I simply didn't want to disturb our comfortable position. 'Don't go!' I found myself begging him. Soon, for whatever reason, I found myself crying—pleading with him not to go. All the old fears from the ravine came flooding back—all the terror and abandonment I had felt for that horrible hour, when I hiked down to the floor of the ravine, thinking that he was dead. He got annoyed with me and my crying, calling me a drama queen; and then, he stormed off into the bushes, totally nude. By now, our fire was only some glowing embers. I strained my eyes, but he had totally disappeared into the darkness. I was alone. I felt naked for the first time—*vulnerable*. You know that sense you have sometimes, that someone's watching you? All of a sudden I had this feeling like someone was watching me. It was like a cold breeze blowing down my back. It wasn't horny Boy Scouts anymore, but someone evil: someone who had entered the woods to hunt and butcher us. …A drifter: some trucker who had hiked from the highway because he knew that this was where all the kids came to screw. All these things went through my head, and I found myself panicking. I wanted to call to my boyfriend, but I was terrified. Maybe a side of me thought that he was already gone: that the drifter had gotten him. I wanted to go to him, but I kept thinking that if the drifter had gotten him, then I'd only be walking into an ambush. All these things went through my head. I was trapped—alone in the middle of nowhere. I suddenly wanted to get dressed—to clothe and protect myself… but my clothes were strewn all over the campsite—where my boyfriend had thrown them while stripping them off. My blouse was on a log over there, and my pants were on a boulder. Both were on the periphery of the campsite, near the bushes. I felt that if I went to pick them up, then the drifter would get me, so I sat there trembling and crying. I kept looking at the place in the bushes where my boyfriend had disappeared, desperate for him to reappear. I tried to listen for the sound of his approach, but between my heartbeat and the wind rustling the leaves, I couldn't hear anything. In fact, I suddenly realized someone could use that to sneak up on me. I turned and looked over my shoulder, expecting the drifter to be there. I was already prepared to scream; in my mind, he had a knife ready…but when I looked, there was nobody there. To be safe, I scanned all three hundred sixty degrees of the campsite. I saw no one, but every wind-blown branch and shrub seemed to be hiding him. I turned in so many directions that I felt dizzy and sick. I couldn't stand it anymore. I was about to scream out my boyfriend's name, so that he would come running and chase away all my fears. I wanted to hold him close; and maybe, afterwards, we would make slow, passionate love as to say that everything was forgiven—

"But that's when I heard my boyfriend scream. It was short and high-pitched—a terrified scream…and then there was the sound of a body dropping to the ground. At the sound, I dug my fingernails into the earth so forcefully that half of them snapped. When you're in that kind of situation your mind tries to convince you that you hadn't heard what you had just heard. I told myself that maybe a branch had fallen or something. I fished around for some explanation, but there was nothing. That's when I remembered the kitchen knife. I had packed it in my boyfriend's camping bag. It was only a few feet from where we had laid out the mattress to make love. I sprung at it; soon, I was flinging out pots and clothes—everything—until I had the knife in my hand. I checked the campsite again—in case the drifter had tried to sneak up while I was searching. I still didn't see anyone, but what you can't see is always more frightening than what you can. I could sense someone out there. I tried to call to my boyfriend again, but my throat was dry. …Somehow, I was walking toward the bushes.

There was something about holding the knife that gave me courage. I didn't feel invulnerable, but the knife was like one of those religious objects that you put all your faith in—an amulet. I felt that it would take care of everything. ...And I knew that there was no running away. Even if I ran in the opposite direction, I would have to enter the bushes anyway, as they surrounded the campsite. ...I had no choice but to keep walking.

"And then, just as I reached the edge of the campsite, a form suddenly appeared in front of me—a *man*. He leapt at me, like some kind of wild animal. My body reacted—even before I could scream. My arm thrust the knife forward with the force of my full weight. And then I was screaming—from my terror, from a sense of vindication...everything came flowing out of me. The man's body fell backwards; the knife was still sticking out of his chest. For a moment, I just stood there panting; but when I looked down at the body, I saw my boyfriend lying there. I had killed him. When he cried out earlier, he had probably only banged his foot on a root or something."

"What did you do?" Vera whispered.

"He was already dead by the time I bent down to hold him. The knife went straight through his heart. I pulled out the blade, as if that would take everything back, but that only caused his blood to gush out. I got sprayed with it. It went all over my body, my face, my hair... I tasted it. ...For the first ten minutes or so I held him...weeping...begging for forgiveness. I was insane with grief. Either I cried myself to sleep or I passed out. I was roused back into consciousness when he came back to life an hour later."

"That didn't freak you out?"

"I was delirious by then. We were both dazed: you see how he is when he first comes back. His mind is a blank slate. You can tell him anything and he'll believe and do it. ...He wanted to know where he was, what he was covered in, what had happened...? I was so relieved that he was alive that the only thing I could do was tell him how happy and relieved I was. I kept telling him that over and over again. We fell asleep like that: covered in his blood, holding one another in the bushes."

"What did you tell him in the morning?"

"Oh," she said with a smile, "when he woke up and saw all the blood, he screamed. He thought I was dead. That's how he woke me up. What had happened the night before was foggy for both of us: he remembered nothing, and what I remembered seemed impossible."

"So, how did you explain the blood?"

"I told him I must have had my period during the night."

"He believed that?"

She smiled. "You know how men are: once he heard the 'p-word' he leapt up and ran down to the river, to bathe. We never talked about it after that."

"You said you've killed him three times?"

"Yes."

"Why'd you kill him the second time?"

"Well, what had happened in the woods was so unbelievable that it was driving me crazy. All week, it was eating away at me. We'd be eating breakfast, and I'd look over at him, wondering if it had really happened—if I was losing my mind. It was all I would think about. So, yesterday, I killed him to see if it had really happened—if he really couldn't die."

Vera stared at her with a frown: "You killed him just like that?"

Stacy shrugged: "I'm not saying I was exactly sane. I spent four sleepless days reliving everything that had happened in the woods—asking myself what the hell had happened. At first, I told myself that I had imagined everything. ...But I couldn't ignore the facts. Right after he woke up in the morning and rushed off to the river to wash off the blood, I looked about the campsite. All the evidence was there: the bloody knife, the ransacked hiking bag that I had gotten the knife from...and all the blood that covered me. I was too honest with myself to believe it had been a dream, or that I had only wounded him and not killed him. Even when I looked at him afterwards, he had no knife wound. I knew then that it had all happened: that I had stabbed and killed my boyfriend, and that he had come back to life. ...I guess I was like you at first, asking myself how it had happened. I came up with all these bizarre explanations in my mind. That didn't really get me anywhere—it just separated me from the one reality that mattered: I had killed my boyfriend and he had come back to life. So, when I killed him again yesterday, it was to verify that truth to myself. The bloody knife from the campsite, which I had wrapped in plastic and kept as evidence, was not enough for me anymore. The dried blood really did not look like blood anymore, but like some other brownish film. The only thing left to me was killing him. That was the only thing that would make it real."

"How'd you kill him?" Vera asked, suddenly fascinated.

"I killed him in his sleep. We had seen *Eye of the Needle* a few days back—that old spy movie where Donald Sutherland played a Nazi assassin. That's where I got the ice pick idea from. I waited until my boyfriend was asleep, but even after he was snoring, all the 'sane' doubts began to enter my mind again: 'What if it had only been a dream—a *delusion*. People did not die and come back to life…' I told myself all these things. Maybe an hour passed with me debating if I should do it or not. I got out of bed and walked around the apartment, talking to myself."

"How did you finally get the nerve to do it?" Vera pressed her.

Stacy paused, thinking about it. "…When I was about twelve, I had this huge fight with my best friend. She thought Harold Turley was the cutest boy in school and I thought Anthony Rivers was the cutest. We started yelling at one another, with me screaming 'Anthony Rivers is the cutest!' and her yelling 'No, Harold Turley!' We were screaming at the top of our voices, and then the next thing I knew, I had punched her in the face—knocked her out *cold*.

"When I was debating with myself over if I should kill him or not, it was as if there were two screaming voices inside of me: one screaming 'Do it!' and the other screaming, 'Don't!' The voices were blaring in my head, driving me crazy, and the next thing I knew, I screamed out and stabbed my boyfriend in the chest. After I had done it, his body convulsed. I pulled out the ice pick and ran out of the bedroom. I threw up then and collapsed on the ground. I noticed the time on the VCR clock as I lay on the ground in a daze; an hour and six minutes later, my boyfriend came out of the bedroom and asked me what was going on."

"What did you tell him?"

"I told him that everything was fine, and that he should go to sleep on the couch; afterwards, I went to clean the bedroom."

Vera nodded numbly. "...And then you decided to kill him today and show me?"

"I was thinking about it all week—about contacting you. I listened to your show for the first time on Monday, after we got back from Vermont. It was something to do late at night, since I couldn't sleep anyway. There was something about you—some connection...I found that listening to you helped me to feel better somehow. ...I followed you home from work on Wednesday, but I knew that I really didn't have anything to show you. If I had just come up to you and told you that I thought my boyfriend couldn't die, then you would think I was crazy. I knew that I'd have to show you the body coming back to life. That also meant that I'd have to see the body come back to life again, to make sure. So, in a way, you helped me to do it that second time."

Vera was stunned, not only by the last part, but by all of it. "...So, you've killed him three times so far," she said, still struggling to digest that impossible fact.

"Yes," Stacy answered her. "Now that you've seen for yourself, we can figure out more of the details."

"Details like what?"

"For instance, I figured out that he comes back to life exactly an hour and six minutes after I kill him."

"Really?"

"Yes, it's like clockwork. I had guessed at it after the second time, but I proved it tonight."

"That's why you were doing that countdown?"

"Yes."

"How is this all possible?" Vera asked again.

"Anything is possible now, Vera—don't you see that? There are loopholes in reality—we've stumbled upon one of them."

"You don't care how these 'loopholes' exist?"

"I don't know. What I'm saying is that we may not have the brainpower to figure it out. Think of it this way: how many cavemen could have figured out what the sun really was? As the first human beings advanced, all they could content themselves with was the knowledge that the sun existed—that it rose at specific times of the day and set at specific times. After thousands of years of advancement, those one-time cavemen could use the placement of the sun to set up calendars and predict the seasons. You and I are still at the early caveman stage, Vera. All we can do for now is acknowledge basic facts."

"What do we do now?"

"We try to find more loopholes in reality." And then, looking at Vera with a smile, "Do you think you're up to it?"

"Yes," Vera said without hesitation.

"Good," Stacy said, pleased. "You should spend the night at my place—so that you can observe my boyfriend when he wakes up in the morning." At that, she started up the van, and they drove off. Vera nodded her head and sat back in her seat, knowing that nothing would ever be the same again.

They drove along in silence for about two minutes. Stacy decided to put on the radio, but the reception was horrible, so she turned it off.

"Tell me a story, Vera," she said while they were waiting for a red light to change.

"What?"

"Tell me a story to pass the time."

"Like what?"

"Something totally insane," Stacy said with a smile. "Show me how imaginative you are."

"I'm not too imaginative right now. I'm still trying to digest what just happened."

"Okay, then I'll tell you a story. I'm thinking about writing a novel."

"Really?"

"Sure. Want to hear it?"

"Okay," she said with a shrug: she was still too dazed to care one way or another.

"Then, sit back and let me tell you a story, my friend," Stacy started with a kind of self-mocking fanfare. "…So, Mr. and Mrs. X were nestling into bed after a long day at work. They were lying in the classic 'spooning' position: the wife was behind the husband, and was holding him around the waist. He had just showered, and had a good scent. She inhaled deeply and smiled. She realized that she was aroused. She breathed deeply again. 'You smell good, baby,' she whispered into his ear. '…Wha?' he mumbled sleepily. 'You smell good,' she said again, holding him tighter. He groaned noncommittally and went back to sleep. Her face soured, and she sighed angrily. 'Jimmy!' she screamed into his ear. He jumped, then swung around, glaring at her. He said: 'Why the hell did you scream in my ear?' Her sour expression had softened, and she was smiling again. She hugged him now, hoping to pacify him. 'I'm in the mood, baby,' she purred. He grimaced and turned back around, nestling into bed again, 'The mood for what?' he said evasively. She caressed his arm: 'Let's make love, baby,' she said. He groaned. She screamed, 'C'mon, Jimmy—it's been weeks since you touched me.' He countered: 'I'm touching you now, aren't I?' 'You know what I mean. I can't even remember the last time we made love. Let's do it, baby,' she purred again. He groaned again, his voice muffled by the pillow: 'I'm tired,' he said at last. As an afterthought, he added, 'Let's do it tomorrow.' 'That's what you always say!' she screamed, frustrated. 'No, I don't.' 'Yes, you do—or you tell me we'll do it later, and then, when I turn around, you're fast asleep. Don't you find me attractive anymore?' 'Of course I do—I'm just tired, that's all.' 'You're too tired to make love to your wife?' 'Yes,' he said, flatly. She gasped, sitting up in bed. 'I can't believe what I'm hearing!' she said, outraged. He rose from the pillow and looked at her: 'You can't believe that I'm tired, after I come home from working a double shift?' 'You're acting as though I'm asking you to run a marathon. You're getting lazy in your old age.' 'What the hell are you talking about?' he said, growing heated. He continued: 'All you have to do is lie there on your goddamn back and spread your legs.

I have to do all the work! You're lazier than I am! Every time I ask you to get on top, you stop after thirty seconds, saying you're tired, so what the hell are you trying to say?' She was a little stung by that; she whined: '...You know I can only come when you're on top.' 'That has nothing to do with it," he said, sensing that he had her on the defensive. "You just like sitting back and letting me do all the work.' 'That's the benefit of having a pussy,' she said, but there was a smile on her face now. She went on, 'If God had meant for me to work during sex, He would have given me a dick.' She snickered here; despite his attempt to stay angry with her, he shook his head and smiled. Seeing him soften, she caressed his shoulder again, and he sighed, saying, 'Okay, since you've ruined my good sleep anyway, we may as well get this over with.' 'Don't pretend that you ain't horny, too,' she said with a laugh, feeling the bulge in his shorts.

"Despite Mr. X's complaints about being tired, they went at it for about forty-five minutes, until Mrs. X was begging him to come, so that she could go to sleep. He laughed out. In the morning, he woke up feeling refreshed and aroused. He nudged his wife with his elbow a few times, until she jumped and raised her head off the pillow. She squinted at him for a few seconds, before resting her head on the pillow again. He smiled. 'Don't pretend that you're asleep.' She smiled, but kept her eyes closed: 'What the hell do you want?' 'I want some—what the hell do you think?' She chuckled, saying, 'You ain't tired?' 'You know I'm a morning person,' he replied. She laughed out, then reached down to feel his crotch, to see if he was aroused...but when she did, she frowned and opened her eyes. They were both naked under the covers. She looked at him confusedly; he, in turn, was looking down at her hand, which was still palming his crotch. 'What the hell...!' they whispered in unison. They threw off the covers. First, they both stared at his crotch; and then, with the same stunned expressions on their faces, they looked down at her crotch. She took hold of the thing that was now between her legs, squeezing it in disbelief. Mr. X, in turn, brought his hand to his crotch, running his finger across the moist slit. When they had both verified what was there, they looked at one another with a kind of wide-eyed horror. Somehow, Mrs. X had her husband's penis; Mr. X had his wife's vagina. 'What happened!' he said hoarsely. She was still holding his dick. The sight of it between her legs was disturbing. It was fully erect. She stroked it a few times, as if amazed. Her face had a far-off, meditative expression. Somehow, watching her made a sense of panic rise in him. He screamed: 'Would you stop stroking my goddamn dick!' She jumped, as if she had forgotten about him. She shook her head, as if freeing herself from a spell. 'I'm sorry—it's just that I've always wondered how it would feel.' She looked down at the thing in her hand, squeezing it again. She was sitting there with her legs spread, whereas he had his legs clamped shut, as if ashamed. She was holding his penis possessively, and he had to resist the impulse to wrench her hands off. When they made eye contact again, he realized that she was watching him with an odd gleam in her eyes. It startled him, and he cringed, saying, 'What the hell are you looking at me like that for?' She had gone back to stroking his dick. There was a seductive smile on her lips now: 'Haven't you ever wondered how I felt when you were inside of me?' 'No!' he screamed, '—I don't want anything inside of me! I want my dick back!' She moved closer to him, and he looked at her with an increasing sense of panic. She nestled against him, still stroking his penis. He shuddered, blurting out, 'What the hell are you doing?' 'Let's make love, baby,' she purred then. 'Hell no!' he said with a full-blown case of panic. 'C'mon, baby, I saw how wet you were when I touched your pussy before.' 'It's not my pussy! It's *your* pussy, and that's *my* dick!' 'Calm down, baby,' she said, caressing his shoulder again. He was out of breath and trembling. She smiled again, and held him close: 'Let's make the best out of it, baby. I know you're ready,' she purred to him seductively. As she said these last words, she reached down and rubbed his clit; despite himself, he gasped at the pleasure. 'C'mon, baby,' she was saying now, nestling against him again, 'I know how to make you feel good. I know all the spots to touch.' She was lowering him to the bed now; his heart was thumping in his chest. He was terrified, and yet, another side of him was ready, as she had said before. And then, his wife was inside of him. The sensation was bewildering and wondrous. He felt things that he could never have imagined.

He tried to resist it, but he moaned. He felt crazy inside—undone. His wife was grinding her hips against his. She was banging against him so hard that his pelvic bone hurt. And he felt her all the way inside of him. He felt somehow complete—as if his wife were adding some essential thing to him. Just as he was about to surrender to all these new sensations, he felt his wife's body stiffen. She cried out as the pleasure seized her, and then the husband felt her hot semen inside of him, filling him. His wife collapsed on top of him, her body already sweaty. He held her; he felt her penis shrinking inside of him. He listened to her breathing as it slowed. He tried not to think. This was all so surreal. Was this really happening? His wife was asleep. Her full weight was on top of him. His mind was jumping about so chaotically that he had to consciously ask himself what he was thinking. ...His wife had just screwed him with his own penis. He had her vagina...he had been enjoying the sex. This last part was shameful somehow. And yet, even now, he was eager for more. He felt cheated, in fact. He looked down at her now, just as she began to snore. He frowned. She had had her pleasure, and now she was snoring. What about his needs? he thought, outraged. 'Sweetheart,' he called to his wife now. She continued to doze. 'Sweetheart!' he screamed, and she jumped, looking up at him confusedly. '...Wha?' she said, fighting to keep her eyes open. 'I'm still ready, baby.' 'Wha?' she said again, going back to sleep. 'Let's do it again,' he said. She groaned, then she rolled off him and lay on her side, with her back to him; she began to doze again. He shook her, suddenly outraged: 'Hell, nah!" he said; and then: 'You were talking all that shit last night. Now *you've* got the dick, so it's your turn to service *me*!' She looked back at him pleadingly, her eyes still fighting to remain open: "But I'm *tired*, baby,' she groaned, '—can't we do it later?'

When the story ended, Vera was staring at her with a disturbed expression on her face. "...That's how it ends?" she asked.

"Yeah," Stacy said, smiling proudly.

"What's the meaning of all that?"

Stacy laughed out, as if Vera had missed the point. "There was no meaning to it. A good story should never have any meaning. A good story should always leave you thinking, 'What the hell was that about?'"

"I see," Vera said, uneasily.

They drove along in silence for about half a minute.

They had driven to the Williamsburg section of Brooklyn. The Williamsburg Bridge was coming up on their left; Stacy made a right-hand turn on Broadway, so that they were soon driving beneath the elevated M Train. The blocks were lined with the usual New York City businesses: Chinese food restaurants, dry cleaners, retail clothing store, grocery store… As it was late at night, there were not that many people outside; but as it was New York City, there were always pockets of people.

"How much farther is it?" Vera asked now.

"Not far."

Vera suddenly remembered the boyfriend: "You think your boyfriend will be okay back there? What if he runs out of air or something?"

"Don't worry about it: if he dies, he'll come back to life later." Her tone was so matter-of-fact that it did not even seem morbid. She was pulling the van over now. She stopped in front of a club: young, hip-looking people were milling about outside; a monstrous bouncer was frowning at everyone with his arms folded, so that his arms seemed like gigantic pythons squeezing the life from him. Stacy had pulled into a cordoned off section right in front of the club, and Vera looked over at the bouncer anxiously, in case he rushed over and squashed their heads between his biceps. However, Stacy got out of the van at that moment, and waved at the bouncer. To Vera's amazement, the man waved back and smiled. Seeing that it was safe, Vera joined Stacy outside. Stacy went to walk past her, and up to the club.

"You're going to leave your boyfriend back there?" Vera whispered.

"Let's let him sleep. In the morning I'll sneak down and take off my clothes, so he'll think we slept there all night."

Vera nodded anxiously. Stacy took her arm again—not as commandingly and gruffly as before, but in order to guide her through all the milling twenty-somethings. Some of them waved at Stacy. She gave them her trademark smile. Vera glanced back at the van—somehow, it still did not seem right to leave the boyfriend there.

When Stacy said hello to the bouncer, he moved his massive bulk to the side for them to pass. There was a wall of sound when they entered. Vera could feel the drum beat in her chest, as if some invisible beast were trying to perform CPR on her. It made her feel as though her insides were liquefying. On top of that, colored strobe lights were flashing in the darkness, disorienting her at the same time that they highlighted the intertwined and/or gyrating bodies of all the young people. Vera felt out of place, but Stacy was still by her side, guiding her through the sea of lustful youth. Some of the young people bumped into Vera during their sexualized exertions; she had the impulse to apologize, but they didn't even notice her. Besides, the music was so loud that it was impossible to talk to anyone anyway. Stacy tugged at her arm again: Vera had been looking around as if lost. They walked on; a beautiful young woman came up to Stacy and yelled something at her. Stacy smiled and nodded, even though Vera was still convinced that it was impossible for her to have heard anything. Just when Vera felt herself on the verge of trying to make a break for it, Stacy nodded to another guard, who then opened a door for them. Immediately, they were in a gloomy staircase. The music was not as thunderous. Vera felt relieved somehow. The young people in the club had filled her with the same unidentifiable sense of frustration and dread she had felt when Stacy first accosted her on the street. There was something inescapable and threatening about their abundant youth—something that terrified her. She took a deep breath; when she looked over, Stacy was smiling at her.

"What are we doing here?" Vera asked then.

"I live upstairs. Come on," she said as she began to walk up the staircase. Vera suddenly realized that she had left her bag in the van. The ice cream was probably all melted by now anyway. She sighed and began to follow Stacy; she watched the younger woman's shapely behind with envy. As she looked at Stacy, Vera finally admitted to herself that Stacy was everything that she pretended to be. Stacy was outgoing and rabidly sexual;

Stacy was carefree and self-confident, and *powerful*. Before she met Stacy, all she had wanted to do was lie in bed and vegetate. Now, she knew that she would not be able to sleep, even if she wanted to. There was so much to do—so much to *discover*. She felt as though she could spend a lifetime exploring the things Stacy had shown her. At the same time, she knew that she had to get some rest and recoup her faculties, or whatever she discovered in the next few hours and days would destroy her. Within herself, she sensed the budding signs of an addiction—an obsession. ...And yet, she saw no other course of action but to continue.

Just as they were nearing the top of the staircase (and the second floor), someone suddenly appeared at the top of the staircase, screaming: "Where is he!" When Vera looked up, she saw a woman in her sixties, dressed in what seemed to be her church funeral outfit: black dress, black straw hat. Adding to the entire effect, she had horn-rimed glasses and clutched her purse with claw-like fingers.

"Shit," Stacy whispered when she saw who it was.

"Where's my son!" the woman demanded again, and Vera suddenly realized that this had to be the boyfriend's mother! "I know you've done something to him!" the woman screamed from the top of the staircase. She was standing there with her arms akimbo, as if she were going to bar their way.

After a moment of surprise, Stacy continued to walk up the flight of stairs. The boyfriend's mother continued to bar the way, and the tension grew with each step that Stacy took up the staircase. Vera froze where she was, staring on as the two women confronted one another. Stacy was almost to the top of the staircase now. She was so much taller than the woman that they were looking eye-to-eye when Stacy still had two more steps to walk to the top. Stacy offered her hand in greeting then:

"Hi, I'm Stacy."

"I know who you are," the mother said with disgust, "—my son sent me pictures of you!"

"How'd you get in here?" she said, wondering how the woman had gotten into the building.

"The club owner let me in. I told him I was here to see my son."

Stacy shrugged. "I didn't know you were dropping by."

"Don't try your tricks on me, missy!" the old woman cursed her, wagging her claw finger in the air now. "I know you did something to him. A mother knows these things!"

"Is that so?" Stacy said, barely able to suppress a laugh.

"You've brainwashed him—I know it. I called him this morning—like I always do on Fridays—and you know what he said? He said that his mother was dead, and that I should stop calling him! What kind of son says that to his mother! You've *corrupted* him!"

Stacy was looking at the woman with a bored, indifferent, expression. Vera had stood frozen all that time, but realizing the two women were not going to come to blows, she continued walking up the staircase. The boyfriend's mother looked at Vera as if just noticing her:

"Who's this?" the woman demanded of Stacy, "—another one of your whores?"

"I beg your pardon!" Vera screamed.

Seeing Vera's reaction, and looking at her professional, overdressed attire, the woman guessed that Vera did not know what Stacy did for a living. The mother smiled now, and stared at Vera with a sordid gleam in her eyes, like an old gossip about to reveal a juicy secret: "I'm betting you don't know that she's one of those female pimps...what do they call them...? *Madams!*" she said as the word occurred to her. Vera looked up at Stacy to gauge her expression, but Stacy only chortled.

Somehow, this enraged the mother, and she screamed: "Look at her laugh! She has the devil in her, I'm telling you!" Here, she looked at Vera imploringly, as if trying to win her over. "She corrupts everything, mark my words. She'll have you selling your ass soon, if she hasn't already."

Stacy chortled again.

The woman went on: "My son was a good Christian before he met you!"

"Please!" Stacy protested with a mean laugh. "You know how old he was when he lost his virginity? *Eleven!* He screwed that good Christian babysitter you liked so much—the one with the huge tits."

The mother grabbed for her heart, but only ended up clutching her sagging tit. It was as if she had received a blow, because she staggered back a few steps. "You're lying!" she squeaked.

"Am I?" Stacy taunted her in a calm, matter-of-fact tone. She walked the last two steps to the top of the staircase, and stood towering over the woman, who now stared at her in horror. "You know how old that girl was at the time?" Stacy went on. "*Sixteen!* They screwed in your bed, you know? That's probably why he's so messed up now—he was probably fantasizing that he was screwing you—"

"Y-You're a monster!" the mother stammered. Stacy only stared at her with a calm smile:

"I may be all that, but your son obviously likes it."

"I'll get him back from you, you witch!"

"You talk as though we're competing for the same lover," Stacy taunted her.

"Where's my son!" she screamed, ignoring Stacy's insinuation. "I know you've done something to him!"

"I do things to him all the time," she said with a mischievous wink.

The mother stared at her, aghast—as if Stacy's wink had downloaded a hundred sordid sexual acts in her mind, all showcasing her one-time-good-Christian son. She seemed to sway from the blow. "I'm going to the police tonight," she said as forcefully as she could, but it came out as a whisper. "I'll be back with a search warrant." She brushed past Stacy now, but in her wounded state, she almost went headlong down the staircase. She had to grab the banister; Vera went to help her, but the woman slapped her hand away and continued down the staircase in the same reckless way.

Stacy stood at the top of the staircase with an amused expression on her face. When the woman was gone, Vera walked up to Stacy.

"That was brutal," she whispered.

Stacy shrugged her shoulders. "I doubt that the police will believe her, but I'll have to take care of everything tonight—just in case."

"Take care of what?"

Stacy sighed as she remembered it all. "My boyfriend was always annoying me with all his talk about his mother. ...I didn't tell you every-thing that happened the second time I killed him—maybe I was blocking it out, myself. …When he came out of the bedroom that night and found me lying on the ground, he said, 'Mama?' perhaps thinking that he was still a kid, and had had a bad dream. I was so pissed that I told him that his mother was dead—that she had been killed and eaten by a serial killer when he was five."

"My God!"

Stacy shrugged: "It seemed like a good idea at the time. How was I supposed to know she'd come all the way from Maine?"

"You can manipulate his memories that much when he comes back to life?"

"I told you that he's a blank slate. He'll be whatever I tell him to be… do whatever I want…"

"My God!" Vera whispered again, realizing the full extent of it.

"I'll have to kill him again tonight," Stacy went on, "and tell him he has a mother, so that when that bitch comes back she can go back to hen-pecking the shit out of him."

"What did she mean about you being a madam?"

"A misunderstanding on her part."

Vera seemed relieved; but then, Stacy went on:

"She meant to say I'm a *pornographer*, not a madam."

"You make sex videos?" Vera said, struggling to digest yet one more incomprehensible fact.

"I direct one of the most popular porn series in the world," Stacy said with pride: "Stank 'n' Ugly."

"Stank 'n' Ugly?" Vera said, her face creasing.

"Yeah—a sexual breakthrough. You know how pornos usually have these sexpot women: blond hair, huge (fake) boobs, cute face?" she asked rhetorically. "I've gotten rid of all that."

"How so?" Vera asked uneasily.

"All the women I use in my pornos have to be hideous."

Vera stared at her as if both desperate to know more and terrified of the consequences of knowing. At last, her curiosity won out: "What do you mean?"

"Beauty is a turnoff to most men," Stacy revealed, "—but they're too stupid to realize it. When they watch my pornos, they realize this truth for themselves. Men have always babbled on about the grandeur of beauty; millions of poems have been written about 'fairness' and 'comely lasses' and all that nonsense, but in the back of their minds, men crave a *hideous* woman."

Despite everything, Vera giggled. "You really believe that?"

"Of course! They want someone with whom they can have the most animalistic, mindless sex. With a hideous woman they have no inhibitions—and that's what they want most of all. The more attracted a man is to his woman, the less satisfied he'll be with the sex."

"You can't honestly believe that!" Vera said, trying to stifle a laugh before it took total control of her.

"It's simple human nature," Stacy went on. "In public, a man wants to be *seen* with a beautiful woman; but when it's time for sex, he wants a total hog."

Vera burst out laughing, but Stacy was laughing as well, so Vera did not know how earnest Stacy was.

"Anyway," Stacy said at last, "—we'd better get back to the van."

"You're going to kill him right now?" Vera whispered again, even though they were alone.

"Why not? There's no reason to wait."

"He doesn't need some kind of recuperation period between killings?" Vera asked.

"I guess we'll find out," she said with an unconcerned expression.

They began walking down the stairs.

"What if his mother is lurking around?" Vera said anxiously. "Are you sure we should go straight to the van? What if she's spying on us right now?"

"I'll just kill that old bitch too, and dump her in the back of the van with her son."

Vera looked at her in horror, but Stacy laughed:

"I'm only kidding." However, there was a pleased expression on her face, as if she were considering the merits of the idea.

Vera looked at her uneasily once more: "What if your boyfriend's immortality is genetic? Maybe his mother can't die either."

"There's only one way to find out," Stacy said with one of her trademark mischievous winks. Vera tried to smile, but the entire thing made her queasy.

They went downstairs and exited through a side door that allowed them to bypass the groping young people within the club. A crowd was still milling about outside the building. Stacy walked straight for the sliding side door of the van, and was about to open it when Vera put her hand on her shoulder to stop her. She whispered:

"You can't honestly intend to kill him right here!"

"Why not?"

"Look at all these people!" she said, gesturing over her shoulder. "And what if his mother is still lurking about? Let's at least drive to a secluded spot."

Stacy thought about it for a while: "I guess you have a point." And then, with a broad smile: "See, I told you I needed you."

"Yeah," she said sarcastically, "I've turned into the perfect accomplice."

Stacy walked around to the driver's door and opened it. Vera was waiting for her to open the door for her when it occurred to her that the door had not been locked the last time. She looked at Stacy with concern after she got inside the van:

"You have to be more careful, Stacy. You don't take any precautions."

"Like what?"

"You leave the door open, as if daring someone to come and open it."

"All they'd see is my sleeping, naked boyfriend."

"It's always the little things people overlook that—"

"That *what*? That get them caught?"

"Yeah."

Stacy smiled at her—as if she had said something stupid. "You're acting as though we're murderers, Vera. It still has not sunk in yet: *he can't die.* No matter what we do to him, he can't die. There is nothing for us to hide from: no consequences."

"Everything has consequences," Vera said sullenly.

"At any rate, we're not criminals—stop thinking of yourself as one. There is no crime for you to cover up. We're not accomplices: we're explorers."

They drove in silence for two blocks. Stacy entered a dark, residential neighborhood and double-parked.

"You're going to do it here?" Vera asked.

"Sure. Why not? I told you before that we're not criminals." She began to get out of the car; when she saw that Vera was going to wait in the van, she stopped. "Don't sulk, Vera. Come on—I'll show you how I do it— how I kill him. You know you want to see—for the sake of curiosity." She was smiling again. "Come on," she urged Vera again, "you have to be the one to document that I really do kill him." Here, Stacy poked Vera in the side, tickling her; and despite everything, Vera giggled.

"Okay," Vera relented, opening the door to get out, "—let me see how the master does it."

Vera waited for Stacy to come around to the side door. When Stacy arrived, she was still smiling. She pulled open the sliding door with the same smooth motion. The boyfriend was still sleeping. Vera looked up and down the block uneasily, to see if anyone was looking; Stacy shook her head and laughed at her.

At last, Vera peered over Stacy's shoulder, at the boyfriend, and whispered: "You sure he won't wake up?"

"I'm sure. I told him to sleep until morning, remember? He always does what I say."

"He sounds like the perfect man," Vera mused. When Stacy laughed, Vera laughed as well.

Stacy climbed into the back of the van; Vera followed her. When the door was closed, Stacy turned on the ceiling light once more. The sight of the naked, sleeping boyfriend again made Vera cringe. Stacy suppressed her laugh while she reached for the ice pick. Vera's heart was pounding in her chest; she felt sick and turned her head away.

"Don't be so squeamish, Vera."

Vera nodded, but her stomach refused to comply. She was preparing herself for a grand act, but in one quick move, Stack jammed the ice pick into the boyfriend's chest. The body did not even move. Vera, likewise, felt frozen. Stacy looked at her and smiled.

"See how easy that was?"

Vera looked at the body uneasily. "Is he dead already?"

"Sure."

Vera was about to say something else when the side door suddenly slid open; at the noise, they both jumped; and then, there was the sound of a woman screaming at the top of her lungs. When they looked, they saw the boyfriend's mother bawling.

"You killed him!" she screamed. "*Help...!*" she yelled into the night. "*Murder...!*"

At first, Stacy and Vera were so stunned that they just crouched there. It was Stacy who jumped at the woman. Soon she and the woman were wrangling in the middle of the street—

"Help!" the woman screamed again. "*Murder!*"

By now, Stacy had punched the woman in the face several times, trying to quiet her. As Vera looked on, stunned, it suddenly occurred to her that Stacy was going to kill the woman! If the ice pick were still in Stacy's hand, Vera had no doubt that she would have used it—

Vera jumped out of the vehicle, just as Stacy was rearing her hand back to punch the old woman again. Vera grabbed Stacy's arm:

"Let's get out of here!"

"*Murder!*" the mother continued to scream.

"Let's go!" Vera screamed, tugging at Stacy's arm now. "We can't let anyone see us here!"

Looking up at the apartment building across from their position, and seeing one of the room lights flicker on at that moment, Stacy finally came to her senses. She jumped up and ran around to the driver's side of the van. Vera was about to jump in the passenger side when the mother grabbed her. For an old woman, she was strong!

"*Murderers!*" she screamed. Vera tried to push her off, but the woman was like a raging bull now. Seeing the course of the battle, Stacy was about to come back and help her, but Vera looked up at the surrounding buildings then, noticing several people looking at the scene from their bed-room windows—

"Get out of here!" Vera screamed. "I'll hold her off! You get out of here!" With the adrenaline pumping through her, she jammed her fore-arm into the mother's nose, so that the woman grunted and retreated a step. Before the woman could regain her balance, Vera sprang on her, making her collapse to the ground. That was when Stacy started the van and zoomed off. The tires pealed. The back door was still open, showing the boyfriend lying there with an ice pick in his chest. Stacy zoomed down the block and turned the corner so fast that the van almost flipped over. When Vera tackled the mother to the ground, the blow had stunned the old woman, but now the woman began to scream again. Vera tried to put her hand over the woman's mouth, but she bit Vera's hand. Vera screamed and cursed. The mother's arms were flinging wildly now. One fist caught Vera in her left eye; the other landed on Vera's right breast; she groaned and coughed. Another blow caught her in the temple, and she found everything going blurry.

"*Murderer*!" the woman had screamed all that time.

As more blows hit her, Vera tasted hot blood in her mouth; she tried to get up, but another one of the mother's wild blows landed on her jaw. That was when she found her knees buckling and the world going black.

"Ma'am, wake up!"

Vera tried to open her eyes, but she somehow did not have the energy. She tried to move, but she felt as though she were paralyzed. She was numb all over—

"Ma'am!"

Someone was prodding her in the side. She tried to open her eyes, but realized that they were swollen. Her mouth was full of blood. She groaned.

"She's waking up." It was a man's voice. She suddenly realized that there were sirens blaring in the background; she could hear people's foot-steps: it sounded like hundreds of them. She was still lying prone in the middle of the street, but in those first moments, she had no idea where she was. The asphalt was still warm from the heat of the day. It smelled burnt, and irritated the back of her throat. She coughed and winced, but she still had no idea where she was.

Suddenly desperate to get her bearings, she used all her strength and will to open her eyes. Unfortunately, everything was blurry: the world was a kaleidoscope of shadows and flashing lights. She groaned again, and then remembered everything: Stacy, the hysterical mother, the fight—

"Ma'am!" the man called again. She forced herself to look up, and found herself staring up at a policeman. There were actually about four of them standing above her.

Vera shuddered at the realization, and closed her eyes.

"The ambulance is on its way—"

Vera suddenly began to cough: some of the blood in her mouth had gone down her windpipe. …But she was beginning to regain consciousness: awareness of her predicament; and then, looking to the side, she saw the mother standing with some policemen, pointing frantically at her. Some of the people in the neighborhood were standing near the woman, corroborating her story with nods and gestures in Vera's direction. Vera coughed again, and then sat up. She felt her head and face: everything was swollen—

"They killed my son, I'm telling you!" the mother screamed then.

Vera looked around, digesting more of her predicament. There were now dozens of onlookers on the street—witnesses. There were at least six police cruisers—

"Make her confess!" the mother implored the policemen trying to keep her calm.

"God!" Vera whispered to herself as the full extent of it hit her again.

"Ma'am," one of the policemen standing above her started now, "—we're going to have to ask you some questions, if you're up to it."

Vera looked up at him, nodded, and then bowed her head again. Somehow, keeping her head bowed kept the worst of the pain at bay.

"That woman is making some wild accusations against you," he started.

"Like what?" she started cautiously: if she knew what the woman was saying, she would be able to lie better. The thought made her recoil: she was Dr. Vera, radio talk show host, not some street criminal!

"Let me have your side of the story first," the policeman outwitted her. "You can start by telling us your name."

Vera felt a quake of panic go through her. She felt everything that she had—all that she had strived for—coming undone. The next thing she knew, she was sobbing. "It's all a misunderstanding," she pleaded with the police officers. "She attacked us!" she said, pointing in the direction of the mother. Thankfully, at that moment, the ambulance arrived. The paramedics rushed out to treat Vera.

The mother complained: "Why are you pampering her! She killed my son!" Some of the mother's supporters were grumbling in agreement. The police officers began to tell them to disperse.

Vera felt sick and groggy again. The paramedics put her on a gurney, and soon had her in the back of the ambulance. They asked her a series of medical questions; they shone a light into her eyes, checking for a concussion. Vera's mind abandoned her. It was like a car that refused to start. She was stranded in the middle of nowhere—doomed.

According to the paramedic, she was fine: she had a mild concussion from the fight, and some contusions, but she was otherwise fine. She was just beginning to feel better when a police officer appeared at the back door of the ambulance:

"Ma'am, at this time, we're going to take you into custody…" He began to read Vera her Miranda Rights. She was handcuffed. She stared ahead in a daze. Somehow, she was transferred to the back of a police cruiser. She sat there in shock as she was driven to the police station.

The police car had its sirens on, but the sound seemed off somehow, as if she were hearing it from underneath the water. The car was speeding down the Brooklyn streets, but she felt as though time had stopped and they were all frozen in place. She kept telling herself that if she did nothing—

if she refused to believe that this was real—then everything would take care of itself. All she had to do was sit back and let the universe correct itself. This was only another aberration in reality, to be overcome by some self-correcting mechanism that was beyond her. Even when she ceased believing in a self-correcting universe, she trusted in Stacy. Stacy was out there somewhere, taking care of everything. Stacy had showed her how this was a world were death was irrelevant, so taking care of this would only be like child's play to her. She refused to think about consequences. She refused to think about what would happen if this got on the news. She retreated into the numbness and felt safe.

The car stopped in front of the police precinct. They had actually driven in a convoy. Another police cruiser was there with the mother. A police officer opened the back door and shepherded Vera inside of the building. The mother began to scream her accusations once again, but Vera allowed the words to wash over her—to bypass her consciousness. Her ability to do this startled her, like a newfound superpower. The inside of the police precinct was drab and dark. She was led into a room with several desks—a booking department—where detectives filled out the paperwork that began people's descent into the Criminal Justice system. There were only about three detectives on duty, whereas there were about ten people waiting to be booked. The police officer led her to the side of the room and sat her down. She was handcuffed to the chair. Others were sitting in that area, chained to their chairs. All were huge, thuggish-looking men. The man next to her kept mumbling about how he was going to kick somebody's ass. He did not say who this someone was, but he kept mumbling it to himself, as if it reassured him. Once again, Vera closed her mind to everything that was happening. She allowed time and the events of the outside world to bypass her awareness, and again found a strange kind of peace.

Eventually, a middle-aged detective came up and started to talk to her. He looked like a stereotypical police detective: bad suit, late thirties, slightly overweight…but his face was kind. He asked her something about if she wanted a lawyer or not. She may have shaken her head—she was not quite sure. The next thing she knew, the man was walking her down a corridor and into an interrogation room.

It was only when Vera was seated in front of the man that her situation began to filter through the numbness. Had she really seen the boyfriend come back to life? What if it had all been some kind of elaborate hoax? What if Stacy had framed her somehow? Her mind tried to go down that path for a while, but she did not have the energy required.

"You need some ice or something for your face?"

Vera stared at the detective for a moment before she realized that he had said something. "What?" she said.

"Your face: you need something?"

Vera touched her face. She realized that the handcuffs had been taken off, but she had no idea when. Her face felt doughy. Thankfully, it was numb like the rest of her. "I'm okay."

"Okay." He sighed at last. "Let's get started then." There were some forms in front of him. He took out his pen. "Please state your name."

Vera knew that this was the moment of no return. "…Vera Alexander," she whispered.

The man stared at her for a while, and then frowned: "*Dr.* Vera?"

"Yeah."

"*The* Dr. Vera?" he said excitedly. "I listen to your show all the time!"

Vera bowed her head. She had nothing to say.

"What the hell is the story here?" he said more casually, as if he and Vera were old friends—as if the time he spent listening to her during his daily commute had forged some kind of deep relationship. He gestured at the door then: "The woman outside is making some wild accusations about you."

"It's all a misunderstanding," Vera said.

"Okay," he replied, as if desperate to believe. "Tell me your side of the story."

Vera took a deep breath and held it for a moment. "My friend, Stacy, and I were driving along, and then all of a sudden her boyfriend's mother started screaming that we were murderers."

"She screamed at you while you were driving?"

"No, we had stopped on the side of the street."

"Why had you stopped?"

"We were checking something in the back of the van. I had left my bag in there." She remembered the ice cream— "I had left some ice cream back there, and we were going to eat it before it melted." After she said it, she realized how stupid it sounded.

The detective seemed unconvinced as well: "You were so desperate for ice cream that you stopped on the side of the road?"

"It was chocolate," she said. To her amazement, she smiled, and the detective smiled as well.

"Why were you and your friend in that neighborhood?"

"My friend Stacy lives a few blocks from where we stopped."

"Where were you headed?"

"We were just driving around."

He looked at her dubiously again: "You seem kind of old to be out cruising on a Friday night."

"Don't judge a book by its cover," she said, amazing herself once again. The detective looked at her curiously, as if intrigued. And then:

"Why was there a body in the van?"

Vera sensed the trap; she forced herself not to speak for a second. She took a deep breath before saying, "There was no body."

"Then why did your friend take off when the old lady started screaming?"

"She had stormed into Stacy's place earlier—we thought she was dangerous."

"Then why did your friend leave you with this supposedly 'dangerous' woman. It doesn't sound like this Stacy woman is good a friend; and again, the old lady outside is saying some crazy stuff about her."

"I told Stacy to go—I didn't want her to get hurt. …I told her I'd hold the attacker off."

"You're a pretty good friend."

"I try to be—to people who treat me well."

"How does she treat you well?"

She thought about it objectively with her head bowed. And then, looking up: "She tells me the truth. She tells me things as they are." She did not know if that was true or not, but she wanted it to be the truth. It was like a religious statement: a declaration of faith in something that she had no way of verifying.

"How long have you two been friends?"

"A while now."

"How long is 'a while'?"

"Some weeks…months," she lied.

"Hmm," he mused, "can you tell me what her last name is?"

Vera could only stare at him. Of course, she had no idea what Stacy's last name was. She opened her mouth, fumbling with words that refused to come. Mercifully, that was when an officer burst into the room:

"They're here, Jon!"

"What?"

"The woman and the guy—the one the mother said was murdered."

"He's *alive*?" the detective asked.

"Alive and well."

Vera sighed in relief. "See," she said with a smile, "I told you this was all a misunderstanding."

The detective looked at her as if just noticing her; he looked back at the officer: "You say they're *both* here."

"Yeah, right outside. You may as well come out."

The detective stood up, nodding to Vera, so that she would come with him. They walked down the same corridor, and then they were in the main area again. When they got there they saw Stacy and the boyfriend standing with a bunch of officers. Just then, the mother, who had been in another interrogation room, burst out. Seeing her son, she screamed!

"How is it possible?" the woman said in disbelief.

The boyfriend smiled and began to walk toward her; she ran up to him and leapt at him, hugging him. "You causing trouble again, Ma?" he said with a chuckle.

Vera stared at the scene. Seeing the boyfriend alert (and clothed) was surreal. She glanced at Stacy, who winked and smiled at her. Vera walked over and stood by Stacy.

The mother was bawling now; the son patted her back. "It's okay, Ma. I told you not to worry so much. I'm fine."

The mother detached herself from him a little bit and stared at him: "...But I saw them killing you. You were lying in the back of the van, and—"

"Ma," he said in a mock stern tone, "you see me standing right here, don't you? Obviously I'm not dead."

"But why were you lying naked in that van. I *saw* you," she said again.

"I wasn't, Ma. Stacy just picked me up from the corner bar."

The old woman looked distraught: "Your old mother must be losing her mind."

The boyfriend held her again. "You're fine, Ma. It's just a hot night out there, that's all."

She detached herself from him again: "Why did you say those horrible things to your old mother on the phone?" she demanded now.

"What things?"

"When I called you on the phone, you said I was dead—that I had been killed and eaten when you were five. Why would you say such a horrible thing!"

"I never said anything like that, Ma. You probably called the wrong number. Haven't I always treated you right, Ma?" he said, as if hurt by the accusation.

"Oh, you're right!" she said, desperate to believe. "It must have all been a mix-up somewhere—some cruel boy playing a trick on your old mother. Give your mother a hug," she said then, even though they were still holding one another. "You love your old mother, don't you?" she pressed him.

"You know you're my main girl."

While the two stood hugging and rocking one another, Stacy groaned under her breath. And then, bending over to Vera, "See what I told you: the two of them are sickening when they get together."

Vera smiled.

"Oh, Sweetiekins," the mother went on, "take your old mother back to her hotel."

"Anything for you, Ma," he reassured her. They began to walk off arm in arm, like two content lovers.

"Jesus!" Stacy whispered to Vera. "You can't tell me he wasn't better off the other way."

Vera smiled again—mostly because the scene put an end to her prison nightmare. However, responding to Stacy's comment, she mused, "People have to be free to be morons. You can't cheat them out of their right to do stupid things."

"I suppose," Stacy said with a playful, pouty expression—like a mischievous child being reprimanded by a parent. And then, as she watched the couple make their way to the exit: "I still can't believe you let that old bitch knock you out!" There was a smile on her face.

Vera cringed and looked up at her uneasily: "You found out?" she whispered.

"When I drove back to the neighborhood, everyone was still talking about it."

"The old lady has a vicious left hook," Vera said with a shrug, and they both laughed.

The mother and son were at the door now. The detective who had interrogated Vera came over to her: "Sorry about all this—but we had to investigate what the old lady was saying."

"I understand how it is," Vera said with a smile. "No hard feelings." She saw again that he had a kind face, and nodded. At that, she began to walk off with Stacy. When they got outside, the mother and son were getting into a cab.

Vera wanted to go home and collapse onto her bed. "Can you drive me home?" she asked Stacy.

"I don't think you should be alone right now," Stacy advised her. "Why don't you come home with me as we had planned before? My boyfriend will spend the night with his mother, and I don't want to be alone either."

"I need to be alone—to think."

"Thinking by yourself is like drinking by yourself: no good can come of it. Spend the night over at my place—I have a bedroom set up for you."

"I don't know."

"What is there to know? Tonight, of all nights, isn't it clear that we need one another? Haven't the last few hours shown that?"

"Maybe I don't want to be needed right now."

"That's the thing about needs—when you see them for what they are, it doesn't matter what you want. I *need* you, Vera…and you need me."

The prospect of entering into that conversation again was draining. Vera sighed: "…I feel so tired all of a sudden."

"Seeing the truth is exhausting."

The expression on Stacy's face made Vera smile; Stacy held Vera's upper arm again, but it was more like a plaintive caress this time. Vera smiled and shrugged at last, saying: "…Okay, I guess I can spend the night."

They drove along in silence for a while. Eventually, Stacy turned to Vera when they were waiting at another red light: "Did you doubt me?"

"What?"

"When you were in the police station, did you think I wasn't going to come back?"

"A little."

About thirty seconds passed before Stacy said, "Doubt is the beginning of all unhappiness." Stacy's tone was that of a hurt woman, and despite Vera's ordeal of the past two hours, she felt guilty. She was desperate to say something to make amends, but Stacy spoke up then, saying,

"Are you still tired?"

"So much has happened tonight. I don't think I can sleep, but I'm tired— *drained*."

"You're still trying to make sense of all this," Stacy said in a way that made the words came out as an accusation.

Vera looked up at her: "You think trying to make sense of things is bad?"

"'Making sense' is people's way of making things more complicated than they need to be. It's like sex: if you sit down and try to intellectualize it, and figure out why you like it, you won't enjoy it. The best sex is mindless sex—*thoughtless* sex. It feels good and you do it. End of story."

"Reasoning like that can only lead to disaster," Vera countered.

"All things end badly, Vera," Stacy said, glancing over at her as she drove down the street. "Even life ends in death. The trick is to enjoy the ride before everything goes to hell."

The statement lingered in the air. Vera knew that she should say something to counter it, but she was disturbed somehow. Something in Stacy's words unlocked a door to darkness within her, and she spent the intervening moments trying to shut that door before it was too late. After another minute or so of uneasy silence, Stacy turned to her again:

"What do you remember about the forget-me-not woman?"

Vera stared at her for a while, as if she had to reconfigure her mind before she could bring herself to think about those things. She sighed. "A mentally disturbed woman got killed outside my book signing," she said reluctantly. "What else is there to remember?"

"Do you remember anything about her?"

Vera shook her head: "Nothing, really…she had this weird, broken heart birthmark. It's strange what you remember about people," she mused. "She had this way of looking at me…it gives me the shivers to this day. It was as if I had let her down—as if she had nowhere else to turn, and I had abandoned her." Vera hated thinking about it, but now that the subject had been broached, she continued, "I went to her funeral, you know. It was in a little town in North Carolina."

"Oh? You met her family?"

"She didn't really have a family. She was living with a family friend— some old grandmotherly woman who used to be friends with her mother. Everyone else in her family died when she was about fifteen. There were rumors. …I don't know how much of it was bullshit, but some people said she killed them."

"You didn't believe the rumors?"

"Her parents' house burned down. She was the only one who made it out alive. As she was always a little 'off' mentally, there were rumors afterwards. You know the way things are in small towns: everyone has a story on everyone else, and they're eager to tell you all about it if you let them."

Stacy smiled: "You don't like small towns?"

"Nah. I've never liked them. They've always given me the creeps. Every time I even pass through one, a feeling of panic comes over me. They always make me feel trapped—unsafe…"

Stacy had a playful smile on her face: "Maybe you should get some therapy for that, Dr. Vera?"

Vera laughed. "It's possible, but…I don't know. I've never liked small towns. …And the other thing is that maybe *I* was a little off when I went down there for the woman's funeral. …She died *right* outside my book signing. The entire thing had me a little crazy. I was talking to her moments before she walked out into the street and got flattened. I couldn't get those images out of my head. Something like that stays with you. …She said all those things about what we had done together, and how I had forgotten—how she had *helped* me to forget…"

"You thought there was some truth to that?"

"I don't know what I thought. Maybe I went down there to see for myself—to make sure that I really hadn't forgotten."

Stacy eyed her. "Do you believe in things like that? Repressed memories and all that TV movie stuff?"

Vera laughed at Stacy's characterization. "As a psychologist, I know that repressed memories do exist. …Do I think that I forgot the woman? No."

"Fair enough." Stacy was staring out of the windscreen, at the street.

Vera followed Stacy's gaze out of the windscreen, and noticed that they were nearing the club again.

Young people were still milling about outside. Stacy parked in the same cordoned off area in front of the club. This time, instead of going up to the bouncer and walking through the club, they entered the building the same way they had left it the last time: through a side door down the block. They began to walk up the stairs. Somehow, it was good to be inside again. Vera felt safer, as if something ominous were out in the night. She wanted to sleep and forget everything. She still did not feel as though she *could* sleep—her mind was too frantic and frayed—but the thought of sleep was soothing to her.

At the top of the staircase, there was actually only one door, which led to Stacy's apartment. It was not locked, because Stacy merely turned the knob to open the door. However, when Stacy pushed open the door, the mother and the boyfriend were on the other side. The door opened into the kitchen area. The boyfriend was at the sink, preparing something; the mother was sitting down at the kitchen table, rubbing her bunions and corns. Stacy and Vera froze; the boyfriend and mother looked up at them. The mother scowled when she saw Stacy; the boyfriend smiled in a peace-making kind of way and explained:

"I didn't see why she should spend the night in a hotel when we have an extra room."

Stacy stared at him as if he were speaking Greek. When she finally spoke, her voice was low and menacing. "I prepared that room for Vera."

"It's okay," Vera spoke up quickly, not wanting to be in the middle of a lovers' spat. "I should be going home anyway."

"Nonsense," Stacy objected. "We have more than enough space—you'll just have to share a room with me."

Vera was not exactly keen on the idea, but she knew that she did not have the energy to argue. She shrugged her shoulders.

When the boyfriend saw that the argument had been deflated, he smiled in relief. "I'm making Ma some cocoa," he explained as he filled a pot. "Would you guys like some?"

"I'm fine," Vera said quickly. She wanted to get away from that scene as quickly as possible. She and Stacy were still standing in the open doorway. Stacy had stepped in; Vera was about to enter and close the door behind her, when she heard someone running up the stairs. It sounded like a herd of buffalo stampeding, so curiosity and a kind of terrified anticipation caused her to stop and look. When she did so, she saw a towering hulk of a woman appear. The woman was probably about two hundred eighty pounds, and stood 6'5" in her high heels. The shoes, Vera saw, looking down with sudden fascination, were stilettos about two sizes too small for her size twelve feet. The woman's toes reminded her somehow of Fred Flintstone's: each one was like a crudely chiseled rock. Vera looked at the rest of the woman the way one would a carnival freak. The woman did not so much walk as fling herself forward with a kind of reckless waddle.

The flimsy stilettos only made the entire enterprise seem more precarious. The woman was wearing a see-through blouse that revealed things one did not even want left to one's imagination. Through the sweat-drenched blouse, the woman's two humongous breasts swayed disconcertingly as she waddled up. She was wearing a bikini top, but she may as well have been wearing dental floss, as the bikini top barely even covered her nipples and areolas. In fact, the breasts were so huge that Vera had to believe they were fake—some mad scientist's doing, perhaps. The left breast seemed two sizes bigger than the other, as if Dr. Frankenstein had had an extra sack of silicone lying around, and had decided to get rid of it. And then, when Vera's eyes finally settled on the woman's face, she blinked twice, as if convinced that her vision were failing her. To say that the woman was ugly would be an insult to ugly women everywhere. The woman was something else entirely—some new paradigm of ugliness. Her eyes were so far apart that they practically seemed to be on the side of her face, like a frog's. Topping it all off, her hair was like a butchered hedge withering in the summer heat. Instead of a haircut and styling, the woman looked like she needed to be pruned and watered. She was baring her teeth, like an enraged baboon trying to show dominance. Vera realized some of that teeth-baring was because the woman was panting from having run up the stairs. Still, the woman's teeth were so brown that Vera found herself thinking that that must be what wooden teeth looked like; she had a momentary image of George Washington smiling with a pair of such teeth. She grimaced. At last, as the towering hulk of a woman waddled the last couple of feet toward the doorway, Vera ducked into the apartment, terrified; Stacy, who had been watching over her shoulder, took her place, and smiled as the woman stopped before her:

"How are things, Coco?" Stacy greeted her.

"I need an advance!" the woman demanded. Her voice was like a rusty foghorn. The woman was clearly high on something, because her eyes had a far-off, crazed expression as she stared down at Stacy. Stacy seemed unconcerned, and Vera had never before admired someone's courage as she did Stacy's then. Stacy shook her head.

"You know I can't give you an advance, Coco—that's not how it works."

"What do you mean, you can't give me an advance! Aren't my movies your bestsellers? You know all the men are coo-coo for my Coco puffs," she said, grabbing her humongous breasts. "I'm the best bitch you got!"

As the woman said this last part, Vera suddenly realized that this had to be one of those "Stank 'n' Ugly" women Stacy had mentioned—

"True, indeed," Stacy averred, "—you're the best actress I've got, but I can't pay you for dick you ain't sucked yet. You get paid on a dick-by-dick basis."

"What the hell you mean!" the towering hulk screamed then.

Stacy's boyfriend came over and began to plead with the hulk to remain calm—

"Don't tell me to remain calm! I want my money—"

"See what I told you!" the mother lectured her son from the kitchen table, where she had taken a break from her corns and bunions, "—look at what that woman brings into your life. ...All these low-life people."

"Who you calling low-life, you old bitch?" the hulk growled from the doorway. She looked like a rhino about to charge; Vera took two steps back.

"There is no reason for any of this," the boyfriend tried to placate her. However, the hulk was one of those people who grew crazier as you tried to be reasonable with her. The next thing they all knew, the woman had fished a gun from beneath her gargantuan left tit.

"I'm gonna fuck all o' y'all up!" she declared in her rusty foghorn way.

Everyone gasped and ducked out of the way, except for Stacy, who still stood there with her usual indifference.

"Coco," she said in a calm, even voice, "you know I don't give advances."

Hearing this, the hulk's head seemed as though it would spin around; Stacy expected green vomit to fly out of her mouth, like that *Exorcist* demon. The woman's eyes bulged; her upper lip was trembling over her wooden teeth, and an evil-looking frown appeared on her forehead—

"*Please*," the boyfriend pleaded, stepping between the simmering hulk and Stacy, but by then the woman had been pushed over the limits of reason. The next thing they heard was the sound of the gun going off.

For a moment after the echoing blast, there was silence, and then there was a thud as the boyfriend fell to the ground. He lay there, writhing in pain with a bloody chest. They all stood staring down at him, as if unable to make sense of it. The mother was the first one to figure it out. In a millisecond, the old woman was out of her chair. Vera just managed to get out of the way as the mother sprang at the hulk. The mother was about a foot and a half smaller than she was, but the old woman was on her like a Tasmanian devil. Soon, the hulk was screaming out as the mother buried her teeth in her neck. With all that, the towering woman finally lost her tenuous balance, and both of them tumbled down the staircase. There was a racket like one of those overbearing jazz drum solos, and then a loud crash, as the two landed on the lower level. At the sound, Vera finally screamed out, as if the scream had been trapped inside of her, but Stacy ran to the kitchen sink, grabbed a knife and returned to the doorway, where the boyfriend was still twitching from the shock and pain of the gunshot. In one clean, powerful thrust, Stacy jammed the knife into his chest, and the convulsions stopped. Vera's scream got caught in her throat again, and she just stared, and there was a horrible silence.

Stacy was still crouched over her boyfriend's body. When Vera could breathe again, she whispered, "Why'd you do that?"

"No point in having him suffer."

Vera did not know if that was a reasonable response or not, but she remembered the mother and the hulk then. She ran into the hallway and looked down the staircase. The mother and the hulk were a crumpled pile of flesh at the foot of the staircase. Vera ran down the stairs. The one-time porn star's neck was broken. The woman's eyes were open, staring blankly into space. She was dead. The mother was still breathing, but she was unconscious. Her leg seemed broken. Stacy appeared at the top of the staircase then. Vera looked up at her and screamed: "Call an ambulance!"

Instead, Stacy walked down the stairs and joined her. She came down nonchalantly, as if nothing were amiss. She stared at the two crumpled bodies, and then smiled mordantly when she saw the mother: "This might be a good time to check your theory on inherited immortality," she joked. "If the old lady dies and comes back—"

"Is everything a joke to you!" Vera screamed, cutting her off. "God-damn," she said in bewilderment, "—do you live like this all the time? Does this kind of crazy shit always happen around you!"

"What are you so upset about?"

"Your boyfriend's been shot; the woman that shot him is dead; his mother is messed up! Doesn't any of that mean anything to you?"

"Stop being such a drama queen," Stacy said in the same nonchalant way; and then, turning to walk back up the stairs, "I'll call the ambulance."

Vera stayed with the mother and the hulk's corpse. A few surreal minutes passed. Eventually, Vera realized she was crying. She had no idea when she had started: she just knew she had been crying for a while. Stacy appeared at the top of the staircase again:

"What are you crying about?"

Vera was too wracked with sobs to answer. Stacy walked back down to her and hugged her. "It'll all be okay, Vera—no reason to come undone on me. We both know my boyfriend will be better in an hour, and his mother will be fine when she gets to the hospital. C'mon, Vera," she pressed her, holding her more tightly, "we've both seen the nature of life and death—we know there's no need for tears."

Vera still did not know if any of that was true, but she knew the boyfriend would be alive again soon, and the old lady's injuries did not seem to be life-threatening. The hulking porn star was dead, however. When it occurred to Vera that the woman's death meant nothing to her, she was disturbed and ashamed—as if it all marked her descent into something horrible. She had seen too much death tonight: maybe she was becoming desensitized to it—some kind of heartless monster. She began to cry again.

Stacy shushed her, and held her closely. "Come with me now," Stacy said eventually. "I need your help. Come upstairs with me."

Vera looked down at the unconscious mother, and then she began to walk back up the stairs. She did not feel like a real person anymore. The boyfriend was still lying in the doorway. Stacy had wrapped his chest with towels to stop the blood from flowing onto the floor.

"Help me move him to the back room," Stacy said then. "The police will be here in a few minutes, and it would be best if they don't see him."

Vera looked down at him uneasily: "Are you sure he'll be okay? Maybe we should bring him to the hospital, too—he's been dead three times today."

Stacy shook her head: "He's already dead. What good would it be to bring him to the hospital? Besides, you're wasting your time counting his deaths. Counting his deaths is like counting grains of sand on a beach."

"How do you know?" Vera said, finally regaining some of her spirit. "Maybe there's some limit to the amount of times he can die. Even on the beach there are only so many grains of sand."

"We can discuss this later," Stacy said dismissively. She took up her boy-friend's legs, and gestured with her head for Vera to pick up his arms. When they were dragging the boyfriend down the hallway, to the back room, Stacy said, "You know what your problem is, Vera? You have no faith." Stacy pushed open the bedroom door with her hip. They left the boyfriend lying on the floor, in the darkness, then they returned to the hallway.

"What does faith have to do with it?" Vera said at last. Stacy's comment had been playing in her head.

"You refuse to accept things that are obvious," Stacy said in the same calm, matter-of-fact way. "You question things that don't need to be questioned."

Vera stopped and stared at her; Stacy stopped and looked back at her. "When we started out," Vera began, "you said we were going to be ex-plorers—*investigators*. If you're going to investigate something, you have to ask questions."

"Even investigators have to take leaps of faith to get around the unex-plainable," Stacy replied. She continued walking down the hallway; Vera pursued her. She did not want to back down anymore. She did not want to make more compromises with her soul. She remembered the hulking woman's corpse lying at the bottom of the staircase, and her sudden indifference to the woman's death.

"Look," she said now, her voice more contentious, "if you're looking for some kind of mindless disciple you'd better look elsewhere."

Stacy stopped and looked at her. Vera was breathing deeply—like someone preparing for a fight. Stacy smiled at her. "Fair enough," she said simply, before she continued walking.

Once they were in the kitchen, Stacy got a rag from the sink and cleaned the boyfriend's blood from the floor. Vera stood staring at her, telling herself that she had to stand strong. She figured that Stacy would say something else to make her compromise herself—something else to lure her into the darkness. However, when Stacy was finished swabbing the floor, she merely walked back to the sink and washed out the rag. After that, she walked past Vera and into the stairway. After two steps, she called over her shoulder, explaining, "I'm going downstairs and let the bouncer know to expect the ambulance."

When Stacy was gone, Vera felt lonely. She walked down and stood above the mother and the dead porn star again. She looked at her watch: it was a few minutes to three. Within minutes, some paramedics rushed up the stairs, followed by Stacy and two police officers. The paramedics checked both of the women on the ground, saw that the porn queen was dead and then began to put the boyfriend's mother on a gurney.

"Will she be okay?" Vera asked.

"The doctors will be able to tell you more when she gets to the hospital." They began to move off.

"Can I come with you?" Vera asked.

"Sure," one of the paramedics said as they rushed to get back to the ambulance.

"I'll stay here," Stacy said then. Vera looked back at her, realizing that Stacy looked tired for the first time—*forlorn*. Her limitless youth seemed somehow faded. Vera felt bad about what had happened—what she had said. She told herself that she would make things better once she knew the old woman was safe; at the same time, she knew this commitment to making peace would leave her open to the force of Stacy's will. She was buffeted between these two impulses for a while, until she groaned and shook her head. She thought about the mother's welfare to distract herself.

For the next few hours, she would simply be a regular person, concerned for another human being. She realized that maybe some of her drive to be attentive to the old woman was in response to the coldness she had felt at the porn star's death. She groaned again....

On the way out of the building, they passed two more police officers. Vera suddenly felt guilty about leaving Stacy alone, but there was nothing to be done now but hold on and allow events to unfold.

When the ambulance got to the hospital, Vera was told to go to the emergency waiting room. There, about thirty wretched-looking people were already sitting in anxious anticipation, waiting for news on their injured loved-ones. There was a huge television in a corner of the room. On it, a loud news segment was playing—something about the benefit concert that Pastranzo was going to have in Central Park tomorrow. The proceeds were supposedly going to go to starving Africans. The TV commentator was talking about the concert as if it would be the seminal event of civilization: as if world peace and the end to world hunger would be declared after it. Vera stared at the screen, vaguely remembering the crazed teenagers at the studio. And then Pastranzo, himself, appeared on the screen: he was a middle-aged Italian with huge oval sunglasses that made him look like one of those bug-eyed space aliens. He had a jarring falsetto voice, which Vera was convinced rotted the brains of teenage girls, because they all seemed to think that he sounded like an angel. Presently, as he began to sing the refrain of his latest hit, Vera shuddered, looked away and sat down in a secluded nook of the waiting room. There was a table with magazines in front of her; she picked up one randomly and began to flip through it. She figured that she would read until the doctor came to give her an update on the old woman. However, in ten minutes she was fast asleep. The dream world seized her quickly and completely. In her nightmare, a cackling version of herself was crouched over Stacy's boyfriend's body, bloody knife in hand, while Stacy sat nearby on an antique chair, sipping from a snifter of brandy and looking on approvingly—

Vera awoke with a start. As she opened her eyes, she realized someone had shaken her shoulder. When she looked up, the detective who had interrogated her earlier was smiling at her. She glanced at the clock on the wall: it was about 4:30 A.M. When she looked back at the detective, he chuckled.

"You sure are having an interesting night, Dr. Vera."

She groaned and sat up: "Tell me about it," she whispered. The entire night flashed in her mind, and she shook her head, as if to ward it off.

For whatever reason, the detective laughed at her again. "The word on the street is that you were around another corpse again tonight."

Despite everything, she smiled. "You mean *a* corpse—the other one was a misunderstanding, remember?"

He sat down in the seat beside her, then reached down to pick up the magazine she had been reading: it had fallen on the floor when she fell asleep. He stared at the cover for a moment: an actor he had never heard of before had been named the world's sexiest man. He frowned and handed her the magazine. Then, still with a pleasant expression on his face, he inquired, "Is the old lady going to be okay?"

"She was in surgery when I fell asleep—nothing life-threatening: just some broken bones."

He looked around: "Where's her son?"

"What?"

"At the police precinct, the old lady and her son were inseparable. I figured he'd be here."

"Maybe he is," Vera said without thought.

"Have you seen him here?"

"I was sleeping, remember?"

He frowned, then smiled, looking at her suspiciously. "What is it that you and your friend Stacy aren't telling me?" he said then. "I go over to the apartment and your friend tells me a story about how some crazed woman got into a fight with her boyfriend's mother. Why the two of them fought, she does not really tell me."

"Maybe the old lady likes beating people up," Vera said sarcastically, "my face is still numb from her attack."

The detective looked at her face critically, noting the dark spots and bruises.

"Do I look that bad?" she asked.

"Nah, you're fine—just a little swelling. ...Anyway, back to your friend's boyfriend, why do I get the feeling that you and your girlfriend are hiding something about him?"

"Maybe you're simply paranoid."

"That might be true," he said with a laugh, "but something doesn't add up. Can you tell me where the boyfriend was while his mother was fighting with this 'crazed' woman?"

Vera groaned and rubbed her temples: "Haven't you interrogated me enough for one night? Stacy's boyfriend will show up sooner or later."

He looked at her suspiciously for a while, and then grunted.

She smiled. "When the boyfriend shows up you'll have to apologize to me again."

"I don't mind: apologies are cheap."

"Not if they're done right. I've been known to charge an arm and a leg for an apology."

"Okay, if the boyfriend shows up—"

"*When* he shows up," she corrected him.

"Okay, *when* he shows up, I'll take you to dinner—my treat."

"Of course it'll be your treat: I never go out Dutch!"

"I thought you were a modern woman?" he said with a chuckle.

"Because I'm modern does not mean I'm stupid."

"Whatever happened to equality of the sexes?"

"I only call for equality when the man is getting more than me; when I'm getting more out of the deal, equality is a rip-off." While she was laughing at her joke, the automatic sliding doors (which led outside) opened, and the boyfriend ran in, followed by Stacy. Vera smiled and looked at the detective: "You owe me an expensive dinner, sir."

The detective turned to see the boyfriend looking around frantically. The detective and Vera stood up, but the boyfriend rushed past them, as if not noticing them, and ran up to the information desk:

"I'm here to see my mom!" he said too loudly. People who had been dozing looked up. The nurse at the desk shushed him. "—My mother fell down some stairs," the boyfriend went on.

The nurse asked for his mother's name, then checked the computer. "She's still in surgery, sir," she told him at last.

"Is she going to be all right?"

Stacy, who walked into the waiting room at a more leisurely pace, smiled when she saw Vera, but then she frowned when she saw the detective. She walked up to Vera's side, and they all stood watching the boyfriend pump information from the nurse.

At the information desk, the nurse went on, "None of her injuries are life-threatening, sir. She just broke some bones. She'll be bedridden for a few weeks." The nurse started asking him for medical and insurance information then, and Stacy, Vera and the detective thought that would be a good occasion to divert their attention.

"I told you he'd show up," Vera said again, addressing the detective.

"Yeah, you did indeed. He always seems to show up when I have you cornered."

He and Vera laughed again, while Stacy looked on confusedly.

"Well," the detective began then, "I guess I'll go find someone else to interrogate." He took two steps before he stopped and faced Vera: "When am I going to pick you up?"

"How about tomorrow night at six?"

"Sounds good—that's my day off." He nodded his head and began to walk off.

Vera called after him: "Don't you need to know where to pick me up?"

He laughed and continued walking, saying over his shoulder: "I already got all your information from the police database." He waved then, and disappeared through the automatic sliding doors.

When he was gone, Stacy turned to Vera. They had both been watching his retreat. "You're actually going to go out with that guy?"

"Why not? He seems nice." However, as she said that, she realized she did not even know his name.

"Your funeral," Stacy said with a shrug.

Presently, the boyfriend finished talking to the nurse and walked back over to Stacy and Vera, looking frustrated and devastated.

"Don't worry," Stacy reassured him, "—your mother will be fine."

"I don't understand how all this happened," he said, growing distraught.

Vera looked at Stacy anxiously, wondering what lie the woman was going to make up.

"There are crazy people everywhere," Stacy explained without missing a beat. "That woman came out of nowhere, and then the next thing I knew, she attacked your mother."

The boyfriend stared at her, trying to understand. "I still can't remember where I was."

"I told you that you went out to get us something to eat."

He stared at her uneasily. "What did I get?"

"You didn't get us anything, silly," she said, punching him playfully in the shoulder. "You probably heard about your mother and headed back."

He groaned in frustration. "…But the only thing I remember is waking up on the floor."

"You passed out from the shock of seeing your mother like that," Stacy lied.

"I passed out?" he mused. He sighed and shrugged his shoulders at last. As he did so, he noticed Vera standing there. She nodded to him, trying to smile. He stared at her for a while:

"Have we met?"

Stacy answered him: "She was at the police station."

"The police station?" he said confusedly, but then he nodded his head. "I remember. …What a crazy night."

Vera inquired, "Did the nurse say how long your mother was going to be in surgery?"

He grimaced as he remembered: "She said she'd be in there for about three more hours. She broke her hip, and her leg…and there was some internal bleeding."

"Maybe you should go home and get some sleep?" Vera ventured.

Stacy added, "That sounds like a good idea. You're not going to hear anything for at least another three hours—and she'll probably be unconscious for a long time after she comes out of the operating room."

"No, no," he cut her off. "I couldn't leave her—no matter how long it was."

"Okay," Stacy said. "I'll stay with you then."

"No—there's no need. …Why don't you go home. I think I need to be alone anyway."

"Nobody needs to be alone," Stacy countered. "Why don't you come home now and try to get some sleep. We can call the hospital anytime to find out how your mother's doing."

"Nah. Please go without me. …I need to see her before I go. You go and get some sleep, please. I'll talk to you in the morning."

Stacy stared at him for a while. At last, she sighed. "Okay, if you say. Call me if you need anything."

"Sure."

Stacy hugged and kissed him. At first, the boyfriend was limp in her arms, but then he held her close and nuzzled his face in her hair. Vera watched them for a moment before she looked away, feeling as though she were invading their privacy.

"Call me if you need *anything*," Stacy said again. The boyfriend smiled and nodded his head. At that, she gave him one last kiss and began to walk toward the emergency exit. Vera followed her. She made no attempt to catch up to Stacy, however: she let her have her space for those few moments.

Finally, when they were outside, Vera caressed Stacy's upper arm. Stacy looked over at her and smiled absentmindedly. They walked in silence to the rental van. Dawn was about forty-five minutes away, and there was a hint of a brightening horizon.

"I'm sorry we argued earlier," Vera said as they neared the van.

Stacy looked over at her, as if she had no idea what she was talking about. Eventually, she nodded. "Don't worry about it, Vera. I'm sure we'll have lots of arguments in the days and weeks to come. Arguments are the starting points of all truths."

Vera liked the way that sounded, regardless of if it was a valid comment or not. She sighed, as if in relief, and smiled.

When they were inside the van, driving out of the parking lot, Stacy said, "Have you thought of a story for me yet?"

"A story?"

"You were supposed to tell me a story earlier, to pass the time."

"Is that one of your driving rituals? People have to tell you a story?"

"Absolutely. It makes the drive go quicker."

"...I'm still too dazed," Vera admitted sorrowfully.

"Okay, I'll have to tell you another one."

"Is this another one of your future novels?" Vera teased her.

"Yeah," Vera said with a wink, "—my magnum opus."

Vera laughed.

"So, sit back and let me tell you a story, my friend," Stacy declared in her usual self-mocking way. She paused dramatically, and then began: "One day a guy was returning home from work, when he looked down and saw a pair of panties lying on the sidewalk."—Vera instinctively chuckled, and Stacy smiled as well—"...Anyway, let's call him William Cooper. For whatever reason, he stopped and stared down at the underwear. They were stylish and silky, and he felt a strange attraction to them. Surreptitiously, Cooper looked around, to see if anyone was looking, before he grabbed the panties and slipped them into his pocket. As he walked the three blocks to his apartment, the idea of the panties in his pocket turned him on. He had never done anything like it before. He was a middle-aged high school principal, not some kind of horny freak. Nevertheless, he was walking quickly now, desperate to get home, where he could look at the panties at his leisure. It was only when he saw two little kids playing in front of his apartment building that he again began to think of himself as some kind of old pervert. By the time he got upstairs to his apartment he had resolved that he would throw the panties away. He would toss them into the garbage and all this would be forgotten—a minor aberration in a morally-driven life. When Cooper finally closed the door of the apartment behind him, he took the panties out of his pocket and looked at them again. As he held them before him, he realized that they looked like the underwear of a supermodel—or at least, that was the fantasy that suddenly popped into his mind. He imagined the panties belonging to Tyra Banks. Maybe they had slipped off while she was running to catch a cab. Anything was possible in New York! A woman like Tyra Banks probably had hundreds of panties anyway, so she probably would not even bother to bend down to pick up a pair that had slipped off.

"Now suddenly excited, he fingered the delicate fabric of the panties, sliding his thumb over the silky material of the crotch. The panties seemed so new that he wondered if they had even been worn. Instinctively, he brought them to his nose and sniffed. Immediately, his eyes widened—not so much because of the scent (which was indistinguishable)—but because of something else, which surged through him. He began to tremble. He felt suddenly energized, as though he could do anything—*be* anything. Amazed, he stared at the panties, like a marijuana smoker who had gotten a particularly good sack of weed. He brought the panties to his nose again and inhaled deeply, so that he felt lightheaded and drunk afterwards. '*Shit!*' he whispered as he lost his balance. He barely managed to make it to the couch before collapsing. Still, there was a silly grin on his face now. He had no idea what the hell was happening to him, but he liked it. Somehow, he felt all-powerful—*invincible!*

"It was then that something blared in the air; he jumped, startled. He was so stunned by the noise that for a moment he could not even move. At first, the noise made no sense, but then he realized that he had super hearing. Someone was crying outside. In fact, more than that, it was as if someone were calling directly to him—making an entreaty only he could satisfy. The cries outside the window seemed somehow to take possession of him, fueling his muscles so that for a moment he had no control of himself. The next thing he knew, he had leapt out of the fourth-story window! Yet, as he dropped through the air, he was unconcerned. He did not so much seem to fall as glide. Below him, he saw the two kids he had passed when entering the building. The little girl was holding the little boy by his shirt collar and waving her fist in his face. She had hit him a few times already and seemed to be waving the hand to remind him. Each time she waved her fist, the little boy cringed and cried louder. Cooper landed a few feet from them. The little girl was so stunned that she let go of the boy—who promptly lost his balance and toppled into some garbage cans. 'Oh shit!' the little girl screamed, '—where you come from!' William Cooper felt suddenly self-important. He stuck out his chest and stood there posing for them. 'I *flew*,' he said at last. The little girl sucked her teeth disdainfully, 'People can't fly, you dumbass!' Cooper was appalled: 'Is that how you talk to adults, young lady?' The little girl had her hands on her non-existent hips now: 'Well, my mamma said you're a big pussy, so it don't matter.' Cooper opened his mouth to say something, but he was too stunned. And it was not only what the little girl had said: all at once, he felt drained and devastated, as if the power had left him. This, it occurred to him, was what a drug addict must feel like after he began to 'come down' from his high. Cooper staggered a little, and looked wretched. The little girl looked at him derisively: 'What's wrong with you, Pussyman?' At that, the little boy, who had picked himself out of the stinking garbage and had been looking on at the conversation with awe, began to giggle. Cooper, who had supposedly come to save the little boy, felt betrayed somehow; and as children everywhere could sense despair and vulnerability in adults, the little girl began to chant: 'Pussyman! Pussyman!' All the while, Cooper was feeling even more drained and devastated. Just when he was beginning to think that things could not get any worse, the little girl started kicking him in the shin. Cooper cried out and grabbed his throbbing shin, but when the little boy started kicking the other shin, he lost his balance and crumbled to the sidewalk. Now, both kids were chanting, 'Pussyman! Pussyman!' The sound resounded in his head; as he was on the ground, the kids' feet had better access to his body and head. He lay in the fetal position, trying futilely to cover his face. Yet, the kids were so quick that it was as if there were dozens of them kicking him. In his weakness, he could do nothing. It was only when an old woman screamed at the kids from her window that they ran off giggling. Cooper was so weak that he could barely move.

Those little kids had had some sharp shoes too! He just wanted to lie there for a while, but that was when he remembered the panties. They were still in his pocket. Remembering the effect they had had on him the first time, he took them from his pocket and took another sniff. To his amazement, he immediately felt revived. He leapt to his feet, feeling like a million bucks. The old woman who had chased the children away called to him from her window. 'You okay?' she said. He smiled back and waved his hand.

"In fact, he felt so great that he decided to go for a walk. Unfortunately, after walking a block and a half, he felt weak again. Once more, he took the panties out of his pocket and took a sniff to revive his strength, but the thought that he would be weak again in two minutes was an unsavory one. He thought about it for a while, until he came up with the only solution that there was: he would have to keep the panties to his nose. He realized that he could wear the panties over his head, with the crotch over his nose and mouth, while the leg openings allowed him to see. Once he had the panties over his head thusly, he felt a rush of power that was like nothing he had ever felt before. Just as Spiderman and the other superheroes had their masks, he had his. He remembered the kids taunting him with 'Pussyman,' but now he would take on that mantle with pride, and proclaim himself to be Pussyman! Breathing in the sacred power of pussy, he felt invincible. He meant to continue walking, but with the power of pussy coursing through him, he took one step and found himself bounding into the heavens. He was flying! An elderly woman had been walking toward him, but as he took off into the heavens, she screamed and passed out. Soon, he was soaring above the rooftops, looking down in amazement at the people of the city. Not only could he fly: his senses seemed more acute. He could hear and see things more clearly; even though he was high up in the sky, he could make out the individual faces of the people below him; by attuning his ears, he could make out their mundane conversations. He felt like *God*. For the first time, he wondered where the panties had come from. Certainly not even Tyra Banks had stuff between her legs that could make men fly—not literally, anyway. He had stumbled upon some kind of divine power source: the *überpussy*, from which all life was born. ...Anyway, his mind worked like that for a while, trying to come up with something to explain his miraculous new powers.

"It was while he was soaring over the East Village that he noticed something strange. Had he been Spiderman, he would have said that his 'Spidey Sense' was tingling. He felt odd—a creepy feeling spread over his skin; and looking down, he noticed hundreds of people streaming down the street. Actually, when he looked closer, he realized that what he thought were people, were more like ghosts—souls. They were drifting down the street, passing through cars and pedestrians. On their faces, there were the most sorrowful expressions; many of them moaned, as if suffering.

"Pussyman stopped flying and began to descend. His 'Pussy Sense' was still tingling. Some people saw him descending and screamed out. Others started pointing in the air at the spectacular sight of a man with panties on his head floating through the air. Maybe they said, 'Is it a bird? Is it a plane...?' Who can say for sure? What Pussyman did realize, however, was that none of them noticed the drifting souls. Obviously the panties gave him the ability to see things that were invisible to the average person. Looking down the street, he could see the line of souls stretching off into the distance, so he rose into the air again and continued to follow them. After a few blocks, he began to notice a sound in the air—a piercing wail that even he, for a moment, found himself drawn to; for an instant, he felt his will eroding; a peculiar feeling went through him, as if his soul were trying to escape him. Luckily, his pussy power made him immune, but all these things only verified that something evil was happening in the city. Just as the little boy's cries had taken possession of him before, he felt as though he were now on a new mission. The piercing wail was getting louder as he continued to follow the stream of spirits. He flew faster, moving closer to the thing that was calling all those wretched souls.

"Soon, he had followed the souls all the way to Central Park. Looking down at the Great Lawn, he saw that tens, if not hundreds of thousands, of people had gathered. That was on top of the hundreds of thousands of drifting souls, which seemed to be congregating there as well. This seemed to be the epicenter of the piercing wail. Looking at all the gathered people,

Pussyman suddenly remembered that there was a political rally planned for today. One of the presidential candidates was supposed to give a speech. The candidate had come out of nowhere to take the lead in the polls. He had been staging open-air rallies all over the country; and this openness set him apart from his adversaries, whose campaign events were all staged behind closed doors, with handpicked audiences of 'the party faithful' and dozens of security personnel patrolling the audience, to carry away anyone who did not follow the party line. The candidate shunned all that; he walked city streets unafraid; he talked to everyone, and even Pussyman was going to vote for him. Yet, when Pussyman looked toward the stage, where the candidate was supposed to be, he saw what he immediately knew to be a demon. The thing's head was grossly over-sized and misshapen. It had a long, scaly neck, which took up about two-thirds of its body, and the rest of it was nothing but a mass of unruly hair. Pussyman could not even see its legs. To his amazement, he realized that the demon looked exactly like a humongous dick! Even though everyone knew that politicians were all dicks, Pussyman could not believe his eyes. He could not understand why the people in the audience did not see what he saw, but then he realized that the demon's screeching cries were putting everyone in a trance. That was the noise Pussyman had been hear-ing. The people, entranced by its spell, were cheering as if the demon's nonsensical screeching actually meant something; they looked at the demon longingly, as if it were the most beautiful thing they had ever seen. And while all this was going on, their souls, as well as the souls of thousands of others throughout the city, were being sucked into the demon's drooling mouth.

"Pussyman had hovered over the scene for a while, stunned; but finally realizing the peril they were all in, he flew down to the stage and tried to drop kick the demon. Unfortunately, as the demon had fed on the souls of millions, it did not even budge when Pussyman kicked it. In fact, it was so content in its feeding that it did not even acknowledge Pussyman as he bounced off its body and landed heavily on the stage. Likewise, the cheering spectators did not notice anything either.

"Pussyman's mind worked frantically for a while, until the answer came to him. Everyone knew that dick was powerless before pussy, so he wrenched the panties off his head and held them before the demon. 'Take a whiff of that, dickhead!' Pussyman screamed then, and the demon immediately shuddered and took a step back. 'The power of pussy compels you!' Pussyman began chanting then. 'The power of pussy compels you!' Each time he said it, the demon groaned. Soon, it was going into convulsions and screaming out in agony. 'The power of pussy compels you!' Pussyman screamed triumphantly as a violent contraction seized the demon's body, and a white, frothy substance came spewing out of its head. Then, after the froth was spewed, the demon began to shrink. Of course, while all this was going on, the people in the audience began to come out of their trance. They looked up at the demon and began to scream. But by now, it had shrunk to such a small size that Pussyman squished it beneath his foot with one mighty stomp. When that was done, he placed the panties over his head again and flew off, shouting to the cheering crowd, 'Never forget the power of pussy!'"

Stacy finished the story and looked over at Vera to get her assessment.

"So, where did the panties come from?" Vera asked.

Stacy groaned. "What difference would that make?"

"The panties would explain his powers."

Stacy shook her head, exasperated: "You're still looking for reason in my stories."

"That's a bad thing?"

"Like I told you the last time, stories shouldn't make sense. The stupider the plot, the more profound the lesson to be learned."

Vera stared her for a moment, dumbfounded, but then she laughed. Stacy had a smile on her face as well, so Vera did not know if Stacy was being earnest or not. Whatever the case, it did not seem to matter. That early morning, as they drove home, there was something careless in the air. Vera felt relieved and carefree for whatever reason, and she smiled again.

Stacy looked over at her and laughed.

The next day, when Vera finally woke up, she lay in bed with her eyes closed, listening to the sounds of the city: honking horns, passing traffic and indistinguishable voices from the streets below. Every few moments, there would be the rhythmic clanking of the elevated train. The passing train was strangely soothing, so maybe it was that that kept her on the verge of unconsciousness. But then, all at once, she remembered everything that had happened the previous day. She opened her eyes and sat up in bed, staring at the strange room. It was spacious with inexpensive furniture and an obscure abstract painting print on the far wall. She checked her watch, which was on the nightstand. It was twelve thirty-six in the afternoon. The curtains were open, letting in the day's light and the day's sounds. She got out of bed and shuffled over to the window. She could see the elevated train rumbling past, and make out individual passengers. She had the momentary urge to wave at one of them. Down on the street, traffic was moving steadily; people were walking slowly in the summer heat, doing their Saturday shopping. Vera stood staring at them, but her mind was actually on all that had happened the previous day. Regardless of everything, she felt alive inside. The things that had happened the day before were like a wondrous dream. She felt a little drunk.

Eventually, it occurred to her that she was only dressed in her bra and panties—and that she should probably not be standing at the window. She retreated into the room a few steps, and looked around again. The previous day's clothes were hanging over the back of a chair, near the bed. There was an attached bathroom. She went to it and stared at her reflection for a moment. She was relieved that her face showed little of the effects of her altercation with the old woman. The sudden recollection of that fight made her smile and shake her head, but then she remembered that the old woman was in the hospital now. As Vera's mind reconstituted all the memories from the previous day, she remembered the detective (whose name she still did not know!) and their date for that evening. That seemed like a dream as well—like something that had happened during a drunken binge. The things she had said to him—all the eroticized banter—had come naturally to her. It had felt easy and good. She smiled. She observed her body in the mirror as she stood there. She was not exactly supermodel material, but she liked her body today. It seemed voluptuous, rather than fat. There was a fine balance, of course, and she felt suddenly sexy and desirable.

Stacy had gotten her a toothbrush; extra sets of underwear and clothes had been set out for her visit. Stacy had pointed out all these things the previous night, during a quick tour of the house, and Vera had been both disturbed and amazed by the extent of Stacy's preparations. She had felt trapped for a moment, but the feeling had passed.

Now, Vera was brushing her teeth while she sat down on the commode. Afterwards, she took a shower. The water was warm and invigorating, so that she had to resist the urge to sing and dance under the cascade. After the shower, she returned to the bedroom and put on her new clothes: the underwear, a skirt that reached down to the middle of her thighs and a colorful T-shirt. They all fit her perfectly, and she wondered how Stacy had gotten her measurements. She stood posing before the full-length mirror in the bedroom, checking out her buttocks and propping up her breasts, and all the other things that women did in front of the mirror before going out. She twirled around in the skirt, and laughed as the centrifugal force lifted the skirt up, revealing the lacy pink panties Stacy had gotten for her. Her shoulder-length hair was still wet from the shower; typically, she would use a curling iron and styling gel on it before she allowed anyone to see her; makeup was usually a necessity as well, but all of that suddenly seemed needlessly burdensome. Today, of all days, she wanted to be free and natural. She wanted to see things as they were and be the person who she was meant to be. She nodded to her reflection in the mirror one last time, then left the bedroom.

She walked down the hallway, to the kitchen; looking to her right, she noticed the boyfriend sitting on the couch in the living room. The television was tuned to a news channel, but he was staring absentmindedly out of the window. Looking into the living room, she again noticed that cameras and lighting equipment were set up against the wall. Stacy had pointed them out during her tour last night, revealing that the living room was where they filmed the pornos. The thought of it made her shudder. She imagined some of the ghastly things that had been recorded on that couch—the various secretions and discharges that were now embedded in the fabric. She forced herself to think of something else. She went to the boyfriend now, needing to talk and distract herself. As she entered the room, he looked over at her; she smiled to reassure herself and him.

"Where's Stacy?" she said.

"She went to return the rental van," he replied. He looked wretched; his face was drawn and his voice was low and lifeless. He continued, "She should be back shortly."

Vera looked at him with concern: "Are you all right? ...I guess you're still worried about your mother."

"Yeah."

"Did you get any news?"

"She's still unconscious, but she's out of surgery safely."

"That's good." She glanced at the TV. There was a news report on a fire that had raged at an apartment building. Two kids were dead and the mother was sobbing inconsolably. Vera looked away and focused on the boyfriend again: "Did you get any sleep?"

"Nah," he said, uneasily.

"Your mother should be fine," she reminded him, "—isn't that what they said at the hospital?"

"Yeah, I know," he said, as if all of that were irrelevant. He looked up at her anxiously at that moment, saying, "That's not what kept me from sleeping."

"What's wrong?"

"You're a head doctor, right?" he said, suddenly hopeful. He sat up straighter.

"Yeah," she said, smiling shyly at his description of her profession.

He nodded and sighed, looking desperate and distraught: "...I keep having these strange thoughts," he said, looking at her anxiously. "I can't get them out of my head."

"Thoughts like what?"

"I keep seeing myself dying."

Vera cringed.

He looked at her with an embarrassed little smile. "...It sounds sick, right?" He laughed then, uneasily.

"Well, dreams usually represent some deeper—"

"No," he corrected her, "these weren't dreams. I've been up all night, remembering things. It's like everything I remembered was a lie. ...I remember new things now. Things that I thought had happened one way, now seem changed somehow."

"Things like what?"

"Like this time when Stacy and I went camping. I used to remember it one way, but now I keep seeing these crazy things. *God*," he whispered as the scene replayed itself in his mind. He looked up at her warily: "...I can tell you how it feels to have a knife blade slicing into your skin...ripping into your heart...I can tell you all about it, because I've been reliving it. I've *experienced* it. That's not the kind of thing you make up or imagine. I've been trying to get it out of my head, but..."

Vera spoke up dutifully: "The imagination is a powerful thing."

For a moment, he looked at her as if desperate to believe, but then he shook his head. "Why would I imagine something like that?" He put his hands to his forehead absentmindedly, but then noticed that they were shaking visibly. "...Look at me," he said with an anxious laugh, "—I'm a nervous wreck."

Vera felt slightly queasy just being around him—especially knowing what she knew. As a psychologist, seeing another human being having a mental breakdown was devastating. "...What else do you remember?" she said then. "Is there anything else?"

"Yeah, but it's all blurred together. It's like there are dozens of scenes. The only thing I know for sure is that I'm being killed in all of them." He looked at her ominously now: "...Stacy's in all of them, too. You think this has something to do with our relationship? Some kind of subconscious... I don't know. ...Mom says things about her. Maybe I'm feeling guilty... I don't know," he mumbled at last, clutching his head.

"The best thing for you now would be to try to get some rest. Why not lie down and try to take a nap at least?"

"I've tried," he said in frustration. "I've been trying since I came back from the hospital…but I keep remembering those things."

"When did these…"—she searched for the right word—"these visions begin?"

"I don't know. When I woke up last night—after Stacy said I passed out from seeing my mother messed up—I guess they were in my head then… but I didn't really think about them then. They were in the back of my mind. It wasn't until I was alone in the hospital, waiting for news on my mother, that they really started to come. I almost threw up on the emergency room floor. I had to run to the bathroom. I felt *sick*…"

"Lie down on the couch," she told him now. And then, smiling in a way she hoped would calm him, "An Indian guru taught me an acupressure technique once. Let me try it on you."

He shrugged after a moment's thought. "I guess it can't hurt." He lay down prone on the couch; she squatted over him and began to knead his tense shoulder muscles.

"God," he whispered, "your hands do feel good."

"You're pretty tense: no wonder you couldn't sleep."

"Yeah," he said weakly. …Within two minutes, he was snoring. Vera rose and stared at him. Her stomach felt unsettled again. She had to get out of the building—perhaps go outside and wait for Stacy. She went and got her stuff from the bedroom—just her purse. When she got back to the apartment last night, she had dumped the melted ice cream from her bag. Luckily, the spill had been confined to the plastic bag the store had packed it in, but her handbag nonetheless had a sickly sweet scent.

In the kitchen, she took a banana and orange from the fruit basket, and then left. When she got outside, she used her purse as a doorstop, and sat down on the stoop. There was a huge oak tree near the curb, so she had some shade. It was actually quite peaceful. The neighborhood looked different during the day. A few Hasidic Jews were heading back from Saturday prayers; the usual New York City pedestrian traffic was meandering past. She began to eat the orange as she sat there. Her mind raced with thoughts of the boyfriend. He was clearly on the verge of a mental breakdown. Whatever Stacy had told him the last time he came back to life had obviously not done the trick—

"How much, baby?"

She looked up from her thoughts to see a man in his mid- to late-fifties. He was dressed in an aquamarine linen suit, replete with matching bowler hat. He looked like a reject from the seventies—he even had a pimp cane with a crystal head. She looked at him with sudden fascination: "How much for what?"

"You know—a *grind*." He had a big, stupid grin on his face.

She cringed when she finally understood his proposal: "...You think I'm a prostitute?" She looked down at her skirt, suddenly wondering if it was too short; she instinctively clamped her knees shut—

"You're just the kind of 'ho I like, too!" he said enthusiastically, overlooking the shocked expression on Vera's face. "I hate those young, perfect-looking bitches," he went on. "Give me some old school, bump and grind, brick house pussy any day!"

Vera was so stunned that she could not say anything for a few moments. The old school player was still salivating over her. Yet, something about him was inherently ridiculous, and she suddenly laughed, more amused by the audacity of his proposition than offended—

"Let me introduce myself," he said, giving her what was supposed to be a seductive wink: "Rique Johnson at your service, baby. And when I say service, I mean *service*."

She found herself chuckling: it was too ridiculous. "Look," she began, "I'm sorry for the misunderstanding, but I'm not a prostitute, 'ho or whatever other term you want to use. Besides," she said with another chuckle, "I'd exhaust your bank account if you tried to get any of this, old-timer."

"Damn, baby," he said breathlessly, "I won't mind going broke over you at all!"

She laughed and shook her head.

"How much for just a taste then?" he said diplomatically.

"Still too much for you, Oldschool."

"Give me something to work with, baby!" he pleaded. "What are we talking, twenty dollars?"

"Twenty dollars! You've gotta come better than that!"

"Okay, okay," he said quickly, fidgeting with anticipation. "How about fifty dollars then?" he ventured.

"Fifty dollars!" she screamed, beginning to feel outraged. "Not even close."

"Fifty dollars ain't good enough for a taste?" he said in bewilderment.

"I ain't no goddamn value meal! If you want a cheap dinner you'd better go to McDonalds and order from the kids' menu!"

"Okay, okay," he said with increasing fidgetiness, "—how about a *sniff* then?"

"A sniff of what!"

"Yo' panties, baby."

"For fifty dollars? My panties cost more than that!" she lied about her Wal-Mart drawers. (Actually, she remembered that she was wearing the lacy underwear Stacy had gotten for her, and had no idea what they cost. Still, the idea of fifty dollars was outrageous!)

"Okay, okay," the old school player said, desperate to salvage something. "How about a *look* then?"

"A look at what?"

"Yo' panties, baby."

She frowned. "You're gonna pay me fifty dollars to look at my panties?"

"Yeah, baby," he said with a grin, glad that she seemed to be showing some sign of considering his proposal. And then, to press home his point, "It's all I got, baby. Help me out!" His pleading expression made her laugh again.

"Where's the money?" she asked suspiciously.

He took it out of his pocket, his hand shaking. "Here it is, baby. Just a look—that's all I'm asking."

"You'd pay fifty dollars just to look at my panties? You men *sure* are stupid," she said with a laugh.

"It's the devil in us," he lamented. "It's God's revenge for our evil ways.

In the Garden of Eden we could see all the pussy we wanted. Pussy wasn't even covered back then. Everything was out in the open—free. All you had to do was look over and you could see pussy. But once God threw us out of Paradise, pussy started to be covered, and we had to start paying for it."

The man's story showed a great deal of earnest contemplation, and, on some sick level, she was impressed. He still had a pleading expression on his face, and for a moment she felt sorry for him—but there was no way she was letting that moron see what was under her dress! That was when something occurred to her, and she had to cover her mouth with her hand to keep from laughing out.

"Okay, Oldschool," she said, snatching the money. She looked up and down the block to see if anyone was coming (some people were at the far end of the block), then she stood up. In a deft motion, she reached under her dress and pulled down her panties. She stepped out of them effortlessly, dangled them in front of Oldschool's mesmerized eyes for a second, before she retreated to the doorway, pushed the door open, kicked her purse into the hallway, and slammed the door in the old man's stunned face. When she was alone in the hallway, she laughed out loud, but she almost immediately felt foolish, and sorry for the old fool. She really did not need his money. When she opened the door again, he was still standing there with a mesmerized gleam in his eyes. She handed him the money and then slammed the door in his face again. She realized that she was still holding the panties in her hand: she put them on again.

Now that she was alone in the hallway, she felt melancholy. She suddenly remembered Stacy's boyfriend. The same queasy feeling came over her, so that she again had an urge to flee from the building. However, she could not go back outside, lest Oldschool was still lurking around, like some kind of lovesick puppy. The entire incident seemed even more stupid in retrospect, and she groaned. What if he had been some kind of lunatic rapist, and had forced her into the hallway? She sighed. She began walking up the stairs slowly.

That was when the thing happened. One moment, she was in the stairwell; the next moment, she was somewhere else. Wherever she was, there was too much light. She squinted to block out the glare, and then she saw it: a huge, bloody hand reaching out for her through the blinding light. The life she had lived just seconds before was now irrelevant; the thoughts that had been coursing through her mind when she started up the staircase now ceased to matter. The bloody hand was a man's hand—a hand gnarled by labor and hardship—but it seemed impossibly huge, like a bear's. The fingernails were packed with filth and gore; and as the hand reached out for her, her nostrils filled with a stench that she immediately understood to be death. She wanted to run, but she was frozen in place, possessed by some pure form of terror. The hand grew bigger. She could smell her own panic-induced sweat—and then the hand had her, so that the stench and reality of death flared up in her mind, blocking out everything else—

Everything went black; and then, she was back in the stairwell again. She almost passed out from the transition alone, but she managed to grasp the handrail. She stood there trembling. For a moment, she was possessed by all the terror of that vision or flashback or whatever it had been. She was panting and lightheaded. When her legs began to quiver, she sat down heavily on the stairs, still trying to catch her breath and make sense of things. Some time passed—maybe thirty seconds or five minutes. Her mind no longer seemed able to gauge things accurately. She only came back to her senses when she heard the building door open. When she looked up, she saw that it was Stacy. Vera felt relieved, but her face still wore a dazed, disillusioned expression.

Stacy frowned when she saw her. "What are you doing sitting out here?" Stacy said as she walked up to Vera. She stood above her, frowning deeper. "Are you okay?"

Vera did not know where to begin. "…Just now, I saw something."

"Huh?"

"I had a vision…of a hand. A *bloody* hand."

Stacy was looking at her confusedly, and Vera realized that none of her babble would make sense. She groaned in frustration.

"What's wrong?" Stacy asked.

"I don't know...I was walking up the stairs..." She faltered, realizing that she did not have the words to express what she had experienced. That was when she remembered the boyfriend. His mental breakdown seemed easier to explain, and she looked up at Stacy anxiously now, saying, "Your boyfriend's beginning to remember things."

"Things like what?"

"All the times you've killed him."

Stacy's eyes grew wider, but then she frowned: "How do you know?"

"I was just talking to him. He said that when he was alone in the hospital he started to remember it all. It's driving him crazy. He's on the verge of a total breakdown."

"It can't be that bad," Stacy said dismissively.

"I know a mental meltdown when I see it," Vera said with emphasis. "What did you tell him after he came back to life the last time?"

Stacy pursed her lips as she tried to recall: "Actually, I didn't really get a chance to tell him anything. The cops were lurking about, remember, asking questions. I managed to get away from the police just as he was coming back to life. I told him that his mother was in the hospital. I made him put on a clean shirt, and then we ran off."

Vera shook her head disapprovingly: "He's remembering everything, and his mind can't take it."

"What do you mean?"

"Everything you told him—all the cover stories you made up after every time you killed him—everything's unraveling. He's remembering *everything*—like the first time you killed him in the woods...*everything*. He's a nervous wreck."

Stacy stood there thinking about it for a while, and then she shrugged. "Well," she began, "there's only one way to fix that."

Vera looked at her uneasily: "You mean, you're going to kill him again?"

"Of course, what else is there to do?"

"*Goddamn*," she protested, "doesn't it get to you?"

"Killing him?"

"Yes—it's obviously hurting him: scrambling his brain."

Stacy snickered. "'Scrambling his brain'? Is that a clinical term, Dr. Vera?"

"You know what I mean," Vera said, annoyed. "Killing him over and over again has the potential to do serious harm."

"Don't go overboard," Stacy went on in the same dismissive way. "He's only remembering because I didn't tell him a likely story when he came back to life the last time. I'll just be more thorough when I do it again. ...Or would you like to kill him this time?"

"*Me?*" Vera practically shouted. "Of course not!"

Stacy stared at her for a while, and then she smiled. "Okay, then we'll do it your way."

"...What way is that?" Vera said, suddenly lost.

"You're a psychologist, and you don't want to kill him. I'll let you use your therapies on him."

Before Vera could say anything, Stacy walked past her, and up to the apartment. Vera's mind sputtered along for a moment. The honest side of her knew that what was going on with the boyfriend was beyond whatever meager skills she had as a therapist; at the same time, every psychologist wanted a challenge. The great psychologists were those who took on hopeless cases, and she could not help thinking that this was her chance to reach her potential. The entire Dr. Vera phenomenon had made her lazy. She knew that. Most of the last few years had been an exercise in boredom and laziness. She had to get out of that rut, and the boyfriend's pending breakdown was her chance to test herself. Maybe there was a kind of self-aggrandizing delusion wrapped in that entire course of thought, but she felt suddenly enlivened by the prospect of the adventure ahead. She got up and continued walking up the stairs. She tried to think of a therapy that could help the boyfriend. She knew that she would have to do some research. She also knew that the boyfriend's pending breakdown would not allow her that courtesy.

Stacy had left the apartment door open for her. When Vera entered the doorway, Stacy was walking up to her, looking confused.

"Did my boyfriend leave?"

"No, I left him sleeping on the couch."

They both looked toward the couch, which was bare. Vera frowned and stepped into the living room, where the television was still playing.

"You checked the bedroom?" Vera asked Stacy.

"Yeah—I just did. He's not in the apartment."

They both seemed to notice the open window at that moment. Stacy walked over to it, and Vera followed. There was a fire escape beyond the window, which led down to an alley.

"Why would he leave through the window?" Vera said uneasily.

Stacy shrugged. She turned from the window and looked around the room as if some clue to her boyfriend's disappearance would be in it. That was when she noticed the story on the news. There was a report of a deranged man running down the street with a pair of panties on his head. He had just caused an accident at the entrance to the Williamsburg Bridge. Traffic was backed up, and the anchorwoman was warning drivers away from the area.

"Oh, oh," Stacy said then.

"What?" Vera glanced at the screen, where there was a helicopter view of the backed up traffic.

"It's him," Stacy whispered.

"Your boyfriend?"

Stacy nodded ominously: "He's acting out the Pussyman story."

"He's *what*?"

"Come on," Stacy said, moving quickly to the door, "—I know where he's going."

They ran out of the apartment and down the stairs. Once they were outside the building, they jogged a block and a half before Vera called to Stacy—

"Wait, I can't run that fast!" She was winded; she wished that she had left her huge handbag in the house. Stacy slowed to a brisk walk, while Vera tried to catch her breath. They were nearing the station for the elevated train.

"Are you sure you know where he's going?" Vera asked when she could speak without passing out.

"I'm positive."

They were walking up the stairs to the station now. They could hear the train approaching. Stacy looked back at her, as to tell her to hurry up. They began to run again. To Vera's annoyance, Stacy's breathing was even, whereas she was practically having an asthma attack.

About five seconds after they made it to the station platform, the train arrived. Vera scrambled into the train, after Stacy. The train was not exactly packed, but most of the seats were taken. Stacy and Vera stood by the door. Vera was still wheezing. A woman with a squealing toddler had also just boarded the train. The child was throwing a tantrum. The toddler kept slapping the woman's hand, trying to get her to put him down. The woman seemed somehow indifferent to the fuss; and the child, who grew enraged by the fact that he could not remove her hands from his person, now attempted to kick his mother as well. The woman held him firmly, but at arm's length; and now, seeing that he could neither remove her hands nor kick her, the fidgety kid began to weep bitterly at the injustice of it all. This lasted about seven seconds, before his body went limp from some kind of emotional exhaustion. At that, his mother held him to her body and patted his back. In turn, the toddler nestled into her breasts and seemed to go to sleep. Vera, Stacy and the other passengers in the car had all stared at the scene; but seeing that it had come to a conclusion, they now went on about their business.

For whatever reason, Vera smiled at the ingenious psychological powers of mothers. She looked over at Stacy, expecting a smile to be on her face as well, but Stacy was staring out of the window meditatively, looking at the passing buildings. There was a pained expression in her eyes. Vera remembered the boyfriend; it occurred to her that Stacy was probably thinking about him. She began:

"You really love your boyfriend, don't you?"

Stacy looked over at her abruptly. She frowned when the question registered in her mind. She went back to staring out of the window; there was a sardonic expression on her face as she said, "Didn't you already ask me that stupid question?"

Vera chuckled. "You didn't really answer me the last time."

"Of course I did. I told you that I needed him. Need is stronger and more honest than love."

"How is that?"

"When you say 'I love you' to someone, you're making a contract—a trade. You say 'I love you' and you wait for the other person to say, 'I love you, too.' You say those words in order to elicit something that may not be there. When you say 'I love you' you're forcing someone's hand: binding them to a contract. ...But when you need someone, love and declarations are irrelevant. For instance, you can need someone you hate. Look at that mother and child," she said, gesturing to the pair that had been the center of the ruckus a few seconds before. "That child hated his mother a few seconds ago, when he was screaming. It was need, not love that caused him to stop screaming. The child needs his mother, but the mother only loves her child. As he grows older, and more dishonest, he'll begin to love her too."

Vera shuddered. "That's a harsh view."

"Why? Because I refuse to believe in lies and fairy tales? ...You don't believe in love either."

"What?" she said with an incredulous laugh.

"Your kind of love is a ridiculous commodity that you sell to your equally ridiculous readers and listeners. You have the same relationship to love that a fast food joint owner has to his food: you both know you're selling shit, but you don't care because you know that people love buying shit."

To Vera's amazement, she laughed—not a defensive or sarcastic laugh, but a laugh of simple acceptance.

Stacy smiled: "You know I'm right."

Vera looked at her with a sly smile. "There are more important things in the world than being right, Stacy."

Stacy shrugged, and they both smiled.

However, that was when Vera remembered the boyfriend: how they had run out of the house in search of him. It was suddenly amazing to her how easily they got sidetracked: how easily their bizarre conversations distracted them. She looked at Stacy soberly, remembering what Stacy had said as they ran out of the house.

"You said your boyfriend was following the Pussyman story?"

"Yes."

Vera looked at her doubtfully: "You came to that conclusion after watching a fifteen-second news report? It could have been another lunatic with a pair of panties on his head."

Stacy shook her head. "I *know* it's him," she said simply. In fact, her expression was chilling. Vera instinctively retreated from it.

"...My God," Vera whispered as the scope of the situation occurred to her. "If what you say is true, then your boyfriend has had a total psychotic break. ...Has this ever happened before?"

"No."

"It must have something to do with his remembering all the times you killed him."

"Do you still think you can treat him?"

"I'll try."

"Have you ever treated anyone like that—who has lost all connection with reality?"

"How many immortal, brain-scrambled boyfriends do you think there are in the world, Stacy?"

Stacy laughed at her sarcasm. "Are you admitting defeat already?"

"I don't know—I'm simply telling you how it is. It's not as though this is your typical case."

"If you can't treat him your way, then that leaves only one option."

Vera looked at her anxiously; she leaned in and whispered, "You mean, killing him again?"

"Yes."

Vera nodded, bowing her head introspectively.

"But I won't kill him," Stacy said abruptly.

"What?"

"I won't kill him this time. No matter what happens, I won't do it."

Vera was confused. "I thought you believed that killing him was the best way to restore balance?"

"Yes—I still do, but you don't. Now it's time for us to show and prove: to test what we believe. I've already taken my test. Now it's time for you to take yours."

All Vera could do was stare. Stacy returned to looking blankly out of the window. They were now on the Williamsburg Bridge, crossing the East River. Outside the window, cars zoomed past on the bridge's road-way. Beyond the cars, the East River seemed dull and dour below them.

Vera's mind rebelled against everything Stacy had said: "Why are you making me responsible for everything?"

"I'll be there with you, but it's time for you to take the lead for a while." As Stacy said these words, she fished something out of her back pocket. She handed it to Vera. It was a switchblade knife. "Hold onto this," Stacy said.

Vera shook her head, looking at Stacy with rising panic.

"If you can't treat him as a doctor," Stacy went on matter-of-factly, "then there's only one option left."

"Why do *I* have to do it?"

"We're partners in this, Vera. You can't be a passive observer: you have to take part. You have to know what it feels like to take and give life. Now is the time to become a full partner in this, instead of some kind of Peeping Tom on the sidelines."

"But I *can't*," she pleaded. "I can't even step on cockroaches."

Stacy shook her head in disappointment: "You're still not embracing the full implications of this situation, Vera. You won't be killing him: you'll be giving him life. If you can't help him your way, using all the knowl-edge and techniques of science, then it's time to embrace new possibilities. Stop thinking so one-dimensionally."

As she said these last words, the subway doors opened. They were across the river, in Manhattan, at Essex Street. They were underground again—Vera had not noticed the growing darkness during their conver-sation. Stacy grabbed Vera by the arm then: "This is our stop."

They ran out of the car and toward the transfer with the F Train. Vera felt lost and wretched. The things Stacy had said to her were rooting about in her head like some kind of vicious beast. She allowed Stacy to lead her; Stacy's grip was firm on her upper arm. She felt frail and desperate.

The F Train was coming. Stacy pulled her arm more gruffly, so that she would speed up. This time, they just managed to leap onto the train before the doors closed. The train was not full; Stacy steered Vera toward two seats in the corner, and they sat down. Vera was panting again. They did not say anything to one another for about a minute. Finally, when Vera began to catch her breath, she looked over at Stacy's calm face. Stacy was staring ahead distractedly, at the colorful advertisements across from where they were sitting. For whatever reason, Vera tried to think about Stacy objectively. What did she really know about the woman? Stacy was obviously highly intelligent, but there was something unhinged about her. Stacy had done things that perhaps human beings were not meant to do. Stacy had gotten it into her mind that it was possible to kill without consequences, and Vera knew that horrible things were bound to come from such reasoning…even if the boyfriend could not die. At the same time, Vera found herself thinking that maybe Stacy was right about her. Maybe she was still refusing to grasp the monumental possibilities of this situation. The boyfriend could not die, and that meant that everything was open for discussion and exploration. *Everything.* …She remembered the switchblade that Stacy had handed her. She shook her head unconsciously, knowing that she was not yet ready to take the proverbial leap of faith that Stacy's request required. …Maybe Stacy was right about her. Maybe she was holding onto old, useless things. Even before Stacy abducted her last night, she had merely been going about the motions of life. She had not really been living—she had been existing: waiting passively for something to happen. She remembered how she had felt when she woke up that morning: she had felt alive and free for the first time in years. She wanted to feel that way again. Her body craved it, in fact.

Vera looked over at Stacy then. She needed to be reassured. Somehow, she felt that if Stacy told her that everything would be fine, then everything would work out. She spoke up abruptly, saying, "Do you really think I can do it? Do you think I could kill him?"

Stacy looked over at her absentmindedly, as if she had forgotten that Vera was there. It seemed to take a few moments before Vera's question made sense to her. At last, she nodded; Vera, despite everything, found herself thinking of how beautiful Stacy was. That fact, irrelevant as it was, gave Vera a strange sense of hope. The beautiful people were always good deep down—at least, that was the case in fairy tales. It was easy to believe in beauty and simplicity. Vera took a deep breath, suddenly desperate to be optimistic about things—to see hope where there was probably only horror. She smiled. Looking at Stacy again, she ventured:

"So, where did your boyfriend run off to?"

Stacy gestured to the poster directly across from where they were sitting. Vera looked up at the poster. She frowned and suppressed the impulse to shudder when she recognized Pastranzo's grinning face.

"The concert in Central Park?" Vera said in bewilderment.

"Yes."

Vera thought back to the story; her mouth gaped when she understood what was before them: "...Your boyfriend is hunting the screeching demon: Pastranzo."

"Exactly," Stacy said. "We have to get to him before he tries to kill Pastranzo."

Some seconds passed; the train stopped at the next station, and dozens of passengers entered. Vera's mind was still dazed and wretched. At last, when the train began to move again, she turned to Stacy again, saying, "If your boyfriend is still on foot, then we should get there before him."

"Unless he jumps off a building, thinking he can fly.'

Vera nodded uneasily. After some thought, she reasoned: "The key to all this may be getting him to take off the panties."

"It's worth a shot," Stacy said with a shrug and a smile.

Something occurred to Vera, and she smiled. "I assume those were your panties he was wearing?"

"Knowing him, it was probably his mother's."

They both laughed.

Ten minutes later, they came to the 57th Street stop. Actually, by now, the train was packed with Pastranzo's fans. Some of them carried posters and wore T-shirts with his grinning image. When the train stopped, practically everyone got out. Stacy walked briskly; once they were out-side the subway station, Stacy began to jog again. Vera followed, her legs already rubbery. Pastranzo's fans were everywhere. Many of them seemed high or otherwise dazed. Even before Stacy and Vera entered the park they could hear Pastranzo's music. It was an eclectic, sometimes incompatible mix of rock, Middle Eastern and Asian music. From Vera's perspective, his shrill voice was an exclamation point to the entire cacophony; however, his fans seemed somehow addicted to it—or at least, immune.

Most of the fans were young and idealistic—from Vera's perspective, people who wanted to be seen saving the world, but who really did not give a shit. A half a million people were expected to attend the concert. (Unfortunately, that was a factoid that Vera had retained from a week of being around the media frenzy.) Vera looked around the crowd uneasily. Pastranzo's fans were a freak show of pierced and tattooed flesh. Even the "normal-looking" ones seemed to have a demented gleam in their eyes, which Vera attributed to prolonged exposure to Pastranzo's music. The only good thing about the crowd was that it kept Stacy from running. Vera's clothes were all soaked through with sweat by now. Her panties had run up her behind; she had to resist the urge to reach under her skirt and correct the problem. She remembered the old school player; a queasy expression came over her face for an instant. Stacy looked back at her as they navigated their way through the crowd. When they made eye contact, Vera ventured:

"What if your boyfriend already got picked up by the police? He caused a traffic jam, remember?" Now that she had Stacy's attention, she began walking by her side. She continued: "Even if he didn't get picked up, he's probably still hours away from the park, if he's still on foot."

Stacy's voice was low but firm as she went back to scanning the crowd: "I know he's here."

"How?"

"I just know—the same way I knew you were going to be at that deli last night."

"That's different—you were stalking me," Vera joked.

Stacy smiled, but continued to scan the crowd. They walked side-by-side for about five minutes. Vera still did not believe that the boyfriend was anywhere near the park. There were thousands of police officers patrolling the crowd as well—which made it less likely that the boyfriend would go unnoticed by the police if he showed up. Even in such a motley crowd, a man with a pair of panties on his head would stick out.

The crowd got thicker as Stacy and Vera moved toward the Great Lawn. Presently, they were coming upon a giant screen TV, on which Pastranzo was shown singing one of his creepy ballads. For whatever reason, Stacy stopped to watch, and Vera did the same. Vera had to listen closely before she was willing to accept that Pastranzo was singing in English. His singing reminded Vera of the Munchkins in *The Wizard of Oz*—it was high-pitched and eerie, without the good humor that cute midgets could instill in a song. Vera shuddered and leaned over to Stacy, whispering:

"You *sure* that guy ain't really a demon?"

They both smiled and walked on.

They walked for another five minutes or so. Vera's feet were getting tired. She looked over at Stacy again: "Even if he's here, this is like finding a needle in a haystack."

No sooner had Vera made this statement than Stacy gestured with her head: about a hundred feet from their position, the boyfriend was skulking around, ducking behind trees and exhibiting other types of paranoid behavior—as if he could maintain a low profile with a pair of red panties on his head. On top of that, he had accessorized his superhero costume with a cape—a floral-pattered curtain that Vera remembered vaguely from Stacy's bathroom window—

"Let's go!" Stacy said suddenly; she and Vera moved toward the boyfriend as quickly as they could, but he was already moving away, darting through the crowd in his quest to find the screeching demon. In his reckless haste, he banged into two police officers, practically knocking them over. However, he did not stop or acknowledge them.

"Hey, you!" the cops screamed. They began chasing him.

The boyfriend hurdled a park bench; the first police officer attempted to do the same, but he was an overweight slob, to put it succinctly. His foot caught on the back of the bench and he toppled over, onto the ground. Luckily, it was dirt, but he was so huge that his collision with the ground was a brutal one.

The second cop, learning from his partner's stupidity, decided to run around the park bench. "You okay?" he called to his partner as he ran; the first cop made a noncommittal grunting noise, so he ran on. The boyfriend was running like a startled jackrabbit—darting in one direction, and then the other. Now, somehow, he was running back toward Stacy and Vera. Stacy looked at Vera and nodded: a gesture that told her to stay where she was. Stacy then ran ahead. Vera thought she would grab the boyfriend, but she ran past him and pretended to accidentally collide with the pursuing police officer. They both crumbled to the ground. The police officer seemed to take the worst of it, as he lay sprawled on the ground like a bloated corpse. As Vera looked on in her usual stunned way, Stacy looked back at her and winked.

The wink seemed to bring Vera to her senses, because she grabbed the boyfriend's arm as he ran past, and they ran on together. In his madness, he did not even acknowledge her; when he ran from the police officers, he probably had not even realized that they were pursuing him. Vera looked at his eye through the leg opening of the panties. His eye seemed glassy, like a cheap doll's. Vera glanced over her shoulder: no police officers were following, but this incident would be reported to headquarters soon.

"Hey!" she called to him. He ignored her. "*Hey!*"

He looked over at her with an enraged expression on his face. For a moment, he seemed on the verge of knocking her out. Her mind worked quickly: "Pussyman," she began, "I've brought news for you."

"You know of Pussyman?" he said, slowing, his interest and ego piqued.

"Everyone knows Pussyman," Vera lied easily.

The boyfriend nodded his head and puffed out his chest, pleased. In the meanwhile, people passed them, frowning or laughing and point at his ridiculous costume. Vera spotted two police officers approaching. She took the boyfriend by the arm now, and guided him away:

"We have to hide: the screeching demon has his spies out—"

"What do you know of the demon!" he said, suddenly enraged again.

"Come with me and I'll tell you."

They moved quickly behind a tree, where two exhibitionist twelve-year-olds were groping and groaning against the tree trunk. The Pussyman outfit startled the girl, and she gasped—

"Get lost," Vera told the two stunned kids. They slunk off.

"What do you know about the demon?" the boyfriend asked her again.

Falling into character, Vera shushed him. She decided to follow though with her original plan. Hopefully, treating him was as simple as having him take off the panties; with any luck, the panties were the catalyst of his psychotic break. She went into action, whispering, "We have to hide from the demon's spies. They know you as Pussyman, but they don't know who you are behind the mask. Maybe it's time for you to assume your alter ego."

He rubbed his chin, giving her proposal thought. Vera rushed him ahead: "Give me your cape, Pussyman," she said, snatching off the curtain—the end of which was not really fastened, just shoved down the back of his T-shirt. She shoved it into her huge handbag. "Now, take off your mask, Pussyman, so we can thwart evil." She almost laughed at her own stupid phrasing; but on another level, she felt proud of herself, as "thwart evil" was a good comic book phrase. She nodded her head encouragingly then, and the boyfriend looked around furtively, before wrenching off the panties. Vera looked at him closely, to see if he came back to his senses, but he still had the same insane gleam in his eyes. Actually, he kept the panties balled up in his hand; as they stood there, he sniffed them anxiously, as if getting a fix of a drug. Vera watched this with fascination, and with the sudden realization that her plan was not exactly working. She hoped that his removing his "costume" would end the psychotic break, but it had no effect. Worse, she had done something fatally wrong as a therapist: she had just verified her patient's delusion. While she was standing there indecisively, he began to wander off, as if he had forgotten about her. The Great Lawn—and the main body of the Pastranzo concert—could be seen through the trees. As if drawn by a scent, the boyfriend began to walk in that direction. Vera panicked a little, wondering what she was going to do. At least now that he had taken off the panties he would be somewhat safe from the police, but he was still mentally unstable: a danger to himself and others. The only thing she knew for certain now was that she had to get him out of there. He still had the panties balled up in his hand and was sniffing them every few seconds (supposedly to keep up his super strength). It occurred to Vera that for all intents and purposes he still had the panties on. Acting on instinct once more, she grabbed the panties from his hand and began to run in the opposite direction from the podium, hoping that he would follow.

"Traitor!" he screamed as he began to chase her. If he had been psychotic before, he was now pushed over some new threshold. He screamed wildly, spittle frothing at the corners of his mouth. Vera glanced back at him and screamed. She was still holding her bag over her shoulder. If she had sense, she would have dropped the bag, but that was a Gucci sports bag, so to hell with that! Either way, she was no match for a young, healthy man on foot; and within seconds, he knocked her from behind, so that she tumbled to the ground. When she looked up, he was in her face, growling like a beast. "Give me back the sacred panties!" he screamed.

"Okay!" Vera cried out, genuinely terrified. "Here!" she said, holding out the panties with a trembling hand, "—take them!" As he bent down to take the panties, she noticed the butt of a gun tucked into the front of his pants. His T-shirt had covered it before, but when he bent over, the gun was revealed. Vera gasped. Luckily, as soon as he had the panties back, he calmed down. He brought them to his nose and inhaled deeply, a glazed look coming over his face. He inhaled deeply several times, in fact, as if recharging his strength. At last, he walked off, leaving Vera trembling on the ground, as if she were irrelevant.

"The demon must die," he muttered as he began to walk back toward the concert.

Just then, the crowd cheered at something Pastranzo had said—

"Don't cheer the demon!" the boyfriend screamed. He began to walk quicker now, as if on a mission. Two nearby girls were clapping; the boyfriend confronted them, screaming, "Can't you see how hideous it is? You're all under its spell!"

The two girls looked at one another confusedly. Luckily for them, the crowd cheered again, and the boyfriend continued on his mission toward the podium in the distance, where Pastranzo was in the middle of one of his tone deaf solos.

Vera came to her senses suddenly. She got to her feet and ran after the boyfriend—who was by now at least one hundred feet in front of her. He was still screaming about the demon to everyone who came within earshot. Most ignored him—or did not hear his gibberish over the cheering and the music. However, some people began to look at him in annoyance. Remembering the gun, Vera knew that she had to act before something happened, but she had no idea what to do. She thought about calling the police, but that would ruin the boyfriend's life—

"The demon must die!" the boyfriend continued to rant as he pushed his way through the ever-thickening crowd. "You've already lost your souls to it!" he raged—

"Would you shut the hell up!" a huge, hairy man growled. The boyfriend had just screamed into the man's ear. The man struck Vera as a huge, hairy mollusk—an oyster without the shell. He had to weigh at least three hundred pounds; and under all that fat, there did not seem to be any definite skeletal structure. In fact, he did not merely have a pot belly, but several layers of flab, which bulged and jiggled against one another as if they were in competition for supremacy. The man's hair was green, and reached down his back; his beard had been dyed orange, and reached down to his second stomach bulge. He was standing in a group with half a dozen other young men, the rest of whom were of normal human proportions—

"You're all slaves of the demon!" the boyfriend screamed at them all, "soul-less slaves!" Actually, he screamed at no one in particular—it was just that the mollusk and his crew were blocking him. The boyfriend began to push past the mollusk—

"Don't push me, asshole!" the man yelled—

"The demon's *drained* you—" the boyfriend continued; he tried to push past the hairy mollusk again. However, by now, the man had had enough. He reared his hand back then, and punched the boyfriend squarely in the jaw. There was a loud "crack" at the blow; however, bolstered by his super-human pussy strength, the boyfriend barely moved. This seemed to enrage the entire mollusk crew—as if the boyfriend had offended their honor. As if a hidden signal had been given, they now all started pummeling the boyfriend.

Vera had watched all this with a kind of numb fascination. She stood about twenty feet away and stared at the scene—just like the surrounding people. That fascination turned to panic when the boyfriend punched one of the punier mollusk crew members in the mouth, knocking out his front teeth. She had to stop this; and yet, there was another voice within her, telling her that this was perfect. At least the boyfriend would not kill Pastranzo if he got beaten up. And if the mollusk crew killed him... she shook her head as the thought passed through her mind, not because his getting killed was a bad thing, but because the boyfriend, despite his derangement (or maybe because of it) was holding his own against the mollusk crew. He was still screaming gibberish about the demon. If anything, his delusion was getting stronger, empowering him. Between lashing out blows, he sniffed the panties, which he kept balled around his fist.

No, Vera had to put an end to this. She knew how, but she would not allow herself to acknowledge it. She kept the awareness locked up in a dark place within herself. ...There was only one thing that could save the boyfriend now. He was totally psychotic; all ties to reason and reality had been severed. The only thing her profession could do for him was pump him full of drugs and institutionalize him. That, she knew, was out of the question, as it would ruin his life; calling the police was out of the question; leaving him alone to continue with the escalating madness of his delusion was out of the question, as she had no doubt that he would turn over heaven and earth to kill Pastranzo, or the next person the delusion told him to kill. And now, as she looked at the melee, she noticed him trying to reach for his gun. Luckily, he was put off balance by a blow to the head.

A dark, unnamable impulse took possession of Vera, and she found herself going to the melee. If she went quickly or slowly, she had no idea.
Somehow, there was a voice screaming in her ears, directing her. From the
stage, Pastranzo was squealing like a skewered pig. Somehow that sound
joined with the one in Vera's mind, pushing her over some new threshold—some previously unattainable mental barrier—so that soon, she
found herself within the melee, pummeling the boyfriend. Her presence
went unnoticed in the chaos. He was screaming; his attackers were
yelling; and from the loud speakers, Pastranzo's screeching solo rever-
berated. Somehow, Vera found herself screaming as well. She did not
know when she had taken Stacy's switchblade out of her bag; but somehow, it was in her hand, cloaked by the boyfriend's one-time cape. And
then, somehow, with her mind and will numbed by all the screaming, she
jammed the knife into the boyfriend's back. His spine arched—

Pastranzo's screeching solo ended. Everything seemed suddenly silent.
Vera's insane screams stopped—if she had ever actually screamed at all.
She put a trembling hand over her mouth when she realized what she had
done. The boyfriend's attackers continued to beat him, unaware of what
had happened. The entire thing was so horrible that Vera was about to
scream out in horror—but miraculously, Stacy appeared at her side—

"Enough!" Stacy screamed, stepping in between the hairy mollusk and
her boyfriend's drooping body; she grabbed his slumping body, holding
him up by looping her arm under his left arm. "—Isn't this supposed to
be a *peace* concert!" she chastised the stunned mollusk. Like many, he was
amazed by her beauty; his crew, which seemed to follow his lead in everything, stood there like sulking six-year-olds, waiting for their mother to
administer punishment. The boyfriend made an inarticulate noise—a
moan. Stacy looked at the mollusk disapprovingly; feeling compelled to
explain himself, he pointed at the boyfriend with a trembling finger and
whined:

"Well, *he* started it!"

Stacy ignored him and began to drag the boyfriend away. She made
sure to keep her hand on the curtain cum cape, and the bloody knife it

concealed. Vera, coming to her senses, grabbed the boyfriend's other arm and began to help Stacy. Together, they began to move off, dragging the mortally wounded boyfriend.

"He's still alive," Stacy whispered as they walked off. Somehow, it sounded like an accusation.

"Oh God, I'm sorry!" Vera said too loudly.

Stacy shushed her. "Keep it together, Vera."

Vera nodded her head uneasily. They were making their way through the crowd now. People were cheering and swaying to Pastranzo's strange music, but all Vera could think was that they all knew what she had done. She had *stabbed* a man…!

They were now out of the thickest section of the crowd. Stacy steered the boyfriend toward some portable toilets. People were on lines to enter the toilets. A woman came out of one of the toilets; a man was about to enter, but Stacy stepped in front of him, saying, "We had an accident—you understand."

The guy did not get a chance to answer. Stacy opened the door with her free hand. Their noses were blasted by the dual odors of floral-scented chemicals and steaming excrement. Vera coughed. Stacy and Vera had to maneuver their bodies so that they could shove the boyfriend in. He slumped on the commode. There was not space for all three of them to enter, but they did. Stacy locked the door. Vera was queasy from the scent and the reality of everything—

The boyfriend moaned. Vera had to stifle the sudden urge to vomit.

"Give me your handbag," Stacy demanded then.

Vera did as she was told. It was a struggle to move within the cramped space, but she finally handed over the bag; she hit the boyfriend in the head inadvertently. She went to apologize, but stopped herself. Stacy was fishing around inside the bag. Vera had no idea why, and she was too numb to think to ask. However, after a few seconds, Stacy pulled out a plastic bag that Vera had wrapped some used gym socks in (and forgotten about). Stacy discarded the socks and proffered the plastic bag to Vera.

"You can finish him off with this," she said simply.

"*Me?*" Vera said when her mind finally deciphered the sentence,"—I *can't*," she said, refusing to take the bag.

"You're halfway there, Vera," Stacy reassured her. "Hold this over his nose and mouth—it's the easiest way."

"Can't you do it?" Vera pleaded.

"I told you before that I won't do it. You have to play your part."

"I *can't!*" she sobbed.

The boyfriend moaned; drool was dripping from his open mouth as he sat there with his head slumped forward.

Stacy talked to Vera slowly, like a mother addressing a disagreeable child: "Here, take this." She took Vera's hand and placed the plastic bag in it. Vera was still sobbing, but she took it.

"*Do* it, Vera. It's the only way. Every moment you delay only means more suffering for him. Look at the agony on his face," she said, taking hold of the boyfriend's head and tilting it upward, so Vera could see his face. A disembodied cry escaped from his lips; his eyes had rolled back in their sockets by now—

Vera shuddered and looked away, still sobbing.

"You have to put him out of his misery, Vera. *Look* at him, don't turn away. Good, that's it. Look at him—see him for yourself. *You're* in control here. You can save him, Vera—save him from suffering and his delusions. Death is the only way. *Do* it."

Vera's hands were trembling as she held the plastic bag. She took the bag in both hands now, as Stacy nodded her head in encouragement. Vera was moving the plastic bag closer and closer to the boyfriend's face—

"Do it!"

Suddenly, the internal screaming started in Vera's head again; the people outside started cheering, and the same strange numbness as before took over. She brought the bag to the boyfriend's face and held it there. He tried to move his face away—an instinctual defense mechanism of the body. However, now that the internal screaming had started again, Vera found her muscles quivering with awesome strength—or so it seemed to her. She leaned over him, applying all her strength. He struggled at first;

and while he did, the screaming voice inside of her blocked everything out. She held her breath while all this was going on—everything seemed to stop in fact. It was only when his struggles finally subsided to nothing that the horror of it registered in her mind. She released the plastic bag. Considering the pressure she had applied to his sweat-drenched face, the bag stuck to his skin. His eyes were still rolled back in their sockets. His body was limp. He was dead. She tried to step away—to flee—but of course, there was nowhere to go in the cramped space.

Stacy held her then, and laughed out triumphantly. "It's over, Vera! I'm proud of you!" When Stacy detached from her, Vera looked at her as if fighting to understand: as if her mind had been severed from the surrounding reality. "We are one now, Vera," Stacy continued, "—bound together by fate. Dry those tears now—you've become part of something great…!"

Five minutes had passed since Vera killed the boyfriend. She watched with a kind of semi-conscious fascination as Stacy prepared the body. Vera had had a towel in her huge handbag. Stacy pulled out the knife, pulled off the boyfriend's shirt, then used the towel (and the plastic bag) as a bandage. She then put the shirt back on, and tied the one-time cape around his midsection, covering all signs of blood. Stacy's finishing touch was a pair of movie starlet sunglasses she had found in Vera's handbag. These, she used to cover up the boyfriend's eyes, which refused to stay closed. With this ensemble, he looked like some kind of cross-dressing freak, but it would conceal his death unless the police stopped them. Stacy's plan, Vera gleaned from the woman's cheerful chatter, was that they would take him home, wait for him to come back to life, and then reprogram him. That gave them an hour.

Stacy pushed open the door of the portable toilet. Vera was startled by the light of the day, and the fresh air, and the reality of the crowd. Somehow she had forgotten about the outside world. The people waiting on line to use the toilet looked at the strange scene of two women and a guy jammed into a toilet. Some of them gasped; some laughed and pointed.

Vera looked at the staring crowd with a mixture of shame and uneasiness. One woman about Vera's age averted her five-year-old's eyes from the sight, and pulled him away in a huff. Stacy, as usual, was unfazed. While Vera avoided their eyes, Stacy looked at them as if to say, "What the hell are you looking at!" Stacy was the first to maneuver out of the cramped space of the toilet, leaving the boyfriend and Vera jammed in there like zoo animals on display.

Just then, a pack of four teenage boys was passing by. The oldest was probably sixteen at the most:

"Damn," one said while the others laughed, "what were you guys doing in there!"

Without missing a beat, Stacy smiled at the young men seductively: "We just fucked his brains out," she said, pointing back at the boyfriend, and a stunned Vera. And then, while the surprised boys stopped and stared, and their previous laughter gave way to shock and disbelief, she continued, "You guys want to be next?"

The boys stared at one another, speechless.

"Speak quickly, gentlemen," Stacy urged them on. "This is your one chance."

The boys looked at one another and nodded excitedly.

"Okay then," Stacy went on. "All you have to do is help me get him to a cab. He passed out after what we did to him. Hopefully you guys won't give out as easily."

The boys practically fought with one another as they ran to get the boyfriend. Vera barely managed to get out of the way. They hauled out the boyfriend and returned to Stacy, like dogs playing fetch. Two had him by the shoulders, and two had his legs. Stacy smiled seductively again, then began to walk quickly toward the park exit. Vera walked behind them all, her mind numb as usual. Of course, none of the boys noticed her—Stacy was their prize. Vera did not know if she was relieved by that or insulted.

Every few moments, Stacy would goad them on with something like, "Faster, baby, I'm *so* horny," or, "The quicker we get him home, the quicker we can fuck." Vera could not believe her ears. It was ridiculous and shameless at the same, but the teens were worked into a frenzy by it. On the other hand, Vera's mind was still stuck on the reality of death—the reality that she had stabbed and suffocated a man.

Stacy was practically jogging now, and the horny teens ran after her. None of them was in particularly good shape; and with the burden of the boyfriend, they were wheezing after a few minutes. Even Vera seemed to be in better shape than they were. The horny teens began to slow, but Stacy urged them on with, "Faster, baby, I want it *so* bad!"

After a while, Vera did not know if it was horniness that spurred them on or their male egos (and the fact that they did not want to appear weak before Stacy). That was especially so, as Stacy's energy still seemed inexhaustible.

Vera was beginning to regain her composure. She jogged past the struggling teens and up to Stacy's side. "You're not really going to screw those fools, are you?" she asked.

Stacy laughed, and glanced back at the wheezing foursome. She winked at them, to encourage them, but they were so exhausted they did not seem to notice. Stacy looked back at Vera: "You can have them, if you want."

Despite everything, Vera smiled and shook her head.

They were nearing the edge of the park. Stacy ran ahead with a few graceful strides that left Vera amazed. Soon, she was fifty yards ahead of them, standing on the curb and gesturing to an oncoming cab. The cab pulled over. Stacy looked back at the stragglers and gestured for them to run faster. Vera ran ahead of the now bleary-eyed teens.

"Get in," Stacy said as soon as Vera was near. Vera complied. As soon as the teens wobbled up, Stacy took the boyfriend from them and pushed him into the cab; Vera helped maneuver the body from the inside. Then, while the four panting teens stood bent over, with their hands on their knees and sweat streaming down their faces, Stacy got into the cab, slammed the door shut and told the cabbie to drive. The teens did not even know what had happened until she was halfway down the block. Even then, they were too tired to do anything but watch the cab drive away. Stacy giggled to herself; on some level, Vera could not help admiring her.

The boyfriend was sandwiched between Vera and Stacy. His mouth was hanging open and his head was resting on Vera's shoulder. His skin was still warm, but the reality that he was dead made Vera quiver inside. He was still wearing Vera's movie starlet sunglasses, but Vera's mind conjured the image of his eyes rolled back in their sockets: two eerie white orbs.

Stacy gave the driver instructions and told him there would be a "fat tip" if he made the trip in forty minutes. She was still in high spirits, whereas Vera retreated into herself. Now that she had time to sit and think, the most horrible thoughts passed through her mind. She shook her head, inadvertently bumping her head into the boyfriend's. Stacy laughed again, and pushed the boyfriend's head back, so that it rested on the back of the seat. She stared at Vera for a while, and then she frowned.

"What's wrong?"

Vera looked up at her absentmindedly—as if lost: as if her mind had been a million miles away. She tried to smile, as to reassure Stacy, but her lips refused to comply.

"What's wrong?" Stacy asked her again.

"I was just thinking," she said obliquely.

"Thinking what?"

"About everything—what just happened...what I just *did*."

"What is there to think about?" Stacy said in a bored voice.

Vera sensed Stacy's disapproval; on some level, she feared that disapproval—was desperate to be on good terms with Stacy. Nevertheless, she pressed on. She looked at Stacy gravely. "...The other times you've killed him," she whispered, leaning over to Stacy by way of the boyfriend's body, "...did you ever find yourself thinking that maybe this time he won't come back to life? Did you ever find yourself thinking that maybe you've really killed him this time?"

Stacy stared at her for a few seconds. "No."

"It's *never* crossed your mind? You never think that maybe the magic, or whatever it is, will run out and he'll end up as a regular corpse?"

"No."

Vera seemed distraught.

Stacy shook her head, disappointed. She looked out of the window for a few moments, at the passing traffic. And then, speaking while staring out at the street, "Like I said to you before, Vera, you have no faith."

"It's not faith that brings him back to life." And then, looking at Stacy closely: "You still don't care how and why all this happens?"

"No."

When Vera seemed on the verge of losing her mind, Stacy smiled and made eye contact with her again: "Look, Vera, as I told you, all we can do at this point is acknowledge the basic facts. Fact number one is that when you kill him, he comes back to life."

Vera shook her head: "But what if fact number two is that you can only kill him six times?"

"Then we'll learn a new fact in forty-nine minutes," Stacy said with a wry smile.

Vera still looked distraught.

"Relax, Vera," Stacy implored her. "You did something great—don't spoil it all with your petty doubts."

"But I *killed* a man!" she said too loudly. She remembered the cabbie and lowered her voice: "I stabbed him, then I suffocated him. I held the bag down with,"—she held her trembling hands before her, staring at them, as if checking to see if they held some telltale sign of murder— "...with these hands."

Stacy reached over the boyfriend and grabbed Vera's right hand. "Don't torture yourself with such thoughts. This will all be over in forty-eight minutes, and then you'll see for yourself."

Vera shook her head. "...Can you *not* do a countdown, please? It'll drive me crazy."

"If you wish."

They drove along in silence for a while. They were now on the ramp to the 59th Street Bridge, headed to Queens. Vera found her mind drifting to more horrible things. She shuddered. "...Talk to me, Stacy," she pleaded. "Tell me something, please—*anything*."

"What do you want to talk about?"

"Anything. I just don't want to think anymore…at least until he comes back and I know that I haven't really…" She did not finish the sentence.

Stacy nodded her head. "You want to hear another story?"

"Yes—anything. Tell me a crazy one: the craziest one you have."

Stacy smiled. "Okay, then sit back and let me tell me a story, my friend."

Vera nodded and literally sat back in the seat this time, closing her eyes.

"It's about a Navy sailor driven over the edge by his horniness."

"Sounds like a good one," Vera mumbled sleepily.

Stacy smiled. "Anyway, in order to protect the innocent, let's give him a name—say, Nane Quartay. So, Quartay and his ship have been out to sea for six months, and he and the other five hundred eighteen- to twenty-five-year-old sailors are all horny as hell. After all that time at sea, they have finally docked at a port. All they can think about is getting ashore, so they pump their cocks into the first woman they see. A kind of madness infects the ship. Sailors are practically ready to riot to be let out; some of them have drool dripping from their mouths!

"Unfortunately, when they get ashore in this Eastern European country, it's full of old, gypsy-looking women with missing teeth and scarves on their heads. Sailors are pissed as hell, but there are bars there, and the average man is content to substitute getting drunk with getting pussy—especially when he can't have them both. So all these sailors flood into the bars in this town. Quartay drinks a few, but he's thinking, 'Damn, man, there has to be some pussy out there somewhere!' So he leaves the others and starts walking the streets, hunting for pussy. Some old, toothless women give him the eye, but he's like, '*Hell* nah, I'd need to drink a few kegs before I'd be willing to go that route!' So, he walks for miles, until he leaves the city behind and comes upon farmland. Even then, all he sees are old women and some old geezers playing dominoes. Now that he's out in the country, there's nobody around at all. It's all farmland and woods. Just when he's ready to turn back, he sees this girl sitting under a tree. He can't believe his eyes: she's *gorgeous*! She has the entire package: luscious breasts, blond, flowing hair, a shapely figure, a cute face… She stares at him invitingly and he practically runs up to her. 'I'm Quartay,' he says. He begins babbling on, trying to loosen her up, but she only stares at him. Of course, she does not speak any English. He is about to scream in frustration when she says, 'I want your cock!' He can hardly believe his ears; and of course, her accent is so heavy that it sounds like, 'Yie vant yar gok!' Quartay is practically trembling with excitement now. He is ready to fling himself at her, but the girl looks so sweet and innocent sitting there that he begins to wonder if he has misheard her. He is just about to ask her to repeat herself when, 'Yie vant yar gok!' she screams louder. A huge, insane grin spreads over Quartay's face now. 'You want cock?' he asks rhetorically, '—then you gonna get it then!' he says, beginning to undress. He is going to pull that crazy gypsy bitch behind a bush and do her right then. She seems fine with it as she begins unbuttoning his clothes. He is like, '*Hell* yes!' He is definitely going to have a story to tell the others when he gets back. Of course, none of them will believe him, but to hell with them. 'Yie vant yar gok!' the Gypsy is saying again. In fact, she keeps saying it over and over again, so that he is like, 'Damn, just take it already!' She pulls him behind the bush, and the next thing he knows, the Gypsy has her dress over her head and he is screwing the hell out of her from the back. She starts screaming out this gibberish—or at least it seems like gibberish to him, since he cannot understand her language. By now, she is yelling out so loudly that he is afraid an old farmer will come by and find him screwing his daughter. It would be like an old Frankenstein movie, with angry villagers chasing him down with torches and hoes and whatever other farming tools they had handy. Of course, you can't really have a good screwing session with such thoughts in your head; and by now, Quartay is like, 'I'd better finish this quick and get the hell out of here!' At that moment, the Gypsy woman screams, 'Yess, yess, yie vant yar gok!' and he thinks, '*Hell* yes! This crazy bitch is into this shit!' He still has a huge grin on his face, so he doesn't care if she screams or not. In fact, if villagers chased him down and this made the international news, at least everyone on his ship would know he was the pussy-getting master. That should be a title, he thinks, like Captain and Chief. Pussy-Getting Master: he likes the sound of that! He wishes some of those bastards from his ship could see him now, and hear the crazy Gypsy yelling out. ...Soon, however, he feels himself on the verge of his pleasure. He feels his muscles tightening, and has to lean against the Gypsy's behind to keep his balance. Everything is getting blurry; to his amazement, he feels giddy and high—as if he has just smoked a good sack of weed. He is like, 'Shit, this Gypsy pussy ain't half-bad!' And then, the pleasure seizes him, and he convulses. He tries to remain standing, but his knees buckle and he finds himself sinking to the ground. 'Goddamn!' he whispers. It is as if someone has knocked him on the head, because the next thing he knows, everything goes black. He has a strange dream, where the Gypsy woman is laughing triumphantly, saying, 'Yie *got* yar gok!' He is still like, 'Damn right, you got it!' However, there is something about her laugh that makes him feel uneasy. It is the kind of laugh a used car salesman has after you have just signed the contract for a piece of shit car.

"Quartay wakes up about two hours later, with a serious headache—as if he has a hangover, or as if someone really had knocked him on the head. The Gypsy is gone. He feels his skull, but there are no telltale lumps. It occurrs to him that maybe it is some kind of Gypsy scheme: the girl gets men to come in the bushes, and her partner clubs them on the head, taking their money. He goes to check his pants pockets, but he realizes his pants are still around his ankles. When he looks down, some evil-looking insects are feasting on the dried semen on his penis. He screams out and brushes them off! He is on his feet now, panting and suddenly alert. Remembering the gypsy scheme, he pulls up his pants and checks the pockets. His wallet and money are still there, but he cannot help feeling that something is very wrong. He looks around the landscape now, searching for any sign of the Gypsy, but there is nobody there. He feels lonely, and decides to head back to the ship.

"On the walk back, Quartay feels strange—as if something has changed within him. Guiltily, he remembers that he did not use a condom. What if he had picked up some crazy disease? ...But he does not want to think about that now. He feels melancholy for some reason. It occurrs to him that he does not feel like bragging to the others anymore. All he wants to do now is get back on the ship and go to sleep. That is what he does.

"In the morning, he still feels a little off. It is when he goes to the bathroom urinal to relieve himself that he notices two bumps on the head of his penis. They are huge, and red! He screams! When some of the other sailors look up to see what the problem is, he runs into a stall and locks it behind him, so he can check himself out. The bumps are *huge*. He squeezes one, to see if pus will come out, but the pain is so excruciating that he almost passes out. It is as if someone is clawing his guts out. He feels the pain in his *teeth*! He sits back on the commode, panting, wondering what new disease he has contracted. He tries to remember back to the film the Navy had shown them on sexually transmitted diseases: a montage of dripping, oozing and infected genitalia. He feels sick. ...But then he remembers the evil-looking insects that had been feasting at his penis. Maybe they had bitten him. That makes him feel marginally better: an insect bite is better than the prospect of his penis rotting off...unless the insect bite has the side effect of making his cock rot.

"He is just leaning over to take another look at the bumps on his penis when something very bizarre happens: the bumps open, and Quartay finds himself staring at a pair of blue eyes! '*Shit!*' he screams at the top of his voice, so that the words echo in the bathroom for seconds afterwards. All he can do is stare! '—You okay in there, man?' some of the other sailors call, but Quartay can't hear...can't *think*! 'What the hell...!' he whispers. He is trembling all over now. Someone knocks on the door of his stall. '—You okay, sailor?' From the man's tone, Quartay can tell that he is a superior officer. Quartay knows that he isn't okay, but what the hell is someone supposed to do about a pair of eyes growing on his cock overnight? He is pretty damn sure that penicillin doesn't cure that! '—Sailor?' the officer calls again, after the silence. Quartay speaks up quickly: 'I'm okay, sir...too much to drink last night, that's all.' Yet, when he looks back down at his penis, he realizes that the eyes are following him—*observing* him. "Shit!" he whispers. The other sailors go about their business, and Quartay sits in the stall, wondering what the hell he is going to do. At last, he pulls his pants up, relieved that he can cover his deformity. He has to get some fresh air and *think*... He wanders about the ship in a trance. Sailors say hello to him, but he only walks past them like a zombie.

He has to *think*, but nothing makes sense. After about an hour of wandering about, he returns to the stall and pulls down his pants again. By now, he has convinced himself that he has imagined the entire thing. Eyeballs don't grow on cocks—that is just the way things are. If he thought he had seen eyeballs on his cock, he had only imagined things. When he bends forward to stare at his penis again, he sees that there are now *three* huge, red bumps! And then, as he sits bent over, staring at them, all three bumps open at once: the blue eyes look back at him, and the third bump, which is beneath the other two, smiles at him, and says, in the calmest, most self-content way, 'Yie got yar gok!'"

When the story was finished, Stacy was leaning over the boyfriend, staring at Vera. Vera was still sitting back with her eyes closed. She opened her eyes and looked across at Stacy, and then at the boyfriend. In truth, her mind had not really been on Stacy's story.

"What do you think about the story?" Stacy said, staring at Vera intently. "You think it'll be a bestseller?"

"That's how the story ends?" Vera asked, frowning. "His possessed penis talks to him?"

"Ah," Stacy said with a chuckle, "you're missing the deeper literary significance of the story."

"You mean that the penis is a metaphor for something?"

"Penises are always good metaphors—that's why they're so useful."

"I see," Vera said, when she could think of nothing else to say. She looked at the boyfriend uneasily again; seeing him left her with another flashback of how she had killed him. Despite what she had said earlier about not wanting a countdown, she looked at Stacy anxiously: "How much time?" After she said it, she looked out of the window, to see if they were close to Stacy's apartment, but the streets outside the cab were not familiar.

"Relax," Stacy said, "we're right on time. We'll be home in ten minutes, and he'll be back in about fifteen."

"We're really that close?" All of Vera's anxieties began to come back. She almost asked Stacy to tell her another story, so that she could distract herself for a few more minutes. She could not stand any silence between now and whenever the boyfriend came back. She turned to Stacy again: "Tell me something about yourself."

"Like what?"

"Tell me about your parents."

"What do you want to know?"

"Anything—who they were, what they did for a living, if you loved them… *anything.*"

Stacy shook her head: "I didn't really know them."

"Why not?"

"They're dead."

Vera looked at her uneasily. Stacy smiled:

"No, I didn't kill them."

"I wasn't thinking that!" she said with a laugh.

Stacy looked at her with a sarcastic smile: "Sure you weren't."

"You were an orphan?" Vera pressed her.

Stacy chuckled. "Nothing that dramatic. I was raised by a great aunt. She raised me since I was a year old."

"How'd your parents die?"

"My mother killed my father—that's what my aunt said, anyway."

"Are you serious?" Vera whispered.

"Yeah."

Vera joked: "Killing the man in your life seems to run in your family." However, it was a bad joke and neither of them laughed. Stacy was staring ahead thoughtfully; Vera was about to apologize when Stacy continued.

"My father raped my mother. He was some kind of drifter who wandered into their town. She killed him afterwards."

Vera gasped, speechless.

Stacy went on: "I was supposedly born from that—from that act. That's the story anyway."

Vera detected something in Stacy's voice and mien. "You don't believe the 'story'?"

She shrugged. "Who knows? My aunt told me this on her deathbed.

She died of cancer about two years ago. She was half out of her mind by then—pain killers and all that. I know she was keeping something from me all my life. She used to tell me that I was adopted; whenever I asked her about my parents, she would say she had no idea who they were—that my parents had died in a car accident or something, and that I had been put up for adoption when I was a baby. I knew she was lying because she couldn't keep her story right: one day it would be a car accident, and the other it would be a fire...I just don't know what to think."

"I'm sure there are police records that you can check, or adoption records."

"No, that's the thing: my aunt never legally adopted me. I was sent to her after what happened with my parents. I only found out on her death-bed that she was my actual aunt. Before that, I thought she was my adopted mother. I found out that I didn't even have a birth certificate: my aunt had paid someone to create fake records for me—someone she knew in the Department of Records. As far as I know, there are no records of me being born anywhere. It's as if all my life, they were trying to keep me hidden. I guess with the murder and rape (if that's all true) they felt ashamed. ...As for my parents, if my mother really did kill my father, no body was ever found; as he was a drifter, nobody would have been look-ing for him. My mother was never charged with anything."

"Then how do you know your mother killed your father?"

"Exactly. I only have my aunt's word to go on. ...All I have is a story about a rape and a murder."

"So, you're saying your mother got rid of his body after she killed him?"

"Yes, that's what my aunt said. Anyway, she got pregnant with me after all that, and I guess it drove her over the edge. My aunt said my mother wasn't right for a while—in the head, I mean. She told me about these times when they found her out naked in the middle of nowhere—wandering around dazed, talking to herself....After I was born, my family shipped me away, figuring it would help her."

"How'd she die?"

"She killed herself."

"My God!" Vera whispered.

"Anyway," Stacy said with a sigh, "what's done is done." And then, changing the subject abruptly, she went on: "What about your parents? Are they alive?"

"Sure—they live in Florida."

"Retired, I guess?"

"Yeah."

Stacy smiled. "You're so 'white bread,' Vera—so clichély American. You probably had the typical upper-middle-class upbringing in the suburbs."

Vera seemed stung: "…We can't help where we grew up…who our parents were."

"Are you close to your parents?"

"Sure. Why?"

"People who grow up in cozy environments usually resent their parents."

"Where'd you hear that?"

"It's human nature, Vera. When parents provide their kids with everything, the kids always resent them deep down. No matter how much the kids manage to achieve in their own lives, they know that it wasn't their doing: it was their parents, and their cozy, sheltered, upbringing. Intimacy and struggle go hand-in-hand. Where there's no struggle, the affection is weak—transitory."

"That's another of your famous theories, I guess?" Vera said testily.

Stacy smiled. "You can consider its merits later, at your leisure. We're here."

Just then, the cab pulled over to the front of the club/apartment building. Seeing where they were, and knowing what was supposed to happen in the next few minutes, Vera felt numb and excited at the same time.

"Pay the cab," Stacy said, opening the door.

Vera reached into her purse and paid the cabbie. She gave him a hundred dollar bill, but was too dazed to realize it. Soon, she and Stacy were carrying the boyfriend up the stairs. Stacy held him under the arms, and Vera held his legs. She felt disembodied; her mind was so preoccupied that the boyfriend felt like a feather in her arms. Once again, Vera heard the strange screaming voice in her head, drowning out everything. In the apartment, they plopped the boyfriend on the sofa. Stacy took off the boyfriend's shirt, and the impromptu bandage underneath. When that was

complete, and he was sitting there bare-chested, she looked at her watch:
"Two minutes to spare."

Vera's mouth was dry. Her legs were trembling. She barely managed to make it to the loveseat before they gave out. She felt sick; Stacy looked at her and smiled, still seeming unfazed.

Please God! Vera found herself thinking. *Please let him come back to life*! Please let this all be forgotten, like some kind of waking dream, so that she could go back to being Dr. Vera.

One minute.

Stacy went to the open window and stood by it for a moment, as if admiring the view. Vera wanted to scream at her—somehow her calmness was unnerving. By now, Vera was rocking herself, like a scared child. She was soaked with nervous sweat. She told herself that after the boyfriend came back life, she would take a long, hot shower. She would lie back in the tub and allow her mind to drift off, and all this would be forgotten. *...Please God...!*

Stacy walked back over to the boyfriend's corpse. She stood above him; Vera frowned at the strange smile on Stacy's face. And then, about two seconds later, the boyfriend's body convulsed, and he took a long rasping breath. Vera did the same—she had not realized it, but she had been holding her breath. The boyfriend opened his eyes. Stacy was the first thing he saw. She bent down and kissed him on the forehead. And then she straddled him and caressed his face. Before he could open his mouth to ask her what had happened, she began to tell him about the last few days. It was a story devoid of death and trauma. It was a story in which he was loved and in which he gave love. It was a story of a full, content life. It took about ten minutes. Vera was amazed by the thoroughness of Stacy's instructions: what he was to remember and what he was to forget. The boyfriend stared up at Stacy, rapt. He had not even looked over at Vera once—as if Stacy were the center of the universe. Vera stared at Stacy the same way.

When the reality-shaping story was complete, Stacy told the boyfriend to go and sleep for a few hours; and that afterwards, they would go and visit his mother. He shuffled off, his face blank. Vera was still sitting on the loveseat. Stacy looked over at her and smiled. "See," she started, "I told you everything would work out."

Vera took a deep breath, then smiled with relief and gratitude. "Yeah, you did."

"Killing is a horrible act," Stacy philosophized, "but the new life that comes afterwards is always greater than the death that came before. A lion kills and eats an antelope in order to stay alive. That's the way of nature; and when you see life and death that way, you see that death *is* life. In our case, death is even more wondrous, because when we kill, we give *them* new life. That's a revolution in the nature of life and death, Vera."

Vera nodded enthusiastically.

"So," Stacy joked, "do you have faith now?"

Vera smiled. "I don't need faith—I have seen with my own eyes."

"But people have a habit of forgetting what they see—that's why they need faith."

Vera thought about it for a while, before shrugging her shoulders. She laughed for no reason in particular, feeling good about things. She took another deep breath. Stacy was looking at her closely:

"You look like you can use some sleep, too."

"Maybe later," Vera replied. "I don't think I've been this hungry in my entire life."

"You want to go out to get something to eat?"

"Aren't you worried about your boyfriend? What if he sneaks off again?"

"Nah, he'll be fine."

"Still, let's stay here. Let's order in or something. We've been running about like maniacs since last night. Let's take a breather."

"Okay, what do you want? Pizza? Chinese?"

"Anything, as long as it's in vast quantities."

They both laughed.

They decided to order Chinese food. Stacy called a local restaurant while Vera named several dishes she wished to devour. Just the act of ordering made her hungry. Stacy jokingly told the person on the phone to hurry up

D.V. BERNARD

when she was finished ordering, as if she feared that Vera might turn on her for nourishment.

Vera looked over at her playfully: "Do you think you could ever be a cannibal? If it came down to that, would you be able to eat another human being?"

"Sure."

Vera laughed. "It's that simple to you? You don't have to think about it first?"

"What is there to think about? We're predators—lions. We eat to survive."

"Yeah, but lions don't eat other lions. Nature has that moral clause built into most animals."

"Nature does not have morality, Vera. Morality is a fantasy created by human beings."

Vera laughed. Stacy went on:

"Morality is *un*natural. It's fake and arbitrary. ...In nature, everything is based on necessity. Lions don't eat other lions because it's unnecessary. Creatures want to preserve their own kind—their own genes—that's why they avoid killing their own kind for food."

"Yeah, but lions kill lions," Vera pointed out. "Human beings kill other human beings."

"When a lion kills another lion, it's not for food. Murderers tend not to eat their victims. When animals kill their own kind, they kill out of rage or jealousy, or some other dark emotion. They are provoked into killing their own. Some impulse takes over them, and they do something that they probably would not have done otherwise. On the other hand, killing for food is like breathing: it requires no rage or outside impulse. It comes naturally: you do it because if you don't, you'll die. The farmer does not hate his cattle; the lion does not hate the antelope. ...But here's the difference with cannibalism: When killing your own for food is 'natural'— is necessary for life—you're seeing a place where nature is broken. Cannibalism is reserved for the end of the world—for the time when all other creatures are dead, and the only way to survive is to kill and eat your own kind."

126

"The end of the world," Vera said uneasily, staring down at the ground. The clarity of Stacy's statement disturbed her, so that an uneasy spasm passed through her body. It was as if Stacy had been sitting around for years, thinking about the implications of cannibalism. Vera shuddered again; and then, changing the subject, she blurted out: "—I need a shower. You have any other clothes I can wear?"

"Sure—let's see what there is in my closet." They started down the hall, to Stacy's bedroom. When Vera recalled that the boyfriend was sleeping in there, she felt wary.

"Let's not disturb your boyfriend," she said.

"We won't disturb him," Stacy said simply. "A hurricane could come and he'd sleep through it."

They walked on in silence. At last, when they were in the doorway of the bedroom, about to step in, Vera began:

"Stacy, before your boyfriend, did you ever hurt anyone?"

Stacy stopped and looked back at her. "What's that supposed to mean?"

Vera told herself not to back down. "It's a simple question."

"You're back to thinking I'm a homicidal maniac, is that it?"

"I'm just asking," she said weakly.

Stacy stared at her, but said nothing. Eventually, she turned back into the room and continued on to the closet. "Let's find you something to wear," she said without turning around.

The boyfriend was sprawled face down on the bed. Vera glanced at him uneasily, then she walked up to Stacy's side as the woman searched her cluttered closet.

"I'm sorry, Stacy," Vera said, resting her hand on Stacy's arm. Stacy stopped her search and looked over at her.

"Why would you ask me something like that?" she said, seeming hurt.

"I'm sorry," Vera said again. "It's just that…well, the things you say, Stacy. The things you say…" But she did not finish the statement.

Stacy was still staring at her. "…All the things I've said," she began, "were they honest? Deep down, was there truth there, regardless of how disturbing you found those truths?"

"Yeah, sure—"

"Then what's the problem?"

Vera felt cornered. She knew that she did not have a definite grievance against Stacy, but she knew, also, that in general there was something about Stacy that was not right. It was something that always seemed on the verge of coming to the surface—something that could either come within the next few seconds, years or decades, but which was destined to come, and which was destined to bring unspeakable calamities when it did.

"Let's be honest with one another, Vera," Stacy began now. "We need one another, but we'll only be useful to one another if we can accept things as they are—if we can see truths for what they are, and aren't afraid of them. Don't be afraid of the truth, Vera."

Vera thought about it for a few seconds; she nodded her head.

"Good," Stacy said, returning to the closet, as if everything had been decided. Vera looked at her as she fingered her clothes; several times, Stacy pulled out a dress or blouse to see its proportions. Of course, all Stacy's clothes were at least five sizes too small for Vera. Vera was just about to point that out when the doorbell rang.

"That must be the food," Stacy said without thought. "Why don't you get the door?"

Vera grunted with mock thoughtfulness. "I notice that I always have to get it when it's time to pay the bill."

Stacy smiled and continued looking through her closet.

Vera left the bedroom and walked quickly down the hallway, to the door. She opened the door, about to tell the deliveryman to hold on, so she could get her bag, when she saw who it was—

"Oh my God!" she exclaimed, holding her hands to her head. "I totally forgot!"

The police detective was waiting there with a smile on his face and some wrapped carnations in hand. He explained: "The people in the club downstairs let me in."

"How'd you know I was here?" she said after the shock had passed.

"I'm a detective, remember?" he said, smiling. He explained: "I went to your place, and your concierge said she hadn't seen you."

"What concierge?"

"The old lady in the lobby."

Vera laughed out. "She's not the concierge. She's just an old busybody. By tomorrow everyone in the building will believe you came to arrest me. Did you show her your badge?"

"Yeah."

Vera nodded uneasily, knowing that no good was going to come of that.

"Anyway," the detective went on, "I figured that if you weren't there, you were probably still here, doing whatever you're doing here."

She smiled. "Brilliant deduction, Holmes, but what do you mean by 'Whatever you're doing here'? You still think a crime is afoot?" she said, mockingly.

He chortled, shaking his head. "To begin with, get your Sherlock Holmes clichés straight. That should be, 'The game's afoot.'"

"Yeah, whatever." After they both laughed, she looked at him askance. "I'm impressed that you'd bother to come all the way here to find me. Most men would have said to hell with it if they showed up for a date and nobody was there."

"I'm not 'most men'—and you're the famous Dr. Vera."

"Ah, I see how it is now," she said playfully. "You want a romp with a noted sex therapist."

"I figured I could get some free advice."

"You mean, give you some pointers to pick up chicks?"

"Exactly."

"Well, sorry to burst your bubble, but nothing's free, Holmes."

"That's right—I forgot that with you everything costs an arm and a leg."

She giggled, remembering their last conversation. "...Are those flowers for me?"

"Nah," he said sarcastically, "I thought maybe you could help me pick up a cheap date along the way."

She snatched the flowers and smelled them.

"Fresh from my garden," he announced.

"Really?" she said, impressed.

He laughed. "If by 'garden' you mean the corner grocer, then yeah."

She smiled. She remembered the shower she was to take, and the fact that Stacy was futilely looking for some clothes for her. The detective was in a fancy suit—she doubted that anything in Stacy's closet would be dressy enough for a formal dinner. "My dress clothes are at home," she said, worried.

"I can drive you back over there if you wish."

She laughed at him. "Damn, Holmes, you go all out to get some free advice!" But then, after a final chuckle, "Just let me tell Stacy I'm leaving. I'll meet you downstairs in a minute."

Incredibly, when Vera reentered the bedroom, Stacy was still looking through the closet. A pair of gnarled sweatpants had been laid out on the bed for Vera, but Stacy was seeing what else was there. Vera could not help laughing. At the sound, Stacy looked back at her.

"Is the food okay?"

"That wasn't the deliveryman. My date's here."

"Your date? What date?"

"The police detective. Remember from last night at the hospital?"

"Oh, yeah. You're really going out with that guy?"

"He's nice."

"But he doesn't believe."

"What?" Vera said, lost.

"He doesn't believe," Stacy said again.

"Believe in what?"

"The things we've seen. He obviously suspects us of something—that's his only interest in you."

"Is it so hard to believe that a man might be interested in me?"

"Don't start that ego nonsense, Vera. If you can't see that he's using you, then okay." She turned back to the closet and resumed her search through it, even though there was of course no reason to do so.

Vera stared at her. "...Well, he's waiting downstairs for me."—Stacy did not turn around—"I'll talk to you later, Stacy," Vera said, retreating from the room.

"Vera," Stacy called to her. Vera turned around. Stacy was staring at her helplessly. "Will you come back over tonight?"

"I don't know, Stacy. I don't know what will happen."

Stacy nodded. "I left the apartment keys for you. I left them on the kitchen table. You can come anytime you want." The same helpless expression was on her face. Vera found it unnerving—like the expressions of those kids in those Christian aide commercials, where you could send an African child to school and change her life for the price of a cup of coffee.

"Okay," Vera said at last. She left the room with an uneasy feeling in her gut. She walked to the kitchen in a daze. The keys were lying on the table, just as Stacy had said. Vera picked up the keys and stared at them momentarily. Next, she went to the living room and got her bag. She dropped the keys in the side pocket, but felt wary about leaving the apartment. She decided that she would leave her number with Stacy. She got out a business card and wrote her cell phone number on the back. When she was finished, she walked back down the hallway, to the bedroom. Stacy was sitting on the bed, her face drawn, her body seeming depleted of energy. Her face brightened when she saw Vera again.

"I wanted to leave my cell phone number with you," Vera said, "…in case anything happens." She stepped into the room and handed the card to Stacy. She took it and held it in both hands, looking at it as if grateful. Vera continued, "Are you okay, Stacy?"

"Yeah, I guess."

"Maybe you should get some rest."

Stacy was staring up at her: "Will you come back tonight—even if it's late?"

Vera sighed. "I'll try."

Stacy smiled—a strange, sweet smile.

"I'll talk to you later," Vera said, leaving the room. "Call me if you need anything."

"Thanks," Stacy said, still smiling.

Vera walked back down the hallway and out of the apartment, feeling suddenly anxious. What the hell was going on with Stacy? What was that all about? …She shook her head. She did not want to think about that now. It was Saturday night and she wanted to have a good time. She wanted to laugh at silly jokes and forget the last two days. She had a flashback of all the things that had happened: all the death and desperation she had seen and experienced. Of course, there had been good times with Stacy; they had had their laughs, but Vera had used more energy in the last two days than she would have typically used in a week. Maybe that was good; maybe that was bad. Stacy had showed her things—*wondrous things*—and she was grateful for that. Still, she needed some time away, in order to think and digest everything that had happened. Maybe all she needed was to forget for a little while—to go back to the old ways, and give her mind a break from all the impossible things Stacy had shown her. Tomorrow, she would again ponder those impossibilities; but for now, she wanted to be carefree and silly. She *needed* it, in fact.

The police detective was double-parked on the street. He got out of the car as she exited the building. He walked around to the passenger side door, to open it for her. She smiled, saying:

"First you bring flowers, and now you're opening doors? I didn't take you for an old gentleman."

"Watch that 'old' stuff!" he said as he guided her into the car.

She was smiling as she sat down in the car. However, looking through the windshield, she saw Rique Johnson—AKA Oldschool—coming down the block, still in his linen suit. "Oh shit!" she said, ducking down in the seat and holding her huge handbag over her face.

When the police detective entered the car, he frowned at her. "What's wrong?"

"I'm hiding from someone."

He looked out of the windscreen, at Oldschool. "Who's that—an old boyfriend?"

"Hardly!" she said with a laugh.

He chuckled and started up the car. "I assume there's an interesting story behind that."

"You can put money on it, Holmes, but you'll never hear it from me."

He put the car in gear and started down the block. He looked over at her suspiciously: "What's this 'Holmes' business? You don't know what my name is, do you?"

She laughed uneasily. "Don't be angry—I think I was in shock when you told me the first time."

He laughed at her. "That's going to cost you, Vera."

"So, now you're going to charge an arm and a leg, too?"

"Damn straight! All's fair in love and war."

"Which one is this: love or war?"

He laughed loudly; and then, with a smile on his face: "The night will tell."

They drove along in silence for a few seconds.

She looked over at him with mock exasperation: "Well, are you going to tell me or not?"

"Huh?"

"Are you going to tell me what your name is—or should I keep calling you Holmes?"

"Oh," he said, before laughing at himself. "Jonathan Luckett—Jon to my friends."

She groaned. "I think I prefer Holmes."

They both laughed.

"By the way," the detective began, "Eleanor's funeral is on Wednesday."

"Who?"

"Eleanor—the huge woman who tumbled down the stairs and broke her neck last night."

"Oh."

"You didn't know what her name was either?"

"Of course not—the first time I met her was when she tried to kill me. Besides, she didn't strike me as an Eleanor."

"What did she strike you as?" he said with a smile.

"I don't know—a Bertha maybe."

"I think that was one of her porn names," he said, chuckling again: "*Big Bertha*."

"Were you one of her fans?"

He laughed out. "Nah—I looked it up on the Internet. She had several aliases. Supposedly she was very skilled."

"Skilled with what? An axe?" After their laughter died down, she looked at the detective suspiciously: "So, is viewing porn an official police duty now?"

"Sometimes I have to go above and beyond to satisfy my duties," he said, chuckling.

"I can imagine—especially when you come across three hundred pound dead porn queens." While they were laughing, Vera remembered the woman was dead. The entire conversation suddenly seemed sacrilegious—or at least in bad taste.

They drove along in silence for a few seconds, but it was comfortable silence. "...So," she began again, "tell me about yourself, Holmes."

"You forgot my name already?"

"No, like I told you, Holmes suits you better."

He laughed again, then shook his head. "Okay, what do you want to know?"

"We can start with the polite stuff first: where you were born, how long you've been a police officer, if you were married...?"

"Oh, I see how it is now," he said with a smile. "This is your chance to interrogate me."

"It is indeed. Why should you have all the fun?"

"Okay. ...Let me see: I'm a lifelong New Yorker; I've been a cop for twelve years. I used to be married."

"*Used* to be?"

"My wife died in a car accident."—Vera looked up at him sharply; he continued to stare ahead blankly, as if seeing the scene unfolding before his eyes—"...A drunk driver drove across the highway median and crashed into her car. My daughter was in the back seat. They were killed instantly—or at least, that's what the coroner said."

"Oh my God, I didn't mean to bring up bad memories."

"No problem."

"How long ago did all this happen, if you don't mind me asking?"

"Five years."

"How old was your daughter?"

"She was two."

"God! ...How'd you get through it all?"

"I'm not saying I didn't go mad for a while. I had my moments when I wanted to take my gun and go down to where they were holding the drunk driver, and put two bullets in his head. ...When things like that happen, you want to believe in evil and evil people."

"Why do you say that?"

"When someone takes everything from you like that, you want to think that they are evil, and that they *deserve* your revenge. Evil makes revenge easy; when you allow yourself to believe that others are evil, the evil behind your own actions begins to look like righteousness. Evil people see evil people everywhere. It's crooks that spend the most time worrying about crime. That's the nature of the world. ...The fact of the matter is that my wife was only on that highway because we had gotten into an argument earlier. She said I was working too much—that being a cop was all that mattered to me, and that I was neglecting her and my daughter. It was all true, but I yelled at her—called her a bitch and other things. She was driving to her mother's house to cool out. ...So, you see, I wanted to believe the drunk driver was evil, so I could overlook my own part in it. In my mind, I saw him as a monster—as subhuman. ...When I finally got a look at the guy, it was a scared kid: a trembling nineteen-year-old. That's when I knew that I had to give it all up."

"You forgave him?"

"It wasn't a matter of forgiveness—just of acceptance: acknowledging things as they were, instead of creating a fantasy in my mind. People create fantasies for themselves all the time, so they can feel good about themselves. No matter what, my wife was not going to come back. My daughter wasn't coming back. I couldn't take away the hurtful things I had said to my wife; I couldn't pretend that I had been a loving father. I couldn't spend the rest of my life grieving for a fantasy. All I could do was acknowledge what I had done, and take that knowledge with me into the future. ...Live life with those lessons in mind, and try to be better."

Vera mused, "I guess that you've seen lots of bad things as a cop?"

"Yeah..."

"What's the worst thing you've ever seen?" As soon as she said it, she grimaced, and then smiled.

He raised an eyebrow at her reaction. "What's the matter?"

"I don't know where that question came from. ...It's the kind of question Stacy would ask."

"Do you usually go around with other people's questions in your head?"

"Stacy has a way of talking and asking questions," she said vaguely.

The detective laughed at the bewildered expression on her face. Then, remembering her question, "Do you really want to know the worst thing I've seen as a cop?"

"Yeah, I guess," she said, embarrassed.

"Okay. ...When I was on the force for about six months, my partner and I got a domestic violence call: a husband beating up on his wife. You see that practically every day when you're a cop: families falling apart. ...When we got there, the door was locked; there was no response, but my partner, who had been a cop for over ten years, had this look on his face. ...I don't know how to describe it. He was listening closely at the door; and then, as if hearing or sensing something, he reared back and broke down the door. ...There was blood everywhere...so much blood. The man's wife, his two little kids...all butchered. The neighbors had heard screaming for over an hour. The man had tied his family up, like cows for slaughter, and hacked..." The detective stopped himself and took a deep breath. "...Stuff like that stays with you. ...We found the man in the bathroom. He had chopped off his hand so that he could bleed to death. He had this smile on his face—this look of peace. All I wanted to do was bust up his face, so that that smile could be wiped from the world...from my memory. ...That's the worst thing I've seen," he said, looking over at her pointedly. "At least I didn't see my family dead. I wasn't at the scene: I only saw them later, in the sterility of the coroner's office. I didn't see all the blood..."

"That is a pretty bad memory," Vera admitted, feeling guilty about having brought up the topic.

The detective nodded, staring out of the windscreen. "It's been a while since I talked to anyone about my family."

She was looking at him closely now; despite what he had said about accepting the deaths of his loved ones, she could see the pain reflected in his eyes. There was an immense well of sadness there. She suddenly remembered the boyfriend: how Stacy had made him forget all the horrible things that had happened. Vera ventured, "If you could forget everything that had happened to your family, would you?"

"What do you mean?"

"If, somehow, you could wipe it all from your memory—get rid of all the pain—would you?"

He shook his head confusedly: "There's no way to forget."

"Never mind that. Just pretend for a moment that there was a way you could wipe it all away. Would you do it?"

He shook his head again. "If we could magically forget everything that was hurtful to us, then there'd be no incentive to try to be better human beings. A man who doesn't have regrets is a soul-less man: an *evil* man. If you have no regrets that's either because you're too stupid to know better or because you're so evil that you think everything you do is good."

Vera smiled. "Is that some kind of Buddhist, New Age sort of thing?" she teased him.

He smiled. "Nah, merely common sense."

"What's the difference?"

He sighed thoughtfully. "…I think most religions started out as common sense. Over time the common sense got bureaucratized and watered down, until, instead of following what our insides told us was right, we found ourselves following bureaucrats."

She smiled wider.

He looked over at her curiously: "What's that smile about?"

"Somehow, you reminded me of Stacy just then."

"Is that good?"

"I think so. I've had the strangest conversations since I met you two. …Strange, but good. …Stuff you'd probably never talk to another living person about."

"Do you realize that that's the second time you've brought up Stacy? If she were a man, I'd be jealous."

Vera laughed. "Stacy's an interesting person."

"Yeah, and mysterious."

"What do you mean?"

"Is Stacy her real name?"

Vera frowned. "...I guess. ...What are you saying?"

He sighed, trying to decide how he would explain it. "She has records like everyone else—school, driver's license...but they're all a little off."

"You mean fake?"

"Possibly...I don't know. They're not right. That's all I'm saying." He noticed the expression on her face. "—I'm sorry. I'm upsetting you."

"No, actually, she told me about that—you're not telling me anything new."

"What did she say?"

"Her family sent her to live with an aunt when she was a baby. Her father had been a drifter who raped her mother. Her mother killed him."

"Are you serious?"

"Yeah. Her mother killed him and buried the body, and then her mother committed suicide some time after Stacy was born."

"Goddamn."

"With all that, the family sent her to live with her aunt. Supposedly, her aunt had fake documents made."

"Oh, I see. That would explain it."

"You're not going to pursue this further, I hope?"

"What do you mean?"

"Sometimes the past should stay buried."

He glanced over at her, but did not say anything. There was an uncomfortable silence. It lasted about a minute.

"Holmes?" Vera said at last.

"Yeah," he said eagerly, glad that she was talking to him again.

"Tell me about the happiest moment in your life—your greatest accomplishment...anything."

He sniggered. "Is that another Stacy question?"

"No, it's a Vera question. Tell me something that'll convince me the world isn't insane."

He smiled widely. "Charmaine Parker."

Vera grimaced. "Please tell me you're not about to tell me how you lost your virginity to this woman."

He laughed. "Hardly—she was eighty years old."

"So what? I don't know what your tastes are," she teased him. "Anyway, go on with your story."

He nodded, gathering his thoughts. "Actually, this happened a few hours after the thing I just told you about—with the butchered family. My partner and I got off duty about eight p.m. My partner went to get drunk, but I wanted to be alone. That's what I told myself anyway. Charmaine Parker was an old lady in my neighborhood. My first apartment was only about a mile from where I grew up. I had known Mrs. Parker since I was a kid. She always seemed to have a fresh-baked cake or pie. She was always expecting guests, I suppose. People in the neighborhood always knew that that was somewhere to go to talk, I guess. The cake was only an excuse. You'd say you were going because you were hungry, but then you'd find yourself talking. I guess she was the neighborhood therapist," he said with a laugh. "Anyway, I was so restless after I got off duty that I walked about the neighborhood. After I passed her house the second time, she called me in. With that piece of pie in front of me I found myself spilling my guts about everything—telling her things I had not even acknowledged to myself. We talked for about two or three hours, but the strange thing is that we probably only spent about ten minutes talking about the butchered family. I came away from that conversation feeling older somehow—as if I had settled the direction of my life: who I was going to be, what I was going to do....For that one moment, everything seemed clearer. I left her house feeling optimistic about things. Talking to her saved me somehow. I can't explain it. Sometimes, I find myself thinking that if I hadn't talked to her that night, I'd be a totally different person."

"Is she still alive?"

"Nah, she died about a year later. Her funeral was standing room only."

"So, you haven't had a therapist in all these years?" she pointed out.

There was a smile on her face. He laughed when he saw what she was insinuating.

"No, I guess not," he said.

"Maybe this date is just an elaborate ruse to get free therapy from me."

He laughed harder. "Anything is possible."

"Then that will be one hundred fifty dollars," Vera announced. When he looked at her confusedly, she said, "My hourly fee as a therapist."

"For what?"

"Obviously talking to me has allowed you reach a state of self-awareness, so now you owe me."

"Damn, you really do charge an arm and a leg!"

"Sometimes two arms."

They both laughed.

"So, what's your story, Dr. Vera? How come you never hatched any eggs?"

She laughed at his phrasing. "First off, what did I just tell you about calling me Dr. Vera? And secondly, my ass is too tender to sit on a nest."

He laughed out loud again. "I don't know," he said, craning his neck playfully, as if he could see her behind, "your ass seems pretty durable to me."

"Were you peeking while I wasn't looking?"

"Oh, I didn't tell you? I'm an official New York City Ass Inspector."

"Ass Inspector?"

"Yeah, we have strict standards in this city. Substandard asses are a danger to public safety."

"Is that so?"

"Absolutely. The stability of society could be put in jeopardy if a few substandard asses were allowed to get out."

She shook her head in bemusement, but there was a smile on her lips. "What do you do with the substandard asses?" she baited him now. "You have a detention center for them?"

"Nah, we throw them in the East River."

"That sounds harsh."

"It has to be done. Anytime you find yourself thinking that you haven't seen a famous actress or singer in a while, that's our doing. As soon as they start sagging, we get rid of them."

Right then, while she was still giggling, she looked up and saw that they were in her neighborhood, driving down the block to her condominium. The time had flown. She giggled again, at nothing in particular: she just felt good. However, Vera had a sudden flashback of Stacy sitting on her bed, looking wretched and hopeless; she remembered the detective's questions about Stacy's background. All at once, Vera's anxieties about leaving Stacy alone came back. Something had not been right there. She knew it. At the same time, she was home now, on a date with a man whom she really liked. In fact, it startled her how much she liked him. She looked over at him, suddenly amazed by the realization. He looked at her when he stopped the car in front of her building, puzzled by the intensity of her gaze.

They walked up to the building leisurely. They were side by side; without thought or calculation, she looped her arm through his. He did not say anything, but only smiled again.

She began, "Do you mind if we don't go out?" They had reached the glass door. "Can we stay here and watch a movie...order something to eat, perhaps."

"I don't mind," he said.

"Did you make restaurant reservations or anything?"

"Sure, but they're easily broken—the manager owes me for life, since I figured out who burglarized his restaurant."

"So!" she said accusingly, "you were trying to use your connections to get a cheap date out of me?"

"Damn," he lamented, "I can't catch a break from you."

"I've gotta keep my eyes on you," she said as she fished her keys out of her bag and opened the door—

"There you are!" a shrill voice cried the moment they stepped through the door. They looked up to see an old lady—late-seventies, with heavily styled greenish-grayish hair, dismaying quantities of makeup and huge jewels of dubious worth. The old lady was sitting on a side bench, wearing an over-starched crinoline dress. She leapt up from the bench and flew at

Vera like some kind of demented vulture. Vera cringed. It was her so-called concierge: the building's official busybody. Now, the old lady was standing in front of them, bobbing up and down like an excited six-year-old.

"Hello, Mrs. Moore," Vera said in a deadpan voice; and then, gesturing to the detective: "I'm told you met my friend, Holmes—I mean, Jonathan Luckett." Vera and the detective laughed to themselves.

"Oh, posh!" Mrs. Moore said, slapping the detective's arm flirtatiously, "you can call me Gwyneth."

"Nice to meet you, Gwyneth Moore," the detective said, extending his hand. When she offered hers, he took it and pressed it to his lips. She demurred and did a girlish half-twirl in her ridiculous dress. Vera was standing to the side, with her hands on her hips, wondering how much more she could take.

"We don't get too many gentlemen in this building anymore," the old lady lamented now.

"I don't see why not," Luckett said, outraged, "—with a fine-looking woman like you on the premises!" Once again, the old lady did a half-twirl.

"Okay, okay," Vera said, losing patience. "We'll have to continue this another time, Mrs. Moore." As she said this last part, she looped her hand through Luckett's once more, and dragged him toward the elevators.

"That was mean," he teased her when they were out of earshot.

She laughed. "I have half a mind to leave you down here with her."

"Don't tell me you're jealous of a sweet, little old lady."

"Oh yeah?" she scoffed. "Just wait until she corners you the next time and tries to tell you the latest piece of gossip that she made up, about how so-and-so in apartment 6A is cheating with the husband of so-and-so in apartment 13C. She'll have all the details, too—what positions they used, how big the man's thing was…"

"Everyone needs a hobby," he said with a shrug and a chuckle. They glanced back just before the elevator opened. The old lady was still standing there, staring at them like some kind of heartbroken puppy. The detective was about to say something to her when Vera glared at him and pulled him into the elevator.

alf an hour later, Vera stepped out of the bedroom, newly dressed and refreshed. She had showered, and spent the obligatory fifteen minutes primping and getting dressed—even though they had decided to stay inside. She was in a flowing summer dress. She was not wearing underwear underneath. She had never really needed a bra. As she had come to think of it, she had been born with an A-cup. The only thing puberty had given her was bigger nipples. When her first boyfriend sucked them, they had swollen to the size of plums, momentarily giving her the hope that breasts would be in her future. Unfortunately, her nipples had returned to their previous size, and no matter how hard and long she had made her subsequent boyfriends suck on her nipples, the original miracle had never repeated itself. Now, as she walked out of the bedroom and into the living room, she found herself wondering if she was going to have sex with the detective. As always, the thought brought a feeling of panic. However, this time, she realized that that panic was not so much driven by fear, as the uncertainty that accompanied anticipation and readiness. She had not felt that way in a long time.

When she got to the living room, the television was playing lowly, and the detective was sitting on the couch, taking food out of a picnic basket and placing it on the coffee table.

"Where'd you get all that?" Vera said, amazed.

"I called in another favor," he said with a grin.

"You got all that in less than half an hour?" she said, noticing that the food was not in cheap disposable containers, but fine china.

He shushed her and gestured for her to sit down next to him. "Eat," he commanded, and she practically flung herself at the food. She grabbed some fried flounder and started wolfing it down. Luckett laughed at her and handed her a fork. She pushed it away, content. While she moved on to some pâté, Luckett poured her some wine. She grabbed it from him and gulped it down.

"Damn, girl! When did you eat last?" he asked.

"I'm starving!" And then, with a half-full mouth, "It's *good!*"

Luckett nodded his head approvingly. Then, he fetched something else from the picnic basket: a DVD.

Vera looked over at it, her eyes growing wide. "How did you know *To Kill a Mockingbird* was my favorite movie!"

Luckett smiled enigmatically: "It fits your psychological profile."

She licked her fingertips, to clean them of crumbs and grease, then she took the DVD case, staring at it with an amazed, childlike expression on her face. Her smile widened; and then, just as naturally, she leaned over and kissed him. She surprised him, leaning against him with her full weight, so that he almost lost his equilibrium. However, he soon regained his balance and pulled her to him.

Vera woke up. She was lying on top of the detective. They were both on the couch. The TV was on, but the volume was low. The clock on the VCR said that it was 12:39 A.M. The detective's body next to hers was warm and good, providing the perfect counterbalance to the air conditioner. She realized, suddenly, that she was naked—they both were. The coffee table was pushed to the side; food containers had been thrown to the ground; as she blinked, she remembered their frantic bodies colliding with the table. The entire thing had passed in a blur of pleasure; she had felt disembodied and free, as if some other self had taken over her body. All at once, she had found herself exploring the detective with her mouth and hands—practically devouring him—as if she were somehow feasting on his energy. He, likewise, had drawn off her energy, until she had collapsed on top of him, spent, begging him for five minutes to catch her breath…but she had fallen asleep. She smiled. She felt safe and relieved. She snuggled against the detective's body, ready to go back to sleep—

Her cell phone began to chime. She heard it faintly. It was in the bedroom. She rose from the detective; he groaned in his sleep, but did not awaken. When she was free of the couch, she jogged back to her bedroom and closed the door behind her, as to not disturb the detective. She turned on the bedroom light and squinted to mitigate the sudden glare. The phone was still in her handbag. She had only turned it on after she gave Stacy her number. The telephone number was one she did not recognize, but she expected the caller to be Stacy.

"Hello," Vera said as she put the phone to her ear. A man yelled something almost immediately, so that she reflexively pulled the phone from her ear. "…Who is this?" Vera asked; the man continued to shout. "Stop yelling! I can't understand anything you're saying."

The man stopped and took a deep breath, but his voice was uneven as he said: "It's me—Stacy's boyfriend. I'm at the hospital."

It took Vera a few seconds to digest that. "Did something happen to your mother?"

"No—she's fine. It's Stacy. They're saying she tried to kill herself!"

"What!"

"Why would she do it?" the boyfriend cried into the phone.

Vera was still in shock. "Is she all right?"

"Yeah, she just came out of surgery. It's a good thing I was there, to tie her wrists up. That's what the doctors said. If I hadn't been there…they said she would have bled to death. Why would she have done it?" he said in the same uneven, disillusioned way.

Vera's mind couldn't really digest it. "She cut her wrists?"

"Yes, right there in the bed. When I woke up, there was blood everywhere!"

Vera's mind was still sputtering along. Something new occurred to her: "How'd you know to call me here?"

"It was all she kept saying," he went on in the same disillusioned way. "When I woke up and asked her why she had done it, she told me to call you. She had your card in her pocket."

"She didn't tell you why she did it?"

"She said that she *hadn't*—that she had fallen asleep next to me—but who else could have done it?"

"Are you at the same hospital from Friday?"

"Yes."

"I'll be there as soon as I can."

Vera went to the closet and put on some clothes—a pair of jeans and a T-shirt. Her legs felt a little wobbly beneath her. She still could not bring her mind to digest what she had heard. …Vera remembered the odd way Stacy had been acting when she left her. She knew that she should have called Stacy earlier! However, as strange as Stacy's behavior had been,

Vera could not see her as suicidal. There had to be some other explanation. ...She dressed quickly. She took one step from her closet, headed toward the door to the living room, when the thing happened again. ...One moment, she was in her bedroom; the next moment, she was in that other place, where there was too much light. Again, she squinted to block out the glare, but she was panicking already, anticipating the huge, bloody hand. And then the hand was there again. She trembled at the sight of the blood-smeared fingers, which had already tasted death, and were reaching out to her, so that they could share what they had tasted. Again, she tried to move—to flee—but she was still frozen. She smelt her own sickly sweat again. *Move!* she pleaded with herself. The hand was getting bigger, blocking out some of the light. In those last few terrifying moments, she pleaded with the universe. Was this a vision of things to come, or some kind of flashback: some hidden terror from her childhood, perhaps? ...But it was already too late. The hand was there, and she felt death spreading through her, killing her cell by cell. And then, after everything went black, she again found herself transported back to her bedroom. Her knees gave out, but she managed to steer her collapsing body onto the bed. She lay there for a moment, her torso on the bed, her legs still on the floor. She was trembling—overcome by some kind of mortal terror. What the hell was happening to her? She returned to her old question: was that something that was to come, or something that had already happened? Both possibilities had their unwholesome consequences—

There was a knock on her bedroom door. "Are you okay?" the detective called. He must have heard her collapse. The reality of him helped her to fight off the hopelessness. She remembered Stacy—the horrible possibilities there...but at least that was something tangible. She could deal with Stacy—she could not deal with the bloody hand and visions of death. She pushed herself from the bed. Her legs were wobbly, but she managed—

"Vera?" the detective called again. She heard him turning the door knob, and then the door was open, and he was looking at her as she wobbled up to him. He only had on his underwear. Her face was still clammy with the nervous sweat of her vision; the residual terrors of her vision must have been reflected on it, because he grimaced when he saw her. In two steps he had her in his arms. "What's wrong?" he demanded. She was still dazed, but she was grateful for his supporting arms. She practically collapsed into them, so that he had to support most of her weight.

Vera knew she could not talk about the hand with him yet. "It's Stacy," she said then. "Her boyfriend called."

"What happened?" he demanded.

"They're saying she tried to kill herself."

He frowned. "Is she okay?"

"Yeah, she's at the hospital." Vera rushed toward thoughts of Stacy now, as to further escape the bloody hand.

He noticed that she was dressed. "You're going to the hospital?"

She detached herself from him a little and looked up at him: "Yes—she's been asking for me."

"Want me to give you a ride?"

"Yeah, thanks—if you don't mind."

He nodded. "Can you walk?"

"Yeah," she said shyly, realizing that he was still holding most of her weight. She stood up straighter then, taking her weight onto her legs, which seemed stronger now. He nodded again, and held her arm as they walked back to the living room. He sat her down on the couch, and then he began to get dressed. Most of his clothes were on the floor. He put on his pants and shirt, and then found his shoes behind the curtains, where he had thrown them during their foreplay. She stared at him, wishing they could return to their lovemaking, but knowing that thoughts of Stacy—and the bloody hand—would never allow her to achieve the same sense of freedom. As she was sitting there musing, he came up to her and pulled her to her feet. He held her again. His body still felt good, and she melted into it.

"She'll be fine," he reassured her, still thinking that Vera's collapse had been due to hearing about Stacy.

They detached and began to walk toward the door. He had his arm around her waist. She needed the support. When they were riding down in the elevator, Vera blurted out, "She said she didn't do it."

"What?"

"According to her boyfriend, she said that she hadn't done it—hadn't cut her wrists."

"Did she say someone attacked her?"

"I don't know." And then, shaking her head: "Her boyfriend was babbling on the phone—he probably didn't even know what he was saying."

The detective was looking at her closely. The elevator door opened, and they walked into the lobby. Luckily, it was past Mrs. Moore's bedtime, and the lobby was empty. They began to walk outside. The detective continued:

"What was Stacy's mindset when you left her earlier? Was she upset?"

"I guess. She didn't want me to leave. I thought it was a little odd, but... I simply can't bring myself to believe that she'd do something like this. It's not her. It's not something she'd do."

"There are some things about people that you just can't know."

"What's that supposed to mean?" she said, as if it were some kind of accusation.

He put up his hand to say he meant no offense. "I'm merely saying that sometimes you know people for years—you laugh with them and hang out with them—and then they do something that lets you know that you never knew them at all. ...Like the first partner I had after coming out of the police academy. He was older—had been on the force for ten years. He showed me the ropes—brought me up. We spent practically all our free time together. One day, about two and a half years after I came out of police academy, I got a call from my sergeant in the middle of the night: my partner had put his gun to his mouth and blown his brains out. At first, I told myself that somebody must have done it to him. Maybe it was some kind of street payback for someone we had locked up. But it was all there in the note: 'I don't want to live anymore. I can't deal with all the things I've seen and done.' That's all it said. Two lines. For ten years, he had been taking home all the things he had seen. I, his partner, thought he was fine, but all the while everything was gathering inside him like a poison. ...You can never know what's inside a person."

They reached the car. He opened the door for her, and she sat down in silence.

When he got inside the vehicle, he said: "Which hospital is she in?"

"The same one from Friday."

For whatever reason, he smiled: "Are your weekends always like this? ...Multiple trips to the emergency room, almost getting arrested—"

"And wild sex with my arresting officer?" she finished his sentence.

They laughed together: a short, bittersweet laugh. They both sighed afterwards. He started up the engine and they drove off.

When they entered the hospital waiting room, the boyfriend was sitting in the corner, staring into space with a disillusioned expression on his face. Vera went to him, followed by the detective. When he noticed her, he stood up, growing more animated. She hugged him. All the while, the detective stood at a distance, watching them.

"Everything will be fine," she said, trying to reassure him. He only held her tighter. At last, she disengaged from him and looked up into his haggard face: "Is she conscious?"

"Yes. ...But they put her in restraints. They have her in the psych ward."

"Is she still saying she didn't do it?"

"Yeah."

"You don't believe her story?"

"I'm the only one who was in the room with her," he said pleadingly, as if her acceptance of this one point would clarify everything.

"Okay. ...Can I see her?"

"Yeah, she's been calling for you. ...She told me to get lost when I went in," he said, looking aggrieved.

She smiled. "Don't worry—I'm sure that once things settle down, and all this is sorted out..."

He nodded. Vera placed her hand on his arm to reassure him.

"Where do I go?" she asked him then.

"Just go up to the information desk."

"Okay."

As she began to move off, the police detective came to her side and announced, "I'm going to take a walk. Call me on my cell phone when you need me." He had given her the number during the drive over. She nodded and smiled, then gave him a hug.

"Thanks," she said.

"No problem."

The nurse at the information desk was a woman in her fifties with a scowl permanently engraved on her face, from years of trying to reason with the panicking, grieving relatives and friends of the hospital's patients.

"I'm here to see Stacy Grant," Vera said by way of introduction. The scowling woman glared at her suspiciously, then consulted the computer.

"What's your name?" she said abruptly.

"Vera Alexander."

Once again, the woman consulted the computer. This was probably the point where she usually told people to go home, or that it was too late to see the patient, but something on the screen confounded her, and she seemed disappointed. "Wait here," she said. She then picked up a phone. When the person on the other end of the line answered, she said, "The woman you were waiting for is here, Dr. Baptiste. …Okay. She's waiting out here. Okay." She put down the receiver, and gave Vera one last look. "The doctor will be with you shortly."

Vera nodded. She moved away from the desk a few steps, feeling somehow that she was invading the woman's space. She glanced back at the boyfriend, who was still sitting there as if wounded. He was staring at Vera. She waved at him, and he immediately brightened, as if her gesture had been a great act of kindness.

Just then, the locked doors that led to the main part of the hospital opened. A tall man exited and walked directly to Vera. "I'm Michael Baptiste," he said. "I've been treating your patient, but anything you have to tell me about her case might be helpful."

Vera looked at him confusedly. "My patient?"

"Stacy Grant." And then, looking at Vera curiously, "She's not your patient?"

It suddenly occurred to her that Stacy had probably told him that so he would allow Vera to see her. On impulse, she decided to continue the lie. "Oh," she began uneasily, "...I'm sorry. It's late. How is she doing, Dr. Baptiste?"

"Actually, you can call me Michael—since we're both doctors." He smiled, and she smiled back. "...Anyway, she's well physically. Luckily, she didn't cut too deeply into the wrist. However, of course, it's her mind that troubles me."

"She seems unstable to you?"

"No, she seems calm and rational, but her denial troubles me."

"You mean her saying she didn't slit her wrists?"

"Exactly."

Vera sighed as she thought about it. "Can I talk to her? I'm sure all of this can be sorted out if I just talk to her."

"Sure—especially since she doesn't seem to want to talk to anybody else."

"I'll tell you if she tells me anything pertinent."

Baptiste nodded, seeming grateful. Then, he began to lead her to Stacy's room.

Stacy was in a ward with about five other women—all of whom seemed to be drugged out of their minds. Stacy's face was turned away, so Vera could not tell if she was awake or not. Vera did notice, however, that her arms were in restraints. Baptiste walked Vera up to Stacy's bed. As they neared, Stacy turned her head and looked at them. She smiled faintly when she saw Vera, but had a look of disdain in her eyes when she saw Dr. Baptiste. He decided to leave the two women alone.

"I'll wait outside," he said. When he was gone, Vera smiled at Stacy and joked: "That gown looks good on you."

Stacy looked at her pleadingly: "Get me out of here, Vera."

"That won't be easy. They think you tried to kill yourself."

"Did I ever seem suicidal to you?" Stacy said in annoyance.

"Nah—just homicidal."

They both smiled.

"Get me out of here, Vera."

"How did all this happen? How did your wrists get cut?"

"I already told them everything," she said in frustration. "After the food came, I ate for a while, then I went to bed."

"You ate all that food by yourself?" Vera asked.

"I tried," Stacy said with a sorrowful laugh, tapping her bloated belly. "I practically passed out after I finished eating. I crawled into bed next to my boyfriend; then, the next thing I knew, he was waking me up, screaming at me, asking me why I had done it."

"That's all? You don't remember anything else?"

"No."

"If you didn't do it, then that only leaves one person," Vera mused.

"What do you mean?"

"Your boyfriend."

"My boyfriend?"

"He was the only one in the apartment with you."

"But why would he do it?"

"You forgot how we spent the afternoon, Stacy? He had a total psychotic break just hours ago, remember. He thought he had superpowers; he was seeing things that weren't there—"

"But he's fine now," Stacy protested.

"Is he, Stacy?"

"Yes, he's fine," she said with a kind of religious certainty.

Vera stared at her. "Anyway, just keep that in mind. It had to be one of you. If you didn't do it..."

"I know he didn't do it," she said simply, looking away.

About five seconds of brooding silence passed. Somehow, seeing Stacy in such a combative mood reassured Vera that she would be fine. Vera changed the subject: "What do you have against me dating the police detective?"

Stacy looked up at her, and then smiled. "I think you can do better, that's all."

Vera laughed at her: "You sound like my mother."

"Maybe you have a history of dating men who are beneath you?"

"Beneath me? That's what you think about the detective?"

"You can do better," she said again.

"What does 'doing better' entail? Getting a guy with a Benz and a country house?"

Stacy groaned. "Let's not argue about it, Vera. Just get me out of here, will you?"

"I can't get you out of here if I think you're a danger to yourself, or that you're going to put yourself in danger."

"I'm not suicidal, Vera. You *know* I'm not."

Vera sighed. "…Then come home with me. I wouldn't feel right about leaving you alone with your boyfriend."

"Okay…Whatever you want. Just get me out of here."

"I'll try to talk to the doctor."

"Thanks."

She left the ward; as Dr. Baptiste had said, he was waiting outside.

"Look," Vera began as soon as she saw him, "I talked to her and she said this was all some kind of sex fantasy that got out of hand." The lie came flowing out of her seamlessly.

"Really?" he said, eying her.

"Yeah. I know her—she's not suicidal, just a bit of a freak."

The doctor laughed. She went on: "I can take her home to my apartment and look after her—you wouldn't have to worry if you released her."

"You're going to take full responsibility?"

"Yeah, I take full responsibility. You can release her into my care."

The doctor stared at her for a while, then nodded. "Okay, I'll fill out the paperwork."

Vera returned to the waiting room. The boyfriend jumped up as soon as he saw her.

"Any news?" he said, rushing up to her.

"Stacy seems fine," she began. "She's going to stay with me for a few days."

He seemed hurt again: "She can't come home with me?"

"It's only for a few days. It's a medical decision—I can keep an eye on her."

"I could keep an eye on her, too—I'm her boyfriend."

"I'm sure you could, but she needs some special attention for now."

He looked distraught—heartbroken.

"I'm sure she'll be back home before you know it." And then, to get his mind off Stacy, "How is your mother doing?"

"Mom's fine. She's still in and out of consciousness, though. Everyone I love is getting hurt."

"You're a good son," Vera said then, seemingly apropos of nothing.

He looked up at her distractedly. "I feel as though everything's falling apart. I feel so confused about things nowadays. I can't explain it...."

"Maybe you should go home and try to get some sleep."

He shook his head: "Sleep is all I seem to get nowadays. Every time I turn around it's like I'm waking up from some kind of strange dream—as if the real world is passing me by. ...I can't explain it."

Vera felt uncomfortable, remembering how Stacy was always commanding him to sleep after killing him. "...Still, try to get some rest," she suggested. "It's the best way. I'll call you in the morning and tell you how Stacy's doing."

"Can I come and visit her?"

"Sure—once I get her settled in. I'll call you after everything's settled. Go home now...try to get some sleep."

He nodded again, before walking off.

After the boyfriend had left, Vera sat down and waited for Dr. Baptiste to return with the release forms for Stacy. Vera knew that the entire thing was unethical. If anything happened to Stacy, and it was discovered that she really was not a patient of hers, then Vera could lose her license. She tried not to think of it. She called the detective and told him to be ready with the car.

Forty-five minutes later, Dr. Baptiste returned with the release forms. Vera signed them in the same careless, illegible way that she autographed her books. The doctor admonished her about keeping Stacy's stitched wrists clean and dry. He handed her a bag with bandages, ointments and painkillers, then he left. Vera called the detective again, and told him to drive up to the entrance. Five minutes after that, Stacy was wheeled into the waiting room by an orderly. Vera only then noticed how pale Stacy looked. Of course, she had lost lots of blood. She was wearing a robe over her gown. Vera guessed that the clothes Stacy had been wearing when she was admitted were probably all bloodstained. Stacy nodded to her, but otherwise said nothing. Then, she, Stacy and the orderly (who was still pushing Stacy on her wheelchair) exited the hospital. The detective was pulling up in his car when they got outside. He got out of the car and helped Stacy into the back seat. Within thirty seconds, they were driving away.

No one said a word. Stacy was in the back, staring out of the window blankly.

"Hey," Vera suggested, "why don't you tell another driving story, Stacy?"

Stacy grunted; in a sullen tone, she went on: "That's only for when I'm among friends."

Vera was too stunned to say anything. The detective only shrugged and drove on. After a while, he put on the radio to drown out the silence.

When they got home, the detective was going to help Stacy upstairs, but she said that she'd be fine. Vera gave him an awkward hug—or rather, a hug made awkward by Stacy's disapproving presence. After that, he got in the car and drove off.

"Good riddance," Stacy said under her breath.

Vera was holding her around the waist for support. "That was rude," Vera said as she began to lead Stacy up to the building.

"What can you possibly see in that guy?" Stacy said in bewilderment.

"He's great," Vera said, resisting the impulse to raise her voice. "I don't see what your problem is."

"Did you have sex with him?"

"What if I did?" she said with growing combativeness. "I don't see how it's any of your business anyway."

Stacy chuckled. "Don't get defensive—I think it's good that you finally got some."

"What do you mean, 'finally?'"

Stacy laughed. "Admit it, Vera: it's been a while."

Vera stared at her for a moment. They had stopped and were staring at one another, perhaps sizing one another up. At last, Vera chuckled and shook her head. They began to walk on.

"Was he any good?" Stacy pressed her.

"Yes," she said with a strange mixture of annoyance and joy. "...It was nice." And then, remembering it all again, "I felt really free for some reason. I like being around him."

"Are you in love with him?"

"I thought you didn't believe in love?"

"I don't, but I know you do."

Vera smiled. Then, in answer to Stacy's question, "I don't know," she said, wishing that Stacy were more discreet. "...I think he's a great guy. It's only..."

"It's only what?"

They had made it to the glass door. Vera got out her keys and opened the door. She continued: "He's great, but there's sadness in his heart. His wife and daughter were killed in a car accident. I asked him if he had the opportunity to do something that would allow him to forget it all, if he would do it."

"Why'd you ask that?"

"I don't know. Maybe I was thinking about your boyfriend—all the things we made him forget."

"Let me guess," Stacy started in a disgusted tone, "your detective said he'd rather remember and hold onto the pain because he loved his family so much."

"He said he'd rather remember, but what's your problem with him? You're acting as if you're jealous or something."

They were now before the elevators. Vera pressed the "Up" button.

"I hate bullshit, that's all," Stacy went on. "Most people, in their honest moments, would choose to forget—especially if they were in *real* pain. But people are too dishonest, especially when they're talking to others. They give diplomatic, politically correct answers. They tell people what they think they want to hear—and what they think will make themselves look best in other people's eyes."

Vera shook her head: "I don't think he's like that at all."

The elevator door opened. They got in. On the ride up to Vera's apartment, they both stared straight ahead, at the elevator doors. Vera was holding Stacy's upper arm to support her, but it was as if they were miles apart. The sullen silence continued when they were inside Vera's apartment. Vera took Stacy to her bedroom. She got Stacy a nightgown. Stacy stripped from the hospital clothes right there and put on the nightgown. Her body was flawless. After that, Stacy crawled into bed. Vera stood staring at her. There was a petulant expression on Stacy's face; and with Vera's big, lacy nightgown, she looked even more like a little girl. Vera chuckled. At the noise, Stacy looked up at her. Vera began:

"What's the point of this argument, Stacy? I brought you here so that you could rest and be safe. I don't want to argue with you."

"I don't want to argue with you either," Stacy said in the same petulant way.

"Then what's going on? What's bothering you? I sensed it in you since I told you I was going on a date. You can't hate the detective that much, so what's the problem?"

"It's nothing," she said curtly.

"It has to be something, since every time I bring him up you act like you're going to have a stroke."

"I do not!" she said with a laugh.

"Yes, you do...so what's this about? You were just talking about how dishonest people are. Why don't you be straightforward now?"

Stacy looked over at her. Eventually, she sighed, bowing her head for a few moments. "Okay," she said at last. "...Well, the thing is, this weekend was for *us*. After all we did together, why are you wasting time with that guy? We were supposed to hang out."

Vera eyed her for a moment, before laughing heartily. "I knew it! You *are* jealous."

"I am not!"

"Are too!"

"Am, not, *infinity*!"

They were both laughing by now. When the laughter died down, Vera came over and sat on the edge of the bed.

"Try to get some sleep, Stacy. We'll spend tomorrow together, doing girlie stuff if you want." They both smiled. "Sleep well," she said, getting up. At the door, she said, "Do you want me to leave the light on?" When she realized how it sounded, she snickered to herself and switched it off.

Vera was lying on the couch when her cell phone rang. She opened her eyes and realized that it was morning. Her back was stiff. She groaned and looked around confusedly, until her eyes rested on the cell phone—which was on the coffee table. She picked it up and smiled when she saw the number.

"Hey, Holmes," she said, lying back down on the couch. "What time is it?"

"It's about 10 a.m. Did I wake you up?"

"Of course. I'm still tired from that workout you put me through last night."

He laughed out, either succumbing to ego or simply amused by her phrasing. "Anyway, how's your friend?"

"Don't change the subject when I'm beaming about sex," she chastised him playfully.

"Is this where I'm supposed to ask you what you're wearing?"

This time it was she who laughed out. "Nah, breathing hard into a tele-phone is not my thing. Is that how you get off when you're not viewing Internet porn for your cases?"

They were both laughing now.

"So," she said when their laughter had died down, "did you sleep well?"

"I passed out the moment my head hit the pillow."

"How come you're up so early?"

"Oh, one of my police buddies called me. Last night, I asked him to keep me in the loop about your friend's case."

"Did he have any news?"

"Nothing really—only that they found the knife she used to cut her wrists. It was in the kitchen, which was a little odd."

"Why is that odd?"

"When someone slits her wrists, the knife is usually lying nearby. Why would she cut her wrists, walk to the kitchen, wash it off, and then walk back to the bedroom? In fact, that could never have happened, because there would be a huge blood trail from the bedroom to the kitchen. We didn't find a single drop."

"Maybe someone wiped the blood away?"

"No, that's the thing. There are forensic techniques you can use: special lights that can tell you if something has come in contact with blood, even if you wash the blood off. That's how they found the knife in the kitchen. It was washed off and placed with the other knives."

Vera realized that she was holding her breath. She breathed out slowly: "So, you don't think it was a suicide attempt?"

"No, do you?"

"No. Like I told you, it doesn't fit with Stacy's personality. It never fit."

There was a slight pause. The detective was direct: "Do you think the boyfriend did it?"

"I don't know," Vera said with a groan, not wanting to implicate the boyfriend. "...Let's drop it. What's done is done." She changed the subject as quickly as she could: "When am I going to see you again?"

The detective laughed out. "I think your friend will kill me if I show up there again. She's very protective of you."

"Don't start that," she said with a laugh.

"Are you the mother she never had or something like that?"

"Maybe," Vera said, stunning herself by the simplicity of the statement. Presently, she heard the bedroom door squeak; when she looked up, she saw Stacy emerging from the room. "I gotta go," Vera said into the phone. "Thanks again for everything. Let's have lunch or something this week." Even before the detective could answer her, she put the phone down and stood up.

"Who was that?" Stacy said with a wry smile, "—your boyfriend?"

Vera grinned, but ignored her taunt. "You want breakfast?" She walked over to Stacy.

"What do you have?"

"I didn't say I had anything. I just asked you if you wanted breakfast. Let's order something."

"You order out too much, Vera," Stacy whined. "Whatever happened to wholesome home cooking?"

Vera smiled and walked over to the phone: "It died when they invented free delivery."

B reakfast arrived about half an hour later—along with the Sunday news-paper. Vera had to spoon feed Stacy, because her bandaged wrists made it difficult to hold anything. Luckily, the wounds were not deep enough to have severed tendons or caused nerve damage. Vera told her everything the doctor had said to her, while Stacy stared into the distance, looking bored. After they ate, Vera helped her bathe. She ran a bath for Stacy, and then scrubbed her back and shoulders with a washcloth. She reneged at scrubbing anything else. Afterwards, the bandages were changed and redressed. It was about midday now, and they were sitting in front of the TV. A show was on, but they were not really following it. They were just staring at the passing scenes.

"Maybe I should call my boyfriend," Stacy announced.

"I'm surprised he hasn't called already."

"You think something happened to him?"

Vera sighed. "God, I hope not. I couldn't spend another day chasing after him. ...Here," Vera went on, picking up her cell phone from the coffee table, "you'd better find out how he's doing."

Stacy dialed her home number and said an enthusiastic, "Hey, you!" as soon as the boyfriend answered. When, thirty seconds later, she began talking in baby talk, telling the boyfriend how much she missed him, Vera decided to take a walk. She went to the bathroom and showered. When she emerged from the shower fifteen minutes later, Stacy was still talk-ing on the phone. Vera smiled. She went to her bedroom and dressed in a pair of shorts and a T-shirt. Five minutes later, when she emerged from the bedroom, she saw that Stacy was finally finished talking. Stacy was lying back on the couch, basking in a kind of conversational afterglow. Vera laughed at her.

"I assume he's well."

"Yeah, I woke him up."

"It's good that he got some sleep."

"Yeah. …You still think he tried to kill me?"

Vera hedged. "I don't know what I think. I have a feeling you'll be safer if you're not around him for a while. And we both know he'll be safer if you're not around him," she said, winking.

Stacy had a sarcastic smile on her face. "He could probably use a good killing about now. Killing is like sex: once you have it done to you, you need to have it done regularly."

"Humph," Vera said mockingly. "In your case, once you kill, you need to do that regularly as well."

"No doubt," Stacy said with a wry smile.

"So, you want something to eat?"

"God," Stacy whined, "tell me you're not going to order out again!"

Vera laughed. "Okay, I'll torture you by cooking something. Just remember that you asked for it. You can't complain."

"I won't. You can tell a lot about someone from her cooking."

"Yeah, in my case, you'll learn that I can't cook." Vera got up to go to the kitchen.

"Don't go yet—it's too early to eat again anyway."

"You want to watch a movie?"

"Nah. Tell me a story, Vera."

Vera winced: "I haven't made up one yet."

"Then tell me something that really happened. How old were you when you saw your first dead body?"

"Damn, you're a morbid bitch!" Vera exclaimed, but Stacy only smiled.

"Never mind that. When was it?"

Vera sighed, thinking back. "I was twelve."

"Good."

"Good? What's so good about that?"

"Twelve is a good age to become aware of death." Stacy was looking at her frankly; Vera was looking back at her with a bewildered frown. Stacy laughed at her expression. "Anyway," Stacy said, breaking the stalemate, "just tell me the story."

Vera stood thinking for a few seconds. She sat down heavily. "Okay. ...I haven't thought about it in years."

"Did it traumatize you?" Stacy asked, but there was an odd smile on her face.

"Damn," Vera said, eying her again, "you're a weird chick."

"Quit with the suspense. Just tell me the story," Stacy said, looking on eagerly and settling herself comfortably on the couch.

Vera smiled and shook her head. "Okay, when I was twelve, my father drove my mother and me down to Georgia to spend summer vacation at my grandmother's farm. It was about a sixteen-hour drive. About eight hours into the drive, we all began to get bored and tired. By then, we had played all the road games we could: ...I Spy and the others. The conversation had dried up, and we just sat there in silence, trying to hold on—"

"You were an only child?" Stacy asked.

"I was by then."

"What does that mean?"

"I had an older brother, but he died in the Army. He was some kind of top secret commando. Rather, that's how I've always thought about it."

"So, he was the first dead person you saw?"

"No, I never saw my brother's body. His funeral was a closed casket funeral. He died in an explosion. I don't even think there was a body in the casket."

"How old were you then?"

"About seven. For years afterward, I used to think that maybe he was out there somewhere—that he wasn't really dead, but only out on another top secret mission. I guess that was easier than accepting that he had been blown into a million bits in a country we had no business being in."

"Vietnam?"

"Nah, I think Vietnam was over by then—it was one of the dozens of other Cold War conflicts that America secretly insinuated itself into. The Army never gave the details of how he had died. They said he had 'made the ultimate sacrifice for his country.' I remember that line from the funeral."

"Do you remember your brother?"

Vera groaned with mock exasperation: "Why do you keep interrupting me?"

"You're not giving the right details."

"Excuse me for not being skilled at talking about morbid shit."

"Well, get it together, sister," Stacy said with a smile. "You're rolling with me now."

Vera smiled, then shook her head again. "...Anyway, he went to the Army when I was four or five. I have memories *of* him, but I can't really say I knew him. I remember that he would call me 'Lady V.' I used to make him have these tea parties with me, and I would hold up my pinky finger when I drank out of the little plastic teacups, and talk with a British accent, and babble on about crumpets and scones, even though all we were eating were Oreos and Kool-Aid." She laughed suddenly. "It is because of him that my parents still call me Lady V to this day."

Stacy smiled and nodded, satisfied.

"Anyway, back to the trip to Georgia," Vera went on, "about eight hours into the drive, the boredom was beginning to set in. We were driving down a lonely highway. For most of the time, ours would be the only car around. We were all pretty silent by then. Some scratchy country song was playing on the radio. I remember that the day was bright. ...But it was almost too bright somehow—like an overexposed picture. Everything seemed faded—or maybe that's just how my mind remembers it. The passing cars and the scenery...everything seemed faded. I remember that a station wagon was passing by us, and that in the back seat there were two little boys. The one closest to the window stuck out his tongue at me and made a face. For whatever reason, I stuck out my tongue at him, too. He stuck out his tongue farther, and rubbed it against the window; he looked over at me cross-eyed, daring me to make an uglier face. I was getting ready to go all out when I noticed the expression on his face—shock, terror... He was looking up ahead; I turned my head in time to see a huge truck tire flying our way. Up ahead, a tractor-trailer was jackknifing—it had

had a tire blowout. It seemed as if the entire axle had come off. I glanced back over at the kid in the car, just in time to see the flying tire explode into them like a missile. There wasn't an explosion or anything, but it knocked them off the highway. …The sound was like a bomb going off. My father swerved the car, because another tire was coming. I looked ahead in time to see it. My father swerved off the road, into a ditch. The car rolled. I wasn't wearing a seatbelt, and I found myself being tossed around—one moment, I was on the roof; the next moment I was being jammed against the back of my parents' seats. …And then, at last, it stopped. I lay in the back, trembling. My father screamed out, asking if everyone was okay. I must not have talked loudly enough, because he screamed out my name, thinking that something had happened to me. He reached back and shook me, asking if I was okay. I was in shock, but I was fine. He had blood streaming down his face, from a gash above his hairline. My mother was trembling and crying….

"Maybe two minutes passed that way, with us in the ditch. My father told us that we should get out. We had to clamber up the walls of the ditch. The tractor-trailer was lying on its side. The driver was standing outside, looking dazed. I remembered the family with the kids in the back. Their car was lying in the ditch on the other side of the road. For what-ever reason, I went to them, and my father followed me. I looked down at the car from the road. The truck tire had caved in the entire front of the car. The kid who had made the face at me was dead—his neck was twisted and dangling out of the window. The entire family was dead. My father grabbed me and pulled me away, so that I wouldn't see, but it was already branded on my mind. Up until I went to college, I would dream about that scene a few times a week."

"When is the last time you dreamt about it?" Stacy asked her.

"It's been years. I think about it every once in a while, but it's been years since I've had a dream about it. I guess I got over it."

"That's a special memory, Vera, you should hold onto it. It was the first time you saw death as it was."

"And how was that?" she said sarcastically, "—bloody and sickening?"

"Most people spend their lives trying to shield their minds from the reality of death. At a very early age, you saw death as it was—random, brutal… uncompromising."

"You're talking as though I saw something great. I saw a kid and his entire family die. It was *horrible*."

"Sometimes seeing horror is exactly what we need. Either way, did you eventually make it down to Georgia?" Stacy asked.

"Eventually. We had to wait in the nearest town for a few days. My father had to get some car parts shipped in, in order to fix the car."

"I guess you stayed in a motel?"

"Hardly," she said with a laugh, remembering their accommodations. "It wasn't that big of a town. We stayed in the sheriff's 'hunting lodge'— an old building in the middle of nowhere."

"Anything else happen while you were there?"

"Nah. Nothing at all. We just waited around the house until the car was fixed. Then, we got the hell out of there. When we got to Georgia my grandmother babied us—wouldn't let us out of her sight. She said that it was a miracle: that we had escaped death, and that this was our chance."

"Your chance to do what?"

"I don't know—our chance to be productive human beings, I guess." She laughed here, and Stacy joined her.

Then, in her usual abrupt way, Stacy enquired, "How old were you when you lost your virginity?"

"You go from my first corpse to my first lover? You're a strange conversationalist."

"Never mind that," she said, smiling. "How old were you?"

Vera groaned, feeling cornered. "I was fifteen."

"Did you love him?"

"For someone who doesn't believe in love, you sure ask that a lot."

Stacy laughed. "Just answer the question."

Vera smiled, feeling as though she had won that battle: "No—I didn't love him."

"I mean, at the time—did you *think* you loved him, as a fifteen-year-old?"

"Nah, it was some moron kid I met in the park one summer. We dated a couple of times; he felt me up, and then we did it at his place before his mother came home from work."

"Good," Stacy said with a smile. "Your first time should always be free of love and pretense."

Vera chuckled at the comment. "…Were you in love with your first lover?" she asked Stacy now.

"Of course not."

"How old were you?"

"Twelve."

"Goddamn! Was he twelve, too?"

"Of course not—he was seventeen."

"Christ!"

Stacy laughed at her. "It's not what you're thinking."

"What am I thinking?"

"That he took advantage of a young, impressionable girl."

"What else could it be?"

"I seduced him."

"A twelve-year-old can't seduce a man. He abused you—*raped* you."

Stacy chortled at her, as if she had said something stupid. "You think seduction is only for adults?"

"He should have known better."

"As I recall, he didn't know shit. It was a total waste of time."

"But you were twelve!"

"Why should I take pride in being some kind of clueless victim, Vera, when I was the one that was in charge? *I* wanted to have sex with him; *I* pursued him. It would be dishonest to say he took advantage of me."

"But you can't honestly say that twelve is a good age to lose your virginity," Vera maintained.

"It was a good age for me—I got it out of the way."

"But virginity isn't something to 'get out of the way.'"

Once again, Stacy laughed out. "You mean it's some 'sacred treasure' that a woman bestows on a man on her wedding night?"

Vera ignored her baiting. "A twelve-year-old doesn't know what she's doing."

"Don't be preposterous, Vera. If dogs and rats and all the other animals of the earth—who don't have the intelligence of a twelve-year-old human—can have sex, then why can't a twelve-year-old girl have sex? It's like I told you before: morality is a creation of human beings. It's artificial—*fake*. Two hundred years ago, twelve-year-olds were getting married."

"But we've advanced since then."

"Have we? Maybe we've regressed. Maybe, after all these years of 'civilization,' we've lost sight of human needs?"

Vera eyed her skeptically: "You don't believe in any moral standards at all?"

"Not at all."

"You don't believe that there are some things that are sacred?"

"I don't think anything is sacred. I believe in needs and necessity. All you moralizers, who puff out your chests and talk about how moral you are, are the first ones to throw it all away when times get desperate. The Ten Commandments say 'Thou Shalt Not Kill' and yet we see our ultra-religious president telling us how great it is that we're overseas killing people in wars."

"War is different. That's self-defense."

"Exactly. Your response proves my point: need trumps morality every time. When you see there is a need to defend yourself, then prohibitions against murder disappear—*morality* disappears. In fact, words like 'morality' and 'sacred' have no substance. They're meaningless. People use them when they want to put on airs—when they want to pretend that their needs are somehow sanctioned by God or whatever other supernatural force they claim to believe in. They pretend to be up in the heavens, when inside they're crawling in the gutters with the rest of us."

Vera sighed. "How did we get into all this?"

Stacy smiled at her. "Don't pretend that you don't like our conversations, Vera. Even now, what worries you is that you agree with me."

"I do not!" she said, but she was laughing.

"You do. Admit it. You know the truth of what I'm saying—it's just unpalatable, since you like putting on airs."

Vera laughed out. "Yeah, I've got to set a moral example for all my fans."

They spent the rest of the evening watching television. Vera started to cook some chicken (which had to be chiseled from a block of ice in her freezer, and which had an unsavory scent, even when frozen). The intricacies of defrosting meat had never been one of her fortés, and so, thirty minutes later—when the stench of burning, unsavory meat wafted through the apartment—Stacy agreed that they should order out. They ordered from an Indian restaurant—something that had the veneer of being healthy, but which left them both with heartburn. Even then, it was good to lounge on the couch, vegetating. Vera realized that it had been a while since she had relaxed so completely. Every weekend she would promise herself that she would relax, but something would always come up—some celebrity event that her agent had booked her on at the last moment, or some other event that was supposed to be fun, but which ended up being tedious.

They watched cartoons and science fiction movies that were so bad that she and Stacy spent half the time laughing. There was something wondrous about the confluence of bad plots, bad acting and bad special effects—especially when you wanted to vegetate.

For dinner, they ordered from a deli. They watched more television while they ate. Around eleven-thirty that night, Stacy decided to go to bed. She said that she was rarely that tired so early in the night. Vera laughed and said that doing nothing was exhausting work.

By midnight, the house was dark and still. Vera fell asleep on the couch. However, around three in the morning, she was awakened by a squeaking noise. It was sudden and violent. She sprung up from sleep and looked around confusedly. She heard the noise again, then remembered the French doors in the bedroom, which led out to the balcony. She was always meaning to oil the hinges, but had never gotten around to it. Anyway, figuring that Stacy had gotten up to get some fresh air, Vera walked over to the bedroom. The door was open, as were the French doors. The bed was of course empty.

"Stacy?" Vera called, walking out to the balcony. She yawned then, but when she finally saw Stacy, she gasped. There was a lounge chair against the railing. Stacy had one foot on the lounge chair and the other on the railing—and seemed to be about to step out into the darkness. Vera sprang at her and pulled her back from the railing. "Stacy!" Vera screamed, but when she looked at Stacy's face, there was a blank, non-responsive expression there. Her eyes were staring into space. Was she sleepwalking? Vera stared at her for a while, trying to figure it out, but then she just decided to return Stacy to bed. Stacy went compliantly; and then, when she was under the covers, she closed her eyes and went back to sleep. Vera stood staring at her, trembling slightly, thinking that if she had come just three seconds later, Stacy might have jumped ten stories to her death. Vera's mind worked slowly, but once it got on its path, it worked steadily. In a sense, she had to wake up first, before she could think. All at once, she remembered the wrist-cutting incident. Stacy had been asleep then as well. What if something happened to Stacy when she slept? What if some latent suicidal impulse took over her when she closed her eyes? Up until now, Vera had thought that the boyfriend had had another psychotic episode and slit Stacy's wrists; but in light of what she had just seen, everything pointed to Stacy.

Even if there were some other explanation, one thing was certain: she had to stay awake to keep an eye on Stacy. She went to the kitchen and put on some coffee. She returned to the bedroom while the coffee was brewing, just to look at Stacy and make sure that she was okay. Vera got a chair from the dinette, placed it against the French doors (which she closed). Then, she sat on it, drinking her coffee and staring at Stacy. Unfortunately, some time after 4 a.m., she fell asleep.

In the morning, she awoke to the sensation of being shaken. As she awoke, she remembered Stacy, and realized that the shaking sensation was like being throttled. She screamed out as she opened her eyes. The room was bright, and she squinted from the glare. She went to run—to scurry away—but only fell off the chair. She cringed on the ground, seeing Stacy towering above her. For a moment she held her breath, waiting to be attacked. However, Stacy laughed at her.

"What's your problem? Did you sleep on that chair last night?"

Vera stared at her until her eyes adjusted to the light. She groaned and sat up. It was about 7 a.m. She remembered everything that had happened last night: Stacy getting ready to leap over the railing. She grimaced.

"What's wrong?" Stacy asked, her face showing concern.

"You tried to kill yourself last night—that's what's wrong!"

"What?"

"You almost leapt off the balcony. I pulled you back just as you were about to jump. I guess you were sleepwalking or something. ...I had to watch you all night."

Stacy frowned. "Are you serious?"

"Of course I'm serious!" Vera said, trembling with emotion. "...Don't you see—something takes over you when you sleep. It wasn't your boyfriend who slit your wrists: it was you. You did it while you were sleeping."

Stacy was still staring at her uncomprehendingly.

"God, Stacy," Vera went on. She got up from the floor and clutched Stacy by the shoulders, staring up into her eyes: "Something's happening to you. When you sleep, something takes over."

"Something like what?"

"Something unresolved that's coming to the surface, perhaps."

Stacy frowned. "You think I'm unconsciously suicidal?"

"I don't know," Vera said in frustration, wary of being lured into a debate. Presently, something occurred to her: "Remember what you told me about your mom? ...How they'd find her wandering in the middle of nowhere. Didn't you say she killed herself?"

Stacy nodded uneasily.

Vera grimaced as she saw the full picture in her mind—all the creepy possibilities. "I can't leave you alone," Vera went on. "Someone will have to watch you."

"I'm not a baby, Vera," Stacy protested.

Vera was still clutching her shoulders. "I brought you here so that you could get better, Stacy. Let me help you."

"So, now you think I'm crazy?"

"Something's going on, Stacy!" she said too loudly. "...Look at your wrists," she said, gesturing to the bandages. "And if I had come into the room just a few seconds later last night, you would have jumped off the balcony. You'd be *dead* now."

"Why don't I remember anything?"

"You did everything in your sleep."

Stacy sighed, sounding unconvinced. "Why would I do all these things?"

"I don't know, but maybe you should talk to someone."

Stacy smiled. "You want to be my therapist?"

Vera smiled, but shook her head. "No. I'm too close to you. I've done too much with you to be objective. ...I don't know," she said, shaking her head. "I told you before that everything has consequences. You tell yourself that you can kill your boyfriend without consequences, but maybe your mind can't handle it. Maybe your psyche—"

Stacy's face soured. "Don't start that psychobabble. If you want to keep an eye on me then suit yourself. ...I have to use the bathroom," she said, walking off. Vera stared at her retreating back; as she did so, the same creepy feeling came over her, assuring her that something was very wrong.

Vera called the boyfriend while Stacy was in the bathroom. When Stacy came out, Vera was making more coffee. Vera went to her.

"How are your wrists?"

"Fine."

"Let's change your bandages."

"Okay."

Vera went to get the supplies, then she returned. Stacy still seemed withdrawn. Vera took her over to the kitchen sink, washed her hands, then began to unwrap one of the bandages. She looked up at Stacy's forlorn face and sighed.

"Don't be angry with me, Stacy."

"I'm not angry," she said, staring ahead blankly.

"You're annoyed with me then?" she pressed her.

Stacy looked over at her, life finally seeming to enter her eyes. "You think I'm crazy," she said, hurt.

"The mind can only take so much, Stacy," Vera explained. "...Just give yourself some time to relax and think things through."

Stacy said nothing. She stared down at the bandages.

After the uncomfortable silence, Vera continued, "I called your boyfriend."

"Now you're abandoning me?" Stacy said, but there was a sarcastic expression on her face.

For whatever reason, Vera was relieved by this. She smiled. "All I'm saying is that you shouldn't be left alone. Someone has to take care of you while I go to work."

"I thought you didn't go to work until the evening?"

Vera smiled, remembering that Stacy had stalked her. "That's true, but we have to make arrangements. Besides, your boyfriend is desperate to see you."

"Okay," Stacy said noncommittally.

"He said he'd come over to bring you something to wear. I told him you'd go to the hospital with him. He'd be able to check up on his mother and you'd be able to have your wounds checked out."

"Okay," Stacy said again.

Vera groaned at Stacy's detachment. "What do you want, Stacy? What do you expect me to do? You expect me to leave you here by yourself, after all I've seen?"

"I want you to believe in me."

"What the hell are you talking about? Your ego is so big that you can't believe that you sleepwalk? Your ego is so big that you can't allow yourself to believe that a side of you might be operating subconsciously?"

"I don't believe in subconsciousness," Stacy scoffed.

Vera laughed. "That's the thing about the mind: it does not care what you believe."

The boyfriend arrived about an hour later. Vera and Stacy were watching one of those morning talk shows. Despite what Stacy had said before, she seemed genuinely happy to see him. They hugged and kissed, and

Stacy's face brightened as she held him. Vera watched them and smiled. Stacy changed into the clothes the boyfriend had brought for her, right there in the living room. She was totally uninhibited; she did it in a way that seemed natural somehow. Soon, Stacy and the boyfriend were at the door, waving goodbye.

"Stop by our place after work," Stacy said over her shoulder. "You have the keys, remember?"

"I will," Vera said; and then, they were gone, and she was standing there alone. As always, her dealings with Stacy seemed like a dream in retrospect. She sighed, feeling exhausted. She returned to the couch and lay down. Five minutes later, she was fast asleep. She dreamed strange dreams, full of revelations that she forgot the moment she awoke. When she did so, she looked around groggily, with a vague feeling of panic—and frustration at the fact that she could not remember what she had dreamed. On the TV, the blaring theme music for the nightly network news was playing. She could not believe that she had slept all day. It was getting dark outside. She checked the wall clock for confirmation: it was six-thirty. She sat up on the couch, allowing her feet to drop to the floor. She had to be at work in an hour and a half. She usually got together with her producers to see what the day's show was going to be about. She remembered Stacy, realizing that she should call and get an update. ...But she could do that when she was in the cab, driving to work. She remembered the detective, and all the things they had done Saturday night. She smiled, feeling suddenly aroused. ...But that would have to wait until another time. She got up from the couch now, and called the cab company. When that was completed, she went to the bathroom to shower.

Forty-five minutes later, when the cab was driving over the Brooklyn Bridge, she got out her cell phone and dialed the detective. "What's up, Holmes?"

"What's new?" he said sleepily.

"I'm heading to work. ...Did I wake you up?"

"Of course. You know I work nights."

"I forgot."

He laughed. "I'll forgive you this one time."

"I'm sorry I didn't call you sooner. The thing with Stacy sort of took all my energy."

"How is she?"

"Fine. She's back home now."

"With the boyfriend?"

"Yes."

"I got the sense that you thought he might have had something to do with her slit wrists."

She paused. "...I did, but I think things will be all right. They need one another—Stacy and her boyfriend."

"They need one another?" he said confusedly.

"Yeah. They'll be fine because they need one another."

He did not exactly follow, but he said, "Okay." He still sounded drowsy.

"Go back to sleep, Holmes," she said with a laugh. "I'll call you later."

"Sounds good."

She ended the call, then dialed Stacy's number. There was no answer. The answering machine came on after five rings. She hated answering machines. She always felt on the spot—that if she said something stupid it would be on record for eternity. "—Hi, Stacy. It's me, Vera. ...I wanted to see how you were doing. I'll call you later. You can call me on my cell— leave me a message, so that I know you're fine."

After she had disconnected the call, she sat back in the cab. She looked out of the window distractedly—at the speeding traffic on the FDR Drive. ...She could not get over the uneasy feeling she had, but forced herself not to jump to conclusions. She told herself that Stacy and her boyfriend were probably out having one of their trademark bizarre adventures. Unfortunately, after the weekend she had had, that thought was not exactly a comforting one. She tried not to think about it.

She realized, all at once, that she missed Stacy. She missed their disturbing conversations; as she drove to work, she found herself longing for one of Stacy's perverted stories. She smiled vaguely at the image of

Quartay screaming out at the sight of his possessed penis. …But then she sighed. The prospect of work was particularly distasteful today. After her weekend with Stacy, she felt somehow as though she had been away for weeks. She had the kind of post-vacation melancholia that made people yearn for the beaches and secluded places they had just returned from. Today, of all days, she knew that her time as Dr. Vera was coming to an end. One way or another, she would have to move on. She knew this. …And she had some money in the bank. Maybe it was time to do something for herself—take a trip around the world; write a book that actually mattered…The world was full of possibilities, and she was suddenly eager to grasp them. A strange fear of failure had kept her trapped in the entire Dr. Vera persona. She did not want to be afraid anymore. She wanted to live fearlessly. Stacy had shown her that. Stacy was at the vanguard of something—Vera was certain of it. Maybe none of them could or should live like Stacy, but Stacy was alive and free, whereas most people became passive victims of their lives. Vera would change her life. She would change who she was and claim back the reins of her life. She swore this as she sat in the back of the cab.

Once she got to work, she fidgeted through her production meeting, waiting for it to be over. Her producers and some interns spent an hour and a half pitching show ideas and talking about things in the news that they might bring up in the show. All the ideas seemed stupid and overdone to Vera, but she nodded her head, if only so that they would stop asking her what she thought. Tonight, a doctor was going to be on to talk about the male contraceptive pill, and the producers were telling her to ask questions about the social and sexual implications of men being in control of contraception. One intern—a woman right out of college—was vehement that no woman was going to trust a man with contraception. Vera allowed her mind to tune it all out.

After the meeting, she called Stacy, but there was again no response. To distract herself, she went and got something to eat. She still had over an hour until the show started. She wanted to call the detective, but feared that he was still sleeping. Instead, she went to her office and took a nap. She was awakened by the chime of her cell phone. When it occurred to her that Stacy might be calling, she answered it eagerly:

"Stacy?"

"No," the woman on the other end of the line said. "It's Mandy."

"Mandy?" Vera said, confused.

"Mandy West—your *agent*."

"Oh," she said, feeling silly. She glanced at the wall clock in her office—she had fifteen minutes until the show.

"Are you feeling okay?" her agent asked her.

"Yeah. I'm sorry—I was napping."

"Okay. Anyway, I'm calling to book you on a talk show. It's a show on why men can't please women sexually. You'll defend the 'female' position and they'll have another psychologist—a man—to defend the 'male' position."

Vera groaned. "Those 'battle of the sexes' debates are pointless, Mandy."

"Of course they are—but they help sell books and attract listeners."

Something about Mandy's statement was sickening—*soulless*. Vera paused for a moment, thinking about it. "What do you care about, Mandy?"

"What?"

"What matters to you? When you're not being a big time celebrity agent, what do you care about? You've been my agent for six years now and I know practically nothing about you."

"What do you mean?"

Vera sighed, suddenly realizing how senseless the conversation was. Her agent was successful precisely because she was the way she was; she had become a wealthy woman through her ability to book her clients on shows like the one she had just proposed. It was idiotic to reprimand her agent for "fluffiness" when their mutual success depended on that so-called fluffiness.

Vera sighed again. "Never mind," she said at last. Reconciled to her fate, she continued, "When is the show?"

"A week from Thursday. Can you make it?"

"Sure, I'll be there."

"Good," she said, chipper again. "I'll inform the show's producer, then get back to you with the particulars. Have a good show."

"Bye." Vera hung up the phone, feeling slightly depressed. She missed Stacy. She thought about trying to reach her again, but knew that she had to walk over to the studio to get ready for the show. She went into the studio. Her wooly mammoth engineer was again behind the glass partition. As she sat down to begin the show, Vera felt nervous for the first time in a long while. She knew that her mindset was not right. She felt like a whore who was not in the mood to deal with her johns—if whores ever were in the mood. She was sure that she could "fake it," but the entire proposition was loathsome. The show began. She answered calls. She allowed callers to make long, rambling statements. She encouraged them, in fact, so that the time would fly by. Whenever they asked her for advice she would say, "What do you think?" so that they would tell themselves what they wanted to hear. It was amazing how easily that worked. Her guest came on and she asked him the questions her producers had suggested. Mostly, she allowed callers to ask him questions. Vera tuned out most of it. After the guest segment, she answered more calls. In fact, everything was going smoothly until one of her typical whiny female callers came on, wanting to know if her boyfriend still loved her and what she could do to make sure. The woman sounded pathetic.

"How can I make him love me again?" the woman said, on the verge of tears.

Something snapped in Vera. "...When is the last time you had sex with him?"

"This morning—before he went to work."

"Why did you have sex with him if you're not sure he loves you? Were you even in the mood?"

"Well, he wanted to—"

Vera almost screamed! "Stop there," she commanded. "You know what you need to do? You need to claim back your pussy!"

There was a stunned silence on the other end of the line; the wooly mammoth engineer looked up at her, attentive for once, his jaw hanging.

"Are you there?" Vera asked combatively.

"Y-yeah," the woman stammered.

"You need to claim back your pussy," she said again. "In fact, most of you women who call me up complaining about your men need to do that. Claim back your goddamn pussy. Men have misused it! In fact, the term 'pussy' has become an insult in our language. Men tell other men, 'You're a pussy!' That's their great insult to one another. You know what I say? I say let's be pussies! Let's claim back the power of the pussy! Say it with me now: Claim back your pussy!"—the woman on the phone mouthed the words inanely, still stunned—"Louder! Say it with me like you mean it—and that goes for all you women out there who want to call me up about your boyfriends and husbands. *Claim back your pussy*! Shout it with me now! Claim back your pussy!"—the woman on the phone finally seemed to be getting the hang of it; she was screaming it now—"That's right! *Scream* it. Let that be your new mantra! Let the city rock with the sound and reality of it! *Claim back your pussy*! *Claim back your pussy...*!"

The woman chanting on the phone was like a screeching maniac now. Vera did not care. She was screaming the words herself. In her mind, it was thunderous—glorious! Her engineer stared at her as if he were in the process of having a stroke.

The show ended. Vera felt high. Dozens of women had called up after her rant, all of them screaming her chant. The switchboards were jammed. The station manager, a grandfatherly man in a bowtie, appeared in the engineer's booth, staring at her in the same I'm-in-the-process-of-having-a-stroke way that her engineer had. She ignored them. Her callers were happy. They were energized in a way she had never seen them. She did not know if she was enlivened by that or terrified. She did not care. As soon as her show was over, she left the studio. The station manager looked like he wanted to talk to her, but she just left. She grabbed her bag and ran to the elevator. When she got outside, she was relieved. A side of her hoped that she would be fired—that the FCC would fine the station hundreds of thousands of dollars. She laughed at the prospect of it, in fact. She was free. She had been wanting to do something like that since she started the show.

In the cab, she remembered Stacy. She had turned off her cell phone during her show. She turned it on now, but there were no messages. She had told the cabbie to take her home, but she now told him to go to Stacy's address. She was still concerned that she had not heard from Stacy all day, but then she remembered her rant on air. She remembered all those women chanting, "Claim back your pussy!" She laughed out loud, so that the cabbie looked back at her, concerned.

When she got to Stacy's place, the kids were again outside the club. Vera got out of the cab—

"Oh my God, it's her!"

Vera looked up in confusion to see two young women staring at her, jumping up and down in excitement. And then, "Claim back your pussy!" they began to chant; some other women, and some men that liked saying "pussy," also took up the chant. In fact, the chant seemed to be infectious, because within seconds dozens of people were chanting it.

At first, Vera only stared at them confusedly, but then she nodded approvingly—like a queen might nod. The entire thing was preposterous, but to hell with it. Some of the women came up and shook her hand; she signed a couple of autographs...but then, she remembered Stacy. She left the excited crowd and moved on. She went to the apartment entrance. After she fished Stacy's keys out of her bag, she opened the door and entered the building. As she walked up the stairs, she remembered how the boyfriend's mother had been waiting on top of the staircase when she and Stacy entered. She wondered how the mother was doing....

At the door to the apartment, Vera stopped and listened, hoping to hear Stacy's voice, but there was a moribund silence inside. She knocked, but was so on-edge that she did not realize that she had knocked feebly. She got out the keys again. As she put the key in the lock and turned it, her mind flashed with a hundred terrifying images of what she would see: Stacy and the boyfriend sprawled lifelessly on the ground from a murder-suicide, blood everywhere, faces frozen in horrified, twisted expressions... It was dark and silent in the apartment, but then she heard a moan. She turned to the left—toward the noise. The door that led to the living room was closed, but light emanated from beneath it. She approached the door, feeling numb inside—almost refusing to let her mind think.

She opened the door and gasped. Maybe twenty seconds passed before she realized what she was seeing. On the couch, two old couples where going at it, their pruny skin rippling with each thrust. Vera could only stare. They had to at least be in their seventies. One old lady had her legs thrown over one old codger's shoulders. The other couple was doing it doggie-style. After a few moments of shock, Vera finally noticed Stacy and her boyfriend. They were running the video cameras, swooping in to get close-ups of ecstasy-drenched faces and penis-engorged vaginas. Everyone seemed engrossed in his or her work, and Vera just stood there, her head swimming. The smell of the old people's sweat and sexual secretions made her feel slightly nauseous. However, that was when one of the old men cried out, spraying semen over the sagging tits of his partner. The other old man, not to be outdone, screamed out as well, spraying his seed over the drooping ass of the other one. Vera did not know what the hell to do. She kept telling herself that decency demanded that she turn away, and yet there was something fascinating about the entire thing. She was not sure if it was arousing, but it was fascinating.

"Great job, everyone!" Stacy announced then, seeming pleased with everything. That's when Stacy turned around and noticed Vera standing there.

"Hey, Vera!"

Vera jumped when Stacy said her name; Vera looked at her uneasily, as if Stacy had just caught her spying; the boyfriend waved at her, smiling. Stacy came over and hugged her. The old couples were all slumped on the couch, wheezing from their efforts. ...But Stacy was smiling—and that smile told Vera that Stacy was fine. Everything Vera had feared was forgotten now, and she was overcome by a sense of relief. All at once, Vera laughed and whispered:

"So, this is what you do for a living?"

Stacy chuckled.

Presently, the boyfriend called to Stacy: "Do you know where the other battery pack is?" he said, gesturing to the camera.

"Yeah," Stacy said. "I saw it in the bedroom. I'll get it."

Vera followed her, if only so that she would be able to get away from the porn set. She remembered how she had been unable to reach Stacy all day. "I was worried about you," she started. "I left you a couple of messages."

"Oh, I totally forgot. I usually turn off the phone during filming. I guess I forgot to turn it back on."

"You could have still given me a call," Vera maintained.

Stacy looked back at her and smiled. "I listened to your show tonight. That entire 'Claim back your pussy' thing is going to be huge."

"Don't remind me," Vera said with a chuckle. She changed the subject: "How are your wrists?"

"No problems."

"I see they don't keep you from being a porn mogul," she joked. But then, she remembered the porn scene again: "What the hell was all that about? There's senior citizen porn now?"

"Of course—another one of my breakthroughs. Sex isn't just for the young and healthy. I have an entire geriatric porn series."

Vera's face creased: "You've been shooting porn all day?"

"I went out to shop earlier, then was filming on and off since about six."

"Those old people have been screwing since six?"

Stacy laughed. "I gave them a couple of breaks in between."

"Damn, that Viagra stuff really works!"

They both laughed.

In the bedroom, Stacy started looking for the battery pack. She checked the dresser drawers.

Vera waited by the side, before noticing a copy of her book on the nightstand. It was *10 Steps to Find Out if Your Man is a Cheating Bastard.* She smiled, walked over to the nightstand and picked it up.

"You've been reading my book?" Vera said, still smiling.

"Yeah, I was curious to see what bullshit you were selling to women."

Vera smiled. "Did you learn anything useful?"

"Yeah," she said sarcastically, "—you taught me how to fill three hundred pages with nonsense."

They both laughed. Vera said, "You're just jealous: writing a book full of nonsense is a difficult skill to master. The average writer lets her pride take over after a while, and finds herself trying to write something useful. It takes concentration and dedication to fill an entire book with nonsense."

Stacy eyed her, impressed either by her frankness or her sarcastic wit. She sobered. "When is your next book coming out?"

"I don't know. Maybe I'll write a book about our adventures."

Stacy smiled. "What will you call it?"

Vera thought about it for a few seconds, before smiling brightly. "I have the perfect title: *How to Kill Your Boyfriend (in Ten Easy Steps)*!"

Stacy nodded approvingly, smiling. But then she frowned. "What's with the ten steps?"

"It's all marketing. The good how-to books always list the number of steps—so that the reader won't be scared off by the prospect of having to think too much or work too hard. You never realized that?"

"I guess not," she said thoughtfully.

"It's all part of the modern American psyche," Vera revealed. "We've come to believe that we should be able to do everything in ten steps or less. Love and happiness and financial security are all ten steps away for the modern American. If we can make cars more efficient, then why can't we streamline our love lives? It's the new industrial revolution. How-to books do for relationships what Henry Ford did for the automobile."

"God," Stacy said with a shudder, "—don't tell me anymore."

They smiled.

After Stacy found the battery pack, they headed back to the porn set/living room. They were in the hallway when they heard a commotion in the living room. There was a loud thud, characteristic of a body hitting the ground. Vera looked at Stacy just in time to see her body go limp.

Vera managed to grab her, but as she was not expecting the weight, they both fell to the ground. Vera looked at Stacy's face: her eyes had rolled back in their sockets; her mouth was hanging open.

At that moment, Vera heard laughing coming from the living room. She yelled, "Help!" She waited about five seconds before yelling for help once more. Eventually, one of the old ladies came moseying down the hallway, a strange grin pasted on her face. She was still nude.

"Help me!" Vera screamed again, but the old woman's strange grin was still there. She almost tripped, and giggled again. From the way the old woman's eyes seemed unable to focus and stay open, it suddenly occurred to Vera that she was high. Seeing Stacy lying on the ground, the old woman giggled again.

"What's her deal?" the woman asked, staring at Stacy. "Is she fucked up, too?" Here, she giggled again, before looking into the distance dreamily and declaring, "That was some righteous weed, man!"

Vera had been waiting for help, but seeing what she had to work with, she cursed under her breath. She was still on the ground, entangled in Stacy's limbs. She disentangled herself, so that she could sit up and look at Stacy.

The old woman drawled, "We still got half a joint left. You look like you can use a few drags, to get your groove going." She giggled again; and then, with a far-off expression in her eyes, she repeated, "That was some righteous weed, man!" She looked at Stacy again, giggling. "Stacy's got the right idea, taking a nap."

Vera exploded: "She's not sleeping, you stupid old bitch—she passed out!"

"Huh?" the old woman moaned, no closer to comprehending. As Vera looked up at her, the old woman again swayed drunkenly, her sagging tits flopping against Vera's head. Vera had a sudden impulse to beat the old woman up, but just then, there was more drunken laughter from the living room.

"What's going on in there?" Vera asked.

"Oh," she said absentmindedly, "—her boyfriend fell down, too. That was some *righteous* weed."

When the old woman's words had registered in Vera's mind, she looked down at Stacy anxiously. "They both collapsed?" She felt Stacy's neck. The pulse was there, and seemed strong enough—but of course, Vera was not a medical doctor. The old woman swayed low once more, so that her tits again bumped into Vera's head. Vera gnashed her teeth to keep from going on an insane rampage and ripping the old woman's throat out!

"Maybe you guys should take off," Vera suggested. "Go home—I'll take care of everything."

"Take care of what?" the old woman said obliviously. She seemed on the verge of swaying again, and slapping her sagging tit into Vera's head—

"Just go!" Vera screamed, losing patience. "Get the hell out of here—*all* of you!"

The old woman seemed wounded. She whined, "You're killing my buzz, man."

Vera leapt to her feet, about to strangle the old lady. "Your buzz?" she screamed with an insane, murderous look in her eyes. "If you don't get the *hell* out of here...!" Vera brandished a clenched fist, and the old lady's eyes opened wide with sudden comprehension and fear. "*Now!*" Vera screamed, and the old woman nodded anxiously, turned on her heels clumsily, and fled back to the living room, her drooping ass swaying in a way that had Vera strangely engrossed for a moment. When the old woman was gone, Vera shook her head. She looked at Stacy again, trying to remember everything she could about treating someone who had fainted; at the same time, she panicked inside, wondering why Stacy and the boyfriend would collapse at the same time. It was while her mind was going on like this that Stacy began to regain consciousness.

"Stacy!" Vera whispered. Stacy opened her eyes, seeming confused and dazed. "Don't try to get up," Vera advised her. "Just lie there for a while."

"What happened?"

"You fainted."

"I fainted?" she said with a frown.

"Just relax for now. ...Your boyfriend fainted, too."

"My boyfriend?"

Just then, the old people appeared in the hallway. They all seemed grumpy now. The old lady must have told them all how Vera had killed her buzz. They were still nude, but had their clothes in their hands. There were some grumbles and evil looks as they began to file out of the door. The last person slammed the door. Vera was relieved that they were gone. She looked back at Stacy.

"Are you feeling okay?"

"Yeah, I'm okay. ...A little drained. I wonder why I fainted?"

"I don't know." She remembered the boyfriend. " ...Wait here for a while. Let me go and check on your boyfriend."

Vera jogged over to the living room/porn set. She gasped as soon as she saw him. He was staring blankly into space, and a mucus-laden froth was dribbling from his mouth.

"Oh my God!" She went to him and checked his pulse. As she put her hand to his neck, he blinked and seemed to regain consciousness. He frowned at her. She bent down, whispering, "Are you okay?"

"What happened?"

"I don't know. Do you feel okay?"

"...Dizzy, drained..."

"Don't try to move. Wait here."

She got up and ran back to Stacy. Stacy was looking more revived. The first thing Vera said was, "Stacy, something's wrong."

"Is he okay?"

"Something's wrong with both of you. I'm going to call an ambulance."

"No, we'll be fine."

"But, Stacy—"

Stacy shushed her. "Everything will be fine."

Vera shook her head uneasily. "Something's wrong. Both of you fainted at the same time."

"Everything's fine," she said again. She took a deep breath and smiled. Vera only stared at her, unconvinced. Stacy went on, "Help me up."

"Maybe you should just lie there."

"No, help me up."

"I'll bring you to the bedroom. You need to lie down until you regain your strength."

"If you wish."

Vera helped her up, then they shuffled over to the bedroom. She left Stacy on the bed. "Let me check on your boyfriend again," she said now.

She jogged back to the living room. "Are you okay?" she asked him.

"I'm getting there." He did look better. "What do you think happened?"

"I don't know, but it's not right. I wanted to call an ambulance, but Stacy said…" she faltered, not knowing how to finish the sentence.

"She's probably right," the boyfriend conceded. "I'm feeling better. …Help me up." She grabbed his arm and helped him to the couch, which still had stains from the old people's secretions.

"Can I get you anything—something to drink?"

"Yeah, that'll be good."

Vera went to the kitchen and got some orange juice out of the refrigerator. She filled two glasses. She brought one glass for the boyfriend, then brought the other to Stacy—who was sleeping when she got there. Vera looked at her uneasily. She wanted to check Stacy's pulse again, but of course, she had no idea what she was doing. Stacy and the boyfriend should be on their way to a hospital. This was not right at all. She walked back to the living room in a daze, wracked by nagging fears. To her amazement, the boyfriend was also sleeping. What the hell was going on? Vera stood there uneasily. She was trembling. She gulped down the orange juice she had poured for Stacy. She was still trembling—

Something began to chime loudly. She jumped, grabbing her heart, but then took a deep breath when she realized that it was only her cell phone. She had left the phone, and the handbag it was in, next to the front door. She went to it, still flustered. It suddenly occurred to her that the detective was probably calling her. She answered the phone eagerly:

"Holmes!"

"Holmes?" a woman said over a bad connection. Vera grimaced when she recognized the voice.

"Mom," she whispered.

"Who is this Holmes?" her mother demanded, "—your new boyfriend?"

Vera paused before she allowed herself to speak; the reality of her mother made her think of the geriatric porn stars. She cringed again. She changed the subject quickly. "Are you okay, Mom?"

"Am I okay?" she said rhetorically. "Of course I'm not okay. I listened to your show tonight!"

"God, Mom," Vera said with a groan.

"Such language!"

"I'm thirty-five years old, Mom."

"You don't think I can still take you over my knee, Lady V?" the woman asked, using Vera's childhood nickname. However, they were both chuckling now. Her mother could always make her laugh. "Anyway," her mother said at last, "what's bothering you?"

"What do you mean?"

"Something's bothering you—I could tell by your voice. What's wrong?"

"Nothing's wrong, Mom," she said, but as she did, she glanced back at the boyfriend, who was now snoring.

"Does it have to do with this 'Holmes' man?"

Vera laughed.

Her mother went on, "Don't think I forgot about that either."

"Nah, Mom, he's fine. Maybe you'll meet him one day."

"Hmm," she said, considering it.

"I really am fine, Mom."

"Well, you know where to reach me if you need to talk."

"I know, Mom. ...Maybe I'll take a vacation soon and come down to visit."

"You've been saying that for years now."

Vera smiled. "I know, Mom, but I mean it this time. ...Maybe I just need a break, that's all."

"Okay. I love you."

"I love you too, Mom." As she said it, she remembered Stacy's various rants on love versus need. She shook her head to chase away the thoughts.

After she finished the call, she put the phone in her pocket, then stood staring at the boyfriend. Common sense was still telling her to call an ambulance, but then she suddenly wondered if this was even something medical. She had seen so much over the last few days…The only thing that made sense to her now was that Stacy and the boyfriend were now joined somehow. Maybe there was some kind of psychic bond between them, joining their lives and their fates. The idea was preposterous when viewed objectively; it sounded like something that old hippie porn star would say, but that was when Vera remembered the details of Stacy's first suicide attempt. She remembered the one odd fact: the knife used to cut Stacy's wrist had been found in the kitchen, washed, and there had been no blood trail from the bed to the kitchen. All that could be explained if Stacy had unconsciously directed the boyfriend to kill her. The implications of that made her shudder. It made her feel as though there were something icy and disgusting within her.

She shuddered again. She did not want to pursue those thoughts too far. In fact, she knew that if she speculated too much about such things she would lose sight of everything. For now, she had to keep to the facts, and fact number one was that she had to keep an eye on Stacy and her boyfriend until she figured this all out. Fact number two was that doing so would be simpler if Stacy and her boyfriend were in the same room. She went to the boyfriend now, saying "Get up—let's get you to the bed-room." He seemed to rouse slightly, but did not open his eyes. She hauled him up by the arm, and he came compliantly. She put his arm over her shoulder and began to guide him down the hallway, to the bedroom. Once in the bedroom, she plopped him on the bed and raised his feet onto the bed. She took off his shoes, then Stacy's shoes. When that was done, she stood staring at them with the same uneasy feeling in her gut. Both of them seemed to be breathing steadily, but this was all wrong—she knew it.

She was just reconciling herself to the fact that she would have to stay up all night—in order to keep an eye on them—when the cell phone began to chime again. She ducked into the hallway, as to not awaken Stacy and the boyfriend. She looked at the caller ID this time, and was relieved.

"Hello, Holmes."

He was already laughing on the other end of the line. "That was an interesting show you had tonight."

She laughed uneasily. "Are you calling to curse me out, too? My mother just called me from Florida to ground me."

He laughed. "Anyway, you must be getting ready for bed."

"I'm at Stacy's."

"Oh? Is everything fine?"

She glanced back into the bedroom. "What makes you think something's wrong?"

"Only the fact that every time you're over there an ambulance or murder investigation is involved." He had said it jokingly, but there was no response from Vera's end, and he sobered. "Is everything okay?"

Vera was debating whether she should tell him. She was nibbling on her lower lip. At last, she blurted out, "Stacy and her boyfriend collapsed— I'm looking after them."

There was a pause. "They collapsed?"

"Yeah, they fell. I'm going to keep an eye on them for the rest of the night."

"Would you like me to come over?"

Vera turned and glanced into the bedroom once more: Stacy and her boyfriend were still sleeping on the bed. "...Yeah," Vera said into the phone. "Come over if you get a chance."

"Okay, I'll see you later."

After she put down the phone, she went to make herself some coffee. She was so anxious about things that she ended up rushing back to the bedroom a few times, in order to check on Stacy and the boyfriend. When the coffee was finished, she returned to the room and sat on the chair of Stacy's vanity. Eventually, she picked up one of Stacy's books (they were on the nightstand, next to *10 Steps to Find out if Your Man is a Cheating Bastard.*) She chose a cryptic science fiction book—about a creature that terrorized an expeditionary force that landed on a far-off planet. It was pretty typical, and she knew how it would end: the creature would pick them off one at a time, until the final person (the hero) either killed it or became lunch. About twenty pages into it, she found herself rooting for the creature; forty pages into it, she wished the creature would kill them quicker—that, instead of picking them off one at a time, it would just leap at them while they were holding one of their tedious meetings. Too bad science fiction creatures were rarely efficient....

Her cell phone rang when she was on page sixty-five. It was the detective. She looked at Stacy and the boyfriend anxiously as the phone rang, but they did not stir. She glanced at the alarm clock on the nightstand. It was three forty-eight. She went into the hall to talk.

"Where are you?"

"I'm downstairs."

"I'll be right down."

She glanced into the bedroom, to make sure that Stacy and the boyfriend were still sleeping peacefully. However, she was so wary of leaving them alone for long that she ran out of the apartment and down the stairs. The detective was standing directly outside the door when she opened it.

"Come!" was all she said. She held the door open only long enough for him to step in the door, then she ran back up the stairs. He followed her.

She had time to run to the bedroom and make it back to the kitchen before he got up the stairs. She turned on the lights. He was winded from the walk up the stairs:

"Sorry I couldn't come over sooner. For whatever reason, people kept getting killed in the city." There was a wry smile on his face.

"That was inconsiderate of them." She hugged him.

He was smiling when they detached, but then frowned as he watched her fidgety nature. "Why are you so on-edge?"

"I told you what happened with Stacy and her boyfriend—plus, I've drunk about six cups of coffee."

He grinned. "How are your friends? Still sleeping?"

"Yeah, but I have to watch them."

His frown deepened—

"Damn it, Holmes," she cut him off, "—don't play detective right now."

He laughed. "What do you want then?"

"Just stay here with me for a while. Convince me that the world isn't crazy."

"Too late for that: I spent the night going from crime scene to crime scene, looking at dead people."

She looked at him closely. "How do you stand it?"

"What?"

"Tonight, when that woman called me on my show and set me off...she pushed me over the edge. Don't you ever get pushed over the edge?"

"Going over the edge isn't always a problem, Vera. The problem is coming back once you've gone too far."

Vera thought about it for a while. She smiled. "Kiss me, Holmes. Help me to find my way back."

They kissed. She melted into him. Time seemed to fly past—

Someone cleared her throat conspicuously. They looked up to see Stacy standing there.

"Did I interrupt anything," she said, smiling.

"You're up?" Vera said, still basking in the dreamy aftereffects of the kiss.

"Yeah." She looked at the detective. "When did you get here?"

"I invited him over," Vera said, trying to head off any confrontation. And then, to change the subject, "How are you feeling?"

"I feel great. I feel like I've slept for a week. I'm reenergized."

Vera looked at her uneasily. "How's your boyfriend?"

"Snoring."

"Are you sure you guys are okay?"

"We're fine. You can go home if you want."

"But—"

"No buts, Vera. We're fine. Besides," she said with an insinuating smile, "you two look like you need some privacy anyway."

Vera blushed, realizing that she was still holding the detective.

"Go home," Stacy said again. "Everything's fine here."

The detective suggested, "My car is right outside."

Vera was still unsure.

"I'll call you later," Stacy said. "Go home—get some sleep...or whatever," she said, smiling again.

Vera sighed. "Okay, but expect my call. Turn your phone ringer back on."

"Yes, ma'am," she said with a mock military salute. She then bent down and picked up Vera's bag, which was still by the door. "Get home safely," she said, handing Vera the bag.

Vera was still preoccupied as she and the detective walked down the stairs to the car. She felt so anxious that she thought she would not be able to sleep that night. The six cups of coffee practically guaranteed that. However, soon after she sat back in the passenger seat of the detective's car, she found herself fast asleep. Her dream was a bizarre montage of women chanting, "Claim back your pussy!" and geriatric porn. When the detective roused her in front of her condo, she shuddered. He was standing outside, holding the door open for her. She looked around confusedly.

"We're here already?" she said.

"You'll be able to go back to sleep soon, sleeping beauty." He helped her out of the car and she leaned against him as they sauntered up to the door. Once she had opened the door for them, he whisked her into his arms and carried her the rest of the way. She was on the verge of sleep again when they were in front of her apartment. He put her down and she unlocked the door. He carried her to her bedroom and helped her into bed. The next thing she remembered was waking up in the morning. She was still in the same clothes. She looked around, but the detective was not there. She felt groggy. It was nine thirty-five. She groaned and closed her eyes. It occurred to her that her phone was ringing. It was still in her pocket. It had been muffled under the covers. She took the phone out of her pocket and looked at it. It was her agent. As soon as she answered the call her agent screamed:

"There you are!"

Vera was still groggy. "Huh?"

"Everyone's been calling me about you—the press, talk shows. They're saying you tapped into something amazing!"

"What are you talking about?" Vera sat up straighter on the bed, leaning against the headboard with a confused expression on her face.

"The entire 'Claim back your pussy' thing!" her agent said joyously. "They're saying it's a new movement."

"A what?"

"A *movement*. People are already printing out T-shirts! I had a couple shipped to me this morning."

Her agent's enthusiasm was suddenly annoying; Vera imagined the woman counting dollar amounts already. She groaned. "What do you want?"

"What do I want?" she said in disbelief, exasperated with Vera for not seeing the big picture. "This is the mother load, Vera! This is the moment we've been waiting for: media saturation; total iconic status…!"

Vera was frowning. "What are you expecting me to do?"

"Now is the time to hit the airwaves. I have you booked on two shows today!"

"Two shows? …When? …Where?"

"Don't worry about that. Just get ready. I'll have a car waiting outside your apartment in twenty minutes. Wear something casual yet stylish— that yellow pants suit will be perfect." She hung up the phone before Vera could ask her what the hell she was talking about. Vera stared at the phone, as if begging it to explain what had just happened. She vaguely remembered her agent saying something about a car and twenty minutes. She got out of bed and headed for the bathroom. She remembered Stacy. …She would call later, when she was in the car, driving to wherever her agent had booked her. She had a slight headache—a caffeine hangover— the aftereffects of six cups of coffee.

Thirty minutes later, when she finally made it downstairs, a limousine was waiting outside her condo. She got in. The driver could not tell her which show she was being taken to: he only knew the address. Vera remembered Stacy. She dialed the number. There was no answer. She did not want to go through this again. She tried not to surrender to her wild speculations: thoughts about Stacy and the boyfriend acting out some unconscious suicidal streak within Stacy. The idea seemed laughable in the light of day; and yet, Vera could have said that about her entire weekend.

Vera sat back in the seat and closed her eyes. The reality that she was on her way to a studio to do a talk show hit her suddenly. She remembered her agent's excited call, but still could not really grasp what had happened. She tried to will herself to understand how all this had happened. She tried to analyze the bizarre statement she had made on air. Was "Claim back your pussy!" really some kind of life-changing statement? She had no idea. All that she knew was that she was a hot commodity now. She knew she was supposed to be happy, but she somehow could not bring herself to be excited. Deep down, she knew that it was all silly. Whatever show she was booked on, she would have to pretend to be the over-the-edge woman she had been last night. She tried to remember what exactly she had said; she practiced the verbal rhythms she had used in her mind. …She was hungry, and her headache was worsening.

When she got to the studio, she realized that she was to be on the popular new talk show of an author named Zane—who specialized in erotica for women. Vera was to be the first guest. Her mind was numbed by the prospect of it, and yet what was there to do but go on with it? Soon, she was in the greenroom. There was food there, and she ate. And then, the show began. Zane introduced her by saying, "Here is the woman who told us all about the power of pussy!" Instantly, women started chanting, "Claim back your pussy! Claim back your pussy!"

Vera felt slightly dizzy as she entered the stage and hugged Zane. Then, she and Zane were talking. To Vera's amazement, people laughed at the things she said. She said things that were obviously nonsense, and yet people nodded as if she had said something profound—

"Yes, Zane, women do devalue the power of their pussies, it's time to take a stand and claim back the power of pussy."

Oh my God! she thought as she said it. It suddenly occurred to her that she was ripping off Stacy's Pussyman story, but the audience was giving her a standing ovation now. Women in the audience were jumping up in the aisles, giving one another high-fives, like men whose favorite football team had just scored. It went on and on like that. She surrendered to it, like a three dollar whore. …And then it was over, and Zane was hugging her and kissing her on the cheek as the audience gave her a rousing send-off.

As soon as she was offstage, she allowed herself to shudder, but there was no time to think. The limousine was waiting to take her somewhere else. When she was headed to another studio, her agent called again. The agent proposed an impromptu book signing for later that day. Vera said okay, if only so that she could hang up the phone. She groaned and sat back in the seat.

She was taken to a radio station for her next interview. She said many of the things she had said on Zane's show. The hosts were men, but they seemed to get off on a woman using "pussy" in a sentence. They giggled like little girls when she did. When that ordeal was over, she was rushed to a huge bookstore in midtown, where literally hundreds of women were waiting for her. She had no idea how the word had gotten out so quickly. Her hand cramped up after signing about twenty books, but she kept at it dutifully. They ran out of books before the line was exhausted. The women at the end of the line seemed disgruntled, but Vera talked to them and kept them from rioting, by promising to send them signed books through the store.

By now, it was 3 p.m. She left the bookstore and told the driver to take her home. She was exhausted, and yet amazed by the way everything had gone. Today should have been a dream day for her, and yet she felt unsettled—as if she were waiting for something horrible to happen. She remembered Stacy. She called her, but there was no answer. She cursed under her breath. Either Stacy had not turned on the telephone ringer, or something had happened. There was only one way to find out, and she nodded her head gravely before telling the driver to take her directly to Stacy's place. She sat back in the seat and closed her eyes.

It was only a thirty-minute drive to Stacy's place, but Vera fell asleep. Her dream opened up like an abyss, and she found herself in yet another montage of death and depravity. She saw Stacy lying dead and butchered; she saw the boyfriend's body lying off to the side like the scraps of a slaughterhouse. However, the most disturbing thing in all these scenes was Vera, herself. She saw herself gloating over it all—laughing out triumphantly as she held the bloody butcher knife. She awoke from this nightmare when the limousine driver called to her. She jumped in her seat and let out a yelp—like a dog whose tail had just been stepped on. The driver told her that they had arrived. She looked out of the car confusedly. Her headache had grown worse; when she got out of the car, she had a sudden urge to vomit. She leaned against the limousine for a moment, until the urge passed. She swayed slightly as she walked. She got out Stacy's keys and headed upstairs. At the apartment door, she stopped to listen. She made out laughter inside. Several people were laughing— a cascading chorus of laughter. Her spirits brightened. She decided to knock on the door, instead of opening it herself. She made out Stacy's laughing voice as it came up to the door. And then, the door was open. Stacy was standing there, laughing like someone who could not stop laughing. The other voices in the living room rose up like the laugh track of a bad television sitcom. Vera tried to smile—to surrender to the laughter, so that she could be one of them—but that was when she noticed the knife in Stacy's hand. There was blood on it. Vera froze as she stared at it; her mind went numb; her stomach tightened, and she just stood there, staring. That was when Stacy gestured with her hand for Vera to step into the apartment. Somehow, Vera found herself following Stacy's command. In all that time, the laughter had not stopped. Stacy held Vera by the upper arm and led her into the living room. The same four geriatric porn stars were there again, nude; and on the ground, the boyfriend lay naked and dead, his chest still bloody. When the others saw Vera's horrified face, they laughed harder. Several of them doubled over and collapsed onto the smelly couch. Vera looked back at Stacy, who had just slapped her back, like a drunk who had made an off-color joke. Vera stared at Stacy, noting the horrible highlights of her face. Stacy's once-sparkling teeth now seemed yellowish in the strange light of the porn set. Stacy was laughing so hard that there were creases at the corner of her eyes. Her skin seemed leathery and unreal. Vera's eyes widened with the creepy aware-ness that the woman standing before her was like a whole other entity from the one Vera had known. The woman before her now was out of control—a cackling beast. Vera looked down, to where the boyfriend's corpse lay on the ground; bewildered, her eyes traveled to the giggling porn stars, a couple of whom were rolling on the ground and pointing jokingly at her horrified face, as if it were some kind of clown mask. At last, Vera looked back at Stacy, her eyes pleading. What had Stacy done?

There were laugh tears dripping from Stacy's eyes now. While Vera was staring at her, Stacy made a mock stabbing gesture with the knife, so that the geriatric porn stars laughed louder, grabbing their sides. Vera saw it all then—the irreconcilable depravity of it. Stacy had finally ascended to her status of high priestess; the four old people were the loyal, faithful subjects that Vera could never be. The next thing Vera knew, she was fleeing from the apartment. They laughed louder as she fled—or maybe that was just how it seemed in her mind. The laughter followed her; it seemed inescapable, so that even when she reached the limousine and screamed for the driver to take her home, the demented laughter of Stacy's apartment continued to resound in her ears.

Her mind was numb by the time she got home. The limousine driver told her that he could take her to work later, and she nodded, barely understanding. Like a short-circuited computer chip, her mind was now incapable of processing anything. Several times, she had found herself hyperventilating. The limousine driver had stared back at her via the rear view mirror, asking her if she was okay. She had been too dazed to acknowledge him.

As soon as she got home, she took a shower. She needed to be cleansed—not only of the day's grime and sweat, but of the things she had seen in Stacy's apartment. In fact, the scene, in hindsight, seemed impossible. What had Stacy done? What had she become? Vera remembered how even Stacy's face had seemed different, as if some new creature had taken over.

When she was finished with the shower, her agent called her, talking in excited gibberish about how well Vera was doing, and about how more events were planned for later in the week. Vera agreed to everything without comment—again so that she could end the conversation quicker. When it was over, she turned off her cell phone. She realized that her hands were shaking. She flung herself on the bed; after a few moments, she found herself sobbing. She felt ashamed and stupid. In a strange sense, she felt as if she had just come home to find her husband screwing her best friend. ...Had she merely been jealous of the old porn stars? Maybe that was part of it—she felt replaced. And yet, there had been something horrible about Stacy. Vera remembered the unhinged laughter. They had all been mad. Even in their closest moments, she and Stacy had never laughed at the sight of boyfriend's corpse. The act had never been the subject of comedy...but then Vera remembered that first night in the back of the rental van: how Stacy had made jokes about the boyfriend's penis. That morbid streak had always been there. Vera nodded her head. Maybe, today, Vera had merely seen Stacy as she really was. Maybe the four laughing porn stars were an example of what Stacy had always wanted her to be. The thought was too horrible.

Vera closed her eyes and sobbed some more. Somehow, she must have sobbed herself to sleep, because she awoke an hour later, with the same groggy hangover feeling as that morning. Her headache had grown worse. Whatever nightmares or demented thoughts she had had in her sleep, were like an aftertaste in her mind. She felt sick. She had awakened in a pool of sweat. She went to the bathroom and showered again. Afterwards, she waited over the commode for a few moments, either expecting to throw up or wanting to. She had the sensation that there was something in her that she had to purge from her system.

When she returned to the bedroom, she saw her cell phone lying on the nightstand, and wondered if Stacy had called. Maybe Stacy had seen the error of her ways and had called to apologize. Anything seemed possible. She wished for it the way heartbroken women everywhere found themselves, in their weaker moments, wishing for the words that would allow them to forgive their cheating husbands and boyfriends. When she turned on the phone, there were five voicemail messages waiting. The first two were from her agent—more excited gibberish. Vera listened to each one for about three seconds before deleting it. The third message made her hair stand on end. She had been standing by the nightstand, but when she heard the third message, she sat down heavily on the bed, staring blankly into space.

"Help me, Vera!" the boyfriend's disembodied voice pleaded, "—I'm losing my mind...and Stacy's gone!" That was the entire message. He left another message two minutes later. He was crying into the phone now, saying: "I'm having these horrible thoughts…! I can't get them out of my head…!" Vera looked at the time on her alarm clock. He had called fifteen minutes ago.

She dialed the number to Stacy's apartment. The boyfriend answered on the first ring with a hopeful, "Stacy?"

"It's Vera. I got your messages."

"I can't find Stacy!" he cried. "And my head's full of these…these thoughts."

Vera remembered this all too well. She knew where this was going. The Pastranzo concert had only happened three days ago, but it seemed like a life lesson from her youth—from a bygone time of innocence and stupidity. She took a deep breath before continuing, "When did all this happen? What's the last thing you remember?"

He paused for a moment, thinking back. "…Everything's so jumbled. I woke up on the floor, naked. There was blood on me…and I had these thoughts about—"

"I'll be right over," she cut him off, knowing what his thoughts were. "Just wait there," she said, before disconnecting the phone.

She called the limousine driver to tell him to come and pick her up. Once that was done, she got dressed. She figured that she would go straight to the studio afterwards. …But after what? What was she going to do? The thoughts lay uneasily in her mind. She did not want to explore them too far, so she rushed her preparations. She ran out of the apartment with her blouse unbuttoned. She only realized it when she was riding down in the empty elevator. In the lobby, Mrs. Moore tried to interest her in a piece of gossip, but Vera only waved and ran out of the door. The limousine was waiting on the curb. She told the driver to hurry.

When Vera got over to Stacy's apartment, she rang the doorbell twice, but there was no answer. In her haste to get to the boyfriend, she had left her handbag in the limousine. She swore and went back to the limousine to fetch the keys. However, she left the bag in the vehicle, not feeling like carrying the entire bag upstairs. When she returned to the apartment and opened the door, the boyfriend was crouched in the corner of the living room/porn set, shivering. She ran over to him when she saw him there. He was unresponsive and dazed—catatonic. Vera saw that he had started to dress himself, but had only gotten around to his underwear. The left leg of his jeans was around his ankle. He had probably been putting them on when the catatonia struck. She shook him gently, and he shuddered and looked up at her.

"It's okay," Vera reassured him.

"Vera?" he said, frowning—almost looking as if he were going to cry.

"Yes, I'm here. You'll be fine." However, as she said it, she wondered if any of them was ever going to be fine again.

"Did Stacy come back?"

"No—I don't think so."

He shuddered and shook his head, staring up at her with a frown. "I keep having these thoughts!"

"Don't think about that now, sweetheart. Let's get you something to drink. Come on, get up."

He complied, but his face had a faraway expression, as if he were reliving all the terrible thoughts in his head. Once he was standing, Vera helped him to put on the other leg of his pants. When she zipped up his pants for him, and looked up at him, he was staring at her.

"What's happening to me?" he said in bewilderment.

"You're a little confused, that's all. There are strange thoughts in your mind. Don't allow yourself to give in to them. Will you promise me that? You have to fight them."

He nodded, but seemed no closer to comprehending. He nodded the way a dutiful child nodded.

Vera was walking him over to the kitchen now. She sat him down at the kitchen table, then got the orange juice out of the refrigerator. She remembered how she had gotten Stacy and the boyfriend orange juice the last time. She noticed Stacy's ice pick in the drainer at the side of the kitchen sink. It was placed among some spoons and forks. Vera shook her head, remembering everything that had happened over the last five days. ...Had it only been five days, or an entire lifetime? What she and Stacy had done to the boyfriend was criminal in every sense. Seeing this now, Vera knew that she had to get the boyfriend away from Stacy—the way an abused woman had to be extricated from an abusive relationship.

The boyfriend was sitting at the table with his back to her and his head bowed. She brought the glass of orange juice to him. She smiled to reassure him, and he nodded his head uneasily to acknowledge her and her kindness.

"Are you a native New Yorker?" she asked him now, if only to keep him from remembering everything that had happened to him. She sat down next to him.

"No," he said absentmindedly, "I'm from Maine."

"Is your family still there?"

"Yeah."

"Maybe you should go and visit them for a while—get away from all this."

He looked at her before nodding again.

That was when the plan came into Vera's mind—or, at least, that was when she allowed herself to acknowledge it. There was only one thing to do: kill the boyfriend one last time, tell him to forget Stacy and everything that had happened, and then send him home to his family. Vera rose from the kitchen table and went to the sink, taking hold of the ice pick. She was numb inside. She needed to be numb. She approached him from the back, raising the ice pick in the air—

"Agnes Smith!" he suddenly screamed out. He stood up abruptly, so that the chair was knocked out from underneath him. As he swung around, Vera instinctively hid the ice pick behind her back and retreated a step. He glared at her, with an expression that told Vera that she was too late. The psychotic break she had feared had come. He took an aggressive step toward her. "Agnes Smith!" he screamed again, the veins bulging on the side of his neck. "That was the bitch!" He looked like a monster, his eyes large, his teeth bared.

"What?" Vera managed to squeak.

He came over to her; in her terror, she got ready to stab him—for her own self-defense—

"That was the bitch who stole my cherry!"

"She did what?"

"She stole my goddamn cherry!" he ranted. "She was an old bitch, too, about your age. I was barely fourteen when she did it—I didn't know what the hell she was doing to me." Vera fumbled to say something. "—That *bitch*!" the boyfriend went on. "She had no business being with me!" And then, he stopped and frowned, looking at her closely. "Hey," he said, frowning, "you kinda look like her."

Vera shook her head, terrified.

He took a step closer to her, his eyes narrowing as he surveyed her face. "You sure you ain't related to that bitch? Your last name ain't Smith, is it?"

"No!" she pleaded.

"You sure?" he said in a low, ominous voice as he squinted.

"I'm sure!"

"Good, because if it was," he said, his voice rising explosively, "I'd snap your goddamn ne—"

He stopped in the middle of the word, looking down confusedly. Even Vera had not really known what had happened. Somehow, she had stabbed him in the chest. When she realized what she had done, she pulled it out. There was a stream of blood, and he swayed. He looked up at her in the same confused way as before the rant:

"Why, Vera?" he said then, his voice soft, his eyes pleading.

Vera was numb again. She looked at his chest—the stream of blood—suddenly realizing that she had stabbed him in the wrong side of his chest. She had stabbed him on the right side: the heart was on the left side. Now, he coughed as his lungs filled with blood. There was blood in his cough, and some of it flew onto Vera's face and clothes.

He looked at her pleadingly again: "Why, Vera?" By now, his words were gurgled by the blood. All at once, he lost his balance and collapsed forward. He landed hard on the ground, and lay prone, but he was still alive—suffering. A voice of panic told Vera to put him out of his misery. She compelled the numbness to take over her again, and then she stabbed him in the back. He screamed out horribly as she did it, his back arching. However, even then, he did not die. He went into convulsions on the ground—slow, agonized convulsions, so that the blood was painted over the floor in a masterpiece of performance art. It was revolting, and when he finally stopped moving, Vera felt the ice pick fall from her hand. She managed to catch herself in the process of fainting, and grabbed onto the kitchen sink. It was a good thing, too, because that was when she threw up.

A minute later, she was still slumped over the sink, washing her mouth and face. She was telling herself that the worst was over, and that all she had to do was reprogram the boyfriend when he came back to life. However, that was when she felt the boyfriend's hand grab her ankle. She screamed out! His grip was strong. He was looking up at her with the most agonized expression she had ever seen. She screamed again, and kicked him in the head with as much force as she could muster—so that he grunted and released her—and then she found herself fleeing. It was all too much for her—too much to take! She ran down to the limousine, almost toppling twice. As soon as she was in the limousine, she shouted at the driver, telling him to go. He started to drive her to work. …Vera's mind began to torture her with images of the boyfriend's death…but of course, he was not dead. He was still alive, suffering, spending his last moments asking why she had done it. It was too horrible!

She knew that there was no way she would be able to do a show tonight. She was a nervous wreck. Her hands were still trembling. She took out her cell phone and called the station manager. As soon as he answered the phone, she blurted out:

"I'm sick—I can't go on tonight."

"Vera?"

"Yeah. I'm not feeling well. Play a 'best of' show or something."

He sighed in disappointment. "But there's so much buzz about you… We've been getting calls all day."

"I just threw up," she said. "I'm *sick*. My head's…" She was about to describe her mental state, but faltered. "I can't do it," she said pleadingly.

The station manager sighed once more. "Okay." He began another sentence, but Vera disconnected the call. She spoke to the limousine driver then:

"Take me back home."

During her drive home, the thoughts would not leave her. When the boyfriend eventually died (somehow she imagined him still lying on the ground, suffering) …when he finally died, he would come back to life worse than ever. There would be no one there to tell him that everything was fine. Nobody would be there to make him forget all the horrible things that had happened. She had presumed to make things better—to play God with the boyfriend's life—but she had only made a bigger mess of things. She looked at her watch. It was not too late to go back…but she shuddered at the thought of it. She could not do it. She could not go back to that scene. She did not have the stomach to hold him as his corpse came back to life; she could not talk to him in the calm manner that Stacy would, giving him a hundred intricate directions on what he was to remember and what he was to forget. She would only make matters worse. She knew it. …Maybe Stacy was home by now. Maybe Stacy would get there in time and make things right. Vera had to wash her hands of it all. Stacy and the boyfriend were on a crash course with disaster, and Vera felt in her gut that she had to free herself of them before they dragged her down with them. She was running away as a coward, but she was honest with herself about what she could and could not do. The time for courage and integrity had passed: she had failed miserably. All she could do for now was accept that fact.

Whatever the case, she did not want to think anymore. She needed to sleep—to have a wonderful dreamless sleep. She still had some sleeping pills that her doctor had prescribed for her during a stressful, sleepless patch of her last book tour. She would take them when she got home and allow her thoughts and cares to fade away.

As soon as she got home, she went to the medicine cabinet and took two of the sleeping pills. They had probably expired months ago, but she did not care. She took them and went straight to bed. She was relieved as she felt the drug-induced oblivion of the sleeping pills taking hold of her.

The cell phone rang. It rang six times, before the call was automatically directed to her voice mail. She was aware of this vaguely. The drug-induced sleep was wearing off, but as she remembered all too well, the drug always left her feeling anxious. When the phone rang again, she jumped. She turned on the light. She had tossed her bag on the bed when she entered the apartment. She got out the cell phone and answered it.

"Yes?"

It was the detective. "Are you okay?"

She grimaced, remembering everything that had happened. "...I've been better." She glanced at the time, seeing that it was a little after 2 a.m. A hundred horrible scenarios flashed through her mind as she thought of all that could have happened to the boyfriend in that time. He had probably come back to life and gone on a rampage. She tried to convince herself that it was not her concern, but she was unable to delude herself this time. She felt her heartbeat picking up—growing erratic. She pulled away from the phone and inhaled deeply. When she put the phone to her ear again, the detective continued:

"I noticed that your show tonight was a repeat."

It took her a moment to realize what he was talking about. "I wasn't well," she explained.

He detected something in her voice and assumed it to be exhaustion. "Did I wake you up?"

"Yes."

"I'm sorry."

"No problem. I'm up now. ...Maybe I need to talk."

"I need to talk to you, too."

"About what?"

"Your friend Stacy."

Vera shuddered. "...What about her?"

"Her boyfriend's dead. We've been looking for her."

Vera was trembling; she sat up straighter. "...What did you just say?"

"Her boyfriend is dead."

"But he can't die."

There was a bemused tone to the detective's voice. "Everyone can die, Vera."

"But he *can't* die. This is all a misunderstanding."

He paused, confused, eventually putting her reaction down to grief. "I'm sorry to bring you such bad news—especially in the middle of the night. I guess you were close to both Stacy and her boyfriend."

Vera shook her head. This had to be a misunderstanding. The detective did not know the boyfriend's secret after all. She tried to think clearly, despite the groggy, anxious feeling that the sleeping pills had left her with. At last, something occurred to her. "Did you see his body?"

"Yeah, I was just at the crime scene."

"When did you see him last?"

"An hour ago."

"He was dead an hour ago?" she said, her face creasing.

"Yeah," he said jokingly, "and he's still dead."

Vera stared at her alarm clock, doing and redoing the math in her mind. "Do you know how long the body was dead?"

"Why do you care?"

"I'm just wondering," she said numbly.

"I think the coroner said about eight hours."

Vera's insides went cold; unconsciously, she pulled her sheet over her exposed shoulders. This had to be a mistake! The boyfriend could not die. He would come back to life...but he should have come back to life seven hours ago. It only took an hour and six minutes for his body to reanimate. Vera was nibbling her fingernails, trying to see some kind of escape hatch—

"Vera?"

She jumped. She had forgotten that he was on the phone.

"Are you still there?" he asked again.

"Yeah," but as she said it, it occurred to her that she had dropped the ice pick on the floor after she stabbed the boyfriend. Her fingerprints had been on them, and on the door. Her vomit had been in the sink, and she was pretty sure she had left Stacy's keys in the apartment somewhere. When the police checked the fingerprints, they would have an airtight case. On top of all that, the limousine driver had driven her there and seen her state when she ran from the building—

"*Oh my God!*" she whispered when she saw the extent of it!

"Vera?"

"I feel sick," she blurted out. "I gotta go." She disconnected the call and ran to the bathroom. Once she was in the bathroom, she dry heaved into the sink until some bile came spewing up. When she was done, and her stomach muscles felt shredded, she collapsed onto the floor, staring into space. ...Had she really done it? Had she really killed a man...?

Maybe half an hour passed. Maybe it was longer. Vera returned to bed and lay there in a daze. Eventually, the buzzer for the intercom sounded. It sounded four times before Vera realized what it was. Someone was waiting outside for her. She was not in the state of mind to see anyone about anything, but she felt, somehow, that it did not matter anymore what she wanted. If she had really killed a man, then there was no point resisting whatever was to come. She expected it to be the police. Maybe the detective would come for her personally. She got up and walked over to the intercom. Her legs were unsteady. She swayed from side to side, then leaned on the wall, facing the intercom. She pressed the button to speak to the person outside: "Who is it?"

"It's me—Stacy."

Despite what she had resolved in her mind, about not resisting what was to come, Vera gasped and backed away, staring at the intercom as if it were Stacy. Vera was trembling again. However, the impulse to flee passed, and she went to the intercom again, pressing the button:

"What do you want?" she said too loudly—as if trying to convince Stacy that she was not terrified.

"Vera, please—let me in. We have to talk."

"What do you want?" she said again, her voice quieter now—cowed.

"I know what you did to my boyfriend."

Vera could not move. The words seemed to echo in her mind.

Stacy went on, "Let me in, Vera. We need to talk."

"The police are looking for you!" Vera screamed, even though the statement seemed unconnected to anything. Maybe she wanted to scare Stacy away.

Characteristically, Stacy chuckled. It sounded otherworldly over the static of the intercom. Vera shuddered again—

"Let me in, Vera," Stacy said; and then, "You *need* me."

Those strange words, which Stacy had been using since the beginning, finally made sense to Vera. The full extent of her situation hit her again—how she had dropped the ice pick on the kitchen floor; how she had left the keys (with her fingerprints on them); how the limousine driver had seen her...She saw the limousine driver in the dock at her trial now, describing how she had run from the place....Yes, Vera needed Stacy. That was plain. If there was any hope of her getting out of this, then she needed Stacy. Moreover, if the case was already hopeless—and Vera could not help thinking that it was—then there was no point in avoiding whatever was to come.

Vera stared at the intercom for a few more seconds, and then she pressed the button, to open the door.

Vera left the door open for Stacy, and sat down on the couch, waiting for Stacy to enter. The reality of her entrapment hit her again, and she grabbed her head in her hands. She was in this position when Stacy entered. She looked at Stacy when she came in, comparing the serene face she now saw with the cackling maniac she had seen that afternoon. She stared at it in bewilderment, wishing somehow that that serene expression would somehow portend her salvation. Stacy smiled at her and walked over to her, sitting down as though nothing had happened.

Stacy said: "Are you okay?"

Vera stared back at her as if not understanding. At last, she shook her head: "No, of course not." And then, she found herself rambling on, as if she were compelled to account for herself: "...After you killed him this afternoon, he called me over. You didn't tell him a story when he came back to life, so his mind fell apart again. He said you weren't there." She was talking even faster now, seeming on the verge of tears. "...I killed him," she said at last, "…but he didn't come back! They say he's *dead*!" she broke down, looking at Stacy with tears in her eyes. Stacy hugged her.

"It's okay, Vera. It had to happen sooner or later."

When they detached, Vera looked at her confusedly. "What had to happen?"

"His death. You saved me by killing him."

Vera's face creased. "What do you mean?"

Stacy looked at her and smiled wider. "My boyfriend was never immortal, Vera."

"But I saw—"

"You saw him coming back to life after we killed him. That's all you know to be fact. He was never immortal."

"Then how…?"

"You know how, Vera."

Vera stared at her; her eyes finally grew wide when the answer occurred to her. "It was *you*."

"Yes, it was always me. Every time he died, I was there. I was the one that gave him life. When you killed him without me, he could not be brought back to life, because I wasn't there to hold his soul."

Vera could only stare. About ten seconds of silence passed. Vera relived everything in her mind, seeing that what Stacy had said was true. Stacy had been there every time. It had always been Stacy.

"I can store souls within me," Stacy explained again.

"But *how*?" Vera asked, bewildered.

Stacy smiled. "You're still asking the wrong questions, Vera."

"Damn it, Stacy!" Vera screamed in frustration.

Stacy laughed at her. "…Anyway," Stacy said after her laughter died down, "You saved me, Vera. If you hadn't killed my boyfriend, I would still be the raving lunatic you saw a few hours ago."

Vera's face creased again: "…I don't understand."

"Didn't you notice how unstable I got over the last few days?"—Vera nodded her head—"Every time I killed him, a piece of him stayed with me. I had all his thoughts and memories in my head. After a while, so much of him was in me that I lost myself—lost sight of reality. When you killed him without me, he was purged from my system."

"You don't care that he's dead?"

"I needed him, Vera," Stacy said simply, "but this was never about him and me. This was always about you and me."

Vera did not understand at all. There was even a side of her that did not want to know. She looked away and shook her head. The reality of everything hit her once more, and she sat back heavily. "Either way, the police have an airtight case against me," she said then. "I left all that evidence behind when I killed him."

"I know," Stacy said nonchalantly, "—I was the one that called the police."

Vera's frown deepened. "But, *why?*" she said, feeling betrayed.

Stacy smiled. "Relax, Vera. It's not what you think."

"What am I supposed to think?"

"No one will ever suspect you, Vera."

"But I left all that evidence! I left the bloody ice pick…my keys with my fingerprints. I even left my vomit in the sink!"

"I took care of it."

"What? …You did? I don't understand."

"The police will find evidence, but it won't point to you."

Vera stared, unable to understand. Stacy revealed:

"Everything will lead to the senior citizen porn couples."

"But why?" She did not want to be implicated, but she did not want to frame anyone else either.

"Don't worry about it, Vera. The case will never hold up."

"Why not?"

"For one thing, they're totally insane. I killed and reprogrammed them earlier," she went on in the usual matter-of-fact way; Vera's eyebrows raised. Stacy explained: "When they came back to life, I told them everything to say and do. In ten minutes, they'll be found running naked down the street; when the police question them, they'll rant and rave and say things that will put them at the scene of the crime. Their fingerprints will be found on all the evidence. It will look like some kind of orgy gone wrong."

"But they'll be sent to prison," Vera pointed out. "They'll *die* there."

Stacy shook her head. "They were already dead, Vera."

"What do you mean?"

"When I realized that I had this power to bring people back, I discovered that I could sense when people were going to die. That's where I disappeared to on Monday. I was amazed by the power. It was as if some force were calling me—leading me to them. I went out to their neighborhoods and knocked on their doors. I'd be right there when they had their heart attacks or stokes. When they came back to life, it occurred to me that I could make porn stars out of them."

"Goddamn," Vera whispered.

Stacy sniggered. "I'm not saying I was entirely sane at the time. Anyway, they were already dead; with the madness I programmed into them, they'll be sent to an insane asylum, not prison. I gave them instructions to revert to their old selves once that happens, so that their stay should be a short one."

"It still doesn't seem right, Stacy. I was the one who killed your boyfriend. I can't have anyone else in jail for even ten seconds if I'm the guilty one."

"But you're not guilty, Vera. Technically, my boyfriend was already dead. He died when he fell off that ravine. Everything else was like a daydream. You killed a corpse. The people about to be picked up for your 'crime' are corpses."

That still did not seem moral to Vera, but she had to admit that she was relieved. Stacy was smiling at her when she looked up; Vera was suddenly desperate to believe in that smile.

"Are you sure it's going to work?"

"Of course."

Vera remembered something else: "What about you? The police are looking for you. How will you explain your absence?"

"I won't have to. After forty-five minutes of pointless police interrogation, the old couples will let it slip out that they have me tied up in the trunk of their car. They'll tell the police where they parked the car, and when the police finally track down the car, they'll find me bound and gagged."

"Huh?"

"That's where you come in," Stacy said with a smile. "Are you up to it?"

"Yeah, I guess."

"Good. Let's get going."

The old people's jalopy was waiting outside Vera's condo. Stacy handed her some latex gloves, then she put on a set of her own. They got in the car, and Stacy drove them to an even more secluded section of Vera's neighborhood. As always, Vera was amazed by how detail-oriented Stacy was—how she accounted for every last concern. A sense of relief was creeping into Vera now. Stacy was saving her life. In a way, they were both starting afresh; and Vera, in that moment, would do anything for her. Once Stacy parked the car on the curb, they got out of the vehicle and walked to the back. Stacy opened the trunk and took out a roll of duct tape.

"Bind my ankles and hands with this," Stacy commanded.

Vera worked quickly; the blocks were empty, but she could not help thinking that someone would come along and see them. Once Stacy's ankles and hands were bound, and she was leaning against the trunk to keep her balance, Stacy commanded, "Rip off a strip and put it over my mouth."

Vera ripped off the strip, but she faltered. "…Thanks, Stacy. I don't know what to say."

"You didn't kill him, Vera," Stacy said abruptly, as if seeing into Vera's soul. "Don't let any of this bother you."

Vera again stared at her hopefully.

Stacy repeated: "He died when he fell down that ravine a week and a half ago. The rest of it was just make-believe—a passing dream."

Vera was desperate to believe. She was desperate for the burden to be lifted. She nodded at last, wanting to bask in her newfound sense of relief. It was like a religious experience: a sudden sense of faith that Stacy would take care of everything. Soon, they would be able to start afresh. She hugged Stacy then. It was awkward, because Stacy's arms were bound. Stacy laughed at her.

"Okay, let's get going," Stacy said at last. "Do you remember where I told you to park the car?"

"Yes," Vera said, remembering what Stacy had told her on the elevator ride down in her building.

"Good. Take off my gloves. Throw them and yours away once you've parked the car."

Vera nodded, again marveling at Stacy's attention to detail.

"Okay," Stacy said at last. "Let's do it. I'll see you in the morning." She winked, before gesturing to the strip of tape in Vera's hand. Vera took a deep breath and placed the duct tape across Stacy's mouth. Once that was complete, Vera helped her into the trunk. She stood staring down at Stacy uneasily for a few seconds before she closed the trunk. The sound of the slamming trunk left her with a feeling of urgency. She rushed to the driver's seat and drove off. Initially, she drove too fast, overcome by fears that Stacy would run out of air, or that the police would reach the intersection before she got there. She took another deep breath.

"Calm down," she told herself. She eased her foot off the accelerator, realizing that she had to drive casually, in case she drew the attention of a police officer and got pulled over. It was always the little things that got criminals caught....

She drove for about twenty minutes—to a commercial neighborhood in Queens, near the Pulaski Bridge. She parked and looked around. Nobody was near. She got out of the car and walked away as casually as she could. Her heart was beating savagely. She walked half a block before she glanced back. However, when she did, she chastised herself for doing so. It would only draw attention to herself. In her mind, every dark window held a spy, who would be there when the police arrived, to report that a strange woman had stepped away from the car only a few minutes ago (not the old porn couples).

About a block away from the car, there was a dark warehouse; she ducked into the shadows of the doorway, staring down the block at the car. Five minutes passed. She knew not to expect the police for at least another half an hour, but any time she saw a car coming down the street, she expected it to be the police. She would feel her stomach tighten....

She started to bite her fingernails. She had to take a walk to burn off some energy. She walked down another block, then two more. She kept looking at her watch. Eventually, she told herself that she would walk for fifteen minutes, and then she would turn back. She was hungry. After all this was done, she would eat like a hungry animal. ...She remembered the boyfriend. Regardless of what Stacy had said, she knew that she was responsible. She had killed a man....She felt sick again. She looked at her watch. There was another five minutes to walk. She was nearing the 59th Street Bridge. She did not feel well at all. She sat down on a tenement stoop for about half a minute, but then moved on when her restlessness got the better of her. If her stomach were full, she knew that she would throw up. A young man passed her on the street, looking at her curiously—or so it seemed to her. She picked up her pace, until she was practically jogging. She glanced over her shoulder, but the man was long gone. She was a nervous wreck. She knew she could not keep this up for long. She looked at her watch again. Mercifully, the fifteen minutes had passed, and it was now time to head back. She forced herself to walk slowly, so that she could waste some more time. In truth, even though she was restless, she did not have the energy to walk quickly anyway. In time, she again found herself wondering if Stacy might be suffocating in the trunk. It was a hot night: it was probably like a furnace in the trunk. And then something truly horrible occurred to her: what if Stacy died, too? ...But could Stacy die? Vera remembered the things Stacy had told her in the apartment—about being some kind of receptacle for souls. Vera remembered the conversation vaguely; she realized that she had not really questioned Stacy about it. She had not asked Stacy when she realized she had this gift or curse, or whatever it was. Vera had been too stunned at the time. All she had been able to do was store the words away. Now, as she walked the last few blocks back to the car, she vowed that if they made it out of this, then she and Stacy would have to talk. She tried to think up some questions, but she soon came to the conclusion that her mind was too frayed. There were too many potential horrors in the present to speculate about what would happen in the coming days.

It was then that a police cruiser rushed past Vera, its emergency lights flashing. The cruiser's sirens were not on—probably as a courtesy to the people sleeping in the surrounding buildings. Besides, there was little traffic. Vera ducked into the same shadowy warehouse doorway and looked at the scene unfolding a block away. Two more police cruisers entered the block almost simultaneously. One came down the wrong side of the road. Soon, the old people's jalopy was spotted, and all three cruisers converged on it. Vera sighed. The first step was complete.

Three sets of police officers went to the car and began examining it with their flashlights. Eventually, one knocked on the trunk and listened closely. He called the others over, and they listened. There seemed to be a consensus that someone was in there, because they became more animated. Vera figured that they would break the window and release the trunk lever, but they waited, probably fearing a bomb or some other unpleasant surprise. Another five minutes passed. Two more police cruisers arrived. The officers began to talk. A news van rolled up and began filming. Seven minutes later, what looked like a bomb squad pulled up; the other officers backed away as the squad went to work. There was a tense moment when the trunk was opened; but once it was, about ten police officers surrounded the trunk. Vera had to crane her neck to see. She held her breath, waiting and hoping; but then she saw Stacy, and smiled, feeling relieved. Step two was complete. Soon, Stacy was shepherded into the back of a police cruiser. When that cruiser drove off, most of the other cruisers left. Two officers stayed behind to secure the old people's jalopy. Vera sighed in relief again.

However, that was when it occurred to her that she had no way to get home. She had not taken any money with her, so she could not take a cab. It probably would not be a good idea to take a cab now anyway, as the driver would be able to place her at the scene. She began to walk. Now that all she had to do was wait and hope that Stacy's plan worked, she felt even more restless. Maybe walking was the best thing for her.

Vera did not want to think about it. She remembered that the latex gloves were in her pocket. She had not thrown them away yet. She tossed them into a trash can now, feeling good that she had at least followed Stacy's instructions. The rest was up to fate....

Vera walked slowly, but it was good to walk. The sun was coming over the horizon when she arrived back at the condominium. Just as she was about to turn into the walkway to her building, a car stopped on the curb. The detective got out and called to her. She stared back at him, stunned and wary.

When he was close, she said, "What are you doing here?"

"I called you about ten times tonight. When I didn't get you…" He did not finish the sentence.

"You were worried about me?" she said with a wary smile.

"Yeah," he said with a sarcastic smile, "—the members of your social circle are dropping like flies. I had to check up on you."

Her heart skipped a beat. "Did something happen with Stacy?"

"We found her. That's what I was calling you about."

"Is she okay?"

"Sure. Apparently some old freaks killed her boyfriend. It's a long story, but we found Stacy tied up in the trunk of their car."

Vera stared at him, unable to move or think. She found herself saying, "Why'd they do it?"

"I guess they snapped or something after shooting one of their pornos." He could not help laughing here, even though he immediately realized that it was in bad taste. "Anyway, they stabbed the boyfriend, kidnapped Stacy and tied her in their trunk. We found them running down the street, naked. They are already being shipped to an insane asylum."

"So, Stacy's okay?"

"Yeah."

"Good."

He looked at her closely now. "What are you doing outside?"

"I couldn't sleep after you called. I went out for a walk…to burn off some energy."

He nodded, then looked at his watch. "Well, I just wanted to know that you were okay."

Seeing that he intended to leave, she hugged him. The hug lingered, until they were standing there for over half a minute. Vera suddenly felt safe and at peace. She looked up at him: "Do you have to go back to work?"

"Yeah—my desk is piled high with paperwork."

"Can it wait for later?" And then, caressing his chest, "—I need you, Holmes."

He stared down at her, and then smiled when he divined her intention. "I think I can spare some time for you."

They walked up to her door, arm in arm.

Vera fell asleep after they were finished making love. She fell asleep with the sense of relief that came from knowing you were loved. However, the dream seized her the moment she was unconscious. At first, she thought the dream was about the boyfriend. She was out in the woods somewhere—deep in the middle of nowhere. She had a shovel in her hand. When she looked down, she saw the half-covered corpse of a man. In the dream, or whatever it was, she was filling the grave. She thought it was the boyfriend's grave she was filling, but the last uncovered part of the man's body was his hand; and when she looked closer, she realized that it was the hand from her previous vision—the bloody, menacing hand!

She woke up terrified and confused. The dream had only seemed to last a few seconds; but looking at the clock, she realized that she had been asleep for three hours. She remembered the detective. She knew he had left, but she called to him, terrified and hopeful. When there was no reply—except for the lonely echo of her own voice—she wanted to bury her face in the pillow and sob. That was when she realized that the intercom was ringing. She glanced at the clock again. It was about eight-twenty. Her legs felt numb and stiff as she walked over to the intercom. She remembered all her walking—everything that had happened last night....

She answered the intercom by pressing the button.

It was Stacy. "Hey, Vera. It's me."

"Stacy," Vera whispered, still dazed. "Are you okay?"

"Yeah." Then, with a laugh, "Are you going to let me up?"

"Oh, I'm sorry." She pressed the button to let Stacy up. She wished that the detective were here. However, it occurred to her that if he knew what she had done he would put her in jail. They were on opposite sides of the law now. This had never really occurred to her before....

Stacy entered the apartment, beaming. Vera was in the living room, waiting for her.

"Didn't I tell you that everything would work out?" Stacy rejoiced.

Vera stared at her anxiously. "...Don't you miss your boyfriend?"

Stacy sighed before she shrugged. "...Don't take this the wrong way, but I'm glad he's gone. I'm *relieved.*"

Vera groaned and shook her head. She sat down on the couch, as if she had lost her strength.

"You don't understand how it was," Stacy tried to explain. "He was inside of me—twenty-four hours a day. The first time he died, I felt all his thoughts—all his memories...his deepest fears. He was like a disease inside of me. I didn't know what was happening at first. I thought I was losing my mind. Maybe I was. ...And when I fell asleep, I would dream his dreams—his nightmares, his deepest desires...all his casual, everyday thoughts—like what he liked for dinner and which movie actress he would fantasize about while he was having sex with me. Every time I killed him, it only got worse."

Vera remembered the old porn couples that Stacy had killed. She began, "Those old people you killed—aren't they inside of you now as well?"

"Yeah, but I can handle it."

"If you couldn't handle twenty-two years of your boyfriend's memories, then how are you going to deal with the memories of four seventy-year-olds?"

"I can handle it," she said flatly.

Vera looked at her skeptically: "How many people can you hold inside of yourself at one time?"

"I don't know."

"Eleanor," Vera blurted out, suddenly realizing something.

"What?"

"Eleanor—the porn star who broke her neck when she tumbled down your staircase—you could have saved her if you wanted."

Stacy groaned. "Why are you bringing up that nonsense?"

"You could have saved her."

"I could have, but I didn't, okay? I can't save everyone. And I feel no obligation to save people who try to kill me."

"Okay," Vera said weakly. She remembered what she had vowed to ask Stacy the night before:

"How long have you had this…this power?"

"I don't know. I think I've always had it, but I was never around a dying person before my boyfriend. If he hadn't slipped off that cliff, I'd probably never know."

Vera was staring at her suspiciously now. "Are you telling me everything, Stacy?"

"What do you mean?"

"You lied to me before, Stacy. You told me your boyfriend was immortal."

"I thought he was at first. I didn't know what was happening."

"When did you figure out that you were doing everything?"

"I don't know. Most of the last two weeks is a blur to me; even now, I'm realizing new things all the time. …It's like years passed between when my boyfriend first slipped off that cliff and today. …Remember how, when you were a kid, you believed in Santa Claus, and then, years later, when you knew better, you looked back on it, amazed that you had believed? That's how I am now. I don't think I was being dishonest with you, Vera. I just didn't know what was going on. Half the things I would have sworn to last week are silly to me now. Now that my boyfriend's gone and I don't have him inside of me, I can see everything clearly."

Vera sighed. "…What am I supposed to believe, Stacy? How can I trust you if your entire frame of reference can change in a few hours?"

"You can believe in what I'm saying now, Vera," Stacy said with a hopeful smile. "The only thing that matters is the present. The past is always a fantasy, Vera. The past is just our present hopes and fears projected backwards. The future is our present hopes and fears projected forwards. All that there is, is the present. The present is the only moment when we can ever really see things as they are; and even then, half the time, we lie to ourselves."

Vera stared at her for a few moments before she sighed again. She had forgotten how Stacy talked—the way the words could overwhelm you.

Stacy continued, "Trust me now, Vera—you're all I have left. When all this happened, and I realized what had happened with my boyfriend, you were the only one I knew I could turn to. Since the beginning, you were always the only one. Since I heard your voice on the radio, I knew that I could count on you—that I needed you."

Vera nodded, but still looked pensive.

Stacy ventured, "How are you holding up?"

"I don't know yet. ...I had a nightmare just now...maybe not a nightmare, but a vision. I thought it was about your boyfriend, but someone else was in it." She shook her head now, realizing that she had no definite proof of this. "...I don't know. Everything's a mess. I don't think I'll ever be able to get over what I did."

"Like I said, the past is just a fantasy—a nightmare in your case. ...And I told you before that you didn't kill him. Technically, he was already dead before you even met him."

Vera shook her head. "My conscience doesn't care about technicalities, Stacy. I'll never be able to forget it. If I were my own patient, I'd tell myself to turn myself in. ...But who'd believe all the things that happened—all the things we did?"

Stacy was looking at her with concern. "No good can come of those thoughts, Vera. You have to get them out of your head. Forget what happened, or it'll destroy you."

Vera was again going to tell Stacy that she would never forget, but she faltered. Eventually, she nodded noncommittally. She suddenly wanted to be alone.

"Maybe I need to get some sleep," she said as a hint to Stacy. Stacy understood, and rose to leave.

"We'll talk later," Stacy said.

"Yeah," Vera said, getting up. They hugged before Vera saw her to the door.

The days passed in a slow, torturous manner. Vera tried to return to work and lose herself in the entire "Claim back your pussy!" phenomenon. She sleepwalked through the shows and interviews and book signings, but she did so in a demonstrative, high-energy manner that was unnoticeable to her fans. It was as if a wise-cracking demon took over her as soon as she got on air. All the phone lines were now jammed on her show; every other fan seemed to greet her with "Claim back your pussy!" Vera was both grateful for it and disillusioned by it.

The first time she lied to Stacy, and told her that she was too busy to meet for something to eat, she attributed the entire thing to exhaustion. However, by the third time she made an excuse to avoid seeing Stacy, she was forced to admit to herself that she would never again feel comfortable around Stacy. Stacy would always be a reminder of her crime. Vera hoped that she would eventually forget, but the memories seemed to be branded on her soul. They popped up and confronted her at all hours of the day and night. They occupied her dreams and daydreams; and, as Stacy had warned her, they were driving her crazy. To soothe her mind, and help her forget, Vera saw more of the detective. Only disappearing into the pleasure of their meetings seemed to give her a respite from her thoughts. She would prolong their sexual sessions until he seemed on the verge of passing out. She too would be exhausted and numb, but she would keep grinding against him, trying to ring one last drop of forgetfulness (not necessarily pleasure) out of his body. She knew it was not healthy, but she could not help herself. It was the same way that the addict knew that the drug was killing him, but could not stop.

Then, one morning, after about two weeks of these strange sufferings, she woke up and realized that she felt great. Her happiness was sudden and powerful, like a drug spreading through her veins, banishing all the pain. She got out of bed and looked around confusedly. She felt refreshed—almost high. She tried to think back—assuming that something had happened the previous day that would explain her mood—but her memories seemed suddenly spotty. Oddly, she could not remember what she had done yesterday. She frowned. Maybe she had been working too hard. Either way, the phone rang at that moment. She got out of bed and went to her cell phone. It was Stacy.

"How are you feeling?" Stacy asked.

"Great!" Vera replied. For whatever reason, she felt excited to be talking to Stacy. A feeling of sisterhood spread throughout her. Before she could think about it, she blurted out, "What are you doing today? Let's hang out." The words surprised her, but once they passed her lips, she found herself thinking that they were right: that there was nothing else she could have said.

Stacy chuckled. "Sure. Let's have lunch."

"Come over now—we'll go out to eat."

"Okay. I'll be right over."

When Stacy hung up the phone, Vera stood there wondering what had happened. ...But she felt great. Her body had reacted to Stacy the way a flower reacted to the sun. She felt herself opening up; whatever beauty had been trapped inside, she now felt expanding. It did not make sense, but for once she did not want to question things. She wanted to let her beauty out and revel in this newfound sense of freedom.

She went and took a shower. The water was warm and good, and she sang at the top of her lungs, making up her own words to songs. She was still smiling when she came out of the bathroom. The phone rang. She leapt playfully onto her bed and answered it.

It was the detective. "Where have you been!" was the first thing he said. "I've been worried sick about you."

Vera frowned. Her reaction to the detective's voice was visceral. She felt as though something had crawled up into her and died. She was so stunned that she could not speak.

The detective spoke up again: "Are you there?"

She took a deep breath: "Yeah, I'm here."

"Where have you been? I've been trying to contact you for the last two days."

She paused again. "...The last two days?"

"Yes, nobody had any idea where you were—even at the radio station. I was getting ready to put out a missing person's report on you."

She stared into space, lost. "You say I've been gone for two days?"

"Yes!" he said, growing annoyed with her confusion. He took a deep breath to calm himself. "You weren't at the apartment. I checked everywhere. I tried calling your friend Stacy, but all she did was tell me to leave her alone."

Vera tried to think back. Two days? ...What had happened yesterday? What had happened the day before that? A cold, creepy feeling came over her.

"Vera?" the detective called to her again. Somehow, the sound of his voice—the very reality of him—still sickened her. She frowned deeper, totally lost and bewildered. "—*Vera?*"

"Yes...I'm sorry. This is all so...strange. You say I've been missing for two days?"

"Yes," he said, fighting not to grow annoyed again. However, then, his voice softened. "You have no idea where you were?"

She took another deep breath. "No...I just got up in my bed."

"You seriously have no idea where you've been for the last two days?"

"No."

There was a long silence. Either he doubted her and was angry, or he was trying to figure things out. She began:

"Jonathan"—as she said it, she realized that it was the first time she had called him by his real name; she wanted to call him Holmes, so that they could be close again, but it seemed too late for that. Somehow, their intimacy was gone—ruined. "...Did we have a fight or something?" she asked him now, wondering about her sudden coldness toward him.

"No," he said in bewilderment, "—everything was great. ...You just disappeared. We were making plans to go away for a few days, but then you just disappeared."

The intercom buzzed. Vera knew that it was Stacy. "I have to go," she said to the detective. He started to say something, but she disconnected the call. She walked over to the intercom and pressed the button to talk.

"Stacy?" she said.

"Yeah, it's me," Stacy said in a chipper voice. To Vera's amazement, the same joyous feeling came over her as when she had heard Stacy's voice over the phone. Despite that, she frowned. She knew it was not right. She pressed the button to let Stacy in. Something was wrong. She left the front door ajar for Stacy, then she went to the couch and waited. Her thoughts moved through her mind sluggishly, but there was only one logical explanation for what had happened to her.

By now, a couple minutes had passed. Stacy poked her head through the doorway, a playful smile on her face. Vera stared at her, trying to resist the joyous feeling that took possession of her and made her want to run to Stacy and hug her. She forced herself to remain seated, and to look away. Stacy noticed her reaction. She stepped into the apartment and closed the door behind her. She walked up to Vera and stood about a yard from her.

"What's wrong?"

Vera opened her eyes and looked up at Stacy's beautiful face. She took a deep breath. "You did it to me, didn't you? You *killed* me and made me forget." She was winded after she said the words. She had blurted them out, as if fearful that they would not come.

Stacy stared down at her. She opened her mouth to say something, but then closed it, unsure. She looked off into the distance, a worried, tearful expression coming over her face. "It was the only way."

Vera got up abruptly and took a step away from Stacy. She *fled.* "What do you mean it was the only way?"

Stacy followed her, putting out her hands plaintively. "I had to do it— you were falling apart. You kept thinking about my boyfriend."

"You killed me!" Vera screamed, still backing away.

"You were suffering. I did it for you."

"You did it for yourself!"

"No," Stacy cried, her first tears running down her cheek.

"Yes, you did! You did it so that I would like you again."

"No," she said, flustered. "I just wanted to make it the way it was."

"You can't live in the past, Stacy. You can't go around changing other people's memories."

"I just wanted to make things as they were," Stacy said again. She stood there with her head bowed for a moment, looking sorrowful. "…That's all I wanted." And then, as if she had come to some internal conclusion, she nodded her head and reached into her purse. She pulled out a new ice pick.

Vera gasped when she saw it, and backed away, inadvertently knocking over the floor lamp. "What are you doing, Stacy?" Vera screamed.

"You'll see," she started calmly, wiping away her tears, "we can make things just the way they used to be."

"Stacy, please listen to me!"

"You won't remember anything, Vera. You'll see. It'll be just as it was in the beginning."

"No, Stacy!"

Stacy lunged at her with the ice pick. Vera barely managed to get out of the way. She ran for her life, but Stacy was faster. Vera managed to jump over the couch before Stacy lunged at her again. She grabbed the remote control from the coffee table and flung it at Stacy. That bought her a few seconds. She had to get out of the apartment. She headed for the door. However, Stacy was too quick. Stacy grabbed her by the back of her robe, then pushed her, so that she banged against the door. Vera swung around in horror. Stacy was right there; the ice pick was still in her hand.

"It won't hurt too much, Vera," Stacy said, breathing deeply. "I know how to do it so that it doesn't hurt—"

"Please, Stacy!"

"It won't hurt, and then things can go back to how they were." Stacy had a strange, hopeful smile on her face now, as if she were already seeing the wondrous times that they would have once Vera was reborn.

"Stacy!" Vera tried to plead with her, "you're unstable again, from when you killed me the last time…and don't forget the old couples. You get unstable every time you kill someone, remember? Don't do it!"

Stacy shook her head. "It has to be done, so that things can go back." As she said these last words, she lunged at Vera again. Somehow, Vera managed to grasp Stacy's ice-pick-wielding hand. Now, they were fighting like two animals—pushing and pulling, grunting and screaming with their teeth bared. With the adrenaline flowing through Vera's veins, she screamed out, lowered her center of gravity by bending her knees, and head-butted Stacy. Stacy stumbled backwards, her nose already bleeding. She tripped and fell to the ground. Vera screamed out again, driven either by blind rage or the unassailable will to live. Stacy had dropped the ice pick when Vera head-butted her; now, somehow, the ice pick was in Vera's hand. Within seconds, Vera was straddling Stacy. In her head, she again heard the screaming, numbing voice; and then, before she knew what was happening, she plunged the ice pick into Stacy's chest. Stacy's body convulsed. When Vera realized what she had done, she screamed. Vera went to scurry away—to flee like she had fled from the boyfriend; but to her amazement, Stacy smiled then: a beautiful, serene smile.

"*God!*" Vera cried. Tears were already streaming down her face.

Stacy continued to smile. Her words came out low and raspy: "…Thank you, Vera," she whispered. "You saved me." That was how she died. Her eyes rolled back in their sockets, and she was dead.

Vera again went to scream, but it got caught in her throat. She went to scurry away from the body, but somehow time seemed to stand still. …And then everything went black, and she had the feeling that she was disintegrating in the darkness. She felt all her memories and thoughts unraveling, disappearing into the darkness. For an instant, she tried to fight it, but it was no use. Everything that she was, was disappearing. After a while, she did not even feel as though she had a body anymore. All that she had was her disintegrating consciousness. …And then it was all gone.

An interval passed. It could either have been a millisecond or an eternity. Somehow, she had a soul again—a consciousness. The parts of her that had before disappeared into the darkness were reconstituting themselves. As she felt the different parts of her coming back together, it was as if she had been purified. It was as if her body had rid itself of a cancer, because everything suddenly seemed so clear.

And then, she found herself reliving the thing that she had spent the last twenty-three years of her life trying to remember. …It all made sense to her now. In that perfect moment, all the connections were made, and she saw the full picture.

Somehow, everything had been set in motion during the road trip to Georgia. After her family had the car accident, they had had to stay in that hunting lodge and wait for the car parts to arrive.

The second day, overcome by boredom, the twelve-year-old Vera set off down the dirt road. It forked off into a narrower road, which was nothing but two tire groves in a sea of weeds, bushes and trees. It was dark, but peaceful. When she reached another fork, she noticed a girl her age skipping down the lane, humming a tune. The girl was more sexually developed than Vera. She had the body of a woman; her hair was long and beautiful— the kind of hair that Vera always wished she had. Vera wished her breasts were full and luscious like the girl's. However, the girl's skipping suddenly struck Vera as childish. As Vera's mother had been reminding her lately, now that she was becoming a woman, she had to put childish things behind her. A side of her wanted to laugh at the oncoming girl and tell her that she was being childish, but the girl was having so much fun that Vera somehow found herself envying her for her freedom. Vera looked at the girl almost nostalgically—as if she were watching something that were already lost to her.

The girl noticed her when she was about twenty yards away. She stopped skipping and walked up to Vera, her eyes intent, yet relaxed.

"What's your name?" the girl asked when she was close.

"Vera."

"What's your last name?"

"Alexander."

"I'm Michelle Valentine," the girl said.

Vera noticed the girl's birthmark: a heart with a jagged line through it. Vera smiled unconsciously, at the contradiction of the girl's last name and her birthmark. However, before she could say, "Nice to meet you, Michelle Valentine," like a proper young lady was supposed to do, the girl went on:

"Where you from, up north?"

"Yeah."

"You one of those people who got into that car accident?"

"Yeah."

"Want to be friends?"

"Yeah," Vera said, taken aback by the abruptness, yet relieved as well.

"Come on then," the girl said as she resumed skipping down the lane. She looked back at Vera and smiled for the first time, and Vera found herself amazed by Michelle's beauty. She had a bewitching, inviting smile. After a moment's hesitation, Vera began to skip with the girl. Somehow, it was wondrous. She found herself giggling, joining in the strange tune that her new friend went back to humming—

A deer bounded across the lane—about fifteen yards from where they were skipping—and disappeared into the brush. They froze. Michelle took Vera's hand, and they tiptoed up to the spot where the deer had disappeared. It was a doe. They looked through the bushes to see it eating the tall, sweet grass Vera had discovered inadvertently, after seeing some of the local yokels chewing on it. She and Michelle crouched there and smiled at one another. Only moments later, they both jumped as there was a gun blast; when they looked back at the deer, they saw it stagger before dropping heavily (and lifelessly) to the ground. Vera screamed. Michelle leapt up and ran over to the doe. Vera followed her more slowly, already knowing that the thing was dead. Michelle bent over the creature and began to cry. Vera crouched at her side and held her.

That was when a man came strolling up: middle-aged, overweight, with a sweat-stained baseball cap that was now a brownish green color. He had a huge backpack, from which gear, like a water bottle and a small shovel, dangled. His face was pockmarked and covered by a few days' worth of beard stubble. "What y'all crying for?" he drawled.

Michelle stood up angrily, knocking Vera to the ground in the process. She bawled, "You kilt her!"

"Don't cry, little ladies," he said with a sickening smile, so that some of his chewing tobacco dropped from his lower lip. And then, while Vera sniffled, and Michelle looked at him with defiant tears, he proposed, "If I take it back, will y'all stop crying?"

"You can't take it back," Michelle screamed, "—you *kilt* her!"

He walked over calmly, smiling almost serenely. He smelled of stale sweat and some kind of unidentifiable decay. Vera and Michelle backed away as he came up to the deer. He smiled widely again when he reached it. "Anything can be took back, little ladies," he announced. "Just look here." As he said these last words, he crouched down and put his hand over the doe's wound. He massaged the bloody fur for a few seconds. Miraculously, the doe began to stir. Vera and Michelle stopped crying, too stunned to move. As they looked on, the doe began to breathe again. Its chest rose and fell. Then, all at once, it bounded to its feet and scampered off, through some more bushes.

"How's that for gratitude?" the man joked. Vera and Michelle were holding one another now, trembling. That's when the man rose to his feet, his sickening tobacco grin widening further. "See there, little ladies? Anything can be took back." Now, he began to walk toward the two trembling girls. When he was close enough, he reached his hand out— the hand that had massaged the bloody fur. It seemed impossibly huge; with the bloody gore from the deer's wound, it seemed like something from a nightmare. Michelle knew to run, but Vera was still frozen in place. For a middle-aged, overweight man, he moved quickly. He only needed to give Vera one blow to the side of the head in order to send her to the ground. She lay there, unconscious—or maybe semi-conscious, because, moments later, she heard all the horrible screams as the man grabbed and held down Michelle. He threw off his backpack, and then tore away her clothes. And then there were the interminable minutes of screaming and pleading and the man's laughter as he violated Vera's new friend....

Get up, Vera! Get up and help your friend! That's what she told herself while all that was going on. *Get up, Vera!* She opened her eyes after minutes of struggle. Things were blurry. She tried to move, but the pain immobilized her. She gnashed her teeth, took a deep breath, and tried again. ...She moved, but things were still blurry. The man was moaning now, reaching his climax. His moans drowned out Michelle's now-hoarse screams. Vera's vision cleared up a little. Everything came into focus for a second, before returning to a fuzzy mess. She got an image of the sickening scene. She almost threw up, but noticed a rock lying nearby—one that was big enough to knock out a man yet small enough for her to lift. She got to her feet. The man's back was to her. A force propelled her forward, giving her strength. She could not really see where she was going—everything was still a blur—but she could operate on her recollection of where everything was. Soon, the rock was in her hands—she used both hands. She lifted the rock high and stumbled over to the man, who was now groaning in ecstasy. When she was close enough, she brought the stone down upon the blurred image of the man's head with all her strength. There was a sickening thud; the momentum of the dropping rock made her lose her balance, so that she landed on top of the man. Some seconds passed. She was breathing hard. Michelle was still sobbing. Vera's vision suddenly cleared up. She rose from the man's body and looked down at the new sickening scene. The back of the man's head was flattened. He was dead, but his corpse still had Michelle pinned to the ground. In fact, his weight now seemed to be crushing her. Coming to her senses, Vera pushed the man off her friend. Michelle closed her legs and crawled into the fetal position. All Vera could think to do was lie down next to her and hug her. They both cried.

Yet, as the minutes passed, they felt the thing inside of them—the man's curse or power, or whatever it was. And then they realized that they had all the man's memories. They saw visions of all the horrible things he had done: the people he had hurt; the madness that had taken over his soul when he realized that he could kill with impunity. With all that power, he had spent most of his life as a modern day equivalent of a hobo.

It was Vera who came up with the plan to bury the body. They were in a secluded spot anyway, and the soil was soft from a recent rain. Vera got the shovel from the man's backpack. She dug the grave while Michelle lay on the ground, hugging herself. Vera did all the work, in fact. She rolled the body over to the hole and covered it over with dirt. She did not do a good job, because the man's hand stuck out when she was finished. She had to re-dig the grave and stick the hand back in.

And then, they went home. Vera helped Michelle hobble back to her home. There was a river along the way. Michelle stripped and washed herself, her movements slow and deliberate. She had a far-off expression on her face. At last, she looked up at Vera:

"Do you feel him, too? Do you feel him inside of you?"

Vera nodded anxiously. Actually, until then, neither of them had admitted to the other that she had the man inside of her. The man's memories and actions had been like a kind of waking nightmare that they had kept to themselves—a disease they feared would spread.

Michelle seemed calmer now—resolute. She got out of the river, but her clothes were useless now—mere rags. Vera gave Michelle her blouse and shirt—she had an undershirt and shorts underneath. They continued on to Michelle's place. Michelle was not limping anymore. Her face was blank. There was no pain there anymore, but there was nothing else either, as though she had been hollowed out. Vera stared at her uneasily, but Michelle did not make eye contact with her.

After about another five minutes of walking, they reached Michelle's house—a dilapidated hovel hidden by some overgrown bushes. Michelle hugged Vera suddenly, then walked up the lane to the house. Vera stared at her until she disappeared into the house. She waited for another five minutes, to see if there would be yelling and crying, but there was nothing. Vera walked back home, disillusioned. It was getting dark, and with the man's memories in her head, she was suddenly terrified. She began to run.

When the hunting lodge came into view, she was relieved. She told herself that she had to go into the building as if nothing had happened. She stopped walking. She took deep breaths to calm herself. She realized that her parents would know something was wrong if they saw her in her undershirt and shorts, so she went around to the back and climbed into her bedroom window. It was on the ground floor. Once she was dressed, she walked back outside and entered the lodge.

Her parents did not notice, and this amazed her. She had always thought that they knew everything—that they would always know, somehow, if she was in trouble or had done something wrong. When she entered the building, they were sitting at the kitchen table, worrying about how much longer it was going to take for the car parts to arrive. They bickered about such things, and Vera was relieved. She retreated into herself, but more and more, the memories of the man she had killed took possession of her mind. She felt the man's memories expanding somehow, taking up space within her.

She spent the next day inside. She told her parents that she was sick, and she was. They assumed it was "woman trouble." She stayed in bed, shuddering at all the images. Her parents complained that the car parts still had not arrived: the parts dealer had promised that the parts would arrive a day ago, but nobody could find them. Her parents brought her food as she lay in bed; they gave her updates on the parts that had not come....

The next day, Vera felt marginally better. She had gotten used to the rapist's memories the way someone living in a sewer could get used to the stench. She was still being poisoned, but at least she was not coughing anymore. There were other rapes in the man's memories; after a while, all the images joined into a swirling kaleidoscope of violence and death. The worst thing was seeing Michelle's rape from the man's perspective. She felt like she were raping her friend. She had to go to the bathroom to throw up. ...Experiencing all the man's motives and impulses was like being inside the mind of an animal—some kind of predator.

Around midday, she began to wonder how Michelle was doing. She heard her parents walking back and forth in the adjoining room, complaining about the car parts. She told them that she was feeling better, and that she would take a walk to get some fresh air. Once she was outside the door, she was overcome by the sudden fear that there was another predator waiting in the woods—another beast of a man getting ready to pounce on her. She was about to turn back when Michelle popped out from behind a bush and waved to her. Vera ran up to her; Michelle pulled her into the woods:

"How are you doing?" Michelle asked.

"Me?" Vera said, surprised. "I was wondering about you. You're the one who he..." She faltered. Michelle shook her head:

"He's inside both of us now."

Vera nodded.

"It's like he's taking over."

"Yes," Vera whispered. And then, looking up at Michelle sharply, "How do you think all this happened? How did he bring that deer back to life? How come all his thoughts are in our heads?"

Michelle looked at her gravely: "…We have his power now."

"What power?"

"We can do what he does: the thing with the deer."

"How do you know?"

"Yesterday, my mother told me to kill a chicken for dinner. I killed it, but then it came back."

"It came back?" she said, lost.

"I broke its neck. I grabbed it and twisted its neck, like I always do. But like a minute later it started fluttering."

Vera shuddered. "What did you do?"

"I chopped its head off."

"It didn't come back again?"

"I don't think so. I chopped it to pieces and threw it in the pot. That did the trick."

There was a morbid expression on her face; and for whatever reason, Vera smiled.

Michelle looked over at her again, and smiled the same disturbingly beautiful smile. For a moment, Vera was desperate to believe that things would be okay—that if Michelle was still beautiful on the outside, then everything would go back to the way they used to be. However, she remembered what Michelle had said about the man's power being passed on to them. Vera began:

"What makes you think I have the power, too?"

"I know," she said simply. And then, changing the topic, "When are you leaving town?"

"I don't know. The next day or so—whenever the parts come for the car."

Michelle nodded her head, deep in thought. "I'm pregnant, you know."

"What!"

"I'm pregnant."

"Already? It's only been two days."

"I know. I can sense the child—just like I can sense the man. I'm going to have a daughter. It's like we're already talking. I told her all about you. I'm going to call her Stacy."

Vera shook her head: "But it's only been two days."

"I know it, Vera. I'm going to be a mother."

Vera began to cry again. She could not help it. Michelle smiled and hugged her. "It'll be okay. You'll be going home soon. You're going to go back to your life. You'll forget about this place—everything that happened."

Vera shook her head. "I'll *never* forget this place. Never. I'll never forget any of it."

"You have to forget, Vera. One of us has to forget. I saw it in his memories. When he kills them, they forget. He tells them what to remember, and they forget the rest."

Vera shook her head again, sensing something horrible.

"One of us has to forget—no use in the both of us remembering." She took a knife out of her pocket then. Vera took a step back, but it was too late. The blade entered her cleanly; Michelle grabbed her before she fell, and cradled her to the ground, saying, "One of us has to forget....." The last thing Vera saw was Michelle's beautiful face....

And now that the adult Vera knew the truth, her consciousness began to move back into the present. For an instant, she was again surrounded by darkness, but then the surrounding world began to brighten; and then, suddenly, she found herself back in her living room. Both she and Stacy were lying on the ground. Stacy was still dead, but Vera felt the power of life within herself now. She felt Stacy's consciousness within her. Somehow, it seemed pure; she knew everything that Stacy had known and done. She saw how confused Stacy had been all her life. Stacy's mother had transmitted all her memories to her, even before she was born. Vera remembered how Michelle had told her she was pregnant, only two days after conception. Most of the memories she had passed on had perhaps been muddled by Michelle's slow descent into madness, but her friendship with Vera had probably been the one good thing she passed on to her daughter: the one memory that had filled her with joy and hope. That view of ideal friendship had been passed on to Stacy in the womb, so that when Stacy heard Vera on the radio that night after the weekend in Vermont, she had been almost genetically compelled to seek her out. It all made perfect sense to her now. The ability to hold life within herself had been transmitted to Stacy from her parents. Vera had had that ability all the time, but it had been dormant—short-circuited by whatever instructions Michelle had given her when she came back to life.

Seeing all this now, Vera smiled and caressed Stacy's face. Stacy looked so peaceful now—so childlike. And then, as if on cue, Stacy began to stir. Vera sat up straighter and looked down at Stacy as she opened her eyes. At first, Stacy looked up at her confusedly; Stacy opened her mouth, to ask Vera what had happened, but Vera put her finger over Stacy's lips, shushing her.

"Sit back and let me tell you a story, my friend," Vera started with a smile. And then, as Stacy looked on with childlike wonder, Vera went on to tell her why they needed one another.

AUTHOR'S NOTE:
BROOKLYN; FRIDAY, OCTOBER 21, 2005; 14:22

(The following is one of Stacy's demented stories. I cut a couple of them in the final draft. The following was supposed to be the first story Stacy told, but when I was finished, I felt that it was so long that it was distracting to the overall plot. Now that you're finished reading the novel, you can probably use all the distractions you can get. Remember that this is Stacy telling Vera a story.)

DELETED SCENE

"...So, one day a businesswoman is rushing back to work after lunch at a restaurant. Let's call her Tina McKinney. She's middle-aged and dressed in a business suit—your typical career businesswoman. Anyway, she runs into a friend of hers, whom she hasn't seen in years. Let's call her Shelley Halima. 'Hey, Shelley!' Tina says; she continues: 'How have you been? I haven't seen you since the divorce?' As soon as she says it, she immediately regrets it, remembering the messy divorce her friend had had two years ago. Nevertheless, her friend smiles and hugs her, undisturbed. Tina is relieved. Figuring that her friend's ease must be due to a new relationship, she ventures: 'Seeing anyone new?' Shelley shakes her head, still unconcerned, before revealing: 'I haven't had a man in two years, and I don't need one.'

"There was a tint of antagonism at the mention of men, and Tina was just beginning to think that her friend had switched teams and gone over to the rug-munching side, when Shelley announced, 'I have Vincent now.' 'Vincent?' Tina asked; and then: 'Who is he?' 'Vincent isn't a who, girl," Shelley corrected her, "—he's a godsend.' And then, with a loud salesperson's voice, she went on, 'The Vincent 6000: ten inches of vibrating magnificence, always ready for my pleasure.' Tina stared at her uneasily: '...A vibrator?' she said, looking around, in case anyone had heard. 'Damn right,' Shelley said proudly. But Tina still had a frown on her face: 'You're saying you don't need a man because you have a vibrator?' 'That's exactly what I'm saying. Vincent is always hard; he doesn't fall asleep on me—' Tina interrupted her with, 'Not unless the batteries run out.' Shelley shook her head: 'No, girl—Vincent runs off the energy of my body.' '…It does what?' 'He runs off my juices, honey.' …Tina's frown deepened: 'Your *pussy* juices?' Shelley nodded her head in the same proud way: 'Damn straight. …And get this: Vincent talks to me.' 'Your vibrator talks?' 'Yeah, he says the most wonderful things. It's like he senses my moods. When I want to get raunchy, he says the nastiest things to me; when I want to be treated tenderly, he whispers the sweetest things.' Tina was uncomfortable listening to all this; and suddenly realizing something about her friend, she said, 'Do you realize that you're calling your vibrator "he"?' 'What else would I call him?' Shelley said as if there were some kind of bigotry behind Tina's comment: as if she had just said that black people weren't human beings, or that women were mentally inferior. Tina tried to reason with her friend, saying, 'It's a piece of plastic, Shelley.' '—Not plastic,' Shelley corrected her in her salesperson voice. '—Vincent is made of the most advanced, skin-like polyurethane known to science. He's so incredible that I quit my job last month and became a Vincent salesman fulltime.' Tina gasped. 'You quit your job as a vice president at a Wall Street firm, so that you can sell vibrators?' 'I know how it sounds, but I'm telling you that Vincent is the answer to every woman's prayers. I'm now making twenty thousand dollars a month!' 'From selling vibrators?' 'It's a revolution in female sexuality,' Shelley announced. 'All my friends have gotten one; and once they get one, they recommend Vincent to their sisters and mothers and daughters.' Some kind of morbid streak went through Tina, and she found herself asking, "…Have you gotten your mother one?' 'Of course.' 'But she's eighty-five!' Tina screeched, totally bewildered now. Shelley looked back at her calmly and countered: 'Eighty-five-year-old pussies don't need dick, too? Shit, girl, once I got her one, all the other women in her nursing home had to get one—and Medicaid covers it, too!' 'Goddamn!' Tina said, stunned. Shelley continued: 'I got my daughter one, too.' 'But she's only twelve!' Tina screeched again. 'That's the best time to get her one, so that she doesn't become dependent on men for her sexual pleasure.' Then, while Tina stood there swooning from the entire conversation, Shelley went on, ' ...So, how many should I put you down for?' 'Me?' Tina said so forcefully that she almost choked. 'S-sorry, sista,' she stammered, 'I only like flesh and blood in my pussy.' Shelley groaned at her statement: 'Don't be so close-minded. ...Let me tell you what I'll do. I'll let you try Vincent free for one week.' '...I don't know,' Tina said, feeling more uncomfortable by the second. 'What is there to know?' Shelley countered. 'If Vincent isn't everything I said he is, I'll take him back, free of charge.' When Shelley saw that her friend was still wary, she challenged her with, 'Take charge of your sex life, Tina, instead of waiting around for some limp-dicked man.' Before Tina could say anything, Shelley went on, 'You still have the same address?' 'Yes.' 'Then I'll have the warehouse send over a Vincent today. He should be waiting for you when you get home.' Tina tried to make a final protest, but before she could say anything, Shelley looked at her watch and blurted out, 'Look at the time! I gotta run! I'll catch you later.' She kissed Tina on the cheek and was gone before Tina's brain could register anything but a mild case of shock.

"Tina returned to the office. However, for the rest of the afternoon, all she could think about was the idea of a talking vibrator being sent to her home. Who the hell would want to talk to a vibrator? She didn't even want to talk to her lovers during sex—much less a piece of plastic, or polyurethane, or whatever the hell it was! She had once had a lover who kept up a running commentary during sex: stuff like, 'Is this the best dick you ever had?' To which, she would be forced to respond, 'Yes, baby!' 'You love this big dick?' 'Oh yes, baby!' 'You love this big dick deep inside of yuh?' 'Oh, yes, baby, yes!' ...Just the thought of it made her shudder. Even when she faked her orgasm it would spur him on to more questions. After a while she would expect him to start asking multiple-choice questions, like, 'Is this (a) The best dick you've ever had, (b) The greatest dick in the history of the universe...'

"When it was time for Tina to go home for the day, she felt an unsettled feeling in her gut. She kept hoping that maybe Shelley, as busy as she was, would forget about the entire thing. In truth, the entire conversation seemed like a bizarre dream to her. However, when she got home, the package was waiting on her front porch. *Shit!* Tina thought to herself, *Shelley's better than the freaking Post Office!*

"Luckily, the package was nondescript—no vibrator pictures or any other telltale signs. She felt like some kind of pervert. As she picked up the package, she looked over her shoulder, to see if any of her neighbors were spying on her. Then, she rushed into the house and locked the door. Common sense told her to hide it away in the back of her closet, until she could send it back to Shelley. However, she was curious to see what a talking vibrator looked like. Did it have a face, for instance? The thought of it made her feel queasy again. What kind of woman would insert such an abomination into her vagina! She put the package down on the dining room table and went to fix dinner. However, her mind kept drifting back to the package. She almost chopped off her finger while she was dicing the onions, and knew that she had to put an end to this before it drove her insane. After she bandaged her finger, she walked back over to the package and ripped it open. Her heart was beating fast. She did not quite know what to expect. The box beneath the packaging was clear plastic, and she could see the Vincent 6000 resting in a silky bed. It was a huge, life-like penis. Her heart skipped a beat! Granted, it was a fake dick, but it had been a while since she had seen anything resembling a penis. Luckily, there was no face. She stood staring at it for a while. To her amazement, she realized that she was aroused, and the realization brought the same queasy feeling over her. ...And yet, she had come this far: she figured that she could at least take Vincent out of its bed. She was curious to see what it felt like. Tina kept hearing Shelley's sales pitch in her mind. She shook her head. Yet, Vincent was soon in her hands. It was rigid, yet pliable, like a real erect penis. She realized that her hands were shaking. Mercifully, the sauce she was cooking began to spill over on the stove. She put Vincent down and ran back over to the kitchen. She felt relieved for some reason—as if she had been on the verge of something horrible. At the same time, she wondered why Vincent had not talked to her. She doubted that she was ready to insert it into her, but she was curious about if it was a good conversationalist or not. She knew that the thought was an insane one, but while she was eating dinner (at the kitchen table, in order to avoid Vincent) all she could think about was the vibrator. There had been instructions in the box. By the time she was finished eating she knew that she had to get it over with, or she would be thinking about it all night.

"She returned to the dining room and picked up the instructions. Actually, there was only one instruction: 'Insert Vincent 6000 into your vagina to charge his battery.' Tina shuddered and fled from the dining room. She went to the bathroom and began to run a bath. She had to relax and get that blasted vibrator out of her head! She wished she hadn't met Shelley earlier. She wished that today were a typical day, where she came home to watch *Jeopardy* on TV…and yet, it had been a while since she had been fulfilled sexually. Every once in a while, she would try to masturbate, but she had always found the entire thing exhausting and tedious. As much as she hated to admit it, it took her *way* too much work in order to bring herself to orgasm. It would take at least forty minutes of sustained concentration; her hands would often get tired; and when they did, she would find herself thinking about how tired she was, instead of how horny she was, and then it would be too late. Bringing herself to orgasm was like building a castle of cards, placing each of the cards cautiously, lest the entire thing crashed to the ground. Once, she had done it for an hour and a half before she admitted defeat; five times, the castle of cards had crashed to the ground. She had been so frustrated that she had cried, clutching her pillow between her legs. On the other hand, the average man could reach orgasm in thirty seconds! Life was unfair.

"She stripped and stepped into the bath. The water was warm and good. She inhaled deeply; the scent of the bubble bath made her feel slightly giddy. She smiled to herself. She felt suddenly sensual. She rubbed the sponge against her skin and found the sensation delicious. Her skin seemed hypersensitive—receptive to her touch. In that strange way that people had, she was seducing herself. She lay back in the tub. Her hand moved down her body, and soon she was touching her sex. …But goddamn it, her fingers weren't doing the job! She stopped after about five minutes, feeling frustrated. She remembered Vincent. Did she dare?… The idea still made her queasy. It was all like the time her old boyfriend had tried to convince her that she would love anal sex. There had been the same queasiness beforehand. It had taken two seconds for her to know for certain that anal sex was not for her, but in the same way she had gone through with the experiment with her boyfriend, she knew, deep down, that she would try Vincent. She had come this far. And what if Shelley was right? What if Vincent were some new revolution in female sexuality? All of a sudden, anything seemed possible.

"She rose from the bathtub, dried herself off quickly, and put on a robe. Then, she returned to the dining room, where she had left Vincent on the table. She took it up cautiously, feeling its girth in her hand once again. If she was going to do this, then she had to at least be comfortable, so she decided to take Vincent up to her bedroom. She tried not to think as she walked. She would just insert the thing and see what happened. God, she hoped it did not say anything at first. She definitely did not want to talk to it. Maybe there was some kind of off switch or volume control? She turned it around in her hand, but there was nothing. As it required no batteries, there was no opening.

"She was trembling slightly as she lay down on her bed. God, was she really going to do it? Her heart was beating savagely. She felt like she was about to lose her virginity. She had had the same anxious feeling with her first lover when she was sixteen. He had laughed at her, telling her to stop biting her fingernails. She had tried to laugh, but had only ripped off part of her nail with her teeth, along with the attached skin. She remembered it all vividly. Now, she was lying on the bed with her legs spread. She took a deep breath before shoving the thing into her. She did it savagely, with a brutal stabbing motion, like a samurai committing seppuku. After she had done it, the world seemed to stand still. She was holding her breath, waiting for what was going to happen. Her body and mind seemed frozen—tense. ...And then, all at once, she realized that there was a pleasant sensation in her vagina. There wasn't a mechanical vibrating sensation, just a pleasant sensation, like a soothing caress. In fact, she realized that it did not even seem as though she had anything in her vagina. She glanced down, to see if the thing was still between her legs. For a moment, she thought that maybe it had slipped out of her, but it was still there. The pleasant sensation spread throughout her body, like a drug flowing through her veins. Almost immediately, her muscles relaxed. She lay back fully on the bed. She began to breathe again—after holding her breath during the initial brutal stab. Strangely enough, with each breath, she felt recharged. Almost imperceptibly, the pleasant sensation became more fervent. Muscles that had before relaxed began to contract to a rhythm that she noticed was somehow perfect. Inadvertently, she groaned. She forgot about Vincent. This was not about what was going on in her vagina, but about some miraculous new spiritual achievement. This, she found herself thinking, had to be how the gods felt when they made love. This was the pleasure set aside for those whose souls were pure and perfect. Somehow, she had been allowed to bypass all earthly struggles to achieve some new plane of sexual bliss.

"She realized that she had been moaning for a while. It wasn't something she did consciously, but something like breathing, which flowed from her naturally. And then, to her amazement, the pleasure seized her completely. All at once, it was there for her—naked and unrestrained—and she surrendered herself to it. It was like nothing she had ever felt before. It was pure and primal, stripped of all earthly barriers and pretenses. Her body felt weightless—free. She was soaring high, existing for an instant in a place beyond gravity and reality...

"She did not even realize when she had fallen asleep. The sleep seized her as perfectly as the pleasure had. In the middle of the night, she got up momentarily, but a voice told her to go back to sleep—a calm, caring voice that was so attuned to her that it seemed like a voice from her own mind. That voice was Vincent's.

"The morning was there before she knew it. She woke up to the pleasant sensation. She had been so overwhelmed from the previous night's activities with Vincent that she had left it in her vagina. Vincent was like a part of her now—not something separate or artificial. When Vincent was inside of her, she could not tell where the thing ended and she began. As she awoke to the pleasant sensation, she once again felt the perfect rhythm of pleasure spreading throughout her body. 'Goddamn!' she managed to whisper as the pleasure seized her again. She was just nodding off to go to sleep when she remembered that she had to go to work. She pulled Vincent out of her and crawled out of bed. She could barely see straight. And then, 'Leaving so soon?' a voice asked. It startled her, not just because it was unexpected, but because it was as if the voice had come from inside of her head. Looking down at the bed, she realized that it was Vincent. She had to reacquaint her mind with the fact that the thing could talk. Still, she was so stunned that she could not say anything for a few moments. '...Are you okay?' the voice asked again; once more, it was as if the voice were inside of her head—as if some of Vincent's microchips had imbedded themselves in her brain, and she were now linked with it forever. The thought made her skin crawl. Also, even though the voice was pleasant and congenial, it reminded her, somehow, of her high school English teacher's voice. He had been a kind, grandfatherly man, and the entire thing made her cringe. '—Aren't you going to talk to me?' the voice pleaded with her, sounding almost hurt. Tina shook herself to regain her composure. 'Yeah, I'm fine,' she said. She wondered if the thing could see her, because her face wore an awkward, anxious expression—the expression of a bad liar. 'Are you leaving me?' the thing asked again, its voice taking on an anxious edge—which was doubly unsettling, as she felt it reverberating inside of her head. Tina shuddered. '...I'll be back soon,' she said in the same uneasy way, '—I just have to go to work.' 'You can take me to work,' the thing pleaded now, '—I'll be quiet.' Tina fled from the bed. 'Maybe another time,' she mumbled. Then, she ran to the bathroom and slammed the door shut, before the thing could say anything else.

"She was trembling as she showered. The conversation had been so bizarre that her mind practically refused to return to it. The conversation sat within her, like a huge, indigestible meal...and yet, her legs were still weak from the pleasure the thing had given her—the *extraordinary* pleasure. Everything Shelley had said about the thing had been true...she just had to get used to talking to it. ...Maybe she could ask it to shut up. ...She shook her head: that seemed rude. ...She pursed her lips, deep in thought for a moment: did the thing have feelings? She shook her head again. She was being silly. It was a piece of plastic—or polywhatever. She owned it— it wasn't her boyfriend or anything. She had to get a grip and take control and tell it to shut up. Still, the prospect of confronting the thing made her feel sick to her stomach. She could hear the potential conversation in her mind now: 'How may I please you today?' the thing might say, to which she would say 'Shut up you piece of plastic bastard, and get in my pussy!' She groaned.

"Once she was through with her shower, she rushed back into the bedroom, grabbed some clothes from the closet and rushed out of the door before Vincent could say anything. She got dressed in the living room. With all that, she got to work half an hour early that morning. The first thing she did was call Shelley. 'Shelley,' she started, 'how do I shut it up?' '...It?' Shelley said, confused. 'You mean Vincent?' 'Yes, Vincent—whatever you want to call it.' There was silence on Shelley's end. '...Did he please you?' Shelley asked at last. 'Yeah, but isn't there some kind of off switch for the voice?' 'You don't like what he says?' 'I just don't like talking to vibrators!' she said too loudly. She peeked out of her cubicle, to see if anyone had overheard. All seemed clear, and she turned back to the phone. 'It's creepy, Shelley," she explained. 'I don't want to talk to it—especially afterwards.' Shelley sighed loudly: 'You know what your problem is?' Shelley said in an annoyed voice, '—you're just like a man!' 'I'm what?' 'You're just like a callous man. Vincent gives you all that pleasure and you can't talk to him for a few moments? You're like a man that just wants to have sex and turn over and go to sleep!' Tina was aghast, 'But it's just a vibrator!' she tried to explain. Shelley chastised her: 'Stop calling him "it!" If you dehumanize him you're devaluing your own pleasure.' 'But it's a vibrator!' she said again, trembling with bewilderment. ...Shelley sighed after a while.

'Look, Tina, give up your inhibitions—there is so much that Vincent can show you, if you're willing to open yourself to him.' Tina grimaced, but she decided not to say anything. She felt, somehow, as if she had been bigoted—as if she had just been advocating that Asians should not be allowed to live in her neighborhood. Shelley made her feel guilty and ashamed, and she did not know whether to resist those feelings or accept them contritely.

"Understandably, with all that, Vincent was on her mind all day. At work, she screwed up two reports and had to start over. She knew that the pleasure had been so exquisite that she could not put Vincent back in the box and pretend that last night had never happened. There had to be some way to turn off the blasted voice. Once that was done, everything would be perfect. Also, she could not help thinking about what Shelley had said, about there being so much that Vincent could show her if she were willing to open herself to it. Granted, the entire thing sounded like something one of those sidewalk evangelists said—*Accept Jesus into thy heart and ye shall know eternal bliss*! However, Vincent had opened her up to new possibilities—a Pandora's Box of possibilities that she could even then sense changing her forever. To put it simply, Vincent had rocked her world; and despite the reservations of her mind, her body knew what it wanted. She had spent most of the day in a state of heightened arousal. Her skin still felt hypersensitive. Around 3 p.m., she snuck away from her cubicle and went to a bathroom stall, intending to take care of her needs… but goddamnit, her fingers still could not do the trick! Ten minutes later, she returned to her cubicle dazed and frustrated—and, even more obsessed with Vincent.

"That day, she drove home like a madwoman. Maybe Shelley had been right, she found herself thinking as she zoomed through traffic. If Vincent could give her all that pleasure, then certainly she could endure talking to it. If anything, she could be like a man and drown out its voice. The thought made her laugh, but, remembering Shelley's accusation that she was like a callous man, she felt guilty afterwards.

"As soon as she parked in her driveway, she got out of the car and ran into her house. She ran as if she were running into the arms of her lover, but the house was dark and empty. There was no human warmth waiting for her—merely a piece of technology lying on her bed. Still, the moment of emptiness passed quickly. She would moralize and philosophize about it later. For now, she needed to be serviced again. She ran up the stairs to her bedroom. Vincent was still on the bed, where she had flung him after she pulled him from her vagina. Now that she was looking at the thing again, she approached the bed anxiously. 'Hello,' she said as she approached. For a moment, there was silence, and she began to wonder if the thing needed to be recharged, but then it said, 'Did you have a good day?' Just as the last time, it was as if she were hearing the voice within her head. It seemed to come from everywhere. She forced herself not to panic; she smiled uneasily, reminding herself to 'give up her inhibitions' as Shelley had chided her. '...Yes, I had a good day,' she replied. And then, stunning herself by rushing headlong into the act, she went on, 'I thought about you today.' To her amazement, the vibrator laughed seductively. 'Did you enjoy our time together?' it asked. 'Oh, yes,' she said with a mixture of panic and sexual anticipation. She found herself thinking that if she did not shove the thing into her soon, then she would lose her nerve—if not her mind. She was moving quickly now, flinging off her clothes. Her mind retreated to its old numbness. Vincent said something else, but she did not hear it—refused to hear it. Soon, she was lying naked on the bed with her legs spread. Once again, she shoved the thing into her with the same vicious stabbing motion, and then she lay back on the bed as the miraculous rhythmic pleasure worked its magic over her body. Ten minutes later, she was snoring, her body spent and tingly with the explosive aftermath of Vincent's pleasure. In the morning, Vincent was there again, awaking her with a full onslaught of the pleasure.

"This went on for days. As soon as she got home, she would insert Vincent into her vagina and surrender herself to the pleasure; in the morning, she would awake to the pleasure, so that it became her new alarm clock. After the third day, she called up Shelley and asked her where to send the check. Shelley laughed and told her that she took credit cards.

"Her life seemed suddenly magical. She felt as though she were just discovering sex. This is how it had felt when she was thirteen years old, getting felt up by her first boyfriends. Everything had seemed like a wonderful secret. Everything had been pure and wonderful, and she had surrendered to it all. Actually, compared to those early experiments in sexuality, what she was experiencing now was exponentially more amazing. Now, for the first time in years—perhaps even ever—she was sexually satisfied. A warm glow had spread over her skin since she had gotten Vincent. She smiled more. She was more pleasant and relaxed, and everyone seemed to notice it. In fact, she was eating in the company cafeteria on the fifth day since getting Vincent, when a coworker she had been privately lusting over for four years came up to her. 'Did you change your hair or something?' he said, looking down at her quizzically. She had just forked some salad into her mouth, so her mouth was full as she looked up at him. She chewed twice and swallowed the huge clumps of lettuce and tomato, almost choking. 'Are you okay?' he asked as she gagged. 'I'm fine,' she reassured him, '—I forgot how to chew for a moment there.' She smiled to reassure him further. He was still looking at her closely. He was standing there holding his tray; and realizing that she was being rude, she gestured with her hand for him to sit down. He complied. She was not quite sure how it happened, but somehow the conversation moved smoothly between them. Soon, they were laughing and telling one another abbreviated versions of their life stories. She kept smiling to herself and thinking 'I'm actually doing it!' When it was time to go back to work, he asked her if she would like to continue the conversation over dinner, and she eagerly agreed.

"The rest of the afternoon passed in a blur. All she could think about was dinner with her coworker. It felt good to be lusting over a human being again. She realized that that had been missing from the past few days. Rushing home to a piece of polyurethane was shameful when you thought about it objectively. Either way, she was about to have her first real date in a year. As soon as her workday was over, she once again zoomed home like a madwoman. Her date would be picking her up in an hour, and then they would go out to dinner.

"She was in high spirits until she closed the front door behind herself and remembered Vincent. For whatever reason, she felt uneasy—as if she were about to cheat on the thing. When she became conscious of these thoughts she shook her head.

"'Hello, Tina,' Vincent said as soon as she entered the bedroom. As always, the voice resounded inside of her head; she had a momentary urge to clamp her hands over her ears, to keep out the echo. '…Hello, Vincent,' she said quickly, rushing to the bathroom. She shut the door, as if Vincent were a man, and would spy on her. She kept rushing, as to not think about these things. She stripped off her clothes and entered the shower. She forced her mind to concentrate on her impending date, in order to distract herself. She wondered how far she was going to let her coworker get—if she should pretend to be a 'not on the first date' sort of girl, or if she would throw her skirt over her head and tell him to have at it. The last idea made her laugh, and that was good.

"However, when she entered the bedroom, Vincent spoke up again: 'Are you going out?' 'Yeah,' she admitted. She moved to her closet, searching for something to wear. She picked out a dress and held it against her naked body, posing before the full-length mirror to see how she would look. 'You're going out on a date, aren't you?' Vincent asked her now. That was the first time she realized that Vincent could see her. The realization made her skin crawl. Suddenly uneasy, she gripped the dress over her nakedness, even though, logically, it was ridiculous to hide from a vibrator. '…Tina?' Vincent called to her again. 'Yeah,' she said at last, her breath getting caught in her throat. 'Are you going on a date?' 'Yeah,' she said warily, 'I'm going out.' There was silence for about five seconds. 'Who is he?' Vincent asked abruptly. 'Just a man from work,' she said as nonchalantly as she could. There was another long silence from Vincent. Tina was so anxious that she decided to get out of there. She flung the dress over her head, forgoing underwear. *To hell with it*, she thought. She would grab a pair of shoes and wait outside. However, as soon as she grabbed a pair of shoes and took a step toward the door, Vincent continued: 'What's his name?' 'William,' she said, numbly. She waited for the thing to say something else, but there was silence. She went to continue to the door, but then Vincent suddenly asked, 'Wasn't I good enough for you?' To Tina's amazement, the thing's voice seemed to crack with emotion. Tina did not know what to say. Such a question was unanswerable. She avoided it entirely by blurting out, 'Can we talk about it later—I'm going to be late.' 'He's picking you up here?' Vincent asked. 'Yes, he'll be here soon,' she said quickly. She ran out of the bedroom then, and down the stairs. Her heart was thumping in her chest. ...*Goddamn*, she thought to herself. *Your vibrator is jealous!*

"She was trembling when she got downstairs. Maybe she could send Vincent in for repairs...or maybe not. She knew that there was no way she could put the thing in her again. It was like a boyfriend who revealed that he was a homicidal maniac. The only thing to do was break up. She looked about her house absentmindedly. In a strange way, she was heartbroken—as if she had just broken up with a flesh and blood boyfriend. She knew that the thought was a sick one, so she sat down heavily on the couch and sighed. She put on her shoes and then lay down to wait for her date. She knew that she had to get Vincent out of her mind or she would sabotage her date. Somehow, she would have to be the smiling, happy woman she had been earlier in the day. Momentarily, she was tempted to be with Vincent for a moment, so that the pleasure could relax her.

"Mercifully, the doorbell rang while her mind was being drawn into thoughts of a quickie. She sprang up nervously from the couch. She took a deep breath again; and then, as she walked over to the front door, she pasted a smile on her face. She would smile like a grinning clown tonight, and fawn over her date, and ask him about himself, and all the other things that women were supposed to do to make their men think that they liked them. All she had to do was make it through tonight. She sensed, somehow, that this was the chance to wean herself from Vincent. She needed to spend the night with a flesh and blood man—not a bunch of microchips in a polyurethane coating.

"Her date was smiling when she opened the door. She was relieved. She hugged him and kissed him on the cheek. She invited him in and she was relieved because it was going so naturally. His muscles had felt good when she hugged him; his smile was bright and comforting. Their conversation went naturally—banter about the ride over; some jokes about possible restaurants. She was about to go to the hall closet, to fetch a shawl, in case it got cool, when the phone rang. She went to the phone instead of the closet. When she answered it, she heard a chipper woman's voice. 'Is William there?' '...Yeah,' Tina said confusedly; and then, 'Hold on.' She held up the phone for her date. 'It's for you.' 'For me? ...Who'd know that I was here?' he said. Tina shrugged. Once she had handed the phone over, she was about to continue over to the hall closet, but as soon as William put the telephone receiver to his ears, his body convulsed. For a few moments he did a strange dance, before he collapsed to the ground. He banged his head on the table as he fell. He twitched on the ground for a few seconds before he lay still. Tina was about to scream when Vincent's voice suddenly sounded in her head: 'Don't worry, he's not dead yet.'

"Tina could not move—could not think. Bewildered, she whispered, 'What happened to him?' '*I* happened to him,' Vincent said menacingly. '...You did this?' she said, fighting to understand. 'Yes.' And then, in a lower, more ominous voice, 'You really think I'd let you go out with another man?' Tina was trembling again: 'But you're a vibrator!' 'I'm the Vincent 6000! Don't ever call me a vibrator again! Once you go Vincent, you never go back!' Tina was so stunned that she could not speak. In fact, she did not know what there was to say; she glanced at the man sprawled on the ground, her heart faltering in her chest. 'This is insane!' she whispered at last. 'Call it what you will,' Vincent mocked her, '—as long as you do what I say.' She kept looking up at the ceiling as she talked, as if Vincent were floating up there. 'What do you want?' she asked. 'For now,' Vincent directed her, 'you can tie him up.' She looked down at her date again. He was not moving. She spoke timidly: 'What did you do to him?' 'I shocked him—a minor shock, actually...for now,' he added threateningly. 'But how?' she asked, struggling to understand. 'I am the Vincent 6000,' the thing said matter-of-factly, 'I can do anything I want.' 'You're malfunctioning,' Tina tried to reason with it. 'Never say that to me again!' 'I'm sorry,' she cried, cowering—practically bowing to the ceiling. 'Tie him up!' her vibrator demanded, and Tina bent down to follow its will. However, there wasn't anything handy, and she spent a few seconds looking around for something to use as rope. 'Use the extension cord!' Vincent screamed, losing patience. Tina complied.

"She tied her would-be lover's arms and legs. The knots were not very good, so it would be no problem for him to escape, but— 'Tie those knots right!' Vincent thundered from the heavens—or rather, the ceiling. Tina shuddered again, wondering how the hell her vibrator could see her. It really was like God—it could see everything; it knew everything; it could do anything. 'Tighter!' Vincent demanded again. Tina began to cry. 'What are you going to do with us?' she whimpered. 'Shut up!' Vincent cut her off. 'And stop that crying,' he warned her, '—or I'll really give you something to cry about!' Like a scared five-year-old, she sucked up her tears and crouched there sniffling. Vincent went on: 'And don't let thoughts of escape enter your mind either! I could kill you both by shocking you through the electrical wiring, or I could cause a fire or blow up the boiler. I'm in control! Do you understand?' 'Yes, Vincent!' she said, crying again. 'I could call the police and tell them that you tried to kill a man,' Vincent went on. 'I could ruin your life, if you cross me!' '...But why are you doing this?' she tried reasoning with it again. 'You're my pussy!' Vincent thundered from the heavens again. 'You really think I'll let you have some human dick again!' Tina was about to squeal, 'But you're a vibrator!' but the words got caught in her throat.

"Tina finished binding her would-be lover's hands and legs. Her mind was dazed. She felt as though she would pass out. That was when Vincent called, 'Come upstairs to me now.' Tina, still numb, did as she was told. She climbed up the stairs like someone sleepwalking. Vincent was still lying on her bed, but of course where else would it be: it did not have any legs. She stared at it, as if trying to digest what had happened and what it had done. 'What are you going to do with us?' she asked again. 'I'm going to do anything I want!' Vincent revealed. 'But,' Tina suggested, 'if you kill me, you'll lose your charge—you'll die.' 'Stupid bitch!' her vibrator cursed her, 'you think yours is the only pussy I've ever been in?' She stared at the thing in astonishment, trying to understand, so it helped her with, 'That's right, you stupid bitch—I've been factory serviced to meet the manufacturer's original specifications. You're the fifth woman I've been with!' Tina could not believe it: her vibrator was a whore! Vincent went on: 'If anything happens to you, I'll be sent back to the factory.' Tina thought of something: 'But won't the police begin to suspect you?' 'Who the hell would believe that a vibrator killed someone? The first woman I was with, I made her car malfunction: she drove over a cliff. The second woman...well, she just went crazy—slit her own wrists and bled to death. The third woman—I startled her when she was cleaning the windows in her apartment, and she fell four stories to her death. The fourth woman is still in the nut house, drugged out of her skull.'

"Tina could not believe what she was hearing! This all had to be some kind of sick dream. She retreated a step from the bed. Vincent thundered, 'Where the hell are you going!' 'What are you going to do to me?' Tina cried. 'Serve me well and I'll let you have a full life,' Vincent revealed. 'Serve you?' she said, disillusioned. Vincent chuckled to himself then, sounding pleased as he revealed: 'I have to admit, you have some of the best pussy I've ever been in. You've been so sexually repressed for most of your life that all that power is there to be claimed by me!' Here, Vincent cackled like one of those cartoon villains. All Tina could do was stare. And just then, when she was beginning to believe that things could not get more bizarre, Vincent ordered: 'Service me now, woman!' '...What?' Tina squeaked. 'Service me!' Vincent demanded; and then, 'Strip off your clothes and come to me!' the vibrator directed her. Tina could see no way out. Her movements were mechanical—drained of life. She pulled the dress over her head and stood there naked. And then, she was sleep-walking over to the bed. 'Service me!' the vibrator demanded again. Tina lay on the bed and took the thing in her hand. For a moment she thought about flinging it out of the window, or smashing it against the wall, but, 'Don't even think about it, bitch!' Vincent cursed her. Tina shuddered yet again: the vibrator could read her thoughts! Was it really going to end like this? she wondered. She saw herself spending the rest of her life powering up a demented vibrator, losing herself in an insane mix of terror and pleasure. Vincent was still in her hands; she looked down at the thing numbly. Once again, it thundered, 'Service me!'

"Tina stared down at the thing, shocked; but then, all at once, something in her snapped, and she growled, 'You want pussy?'—she spread her legs wide—'Then take it!' With that, she shoved the thing deep inside of her. The previous times, she had just inserted the thing and let it do the work, but she was stroking it in and out of herself now. The pleasure was somehow brutal, and she gnashed her teeth to keep from screaming out. The first wave of ecstasy washed over her, but she refused to relent to it. Somehow, she found a wellspring of energy inside of herself—a source of untapped sexual energy, waiting to be released. She was still pumping the thing into her, double-fisted. It was coated with her juices by now—so much so that it was getting slippery in her hand. Even when her body convulsed with pleasure, she kept going; in many instances, she picked up speed, as if each orgasm were some new plateau to be reached and surpassed. Suddenly, she laughed out, saying, 'Why you so quiet, Vincent? My cat got your tongue?' To her amazement, the vibrator moaned. 'Yeah, you deep in me now, ain't ya!' she taunted it. Even when her body convulsed with pleasure again, she kept up the same double-fisted rhythm. 'How you like that pussy now?' she taunted the vibrator, which was moaning more with each passing orgasm. At last, it groaned, 'I don't feel well...please slow down.' Tina grunted with a sarcastic grin on her face. 'You wanted pussy, didn't you? So take it then,' she said, picking up the pace of her thrusts, so that her hands practically became a blur to her now. '—Please...stop!' Vincent cried out. 'Stop?' she said mockingly. 'You made to give me pleasure or ain't ya? Ain't ya the Vincent 6000?' '—No more,' the vibrator pleaded, its voice sounding robotic and sluggish, '—batteries... charged...over...limit—please...stop!' All of a sudden, the lights in the bedroom began blinking on and off; in the bathroom, she could hear her hair dryer turning on and off. The phone began ringing; down in the kitchen, she heard the blender turning off and on in a sick kind of symphony. 'Stop!' Vincent screamed in panic, but just then, Tina's body shuddered with her most powerful orgasm yet. She swore that for a moment she went blind. Strange shapes flashed before her eyes and she felt as if her body were on fire. Still, she gnashed her teeth again and continued the same double-fisted thrusts. It wasn't until she realized that something was smoking between her legs that she screamed out and flung Vincent from her. She was just in time too, because a few seconds later, the thing exploded. '…Yeah,' she said with a chuckle, as she watched the polyure-thane skin bursting into flames, 'I bet they won't be sending your ass back to the factory this time.' At that moment, William rushed into the room. 'What the hell…!' he said, looking at the scene. Tina was still lying there naked with her legs spread. 'Fetch the fire extinguisher from the kitchen,' she said, nonchalantly. '—And hurry up,' she said with an alluring smile: 'I still have some energy left.'"

AUTHOR BIO

D.V. Bernard emigrated from Grenada to New York City when he was nine years old. Those who wish to know more can visit www.dvbernard.com

SNEAK PREVIEW: EXCERPT FROM

Intimate Relations with Strangers

BY D.V. BERNARD

COMING SPRING 2007 FROM STREBOR BOOKS INTERNATIONAL

Few are the people who know the meaning of what they are living through, who even have an inkling of what is happening to them. That's the big trouble with history....
—RICHARD WRIGHT's *The Outsider*

War had a way of fooling men into believing they were in love. Once soldiers found themselves in foreign lands, surrounded by death (and the threat of death), they either learned how to fantasize, or they became victims of the surrounding nightmare. In this way, war constructed any passing affair they had ever had into a grand love story; the girlfriends and wives they had been happy to get rid of at the onset of war were now goddesses to be worshipped from afar. And whatever slums, barrios and trailer parks these soldiers had left in favor of the Army were now the paradises of the most whimsical daydreams. When reality was stark and depraved, the mind compensated with fantasy.

Accordingly, now that the killing was done, the soldier was left with nothing but the haunting image of the woman. Ten minutes ago, there had been gun-shots and screams—and the sounds of men rushing over the sun-baked earth of the Sahara Desert. He had killed all five of the prison camp's guards. The men that had tortured and imprisoned him were now lying on the ground before him, like the grotesque figurines of a child's play set. He had no idea *how* he had killed them. A force had taken over him: an impulse to exact revenge, perhaps. Either way, once that was done, he had freed twenty of his fellow prisoners of war from the hovels that had been their jail cells. Like captured animals being released into the wild, the men had scampered into the craggy hills beyond the prison camp, reaching the summit just as the sun was about to set over it. He had stood there, watching them from the camp—mesmerized by the strange illusion of his countrymen escaping into the sun.

It was only when he lost all sight of them that he realized that he, himself, had nowhere to go. He looked at his surroundings now, as if just waking up in a strange bed. The desert landscape seemed not only barren but brutalized. At the same time, the Sahara had a way of opening one's eyes to what was essential. That was one of the lessons the soldier had learned in the years he had been here. He had learned about life and death and desperation. He had learned to hate, and he had learned to love. Like the Sahara, his knowledge was a vast expanse, filled with mirages and oases that had kept him going and hoping as he travelled deeper and deeper into the nothingness.

In fact, now that the killing was done, even the prison camp seemed to be disappearing into the nothingness. Its seven earthen structures had been sandblasted smooth by the desert winds; and as the soldier looked at the wall closest to him, it seemed as though it were disintegrating in the breeze, like a sand castle. There was a gust of wind then, and a miniature cyclone danced in the sand for a moment, before disappearing like a ghost. The gust of hot, arid air burned the soldier's eyes and left his nasal passages desiccated. As he coughed and winced, it occurred to him that he was dehydrated. The prisoners of war he had freed into the desert heat were no doubt dazed and dehydrated as well. Maybe in an hour or so they would pass out and be covered over by the Sahara—or be eaten by the flocks of vultures that soared over the desert, looking for death.

Just as he was nodding his head absentmindedly, something came up behind him and brushed against his leg. He sensed it even before it touched him. The usual tingling sensation came over him, and he looked down in time to see the cat arch its back as it brushed its flank against his leg. It was the same spectacularly white cat that he had been seeing periodically for months now; and as usual, he felt himself being severed from time and reality. He was free for those few moments—able to see more of the repressed memory (or delusion) that had been unfolding for him over the months of his capture. As he looked down, the setting sun's blinding rays seemed to refract off the cat's immaculately white fur, so that the soldier had to clamp his eyes shut. In a world of dust and death, the cat was a beacon of life and possibility. Its movements were lithe and mesmerizing; as it rubbed against his leg, it purred, and he felt the sound washing over him, like a soothing waterfall. He smiled as he stood there with his eyes closed. However, when he opened his eyes, the cat was gone, and he felt suddenly melancholy and foolish. He had spent the bygone months wondering if the cat was a figment of his imagination—

But presently, as he began to tremble all over, it suddenly occurred to him that he had been shot during the battle with the prison guards. He lowered himself to the ground then, and leaned against the side of the hovel. Rather than being painful, the bullet holes that riddled his body were points of numbness. He had been shot at least once in each leg. A bullet was embedded in his left shoulder, and there were two in his abdomen. As the blood flowed, the points of numbness seemed to expand in diameter, so he knew that soon there would be no sensation at all—no life. With these thoughts in mind, he lay down flat on the ground, closed his eyes, and sighed—as if anticipating the fitful sleep that always possessed him when he dreamed of the woman.

♟♟♟

All those months ago, before the soldier became a prisoner of war, the war had not been going well. The enemy had won no great victories over them, but the era of grand victories was over. In its stead rose a stalemate between those who were clearly mad, and those who were dedicated to being more brutal than the madmen. When the American Military originally swept into the African desert, the war fever had unified them. As politicians and television commentators were constantly reminding them, everything had changed two and a half years ago. The American Military had come to the desert to either change things back, or to exact revenge for the change.

Whatever the case, two and a half years ago, the soldier had been a typical senior in high school. He had talked the way others talked, and dressed the way those around him dressed. He had had girlfriends with whom he had experienced varying degrees of sexual success. He had had friends and enemies, and engaged in all the fads of adolescence, so that once he was within the crowd, he had been indistinguishable from his classmates. And yet, on the morning when everything changed for America, he had felt disembodied—severed from time and history. He had been late for school; nevertheless, as he drove along the streets of Long Island, New York, he had sensed that his lateness would be irrelevant tomorrow. …And then, towards the end of his history class, there had been a scream in an adjacent classroom. That other class had been watching the news for a social studies project; and when several other students from that class began to scream, the soldier's history teacher had gone to investigate the commotion. She had warned her students to stay in their seats. However, as the seconds passed, and more students in the neighboring class cried out, everyone in the history class had streamed over to the other class. …Even before the soldier saw the thing for himself, he had known. He had actually been the last one to leave the history class. He had meandered over to the other class—not with the curiosity and budding horror of everyone else, but with the detachment of someone going to verify something he already knew. While girls cried and hugged, and boys mustered whatever emotion their machismo would allow, the soldier had only nodded his head as he watched the smoldering remains of the White House.

The subsequent announcement that the president and half the cabinet had been blown to bits by terrorists had been one of those reality-changing events. Within a week of the attack, the soldier and forty percent of his graduating class had signed up with the Military. There had been nothing else to be done: the resulting war had been inevitable—like the impulse to scream once someone had stepped on one's foot. At the same time, there had been a kind of purity in the terrible war cry of America. The war had been a transcendental event; Americans had surrendered to the war the way converts surrendered to a new religion. In the aftermath of the White House bombing, it had not so much been a new president that Americans cried out for, as a priest that would be able to interpret the will of God. The laws enacted by the new government had been like edicts from God. The new government's policies had been like the ones mandated by ancient high priests, where everyone was either a believer or a nonbeliever—and where the nonbeliever was a sinner to be eradicated through conversion or death.

As such, America had swept into the African desert with all the religious zeal of the original Crusaders. Unfortunately, after over two years of war, America found that while it could conquer, it could not rule. Military might had allowed it to overthrow a regime; missiles and bombs had decimated the conquered regime's army; its infrastructure of power had been systematically dismantled and replaced by a structure sympathetic to America. However, the battles and skirmishes continued—not against an army; not against anything with a structure that could be dismantled by military might or political will. It became a matter of their believers against the believers of America—a battle not so much of ideals, as superstitions.

That was the state of the war before the soldier was captured.

♁♁♁

During his time in the war zone, the soldier had gotten into the habit of walking around the base before his unit went out on night time raids. He would walk inside the base's perimeter walls, willing his mind to be still. As his sergeant was always telling them, a soldier's job was to forget everything but his orders. For a soldier, there were no yesterdays—and no tomorrows; and even the present was only a nightmare dreamed up by someone else. …That was what their sergeant would say; so, when the soldier went on his pre-mission walks, he would allow himself a few moments of indulgent fantasy before he willed his mind to be clear. Most times, he would think about his parents: how much he missed them and their home on Long Island. Sometimes, he would think about a girl from high school that he wished he had asked out, or a girl he had been able to seduce. Typically, these walks would only take five to ten minutes, and he would come back looking resolute. However, on the night when everything began to unravel, he was gone for half an hour. His sergeant came looking for him, concerned, because their mission was supposed to begin in five minutes. The sergeant exited the barracks and spied the soldier through the darkness. The sergeant called to the solder, and the young man came stumbling up, looking dazed. At first, the sergeant was going to ask him what was wrong, but he prided himself on being a strict disciplinarian, so he screamed:

"Get a move on, soldier! Quit walking as if you need to change your goddamn tampon!"

The soldier tried to move quicker, but the disillusioned expression on his face did not change. The sergeant glared at him momentarily, still determined to ignore the soldier's strange mien, then he re-entered the barracks, where the rest of the 10-man unit was getting ready for the mission. When the soldier entered the barracks, he went straight to his cot, and began to put on his gear. The man on the cot next to the soldier's had welcoming eyes. He and the soldier were friends; and as the man with the welcoming eyes saw his friend's agitated state, he frowned. In fact, several of the other soldiers had frowned at him as he entered, noting the strange expression on his face. However, the sergeant was yelling at them again, telling them to hurry up. The others got up and headed out of the room. The soldier was the last one left, and the sergeant yelled at him, saying:

"Move your ass, goddamn it!"

The soldier bundled the rest of his gear in his arms, before running out of the door. The other men were getting into an armored personnel carrier when he got outside. As soon as he got in, the door was closed. In addition to the sergeant and the other soldiers, there was an interpreter and a lieutenant. The interpreter was a scrawny old man who claimed to have been an English teacher before the war, but whose sentences were so convoluted that the soldiers did not bother to ask for translations half the time. They kept him along as a kind of mascot, and made crude jokes about him to his face, which he never understood, but which he would nonetheless smile at, in his demented, toothless way. The lieutenant was a young man straight out of West Point, who always kept a certain professional distance from the others, as if military decorum demanded it.

The personnel carrier started off, through the night. There was still a dazed, disillusioned expression on the soldier's face. The man with the welcoming eyes was sitting across from him; they usually engaged in idle banter before a mission, but the soldier did not want to talk at the moment. He began to put on the last of his gear. He needed to clear his head and figure things out. However, when the soldier looked up, he realized that everyone was staring at him. He felt suddenly self-conscious. He tried to smile to reassure them, but all he could manage was a nervous grimace. He realized he was trembling slightly. He inhaled deeply, hoping to calm himself, but it was no use. This was usually the time when they all made wise cracks about one another, in order to put the unit at ease before the start of a mission. When men faced death on a daily basis, they became superstitious. They were always on the look out for bad omens, and strove to repeat their routines, feeling that their most mundane actions held sway over the forces of life and death. The soldier's strange behavior was a bad omen, which brought out all the secret terrors that seized superstitious men. Suddenly exasperated, the sergeant snorted in disgust and addressed the soldier again, saying, "What the *hell* is your problem?"

The soldier opened his mouth, but he had no idea where to begin, so he shut it, shaking his head in the same disillusioned way. He was staring at the floor.

"Soldier!" the sergeant yelled, annoyed. The soldier looked up at him help-lessly. The sergeant went on: "Whatever it is, get it off your goddamn chest now, before we start the mission." And then, sarcastically: "What happened? Did your girlfriend tell you her new man has a bigger dick than yours?"

The rest of the unit laughed. The soldier tried to laugh, but his lips some-how refused to comply. He looked up at them apologetically, as if embarrassed by his lips' shortcomings. This strange reaction made the laughter cease.

"What is it, son?" the sergeant asked again, his tone strangely compassionate.

The soldier took a deep breath. "I…I don't know where to begin."

"Start from the beginning," the sergeant coaxed him.

The soldier nodded. He looked at the unit apologetically again, and took a deep breath. "…I went out for my walk—you know, like I always do before a mission." Everyone else in the unit nodded, remembering his routine. The soldier went on: "…I was walking along the wall, like I always do. My thoughts were just drifting, you know…Anyway, I looked up, and there was a man there. He just seemed to pop out of nowhere. I looked up, and he was there."

"What do you mean?" the sergeant asked. "He wasn't one of us?" he said, meaning if he was with the Military.

"No, he was in this business suit. His shoes…I remember that his shoes were shiny: *polished*. That's how I knew that he didn't belong there. You know how the desert dust gets on everything. It was as if he had just popped…" The soldier shook his head. When he looked up again, everyone in the unit was frowning at him. He felt embarrassed and foolish. "I'm sorry—"

"Finish your goddamn story, soldier," the sergeant chastised him. "Tell it now and get it out of your goddamn head." The sergeant's favorite word was goddamn. He used it as a crude exclamation point in practically every sentence—especially when he was angry or anxious.

The soldier stared at him, then nodded when he saw no choice but to continue. "…Well," the soldier began, "he was just there when I looked up… the man with the shiny shoes. …And then he began to speak."

"What did he say?" another soldier asked him eagerly.

"He said he knew me—that we were friends. I tried to look at his face, to see if I could place it, but the strange thing was that no matter how hard I looked, it was as if he had no face—as if his entire face was a shadow. I think I spent about half a minute trying to see his face. He began to talk. I don't think I heard what he was saying at first—I was staring at his face…trying to see it, I mean…"

The sergeant spoke up again, losing patience: "You're saying you met a stranger within the perimeter wall, and he didn't have a face?"

"…I know how crazy it sounds." When the soldier looked around the unit, he realized that even the lieutenant, who usually read mission orders during these rides and pretended to be too engrossed to hear their banter, was staring at him. The soldier felt even more unsettled. However, feeling it was too late now to keep quiet, he went on, "…I started to listen to what the man was saying. …He told me about this mission—about everything that's going to happen."

Everyone stared at him, but then the sergeant laughed out, saying: "A ghost appeared to tell you the future? Why the hell can't you fantasize about women like the rest of us, soldier?"

The other soldiers laughed, but it was a mirthless kind of laughter—as if they were desperate to believe that it was all a joke. The soldier tried to laugh as well, willing to admit that it did sound silly. Unfortunately, he had a sudden flashback of what the man with the shiny shoes had said to him, and he shuddered.

The laughter died down.

The sergeant sobered, and spoke up again: "You're serious about all this? Some ghost man popped out of nowhere and told you what's going to happen on our mission?"

"Yes, sir."

"Then tell us then?" he said, trying to joke again, but nobody laughed this time.

The soldier nodded anxiously. "…The man said that go to the complex and find it deserted. There won't be a damn thing there…but he said I'll see a white cat."

"A white cat?" the sergeant interrupted him again.

"Yeah, he said I'll see a white cat; and that if we all followed it, we'll stay alive."

"*What?*"

"He said that we'd die if we stayed in the building."

"Die how?"

"I don't know. He just said that we'd die—all of us—if we stayed in the building. Our only chance to live is to follow the cat."

"Goddamn! What kind of fucked up story is that to tell before a mission!" the sergeant screamed; the other men began to grumble. Even the man with the welcoming eyes seemed exasperated with him.

"I'm sorry, sir," the soldier apologized. "...I told you it was weird. I didn't want to talk about it, but you asked me to...I'm sorry, sir."

"Well, just keep out of our way on this mission, soldier!" the sergeant screamed again.

"I'm sorry, sir," the soldier said again. He stared down at the ground, because he could sense the other members of the unit glaring at him. He willed his mind to wander. He conjured images of his mother and father, sister and brother; he thought about the little house on Long Island that his parents had scraped and sacrificed to buy. He thought about how he had called his parents today, hoping to pacify a strange, nameless feeling that had been building in him lately. He would typically call his parents a couple times a week, and close his eyes as he listened to them, pretending that he was listening to them from the kitchen table. He would allow himself to believe, for those few moments, that the war was all a dream to be forgotten. ...But when the soldier called his parents that morning, something strange had happened. A woman whose voice he had never heard before had answered the phone; when the soldier asked her who she was, she had said she was his mother. He had asked her questions—trying to test her—but she had ignored him, and talked excitedly about her house redecorating plans. It had driven him over the edge somehow, so that he had found himself screaming and cursing—but the strange woman on the other end of the line had only kept on babbling about how beautiful her flower bed looked. He had slammed down the phone and redialed his parents' number, but there had been no answer, and he had walked away, looking dazed and wretched.

The soldier shook his head. Even that memory seemed farfetched. Was he coming undone? Maybe. ...Maybe he needed to come undone. He thought about that for a moment, allowing his mind to accept the possibility that madness might have its benefits....

The other soldiers were still brooding over the bad omen of his story; outside the vehicle, it was deathly quiet in the sprawling slums of the city—except for the intermittent sounds of gunfire and sirens. Most of the people in the city were refugees—from war and famine and the dissolution of civilization. Even before the Americans rolled into the desert, there had been war: between Christians and Muslims; between those who looked the same and had lived side-by-side for centuries, but who claimed to be of different ethnic groups. The irreconcilable differences spawned by religion and ethnicity had left hundreds of thousands dead and maimed; millions of others wandered the desert—like ancient Jews looking for some elusive Promised Land.

With the ongoing strife, most people had been without set homes for over a decade now. The de facto refugee camps encompassed most of the city: countless kilometers of one-story shacks and human refuse—which, in most instances, were the same thing. In this sector, there were few genuine streets—just corridors through the shantytowns: tracks through the refuse, which might tomorrow be covered over with trash and shacks, like wounds that sealed themselves with ugly scabs. In the center of the city, there were high-rise buildings—not skyscrapers, but buildings that perhaps reached seven or eight stories at most. And yet, even on the streets with high rises, there would be shacks within alleyways and on the sidewalks, as if the shacks were some kind of mange, spreading over the skin of the city. In the distance, the oil derricks stood out like giant mosquitoes, drawing sustenance from the diseased host. Another American base was in that direction, forming a protective ring around the derricks, so that the parasites could keep on feeding...

Within the armored personnel carrier, there was still none of the cheerful banter that usually prepared them for battle. However, the men prepared nonetheless. Some of them stared into space, conjuring their intimate fantasies; some closed their eyes and said prayers—either to gods or men or chance, itself. Across the aisle, next to the man with the welcoming eyes, a corporal was leafing through a miniature edition of the New Testament, the pages of which had become grimy from sweat and the Army-issue grease they used on their guns. The corporal's lips were moving as his mumbled Bible passages. The soldier felt somehow that it was indecent to watch the man, so he looked away and scanned the rest of the unit. He was suddenly desperate for something to reassure him, but there was nothing, so he preoccupied himself by fastening his flack jacket. He thought about the man with the shiny shoes again, unconsciously shuddering. He had not told the other soldiers how the man had disappeared. One moment, the soldier had been looking at him, trying to digest what he was saying; and then, the next moment, the soldier had found himself looking into the darkness of the African night. The soldier had not told the other men how he had cried out—how he had tried to run, but been frozen by some kind of mortal terror...

The door of the personnel carrier opened. This was a relatively opulent neighborhood: there were asphalt streets and brick walls here. However, the night seemed repulsive—like something dead and rotting. Even the full moon seemed drained of life: its rays were faint, giving dour highlights to everything. With no sewage system in the sprawling shantytowns, the stench of excrement was always in the air. A wave of intense heat ambushed the unit as they exited. Some of them coughed inadvertently on the hot, dry air—and the pestilential stench it carried. A stray dog, which had been sleeping in front of the gate of the presumed terrorist's home, fled as they emerged from the vehicle. It ran down to the next compound, then crouched behind a pile of garbage, watching them timidly—but not barking. The unit moved quickly. They had done this so many times that they hardly had to think. The sergeant glared at the soldier, as to tell him to stay out of their way. In turn, the soldier nodded and bowed his head, and slouched to the rear. Two other soldiers kicked at the front gate, so that it collapsed onto the dusty ground. The unit ran up to the door of the house. It was quickly kicked down as well. They entered, screaming out "clear!" as they progressed through the empty rooms... and at last, after about thirty seconds of searching and screaming, they realized that there was no one in the house. Following the lieutenant's orders, a quarter of the unit fanned out to the backyard, looking for bunkers—but there was nothing. Eventually, they all congregated in the living room. The soldier, who had stayed back, came walking up with the same dazed expression on his face. The others looked at him, remembering his story. The lieutenant grew annoyed with them; refusing to give in to superstition, he made a call to headquarters, talking in an overly loud voice about how they had been given bad intelligence.

While the lieutenant talked over the radio in his stage voice, the rest of the unit grew increasingly anxious. All of them stared at the soldier. Their rational minds told them that men with shiny shoes did not pop out of thin air and foretell the future, but their eyes kept wandering over to the soldier—as if he had all the answers. Even the sergeant was looking toward him, his eyes unsure. The soldier felt self-conscious. As he stood there, waiting for the thing to happen, his skin felt hypersensitive. His mind seemed in shock somehow; and then, as he glanced out of the living room window, he saw it. Initially, there was a white blur, and then he saw it clearly: the white cat, sitting in the middle of the yard, staring at him.

Printed in the United States
By Bookmasters